1

SPEAR-WON

A novel of ancient Macedonia

by

D William Thorburn

For my mother and father

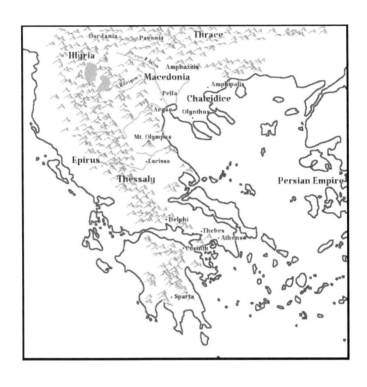

Small opportunities are often the beginning of great enterprises.

Demosthenes

Chapter 1

Thick pillars of smoke rose far in the distance and formed a cloud. The only cloud in an otherwise perfect blue sky.

"How long until we reach Pella?" Philip looked up and asked his mother, squinting into the sunlight to try and see her. His head then dipped back into the shade to peak over the side of the cart and watch the wheels turn. His eyes took a moment to adjust back.

The cart trundled heavily on the rocky, uneven road surface. The ride was bumpy and uncomfortable. The wheels rolled along two parallel tracks that had been worn down by many farmers' carts over time. The road they were on was also well travelled by merchants and traders, but none were using it now. Every now and then a wheel would roll over a pot hole and the bump would be more violent, and all the people in the cart would hold on to avoid being ejected. Their transportation was intended for farmers to move hay and farming tools, not carry people. The lingering stench of moist hay and animal dung was awful; and it filled his nostrils.

It was mid-summer and the day was hot; the sun was high in the sky and beat down on them. The children's skin was starting to burn and their mother kept covering them with a sheet to keep the sun off them, but this meant they were even hotter. Beads of sweat ran down Philip's forehead; he wiped his brow. To add to his discomfort, he constantly had to swat at flies and mosquitoes, attracted by the horses pulling the cart, and the residue of their dung that was stained into the wood.

"I've told you already, we're not far," his mother said. "You are normally so patient Philip, why not now?"

Philip sat up and looked around. Along with his mother, there were courtiers whose faces he recognised, but did not know. Philip shared the cart with his sister and brother Perdiccas, who was older by a few years. He leaned across their mother's lap. "Don't worry, I saw the palace back a bit, shouldn't be long," he said.

Philip's sister Eurynoe, who had been asleep, had been woken up. She yawned and stretched. "I wish Medius could have spared some more comfortable transportation," she said.

"Come now," their mother said. "Medius has gone far beyond what he needed to. When we are back in the palace we will sacrifice to the Gods and pray they watch for his health and prosperity. He has helped us in our time of need and he has proven himself a loyal friend to your father."

"But it's a cart for moving hay," Eurynoe complained. "Surely he could have done better, a-"

"Medius couldn't very well give us all of his horses now, could he? We wouldn't want to hurt his farms; his people might go hungry."

Philip smiled listening to his mother's soft voice, she was kind, and always considered others. He turned and looked down the convoy which snaked back along the road to the south. More similar carts to the one they

8

rode in followed them. The tired soldiers of the army were carrying whatever they could.

"What's going to happen when we get back to the Palace? Will father and Alexander be there?" he asked.

"I'm sure they're already there Philip," she sighed, and squinted into the distance along the road.

Philip looked across in the same direction. They had cleared the mountains a while back, and were now in the plains. Pella would not be far now. The city walls could vaguely be seen through the haze of the heat.

...

As they approached the city, none of them received a welcome; there was not a man to spare. Macedonia was a poor country with many enemies, and had been in a constant state of war with their neighbours, and internal threats, for as long as anyone could remember. It had brought the country to its knees. Philip was young, and he knew his understanding of these things was limited, but he did understand how important it was for his father to return them to Pella. It had been his single focus, and all he had talked about the entire time they had been in exile. He constantly praised Archelaus, their ancestor who had built the Palace at Pella, and how to lose it was the very worst of insults.

The convoy entered through the main gate of the city. There was no obvious damage to the walls or gates, but Pella had suffered from the fighting. Many buildings within the walls had been raided, some were black with soot, and others were hollowed out by fire, leaving only the walls with no roof; smouldering skeletons of the former homes. The embers glowed and the heat rose from them in a wave, the air thick with the smell of charred wood.

9

Displaced people were out in the street, some begging with nowhere to go. A father drifted past like a shade carrying a dead child in his arms, his empty eyes red and swelled with tears.

A group of young women in their undergarments stood outside what was left of some kind of inn that Philip guessed they lived in. The building was almost completely destroyed like the others. An old, tough looking man stood next to them, whom he supposed he was their father. He was talking to passing soldiers while glancing back to his daughters. He took coin from one of them and the soldier went around the back of the building with one of the women, out of sight.

A woman kneeled in a doorway weeping, with a bloodied man lying in her lap. He was most likely dead; Philip guessed it was her husband, and hoped he was just hurt and that he would get better. Their house had not burned, but the door hung half off its hinges and a trail of coin and jewellery was scattered on the street outside.

Philip felt his mother pull him in tightly to protect his young eyes from such sights, but it was too late, he had seen it all. On the journey the previous day, he thought he had seen the worst of the horror of war on the north road from Thessaly to Macedonia. Bandits had attacked the convoy ahead of them. He had not seen any of the fighting, but the bodies had been left on the roadside for the crows. Perdiccas said they should have been crucified, but was told this would have taken too long, as they were in a hurry to get back. The only difference was that on the road it had been soldiers, the enemy, but in the city, it was the civilians; wives, mothers and children. He had been up on the cart and so had not been close enough to get a good look. Philip gulped at the lump in his throat, it did nothing.

The streets were lined with guards and soldiers, out to protect the journey of the Royal family. Somewhere in the train also travelled Philip's half-brothers and their mother, his eyes nervously scanning back along the convoy for them. He would not feel completely safe until he was near his father and his eldest brother Alexander. He could not see them, so he relaxed and cuddled into his mother. Amyntas's marriage to their mother was of less importance than that of his own. She had told him this every day of his life, and he took comfort in this. His brother Alexander was the heir, not Arrhidaeus, the eldest of the three.

They were stopped at a checkpoint, and a Macedonian officer approached the leader of the convoy guards, "There are still pockets of resistance from some of the Illyrian's around the city; the bulk of them have fled, but some are hiding in the buildings, be vigilant," he told him and they saluted each other. As they passed the officer bowed his head at Philip's mother "Queen Eurydice," he addressed her, and she smiled and placed a coin in his palm, "for your loyalty in these difficult times soldier."

The convoy continued, passing a large group of captured enemy soldiers, Illyrians from the North West. These Illyrians were kneeling, their hands bound. They had been stripped of their armour and weapons, which were arranged in a neat pile well out of their reach. They were being guarded by a group of Spartan soldiers, who could be easily identified by their red cloaks.

Philip did not like to think what the fate of these men would be; the Spartans despised weakness and surrender. They would probably suffer interrogation and maybe torture, and, if they were lucky, would become slaves. Although this would be terrible and humiliating, the alternative would probably be far worse than he could even imagine; the Spartans did not have a reputation for being kind hearted to their enemies, especially ones that had surrendered. The Spartans laughed and joked with each other while standing over these broken and frightened men, as if they did not exist. The prisoners looked at the ground, afraid to glance up.

The Spartans, he had once been told by some older boys, were always looking for more slaves. They said each Spartan had fifty slaves. Fifty. It was something about them that Philip didn't understand. Why did they need so many?

For a moment Philip felt pity for them, but then he remembered the stories his father had told him about the Illyrians, and about their King, Bardylis, who was described as a monstrous giant, and led the Dardanians, their strongest tribe, and that he had conquered all the nearby tribes. It was said that they slaughtered enemies who had surrendered, women and children included; they deserved whatever happened to them.

His father had always had fondness for the Spartans and their way of life, and told stories of their bravery to him and his brothers. They were deeply pious and respected the gods and their ancestors, much like himself. King Amyntas would always be careful to pay homage to the Gods and make the correct sacrifices.

He said that Macedonia and Sparta shared common ancestry, both royal families being descended from Heracles, and were both seen as primitive by the Democracies of the South because of it, so it was only natural for them to ally. This had been preached to Philip by his father since he was very small.

The wagon travelled up winding streets towards the palace. A troop of soldiers marched past them down the hill, the pounding of their feet in rhythm echoed around the stone of the buildings. The palace became visible between some of the houses, at the top of the steep hill they were climbing; its fortified walls basked in the sunlight, towering high above the other buildings. When they reached the top of the hill, the walls loomed over them. King Amyntas stood outside where the gate had been, which was now reduced to ash. A half-charred battering ram partially blocked the entrance. Shields and weapons were strewn about the ground.

King Amyntas was not a tall man, but was broad across the shoulders and was as strong as an ox, both in his body and his heart. He wore full military dress, but had removed his helmet now that the battle was over.

He stood in a group of men; the generals who had helped his father retake the Pella. He was trying to remember where they were from: Olynthus and Thessaly he remembered, and Sparta of course, but not the others.

They all wore well-made armour, expensive looking armour Philip thought. The exception was a Spartan, who was dressed very plainly, just a red cloak, the same as his men from further down the hill, although his helmet, which he carried under his arm, had a transverse plume instead of the front facing plume of the regular soldiers. This identified him as a high-ranking officer, part of the nobility, probably not a king but maybe part of the royal family. He was probably the richest one there, but had the poorest clothes. Philip found this curious. The Spartan stood tall and steady like a statue of stone, his long beard and hair swayed in the breeze. His upper lip was clean shaven like all his men. Philip had asked his father once why they wore no moustaches; he had simply said, "I wouldn't know how to ask them. They have so many strange rules."

The group were looking out over the city, their hands cupped to shade their eyes from the sun. They were talking, and directing the Macedonian officers who came and went, trying to establish some order in the city.

Most of the group gave short bows and departed, leaving only the Spartan, the King and to his other side his eldest son, Alexander, who was shadowing him. He was only sixteen, but was already becoming tall and athletic. He was a smaller silhouette of his father, strong and silent, only speaking when necessary.

Amyntas nodded to them as they passed. He was always an incredibly serious man, not that this was not a serious time. However, even in private when the day's business should have been forgotten, his father never laughed or joked with any of them anymore. Philip had fond memories of him chasing him and his brothers and sister when they were small, pretending to be the cyclops Polyphemus and they were Odysseus and his men. He would catch them and tickle them on the floor. He smiled a lot then.

Philip always thought he was like Atlas, the titan from the myths, doomed to carry a heavy burden; for Atlas, it was the sky, for his father, the kingdom and all its problems. Although he was still very young, he knew that it saddened him that they did not lead a simpler life.

The wagon jerked to a stop and they were helped down from the cart by two of the king's Royal Guards. Philip kicked the loose dirt on the ground while the soldiers spoke to his mother and unloaded the baggage.

As his mind drifted, there were suddenly screams and shouts that dragged him back into reality.

"Look out!" a voice shouted.

Philip looked up to see a group of Illyrians, five of them, break out from behind part of a damaged wall.

They ran as fast as they could, and headed straight to the king. One broke from the others and headed directly for him and his mother. She did not flinch, but stood up tall and shielded her children from the approaching attacker. As she did, the Royal Guards formed up in front of her, bracing behind their large round shields, spears pointed at him.

He raised his sword high above his head to strike, but an arrow shot from the top of the palace wall whistled through the air and struck him in the armpit. The arrow penetrated deep into his chest and he stumbled. His momentum carried him forward and, weakened by the arrow, he clattered off the guard's shields and fell flat on his back.

The guards surrounded the fallen man and stabbed him with their spears to finish him off. Philip stared over at his father and the Spartan general who had fought off the other four long enough for more of the Royal Guard to arrive. They struck the Illyrians from all sides and hacked them down.

The Spartan casually walked after the last living Illyrian, who was badly wounded and crawling away from them. He drew his weapon and calmly stood on the middle of the man's back, in-between his shoulder blades, pinning him to the ground. The Illyrian tried to say something over his shoulder, pleading; Philip couldn't make out what he was saying. The Illyrian struggled weakly with the little strength he had left. The Spartan watched him for a moment with a blank expression; he then bent forward and firmly pressed the tip of his sword into the back of the man's neck, between the bones of his spine. He instantly stopped struggling and went limp, face down in the dust.

Philip stood frozen, aghast at the calm efficiency of the kill. Eurydice had tried to shield her children's eyes, but Philip had seen everything.

The Spartan turned to Amyntas and smirked, amused.

Amyntas smiled back a half smile, but Philip could see the distaste clear as day behind the smile. He thought he heard the Spartan say, "He did not die well."

Their father came to them. "Husband," his mother curtsied.

Amyntas looked furious, but had a pleading in his voice "I told them to wait another day," he said, and gave his wife and children a brief embrace. "The city isn't safe yet. Are any of you hurt?"

"I'm sorry," she said. "The message wasn't received"

"Get the children inside the walls, it's safest there. I'll come and see you later."

Chapter 2

They were escorted into the courtyard of the Palace; the grounds were largely intact. It was a vast garden surrounded by a stone walkway around the perimeter, with the palace walls rising up on all sides. The grass in the middle of the garden was dotted with cypress trees and water trickled out of fountains built of white marble; the courtyard was surrounded by white pillars on all four sides. Balconies on the upper floors had views of the garden and lush green vines draped over them. Philip looked around: it was beautiful, a paradise compared to where they had been living. He understood now why his father wanted it back.

Inside the walls he felt safer, and began to calm down, his racing heart began to slow down, and the thumping in his chest shrunk until it was unnoticeable.

The garden statues of the Olympian gods were all untouched, but their paint was cracked and weathered, exposing the white marble beneath. Father Zeus stood in the centre, holding his thunderbolt high above his head like a javelin, his lean muscles taut and flexed. No mortal man would dare to anger the gods by desecrating any of these great tributes to them. Did the Illyrians worship the same Gods? He didn't know. The usurper they had sponsored was Macedonian, so wouldn't have allowed them to anger the gods.

"Can we explore?" Philip looked to his mother; she frowned and looked at the officer of the Royal Guard.

"It is safe within the walls my Queen," the officer said.

"Please?" begged Perdiccas.

"I want to stay with you," Eurynoe said, clinging onto their mother's hand.

"Very well," she said, "but stay on the ground floor".

The boys ran off, their rapid footsteps pattered off the courtyard stone.

They ran around the vast labyrinth of corridors and peaked into different rooms.

In one room there were men standing around with a whole manner of instruments, measuring the cracks and damage that had been done to the palace; it had been neglected. One shouted something at them and they ran off. Philip could not make out what he had said; he looked back at Perdiccas and smiled. He felt alive and free. They had snuck in to an older part of the palace, which was run down and dilapidated; they had not expected to find anyone in there, but their father must have got these men in to start restoring it, as had been his ambition for more than a decade now.

They eventually came to the bottom of a grand staircase stretching up into the distance.

"I'm going up," Philip said.

"No, we were told not to," Perdiccas said, tugging on his arm to head back, but Philip was drawn towards whatever was up there. He felt like he remembered his way around, but it had been a long time since he had last been there and he had been very small, but the corridors and hallways were embedded deep somewhere in his memory. They had spent a year or so moving around and living with one of his father's allies, then another, not knowing whether they would have to leave at a moment's notice. It had not been easy.

He left Perdiccas at the bottom of the stairs and vaguely heard him shout, "I'm getting Mother!", but ignored him.

Passing through some hallways and around some more corners, he came to a heavy wooden double door, braced with iron studs. This was the only closed door that he had noticed, and was curious about what was behind it. He imagined himself as Theseus, about to enter the Minotaur's lair. What lurked behind here? Slowing his pace and trying to make as little noise as possible on the tiled floor, he turned the door handle down and it slowly creaked open.

He jumped as it swung all the way open with a loud bang.

He crept into the doorway and froze when he heard shouts and bangs echo around the walls from downstairs. He waited, and waited... nothing... He entered the room.

The room was a vast atrium, with another door on each wall. The roof was partially fallen in and vines hung down like stalactites in a cave. A pillar of light shone down from the hole, revealing how the air was filled with dust. After inhaling it Philip had to sneeze.

He stared at the floor, which was laid out with an intricate mosaic of his ancestor Heracles, bordered by a wave pattern of key, a symbol of wealth and power. The hero was performing one of his twelve labours. Moss had grown over a large portion of it.

Heracles wrestled the Nemean lion. The beast had raised itself up onto its powerful back legs, leaping for his throat. Heracles half squatted down, hooking his arms under the lion's armpits, his muscles bulging, ready to make a throw. Philip found himself lost in the picture, imagining the age of heroes.

"I thought I told you not to come up here,"

He jerked, it was his mother's voice from behind, but it startled him, and he turned to see her, ready to try and make up an excuse when he realized, she was smiling.

"You found it; I always told you we would return."

19

They looked at the mosaic on the floor together.

"This part of the palace has been abandoned for some time," she said.

"Why?"

"Money; but you don't need to worry about such things Philip, you are only a small boy." she said, kneeling down and putting her arm around his shoulder.

"Please tell me," He pleaded.

"Macedonia is not as wealthy as it once was. There is too much fighting."

His mother, Eurydice was beautiful, and her smile warmed Philip's heart. He had only the vaguest of memories of the palace, but she had told him stories.

"You don't need to worry about such things though, your father is working hard to return it to the way it was."

"Do you think father will be happier now that we are home? Will the fighting stop?" he asked, praying that it would happen, but knowing in reality it would not.

"I hope so, but you know your father is a very busy man, and will never rest until all of Macedonia is under control and safe," Eurydice sighed, and moved over to her son. "We can only pray to the Gods that they favour us."

Eurydice was from an old and respected Macedonian house, but she had been born in a northern territory that had been lost to Macedonia a long time ago. Pella was in the lower region of Macedonia, near the coast, and its territory and influence had receded to the Illyrians and other tribes. She had told him a long time ago about how, after she had married his father, there had been fighting and, he couldn't remember exactly, but it had been taken. He didn't want to ask her to tell the story again, he knew how upsetting it was for her.

"Go back down and find your brother, I'm going to speak to your father. I'll come find you both soon." She knelt down and kissed him on the cheek.

Perdiccas was stood halfway up the stairs when he came back down.

"What did you see?" he asked as Philip approached, and passed him heading for the bottom.

"Nothing," he said. "Mother says we're to stay downstairs."

…...

Back outside, they stepped down a step and through a doorway in the partially collapsed walls where they were met by Ptolemy, the nobleman's son who was their sister's intended. He leant against the wall. He was older than them, already had his sword belt, so was a man grown. Tall and handsome; he was universally admired. He ruffled Philip's hair.

"What are you little shits doing running around with no guards? If any of those Illyrians are still about, they might bugger you." He said, wearing a wide grin.

"And what are you doing here? Shouldn't you be kissing our father's arse?" Philip asked. He liked Ptolemy a lot; he always teased Perdiccas and himself playfully. He was always jesting.

"Ha, ha," he said sarcastically, then quickly moved on. "No, I haven't seen him all day. He's mostly been dealing with the Spartans and Olynthians".

"Have you seen any of the fighting? How many Illyrians have been chased? Did you kill any of them?" Philip asked.

"I didn't see much of the fighting, I was kept back; your father said I was too important."

"Why? Surely they need as many men as possible?"

"I hear they were greatly outnumbered," Philip said, frowning.

21

"Because," he said, pausing to take a drink out of his skin, "I'm marrying your sister, and that will consolidate my family's loyalty. Do you think Pella being retaken was only because of the army?"

Philip and Perdiccas looked at each other, not really understanding.

"It was also because of the alliances your father has formed with the Thessalians, Olynthians and Spartans. The Usurper that the Illyrians put on the throne could not keep the nobility under control, including my family in Aloros. When he realized he could not hold Macedonia, he fled."

"So, it's not you that's too important to father," Perdiccas teased him, "It's your marriage to Eurynoe."

"No, you little bastard, I-" Ptolemy said, and tried to clip him round the ear, but he dodged it, laughing. Ptolemy tried to continue, but Perdiccas continued to mock him.

Philip was interested in what he was telling them but, although he liked Ptolemy, he always thought that he over-explained everything; Philip lost interest and stopped listening once it got too complicated. He looked around at the palace and the soldiers.

Lecturing a thirteen-year-old and fifteen-year-old on the politics of the kingdom, how much does he think we understand?

Perdiccas stopped and let Ptolemy continue.

"Well, not just that. Our fathers have always been friends, and my father could not tolerate someone other than Amyntas being on the throne," he said.

"Did you see the Spartan? We watched him kill a man like you'd step on an ant."

"Ah, yeah, he's a cold man; Spartan's are all like that, the one's I've met anyway."

"How many have you met?"

22

"Just a few," Ptolemy said, "You'd be best to stay out of their way. You know what they do to young boys in Sparta?"

"No, what do you mean?" Philip asked.

"Never mind that, just be glad they're on our side, or we'll all be in Hades before this is over. Anyway, I'm off to find your father. You two stay out of trouble. I think your half-brothers are about. Little shits."

……

That night Philip lay back in his own bed. The night air was warm; the tall balcony doors were open, letting in a cool breeze from outside. Although the night was peaceful, and he was exhausted from the long journey of the day, he found it difficult to sleep. He lay flat on his back staring up at the high ceiling; the perfect, clean white stone was a blur in the darkness and he was barely able to make out the key pattern carvings around the edges, or the mural that was visible in the daylight. He had not slept in this room for years because of the family having been in exile, but it was familiar to him, it almost felt as if he had never left.

Now he was older, but his bed was still meant for a small child, and he had grown a lot while they had been absent. He was almost too tall for it; his feet nearly hung off the end. His mother had assured him he would get a bigger bed as soon as she could start to organize the household.

For now, he would have to put up with what they had. His bed linen composed of only a thin sheet because it was summer, and the heat from the day was still diminishing. The sheet had been cleaned by his servants earlier in the day and they had aired it outside, so it smelled faintly of smoke. When he closed his eyes, he kept seeing the fire, the pillar of smoke billowing above it, the displaced people weeping, and then his

23

thoughts eventually moved onto the dead; the dead littering the roadside; they slowly stood up, opened their eyes and stared at him.

He cleared his thoughts and was almost off, when he heard a creak in the corner of the room. The sound jarred his eyes open; his body froze. He slowed his breathing, but his heart thumped in his chest. He squinted into the blackness, trying to make sense of the dark shapes around the room. The drapes swayed gently in the breeze; crickets chirped outside. He could hear the crunch on the gravel of his father's sentries walking their patrol below the window. He would be humiliated if he were to run and seek their help over a few noises.

He waited for the noise again; nothing. He relaxed and closed his eyes.

After a few moments his thoughts began to wander again. A million images ran through his mind, all the nightmare creatures from the myths: the Hydra, the Minotaur, and the Gorgons. The latter had not so long ago been told to him as his bedtime story by his mother; those terrifying sisters with snakes for hair, who would petrify warriors with their stare, turning them to stone.

He lay on his side, the bed was positioned in the middle of the vast room; he felt open, exposed; the only object in the centre of a void. He felt as if something was behind him, but he dared not turn to see. He wished his bed was against the wall so he could put his back to it.

He waited. And waited. No more sounds came. No movement; nothing.

When he managed to get these thoughts out of his head, he felt embarrassed. Embarrassed for not being brave, ashamed of what his father would think, a father who already thought of him as weak and a coward, the puny third son. Exhaustion overcame him and he eventually drifted off to sleep.

He was jarred awake when something gripped his ankles hard and he was dragged out of bed. He thought it was a dream, but then he landed hard on the tiled floor; the cold of the tiles stabbed his body like an icicle. He opened his mouth to shout, but a strong hand clamped it shut, the taste of dried sweat was on his lips and the stink filled his nostrils. He squirmed to try and get away, but a shin pressed hard across his upper thighs, he was flattened out, pinned, with his back to the ground.

He looked up, and his eyes met the cold grey eyes of Arrhidaeus, his half-brother. Arrhidaeus' thin face sneered down at him with cold malice, illuminated orange and red, the light dancing on it giving him the appearance of some fire demon from Hades. Philip's gaze darted around the room, desperately looking for help. Two more figures stood in the darkness, but they could not clearly be made out. One held a torch, and they were hidden behind the red halo of light, the other carried what looked like a coiled length of rope, but it was too dark to tell. They were not here to help him, that much was certain. They must have been Menelaus and Archelaus. They were all sons of his father's second wife.

He tried to shout again, this time at them, but the sound was smothered by the hand again, and a clenched fist came down hard on his stomach. His muscles tightened up in pain. His reflex was to curl up in a ball, but it was halted by the shin across his legs and the hand on his mouth forcing his body to stay straight, the muscles in his abdomen flexed, but could not move. It was agonizing. They felt as though they were being torn apart.

25

He breathed in as hard as he could through his nose, but it was not enough. Gasping for air, his lungs were on fire. He convulsed and his mouth gulped at the hand clamped over it, unable to draw a breath.

The weight finally released him from the pin and he rolled onto his front with a thud, and took in a long cleansing breath, fresh air filled his lungs and time slowed in a serene moment of respite. Cool air, in, and out; in and out.

Then reality returned.

"What's wrong you little shit? Want to go running to your bitch mother, that foreign whore?" came his voice, an angry, raspy whisper, shattering Philip's moment of tranquillity. Something else struck him, this time in the side, a foot. A sharp pain tore through his chest when he breathed. Cracked ribs?

"What… are… you… doing?" Philip gasped between deep breaths. Struggling to get the words out, he was breathing hard, his lungs trying to catch up and his forehead throbbed.

He turned over and sat up, strong hands came from behind, fed under his armpits and grabbed the back of his head; the hold locked both of his arms backward and forced his head forward, in a position too weak for him to pull away. The strong finger tips pressed into the back of his head, the nails digging in, stinging.

Arrhidaeus knelt down in front of him holding a leather belt; he lifted it to Philip's face and started to gag him. Philip glanced around the darkness to look for help; when he could see none, he threw his feet up into the face of his half-brother who fell back, enraged. The force had pulled whoever was holding him from behind forward, weakening his grip. Philip threw his head back, butting him in the face, the grip was lost and he fell

26

back. They all pounced on Philip and kicked and punched him until he was curled up in a defensive ball like a tortoise in its shell.

Once they had him under control again, Arrhidaeus knelt back down in front of him. He snorted back and spat in Philip's face. Blood and mucus dripped from his cheek and he wretched in disgust.

"Whatever you're planning, you won't get away with it. Father will find out, and you three will be exiled along with your mother," he said; after doing the best he could to wipe his face on his shoulder, "or worse."

"We were going to sell you to slavers, but now we're going to tie you in a sack and throw you in the river," Arrhidaeus said, looking coldly at Philip's young face, delighting in his fear.

"Eh, Arrhidaeus," came the voice of Menelaus, "that's not what we agreed; if father finds out we've killed him- "

Arrhidaeus head whipped round like a serpent. "Do you want to join him?" he hissed, then turned back to Philip. "Once we've done away with you and your brothers, our mother, who is from the true Argead line will be queen and your foreign whore mother will be discarded, like ours has been for so long."

"Why me? You stupid bastards know that Alexander's the heir?"

"Wolves start by picking off the weakest sheep in the flock," Arrhidaeus said without a moment's hesitation.

"And my mother is still Macedonian. You think you'll be able to jump Alexander and Perdiccas like this? You'll never be able to kill them."

They sniggered at his words, then stuffed a cloth in his mouth and gagged him. As they tied him up, he thrashed as much as he could, but after a while his

27

energy gave out, the burn of the ropes on his skin became too much, and he stopped struggling. They were preparing a sack to put him in.

They all paused when they heard footsteps. The sound was of bare feet on the tiled floor.

"What the fuck do you think you are doing?" came a deep voice from the doorway, as they were dragging him toward the window. They froze and looked up. Philip's brothers Alexander and Perdiccas were stood in the doorway. Their silhouettes contrasted each other, Alexander, broad and muscular, Perdiccas, lean and slight. Perdiccas must have stayed awake late, reading Greek scrolls as he often did, heard the commotion and woke Alexander, thank the Gods.

"We were just…" Menelaus, the most cowardly of the three muttered as he slowly backed up, ready to step behind his brother should it come to blows. Menelaus would sell out his brothers in an instant if it meant saving his own skin.

"It'll be interesting to hear how you explain this to father," Perdiccas said, as they entered the room.

"Untie my brother," Alexander said through gritted teeth, not raising his voice louder than a whisper; "Now!"

Arrhidaeus' eyes lingered on Alexander's hand, a glint reflected the dancing orange and red torchlight; iron. A dagger. Held relaxed by his side. They slowly backed away from Philip, who lay tied up on the floor. As they did, Perdiccas moved to Philip to help him up and started on untying the ropes.

Arrhidaeus straightened up and looked side to side to his brothers, standing tall, and chest out.

"You won't cut me with that," he said.
"Are you sure?" Alexander said.

Without warning, he then sprung forward to strike Alexander.

Alexander reacted with lightning speed, his knees were slightly bent, his posture always ready to move his weight quickly, learned from years of wrestling in the gymnasium.

He shot forward as fast and straight as an arrow to meet his opponent. His head slipped to the side of Arrhidaeus' punch and he slammed the hardest part of his open palm hard into his chin. Arrhidaeus took the hit badly, and staggered back dazed. When he regained his composure a few seconds later he felt his face and neck. He then looked relieved when he realized it hadn't been the blade that had struck him.

"You piece of shit," he hissed, holding his mouth, feeling his jaw. "You'd better never turn your back on me."

Alexander took a step toward him and he took a step back, keeping the distance between them the same. Alexander kept a completely straight face, never breaking eye contact; he was feared by all three of his half-brothers.

The three of them slinked around him to the door, keeping facing him, backs to the wall, and then fled the room.

Philip, now untied, moved to embrace his brother and thank him, but he took a step back, refusing the contact.

"No Philip, there's no room for weakness here. We have enemies everywhere. You think they're the worst of it? We are back in Macedonia now. It's a nest of vipers here, and it will only get worse. From now on, sleep with a weapon close. Take this." He placed his dagger on the night stand next to Philip's bed, then started to turn to leave, but stopped and looked back.

29

"And don't bother father with this, he has enough to worry about."

"Alexand-" Philip said, but he had turned and was heading for the door, dismissing Philip with a wave over his shoulder.

Alexander's footsteps faded and Perdiccas and Philip were left standing in silence, leaving only the flickering sound of the torch Menelaus had dropped before he ran.

Chapter 3

Amyntas had his court up and running and it was beginning to function after a few months; his sons resumed their studies on all the subjects they had been learning before the exile. Lessons on politics and economics; physical training in the gymnasium, wrestling, boxing and sprinting.

All of them were proficient athletes but had only trained intermittently in the time spent away from Pella. Now it was time to re-establish themselves as the Royal family of Macedonia in practice as well as in name. This meant the boys had to be able to compete in or adjudicate in the games. Amyntas saw this as essential and Philip was happy to see the start of a return to normality.

Philip made his way from his morning lessons, across the grounds just outside the palace. Walking with some of his classmates, he looked up at the sky and shielded his eyes. It was now the peak of summer and the mid-afternoon sun was at its highest. A bead of sweat ran down the side of his face, and he wiped it with the back of his hand. Any part of the walk that was not in the shade quickly became unbearably hot.

"Are you coming to the gymnasium with us Philip?" Polyperchon, one of his classmates asked.

"No, it's too hot today," Philip said.

"That's never bothered you before."

"Sorry, I've got other studies to be getting on with," he said.

"Really Philip? Like what?" Polyperchon let out a short laugh.

"Politics."

The boys all looked at each other.

"Politics? …Over the Gym? ... That's not like you?" Polyperchon said, staring Philip in the eye, his eyebrows lowered. The other boys also frowned.

"Yes, Politics…I've been told it's a subject I need to work on more," he said, trying to sound as convincing as possible. There was an awkward pause.

"You said only last week that you had no interest in getting involved in politics, that you want to be a general for your brother one day."

"I don't want to but my father has spent years trying to consolidate my family as a worthy Royal line, so I may need to do politics, I'm a capable enough athlete."

"You are, but you still need to practice, and we love having you there. Politics can-"

"Not today, I just, have to go," he said.

"Very well then, we'll see you tomorrow?" Polyperchon continued to look sceptical.

"Yes, see you then." Philip said and excused himself. He headed back towards the palace on the dirt road, glancing over his shoulder. Once the other boys were out of sight, he turned and headed towards the stables.

His favourite horse, a beautiful brown stallion, had been prepared. It was hitched to a post by the reins waiting for him, with a saddle cloth thrown over its back. One of the stable boys was aware of his routine of late and had prepared the horse. He had also hung up a wide brimmed straw sunhat, the kind favoured by farmers, which would help hide his identity. Philip placed it on his head. The stable boy was across the other side of the yard, brushing another horse. Philip gave him a wave and he smiled back.

He headed out of the palace, through the houses and bustling streets of Pella, and out of the city gates.

On the dirt road the hoofs of the stallion beat the ground like a heartbeat. The cool air rushed over Philip's skin, soothing it. Tightening his grip on the reins he dug in his heels and picked up the pace; riding along the main road north east, which followed the Axios river, it was wide and fast flowing at this time of year. The trees on his side of the river became a blur as he galloped past them, but the ones on the far bank were clear, beautiful, green and lush.

Before long he arrived at the gates to Arsinoe's family's estate. He dismounted and led the horse, his feet crunching on the gravel path. The wall was made of brown dirt and only rose just higher than his head, not fortified like the walls of the palace at Pella, or even the walls of the city. It was just a boundary to keep wolves and other wild animals out and the livestock in.

Philip stood on a rock and peered over, keeping his head low in case anyone was on the other side. Rows of vineyards stretched for miles in all directions. The family's workers walked up and down the rows of vines, carrying large wooden buckets, collecting the grapes. He could see the house in the distance at the top of a low hill, a two-story villa with a veranda and a balcony, with flowing drapes outside. On the other side of the house there were several beehives, with more workers in broad, netted hats collecting honey. Arsinoe's family was wealthy. One of the grape collectors turned toward him and he ducked down so as not to be seen. *Where was she? She was normally waiting right here for him.*

"Hello stranger," came her voice from behind him, soft and pure as Aphrodite's.

Philip turned, and saw her, Arsinoe, the girl he'd been meeting with for a few weeks now. She stood with one hip cocked; a long white chiton flowed over her toned form. Her hair was as dark as ebony in complete contrast to her pale alabaster skin. It curled and spilled over her shoulders. Philip could not help but stare.

"So, what do you want to do today?" she asked, causing him to come out of his daze.

"I.. I.. don't know," he said, unsure how to answer. He stood dumbfounded, bewitched by her beauty. He was not used to girls being interested in him and Arsinoe was the first who had been forward with him. Most of the girls in the court were interested in his brother Alexander, or even Perdiccas, but not him.

"I love your horse. He's beautiful," she said and walked over and began stroking and patting the horse's neck. She tilted her head so it rested against the horse's neck, as the animal relaxed and its breathing slowed down. She looked up at him, her lips curled up into a smile, warm and genuine. Philip was frozen, unable to move or think completely drawn into her green eyes, under her spell.

"Will we go for a ride like we did the last time I saw you?" she asked.

"Of course," he said.

Philip stepped down from his stone, and beckoned her to come with him. He climbed onto his horse and then he helped her up. She sat behind him and wrapped her arms around his waist. He took the reins, dug his heels in and they rode off.

Philip kept the pace at a trot, so as to let them talk, feeling more comfortable talking to her now that he didn't have to look into her eyes. At these meetings, she had asked Philip all sorts of questions and he was happy to answer them for her. She enquired about his family, and asked about their health. She was popular in the court and always talked about the latest piece of gossip she had heard and Philip listened to her intently, even

34

though he had no real interest in the subject, Arsinoe's voice keeping his attention.

They continued along the road beside the river which led up into the mountains. At points when the road was closest to the river, they would be splashed by the spray of the water dashing off the rocks; it was beautifully refreshing. They passed by farmers pulling hay carts, who gave the couple curious looks. Did any of them recognise him? Possibly, he thought. A short while later, they ended up just outside the farmland, the foothills of the mountains were visible in the distance. Upper Macedonia is on the other side of those mountains, my mother's old country, he thought.

It was wild country once you crossed into those mountains, he had once been told by Ptolemy; if you ever go over there you'll be captured by Thracians, and Thracians eat their captives, paint their bodies with their blood and make cups from their skulls. The stories had scared him as a child, but it seemed like nonsense now. Still, seeing the mountains always gave him a feeling of foreboding, and he shivered.

"Are you alright?" Arsinoe asked him.

"I'm fine," he said, and turned his attention back to the closer plains and rolling hills.

If he squinted very carefully, he could see herdsman and their goats in the hills. The heat haze rose above the ground and made everything blur; they were just visible as tiny white dots on the hillside.

They dismounted and walked along the road for a short while. He allowed her to lead the horse by the reins and listened to her talk about her parents and that led to her talking about other members of her family, then gossip about her friends and their relationships. Philip joined in when he had something to contribute.

The country was hilly and covered in patchy grass, with grey rocks punctuating the hillside. There was a copse on the brow of the hill with a small clearing where the ground was covered in soft grass. Arsinoe led Philip there with the horse. They had been here the last couple of times, laid in the sunlight and talked. She had moved to the shade after a while, complaining that she didn't want her skin to darken, because she would look like one of the lowly vineyard workers.

Once they were out of sight of the road, she tied the horse's reigns to the branch of a tree, and took Philip by the hand. She led him over to a cool, shaded spot covered in lush green grass, the sunlight peaked through the branches of the trees and felt warm on his skin.

She stared into his eyes. He was unsure what to do, she placed her hand on his jaw and turned his face towards her. She drew his mouth down towards hers gently, and kissed him on the lips. They were soft and exquisite. Philip was lost in the kiss; time seemed to slow down, He never wanted it to end. They both lowered to a kneel.

"Will I be yours forever?" She asked softly, "No matter where life takes us?"

He nodded.

They kissed again, and he felt her place her hand just above his knee, and slowly begin to work its way up. He turned slightly to avoid her feeling the cut on his leg. Her hand reached his upper thigh, and pain shot up his body. He winced and the kiss was broken.

"What is it?" She asked.

"It's nothing."

"Nothing?" She lifted his tunic a little to reveal the cut which ran around the outside of his leg, which was beginning to scab over. When he had turned, part of it had cracked and bright red blood seeped out. She recoiled. "Your half-brothers again?"

"The bastards tried to hamstring me, but it's only superficial, barely even broke the skin."

"Philip, you need to tell your father-"

Philip's horse began neighing and became increasing agitated, kicking its front legs.

"Whoa boy, whoa boy," Philip said and stood up. Arsinoe sat back and folded her arms, shaking her head. Philip made his way over to the horse to calm it. "What is it boy? What's the matter?" He stroked the animal's neck and it quietened down.

"You hear drums?" Arsinoe asked as the horse became silent again.

"I hear nothing," he said standing perfectly still, apart from his arm stroking the horse's neck. He couldn't hear anything except for some birds chirping, and a tiny lizard scurrying up a tree.

"I definitely hear drums," she said, standing perfectly still, looking from side to side "It's very faint, just in the distance."

The two of them made their way over to the brow of the hill and laid down, from here the road was visible. Far in the distance the road snaked up along the flat plains and up into the mountains. There were men, marching along the road on the horizon. More continued to come over the mountains as they watched. "Gods protect us," she said, getting up, ready to run. "It's a raid!"

"No, it can't be," Philip said, reaching out with his hand but without taking his gaze from what was now becoming an army marching down the road. "Those are Macedonians. Look at the shields of the leading men, they bear the sixteen-point Argead star of my family."

"What are they doing?" she said, settling down next to him.

"My father is on a campaign in the East at the moment, he said they were going to attack Olynthus. He left with their Spartan allies only last week," he said, concern in his voice.

"Why were they attacking Olynthus?" Arsinoe asked.

Philip didn't hear her, all his focus was on the approaching soldiers, trying to catch a glimpse of his father. By the gods I hope he's okay, they haven't been gone long.

"Philip?"

"I don't know, they're fighting all the time. I've completely lost track of who and why. He broke with Olynthus almost immediately after they helped retake Pella, but it's usually Thracians raiding for our animals, or the Illyrians. My father hates them."

"Hates them?"

"Yeah, their King Bardylis, my father hates him with a passion; he's caused us nothing but trouble."

The army had reached the road just adjacent to where they were watching. The men look tired, beaten. The mood was sombre as they marched. The drumbeat that was being kept only added to this. There was no triumphant playing of trumpets or anything of that nature. They watched column after column of men march past, many injured and needing help walking, others simply looked defeated. They were followed by carts loaded with bodies, fresh corpses from the fight being brought back for burial. Arsinoe gasped and raised a hand to her mouth. Philip put his arm round her.

"I can't see my father," Philip said, standing up, the thumping in his chest rising. "We need to go."

She nodded in agreement and the two of them returned to their horse. He rode as hard as he could back to her home, she was upset to see him leave, "I will come see you soon." he said. "Try to put it out of your mind, spend time with your family."

They kissed and he set off back to the Pella. He rode back to the palace. By the time he got there, his thighs burned and blisters had formed on the inside of his legs, and had been rubbed off. It stung and blood had matted into the horse's flanks.

He rode straight into the courtyard, the hoof beats echoing off the stone. He rode past the guards, who recognised him, but always ignored his movements. He threw one leg over the horse and wasting no time slid off, leaving the horse standing in the courtyard. One of the palace guards ran and took the reins as he made off; he didn't look back.

He could barely stand he was so out of breath. His legs weak, his chest heaving, he marched hard through the corridors to the royal apartments, where his parents would be. One of the guard officers caught up with him and tried to talk to him "He's fine young Philip, everything is fine, he says he's not to be disturbed."

Philip nodded, but kept walking "I have to see him," he said. "Leave me."

The guard waited where he was, and Philip stopped outside his father's chambers when he heard voices. The heavy wooden door was ajar; Philip slowed his breathing and turned his head to listen. He could make out his mother and father's voices, and a third voice that Philip didn't recognise, a man's voice.

"Why don't you give these attacks a rest?" his mother said, "It could have been a lot worse this time. Leave it for the Spartans."

39

"I can't, I don't want to leave them unchecked to get a-"

Philip leant closer to the door, and peaked in, feeling the draft on his face. His father sat in a chair, with the Royal physician wrapping his arm in a bandage; it was speckled with red, blood seeping through.

"I will come back and change the dressings in an hour your Majesty."

"Thank you, you may go."

The physician gathered up his bag, and headed for the door, Philip moving quietly as a shadow behind it as it was swung all the way open. He held his breath as he watched the man walk away down the corridor. He then resumed listening, although the door had been closed so the voices were far more muffled. He pressed his ear onto the cool wood.

"We must keep attacking. If we lose the ground, we will never retake it. If we lose the ground, Athens will look to whoever controls the territory to buy their timber from. They don't give a shit who has-"

"But you could have been killed Amyntas. Where would Macedonia be then? Your sons would fight each other for the throne. You don't want them to kill each other yet surely?"

"Of course not," his father said impatiently, "but if Athens stop buying it, we are done."

Philip moved away from the door, relieved that his father was alive and well. His injury could not have been so bad if he was able to argue with his mother. He moved off and headed back towards his own bedchamber.

Chapter 4

Several days passed and Philip now walked down the path toward the gymnasium, it was morning and he could tell the day would be another extremely hot one; there was not a cloud in the sky. It was early, so the sun was still low and the air was cool, the leaves of the plants bowing under the weight of the dew that dripped from them. He stopped and leaned against the waist high wall that ran along the path, shaded by a cypress tree. The path led from one end of the army parade grounds to the other, and was the main route from the palace to the gym. A few other people pottered about their business.

He kicked some of the loose dirt with his sandal and waited. A little time passed. "Where is she?" he said to himself, then quickly glanced around to see if anyone heard when he realised he'd said it out loud.

He waited on this spot every day before training to catch a sight of Arsinoe as she went to her tutoring with her friends. It was how they had first met. She had passed with her friends and immediately caught his eye, and when she had smiled at him, he was hers. Her presence was intoxicating. After a few of these encounters she had eventually come over and spoken to him.

He waited a short while longer. Where was she? The group of girls she was normally with passed, talking and gossiping away. A few snuck glances at him and this led to more whispering and tittering. She wasn't with them, so he shrugged his shoulders and headed off to training.

The gymnasium was a vast rectangular field, surrounded by long white pillared buildings on all four sides. As he came to the large double door at the entrance of the gym, he stepped off the dry dirt ground into the shade and onto the cool marble floor of the atrium building.

It was dimly lit, and he paused for a second, unable to see. Once his eyes adjusted, he looked to his side where there stood a stone statue of Hermes, the messenger god, tall and athletic wearing his winged helmet and sandals. Philip paused to look up at the statue; he lowered his head with respect. Hermes was god of athletes along with many other things, known for his speed and cunning, traits that Philip greatly admired, but also for music and poetry, which he was not interested in.

He walked out the other side and into the open air of the gym, took off his sandals and dusted his feet. As he emerged from the entrance building, out into the bright sunlight, he shielded his eyes. The field stretched out in all directions, the air was still, any breeze was blocked by the walls. A stone walkway ran around the perimeter, and as he stepped onto it, he immediately pulled away his foot. The direct sunlight had made it feel as hot as a forge. He placed his foot down and gradually applied more pressure; giving it a moment for the sole to adjust.

In the corner of the vast, flat field, a large area was separated out from the running track, discus and javelin throwing areas. It was covered in sand and this was the area for wrestling and boxing. There were small rooms on all four sides of the gym, under the shade of the roof. Philip glanced into one as he passed, where there were athletes lying prone, having their backs massaged with oil.

Philip moved along to the end and past several groups of boys already training. His brother Alexander drilled with his peers in wrestling. They were pummelling with their opponents, reaching over the top of each other's arms and gripping the triceps. Then, when the timing and balance was right, they would turn into their opponent, levering them over their hip to throw them to the ground. They would then squat down and lift their opponent back to his feet and repeat the drill. Most of their mouths were wide open, taking deep breaths.

Philip passed several other groups of boys he did not recognise, and then noticed his brother Perdiccas among them. The boys his age were doing a similar drill. Perdiccas was a great technical fighter, and although his athleticism was not a match for Alexander, he more than made up for it with precise leverage and excellent technique. This was something that Philip greatly admired about him, his use of feints and misdirection. They had sparred many times; he was very difficult to read.

Philip arrived at the group he was going to train with, about ten boys the same age as him. They stood around loosely, some of them awkwardly. They did not all know each other. The nobles at court were constantly changing. They were landowners so had to come and go to attend to matters in their land. As they came and went, their sons often came and went with them, so there were often new faces, and familiar faces disappeared.

Their instructor arrived, Antipater, who was a bull of a man with arms, legs, waist and neck like tree trunks. His thick black beard was wild and unkempt, and streaked with grey. A hairline of the beard was bald with a visible scar below running along his left jawline. His nose was crooked and misshapen; clearly it had been broken many times. His brow and the hollows of his ears were thick with scar tissue after years of competing. Philip felt his own ear, it had small lumps of scar in it from when it was knocked in training, he wondered if his ears would look like Antipater's in time.

Under his arm Antipater carried a short, hardwood stick. This was used mostly to nudge the boys to refine their technique, but he had been known to hit with it on occasion, if the boys needed disciplining. Philip squeezed his fingers, recalling a time when they had all been struck across the fingers for taking too long to fall in.

"Some new faces here. More of Amyntas's friends returning to court I expect. Good," he said, his voice deep and gruff, his accent strange. It sounded as if he was from Epirus, a kingdom to the west of Macedonia, but none of the boys dared ask where he was from.

His eyes surveyed the group.

"For those who don't know me, I'm Antipater, and I'm here to turn you boys into men. Let's get started."

"He's a man of few words," the boy standing next to Philip whispered in his ear; he was tall, and had some muscle, but had a stomach like baker's dough. Philip nodded in agreement and smiled.

Antipater's ears pricked and his gaze whipped over to the boys.

"Something you want to share with everyone else?" he asked, and both Philip and the boy who whispered to him froze. "No? Good. I will continue then."

Antipater started the warm up. They began by running around the outside of the gymnasium, and then came back in to do push-ups, sit-ups and many different jumps. Some of these involved jumping and tucking your knees up to make yourself into a ball, and jumping and drumming their buttocks with their heels. This took a lot of effort and Philip's skin prickled as he started to sweat. The boys were then told to pair off and they were shown how to stretch with their partner. Philip was working with the boy who had whispered in his ear; the boy's presence made him feel comfortable and relaxed.

"A volunteer," Antipater's voice boomed, no one volunteered immediately, the boys all looking around to see if anyone else would volunteer. "Fine. You then." He motioned for Philip's partner to come forward.

"We're going to practice fighting fundamentals, starting with basic combinations against vulnerable parts of your opponent's body," he said; some of the boys sighed. Antipater's gaze whipped around, his stare was intense, his voice deepened, "No champion wrestler, or boxer, or warrior, ever got to the top without having a strong grasp of the most basic techniques."

Philip caught his stare and nodded.

"We will slow fight," he said. Among the boys some seemed familiar with this and nodded, others looked at each other. Philip was unsure; he had never done "Slow fighting" before.

"With your opponent," Antipater's voice boomed "you will fight slow, pick vulnerable targets and kick, punch or knee at them. He pointed to the boys chin and throat, "Make contact, but just enough so you both feel it. I don't want anyone losing teeth or eyes in training. The aim of this is to train yourself to pick targets better, and after practice, faster."

He demonstrated the slow fighting with the overweight boy for a few moments, making enough contact with him to make him turn and avoid the discomfort of bone on bone. He then told the boys to break off to find a space to work with their partners. Antipater nudged the boy he'd been demonstrating with to pair off with the nearest boy, and Philip, who had been heading over to pair off with him, stood looking for someone else to work with.

There was another boy standing back that everyone seemed to have avoided partnering with. Philip had seen him around the court, but they had never spoken. He nodded awkwardly to him and the boy nodded back, his face straight. It was very hard to read, Philip thought. The boy was tall, a lot taller than himself, and he could tell he was far stronger; he was made up of dense muscle that while not bigger than men who had trained with the weights, he held far more strength. The boy was lean and the separations of the muscles in his forearms and the veins were visible. His hair was black and cut short, a lot shorter than was normal for a Macedonian youth, it showing the shape of his skull, making him look extremely tough.

"I'm Philip," Philip said trying to break the ice.

"Antigonus," said Philip's partner. No more words were exchanged. Philip let out a slow breath and drummed his leg with his fingers, uncomfortable with this young man, and the feeling seemed to be mutual. He wished for his other partner back.

They raised their hands up in a boxing stance and slowly circling each other, began to slow fight. They slowly struck at each other faces, stomachs and ribs. They kicked each other in the knees and stomped each other's feet, all with slow, deliberate movements, like the dance of a cult belonging to some bizarre God.

After a while the speed began to build and build and the hardness of the strikes began to escalate.

Philip stepped to one side and swung his arm up in a right hook, Antigonus stepped into it and it hit him harder than the light strikes they were meant to be making. Antigonus shook his head, facing away and mumbling something to himself.

46

"Sorry," Philip said, but thought, why is he so annoyed? He was so strong, did it even hurt him? Philip wasn't sure if that was what he had done to annoy him, or even if he was annoyed at him. Antigonus didn't acknowledge the apology, he simply raised his hands again and continued the slow fight. He raised his hand and palmed Philip across the jaw. Philip rolled his head with the blow and came back with an uppercut to his ribs.

Just like before, the pace from all of the boys inevitably sped up as the excitement escalated; from time-to-time Antipater could be heard shouting "Slow down!" or "Keep it slow!"

They trained for a while and Philip stepped forward and brought his fist up in an uppercut and again, by accident, he struck Antigonus with a little more force, this time on the mouth. Philip apologised again and Antigonus again stepped away and gave his head a sharp shake and sucked his lip.

"One day it's going to hurt," he said, while his lips widened and flattened as if he was trying to force a polite smile.

Philip was confused about what to do because of the calm reaction. This was building to something bad. He imagined the boy hitting him back and knocking him to the floor, knocking his teeth out, really hurting him. From the little training they had done together, he knew that Antigonus was bigger, tougher, stronger and had better technique than him.

I am scared of this man, Philip thought, far more than my half-brothers scare me, I feel like he could beat me to death and if I tried hitting him back with everything I've got, I wouldn't even hurt him, he would just keep coming. Even though the punches he was throwing were slow and the contact was light, he felt immovable; it would be easier to move an ox.

Antipater strolled around with his stick and coached the pairs of boys separately. Philip saw him poking one of the boy's feet with his stick to move his stance into a more stable position. He corrected the technique and gave small demonstrations.

Philip and Antigonus resumed their slow fighting, and Philip took extra care not to repeat the accidental hits.

The boys took a short break, and Philip moved off to the side to get some water; back on the stone path, he sipped from a skin. His thoughts were only on Antigonus and how much the thought of fighting him for real filled him with dread.

I want to make him my friend, he thought, I don't want him to be my enemy.

After he finished his drink, he leant down to place the skin against the wall. His feet were yanked out from under him and he fell flat on his front. His hands and knees cracked the stone floor. He reacted quickly enough to turn his head, so that only the side of his face was struck, but his chest landed flat on the skin and it burst, spilling water everywhere.

Dazed, he turned his head and looked up to see the back of his half-brother Menelaus walking away. He looked back and smirked. Not sure whether to get up or not, Philip felt the side of his face, his hands stinging from slapping the stone, and his cheek throbbed.

As he looked at the marble floor, he felt his breath coming back. How many people saw that? Humiliated, he peeled himself up off the ground and turned to leave the gym, his knee and hands throbbed. As he started to walk out a voice boomed at him from behind "Where do you think you're going?"

It was Antipater shouting him back.

He froze to the spot, and felt the heat in his cheek, imagining them turning scarlet; he tried to relax the muscles in his face. He was about to be chastised in front of the other boys and didn't know if he could take it. Should he run? No. Never.

"Come here!" he bellowed, then looked around at the other boys, some of whom had stopped to look. "The rest of you, back to training!"

Philip walked sheepishly over to Antipater, glancing from side to side to see who had seen. He could make out Antigonus in the corner of his eye, watching and sipping a skin.

"What will you do now?" Antipater said, who, to Philip's surprise, put his hand on his shoulder, and spoke softly to him.

"I… I… was," Philip said. "My heart isn't in it."

"Good. There is never a better time to train. I don't think anyone saw it. You need to stand up to them though, or they will do this your whole life. How long has this been going on?"

Philip felt his cheeks start to flush red again. Antipater looked him in the eye and sighed.

"Look around Philip," he said leaning close to him, glancing over his shoulder and lowering his voice to make sure no one else was able to hear. "How many years do you think your father has left? When he dies, there will be fighting, and blood will be spilled. You need to be ready...they seem to feel it." He trailed off, staring intensely into Philip's eyes.

Philip was shocked; he had never for a moment considered what would happen if his father died.

"I have been training young men in Macedonia since before your father. Macedonian kings do not normally die of old age; and none has lived as long as Amyntas.

One day any of you or your brothers could get a knife in your back."

Philip's thoughts flashed to images of Arrhidaeus' face the night they had first come into his room to try to kill him; the eyes, glowing in the torchlight.

"It could come from anyone. Your brothers may even try to have you killed," he continued as if he had read Philip's mind.

"He wouldn't hurt us, would he?" Philip whispered. "That would be a blood crime, it would bring down furies on him beyond our imagination."

"Do you know how Zeus came to power on Olympus? The King of the Gods was Ouranos, his grandfather. He was challenged and defeated by his son Cronos. Then Cronos was challenged and defeated by his son, Zeus, who made himself king. Your father will be keeping a careful watch on all of you, and no doubt Alexander will be doing the same thing."

Philip looked down to the other end of the gymnasium, at his brother Alexander, wrestling with his group. He threw his opponent flat on his back effortlessly, and his peers cheered and raised their arms, the sound lost amongst the noise and chatter of all the other goings-on in the gym.

Alexander smiled warmly at his friends; they patted him on the back. He was incredibly popular with all the other nobles' sons. He looked up and met eyes with Philip, his smile faded.

Philip looked away and suddenly felt more alone than he had ever felt in his life.

He had never been friends with Alexander, but the idea that he would kill him and their brother Perdiccas was unreal until now. As a young man he had not thought beyond this family doing anything other than staying the way they were. His thoughts went to their half-brothers, and his murderous hatred for them, made ever more intense by what had just happened. The pain in his knees and hands throbbed again.

"But Zeus fought Cronus to protect his brothers and sisters," Philip said. "I know Alexander doesn't like me, but he won't kill me."

"I'm not saying that he would. Only that you must be ready. Your half-brothers will almost certainly kill or be killed. Rival claimants to the throne will not be tolerated." He sighed again. "You're a great athlete, strong and capable, but I have seen what happens to you when they push you around, you freeze. When your father dies, you'd better believe that they're going to come for you." "What must I do?"

"When they do come for you, you have two choices: you run, leaving your brothers, your mother and sister behind." He paused. "Or you kill them before they kill you."

"And what if- "

"Enough for now. Think about what I said. Now you must get back to training. The other boys are waiting."

The rest of the boys stood waiting for instruction in a loose group, some of the more industrious ones starting to run up and down the width of the gym and stretch their muscles to keep warm.

Despite the pains in his body and a thumping headache that had come on, he continued to train, but his mind was not on the lesson. He returned home to the palace. There was much to think about.

Chapter 5

Amyntas spent the winter recovering from his injuries, and planned to attack Olynthus again in the spring. Philip observed various representatives of the king's allies coming and going and overheard their conversations about who was offering what in terms of troops and funding for the campaign.

The following spring, Ptolemy and Eurynoe were married. Philip left Pella with the entire court for the old capital at Aegae. The royal family only returned there for weddings and burials. Philip vaguely remembered going there for his grandfather's funeral games. Amyntas was excited to bring Ptolemy into the family, having overheard him saying that his family's influence would be most useful, confirming what Philip had gathered about Ptolemy, that it was not Ptolemy himself that was the reason, but the family connections

The ceremony was a huge event and had many people from all around to catch a glimpse of the couple. The common people were everywhere, sitting on walls and rooftops to catch a glimpse of them; women in the street gossiped about what Eurynoe's gown would be like and how beautiful she would look.

On the first day of the three-day celebration, the bride and groom were apart, with Eurynoe spending the last of her unmarried time with her mother and her female relatives, while the men spent the day drinking together and making the sacrifices to the gods.

The ceremony took place in the temple of Hera under the statue of the goddess herself. The room was full of nobles from all over Macedonia, and the most powerful men from Amyntas' Greek allies. Some seemed unhappy at the wedding. Had their own sons been declined a union with Eurynoe?

The following day, Philip stood next to Perdiccas during the ceremony. He didn't pay much attention to what was being said. Although they were in the front row, this was not a theatre and the acoustics made it difficult to hear. He wasn't particularly interested in what was being said anyway, and his head was sore from the drinking the day before; he could not get the taste of dryness out of his mouth, no matter how much water he drank. Instead, he studied the statue of the goddess. She held a pomegranate in one hand, and a staff with a lotus leaf on the tip. He wondered what the significance was. He was more interested in the warrior gods like Zeus and Ares. Hera, whose domain of marriage and home held little interest for him.

He looked over at his father and his brother Alexander who were up next to the couple. The men were all separate from the women. Eurynoe stood veiled in the centre, between Amyntas and Ptolemy. She held her father's hand. The priests said some words; she was unveiled and changed to holding hands with Ptolemy.

The two stepped toward the statue of Hera, heads lowered. A priestess handed Eurynoe a bag. She took out the contents, some of her childhood dolls and clothes. She placed them on the altar as an offering to the goddess. The couple then backed away from the statue for a few steps, then turned and walked back down the central aisle of the temple towards the entrance.

As they walked, the crowd of guests parted and confetti made of violets and roses was thrown over them; they both smiled and laughed happily. Philip was happy for his sister. Even though the wedding was political, Eurynoe looked so content, her smile shone like light from Olympus. Of course, Ptolemy had been around since they were small, so in a way was like an older brother to them.

"She looks happy," Philip said to Perdiccas while still facing forward.

Perdiccas whispered, "It's all political though."

"I know that, maybe for Ptolemy, but not for Eurynoe. He's just trying to elevate himself and his family. That's the reason royals have been getting married since the beginning of time."

"Yeah, but he's getting a lot out of it, more than we are. I mean he's-" Perdiccas said, but then stopped himself.

"What do you mean by that?" Philip whispered back, leaning in, raising his voice a little so they could hear each other over the cheers. He finally turned to look at him when he didn't answer.

"Face forward," he said, and Philip obeyed. "His family are getting to marry into our line; he could even be heir someday. But on the face of it, yes, it's political, protect our borders, more manpower etc. you know. Father surely discussed it all with you too."

He had not. Why had their father told Perdiccas about many of the implications to the borders and alliances the union held, but not him? He found it extremely frustrating that although he was not interested in Politics, whenever he did show interest, his father did not keep him informed. Did they think he was useless?

"Yes, but how far does he want to elevate himself?" Perdiccas asked. "That is the question,"

"He wouldn't try and usurp Alexander. Would he?"

The two watched Ptolemy closely as he left with their sister, now newlywed. As they passed, the couple smiled at them. Perdiccas and Philip smiled and waved back. Their smiles faded after the couple had passed however, and they awkwardly turned and looked at each other. There was a long pause while the two thought about what had been said.

"Never, he's always been our friend and ally," Philip said, breaking the silence. "You're paranoid. Arrhidaeus, Archelaus and Menelaus are the real problem. They've already tried to kill us, and they would have succeeded by now if they weren't so afraid of Alexander."

"I have no intention of trying to take the throne from our brother," Perdiccas said.

"Gods, keep your voice down," he whispered sharply.

Philip was then rendered speechless, the idea that his brothers would kill each other being unthinkable. As the third son, this was unlikely to even be an issue for him. Third in line, the highest status he would ever get would likely still be a prince, maybe governorship of a city or province. When Alexander had a son, he would be the heir.

He thought about it from Perdiccas's point of view, his life having been spent living in the shadow of Alexander, and the thought that he would only be one of his generals, or regent, never King, unless something happened to Alexander. He could be taken by illness or maybe killed in battle.

Perdiccas was sharp. He always seemed to be one step ahead of Philip. "Do you really think Ptolemy is up to something?" he asked.

"I'm not saying that he is, it's just that Antipater, he has made me suspicious of everyone" He paused for a moment. "Everyone except you."

"I feel the same, he had words with me too…. so what do we do about them?"

Philip had felt closeness to Perdiccas that he didn't have with any other person he knew. He had felt this since he was a small child. He could trust him with anything, a huge weight being lifted off his shoulders to learn that this was clearly shared. From early childhood there had always been a distance between them and Alexander; he was the heir, and had always kept them at arm's length, never letting them get close. They were a threat to his succession.

Once the ceremony concluded, people were free to stroll around the gardens and more public areas of the old palace. Philip spent some time milling around, making polite conversation with guests; they would usually talk about the same things: his sister; how happy they are; what a beautiful day on which they were getting married; hopes that the gods would favour them with a son. After quite a while of this he found himself going back into the temple of Hera. He walked up the white steps at the entrance, looking up at the broad white pillars that were on all four sides of the building. The building itself was extremely tall, stretching up into the sky. The air above it was clear except for one or two clouds that slowly floated past making the building appear to levitate. It seemed surreal. He headed up the staircase, had a quick glance around to see if anyone was watching him, then headed in.

He trod carefully to stop the sound of his feet echoing on the marble floor, paused, and took a sip of his wine. In complete contrast to how busy it was earlier, the temple was now serene and quiet. It would be perfect for contemplation, he thought. Now that there were no wedding guests, he could see around the inside of the temple better. No one was there apart from the odd priestess, each wearing a white cowl, quietly going about their business, whispering to each other. There were bowls with incense burning in them along the central walkway that led up to the statue of Hera. Some had burnt out. Philip took a sniff of the floral smoke into his nostrils, deep into his lungs, and let a slow breath out.

His gaze was drawn to the statue of the goddess. He paused for a moment; she now seemed to be staring at him, beckoning him towards her. There were no priestesses around now, so he approached the goddess.

Standing under her, looking up, he wasn't sure what to do. There was a mixture of items laid out at the foot of the statue, dried flowers, and small animals that had been sacrificed. He heard a rustling noise and turned to see some cages, stacked to about waist height containing different animals; immediately he noticed a white rabbit. He thought about the statue of Hermes at the gymnasium in Pella. He often thought of sacrificing something to the God, to ask for help against his half-brothers, but could not get hold of animals like this. If he were to try and buy one, he would be recognised, and his father would find out.

Philip glanced around and took a slow breath. There was still no one around. He bowed his head to the goddess, poured his wine onto the floor at the feet of the statue and gently placed the cup on the alter. He picked up one of the priestesses' cowls that was over a chair in the corner and threw it over the box containing the white rabbit. He picked up the box and headed out of the temple with it. He paused on the threshold, looking back at the statue of the goddess; he waited for something to happen, to be spoken to, stopped by one of the priestesses, anything. Nothing did, so he headed out of the temple.

Wanting to avoid any guests, he didn't go down the main stairs at the front, but instead skirted round the

57

outside of the building, in the opposite direction from where the celebrations were happening, staying on the inside of the pillars. Once he was round the back of the building, he headed across and into the palace, placing the white rabbit, still in its box, with his baggage. This baggage would be taken back to Pella the next day by his servants.

He then headed back to the tedious conversations of the wedding.

. . . . . .

The celebrations continued well into the evening. People had been drinking for a while now; the wine was flowing. The Royal Guards were everywhere, straight faced and serious, scanning the crowds. The guests, however, were being extremely peaceable; they were just celebrating, talking and eating. They were getting louder, but there was no trouble. That won't last, Philip thought.

He stood with Perdiccas and took a sip from his cup. They looked around at the mix of guests who were attending. Some of the Greeks stood at the wine servers, after a sip they looked into their cups and screwed up their lips in irritation. The wine was very strong; Perdiccas had told him to watch the Southern Greeks when it came to drinking that night. He said some of the older boys told him they were lightweights and watered down their wine. This was neat, the Macedonian way.

"They still look down on us, they always will, they think we're barbarians; what will it take to make them accept us as Greek?" Philip said, and Perdiccas nodded.

His gaze moved across the crowds to a group of some of the other Macedonian nobles, who had stayed in the one spot the whole day and hadn't moved. They kept glancing over to another group of nobles who were doing the same thing, staying in their protective group.

One of the younger ones, about Philip's age, was staring intensely at them. Philip tried to recall his name, Argeus maybe? He seemed to remember the youth being mocked because he shared the name of the usurper, who Philip's father had driven out with the Spartans, and the Olynthians, when they were still allies. He was still on the run, with a bounty on him. This Argeus had clearly drunk too much, the whites of his eyes were visible and his chest was out, but his balance was off. He swaggered towards the other group; an older man, his father maybe, put his arm round him and pulled him back, taking him to the side to scold him. Blood feud, Philip thought. Macedonia was rife with all these old rivalries. Hopefully it won't turn into a brawl after they've all had too much to drink; surely not at a royal wedding? Who knows how his father would react if they fought, or if the daggers came out?

Another youth who looked tired and drunk slouched down on one of the couches. One of the elders from his group grabbed him by a clumped fist of his tunic and pulled him to his feet, and, just like Argeus, he got a stern lecture. Philip noticed the youth had no sword belt; he was not a man yet. He was not yet permitted to sit at feasts. Philip made fists with his toes as his own feet were a little achy from standing. He had often been tempted to sit at a feast, but as a son of the king, he would have to set an example.

Philip and Perdiccas had been joined by Polyperchon, the youth who they knew from their classes. He was about the same age as Philip, and he had noticed that he was an intelligent young man who showed great aptitude for politics and history, and he

59

enjoyed the conversations that they had. He always looked dishevelled, his hair looking as if it has been combed but then he had scratched his head, and a tuft protruded out the side. Today he had obviously already had too much to drink; as he approached the scent of wine on his breath was overpowering at first and his speech was a little slurred.

"Your sister looks beautiful," he said, looking at her while he spoke. He appeared to be having trouble keeping completely stable. "Why is she marrying him anyway?"

"You seem quite jealous?" Philip said.

"Not at all," He snapped back.

Polyperchon asked about Philip's half-brothers, seeming not to like them. The three then realised that they were being watched from across the room by Menelaus. He stared at them through the bustling crowd, unblinking. He stood on the other side of a circle of boys that Alexander had told them to stay away from. "Never trust them," he had said, "even if they appear friendly. Like wolves separating a sheep out from the herd, they will lead you away to where you can't be protected."

"Even at our sister's wedding, those bastards never stop do they?" Perdiccas said.

"Not their sister," Polyperchon said, making the others pause to think.

"Yes, but they still grew up with her too," Philip said.

"But if she marries and consolidates alliances with Ptolemy's family and their lands fall under your father's influence, this only weakens their claim to be the first family, doesn't it?"

Polyperchon then started to talk about Ptolemy; he was very interested in the politics and the strategies of running the country, which first made Philip suspicious.

Why would someone who is not in the royal family be interested in his father's alliances? But after listening to him for a short time, he went off on tangent after tangent, his mind working faster than a bee. He ended up talking about how the Greeks made alliances back when they were at war with the Persians. Philip then realised that Polyperchon just liked to talk, and his first impression that he liked the sound of his own voice was wrong, he was just interested in everything and talked intensely. He could talk nonstop on the subject, but when someone else interjected, he would stop and listen intently to what others had to say, and took it all in.

"Would Ptolemy's army be any good for fighting Bardylis and his Illyrians?" Polyperchon asked Philip.

Philip paused, again caught off guard by how much Polyperchon knew about his father's affairs, but decided that it was no secret. "I don't know, I hope so," Philip said, "we need all the help we can get these days it seems."

"Hmmm, numbers always help I suppose. Hmmm, I heard a rumour that your sister's bride price was ten talents." Polyperchon said, kneading his chin.

"I have no idea, but I doubt it. That sounds far too high," Philip said, the feeling of intoxication was building up in him now. Trying to concentrate on what Polyperchon was saying over the noise and chatter of the room was hurting his head.

He glanced around the room while Polyperchon continued to talk. His father and mother were at the head table, feasting with the bride and groom. The place was alive with the sound of talking and drinking. The celebration was in full swing.

"Some beautiful women here," Polyperchon said, looking over at a group of young women who stood near where the wine was being served, "especially that one,"

Perdiccas and Philip both looked over and saw the girl he was talking about, she smiled over at them.

"She would rival Aphrodite herself. I think she's smiling at me," Polyperchon said.

"Ha-ha, that's Arsinoe," Perdiccas said, glancing at Philip "you might be out of luck there."

"Why do you say that?" Polyperchon asked.

Arsinoe was looking at them across the room, and the three stared at her as she made her way towards them through the crowd of people. She paused to take a sip of wine from her cup and licked some off her lips; she then came over and stopped in front of the three boys. Her head was low, but her eyes looked up at Philip and she smiled showing her teeth, white as polished ivory.

Philip felt a lump in his throat, not expecting her to come over, as their relationship was still a secret. "Hello" he said to her. "Arsinoe?"

"Hello Philip," she said. There was a pause and time seemed to slow down. Polyperchon's jaw hung down, his mouth wide open. Perdiccas nudged him and he closed it.

Arsinoe lightly placed her hand on Philip's chest and whispered into his ear to find somewhere private; the scent of alcohol was heavy on her breath. Philip was torn, he wanted nothing more than to go away with her. He glanced around. Certain people would be watching this meeting and Philip did not want their relationship to be known about. Too many in this room that had their eyes on the throne.

"I can't," he whispered.

Arsinoe recoiled, clearly hurt, obviously confused at why he didn't want her. She looked angrily at Philip and stormed off. Don't worry, Philip thought, I'll explain everything the next time I see her and she'll understand.

Polyperchon was speechless; he then took a swig of his wine and let out aloud breath, "Are you two?" he asked.

"No," Philip said bluntly, watching her walk away.

Polyperchon frowned. "Nice acting. Be careful you don't put a bastard in her belly though."

Philip was taken aback; he turned his head. "What do you mean by that?" he asked. His eyebrows lowered.

"What *do* you mean by that?" Perdiccas asked. Both of them leaned closer in to him so they could hear his answer over the din of the celebrations.

Polyperchon was in the middle of a deep swig from his wine and startled at Philip's reaction, pulled the cup from his mouth and spluttered. His cheeks went red. Abashed, and defensive, he leaned away from them slightly. "I didn't mean anything by it, I'm not saying she is…"

"She is what?" Philip asked and grabbed a handful of Polyperchon's tunic in his fist. He leant back further, almost about to fall over.

"Well, you know, this is a court, there are a lot of ladies around here who are, you know..."

Philip and Perdiccas looked each other. "No, we don't know, tell us."

"Well, there are already enough claimants to the throne in this kingdom, without adding one more. I'm just guessing, she might be trying to elevate her status, you know, like Ptolemy up there, although women usually don't have armies, so they tend to use what's between their legs. A son of a prince in her belly might certainly do that," he said.

Philip guessed he wished he hadn't said anything now. He released his grip and Polyperchon sighed with relief and adjusted his tunic as he straightened up.

Both Perdiccas and Philip took a step back to think. This hadn't crossed his mind, and by Perdiccas's reaction he hadn't either, but now it made perfect sense. Philip thought about her, her smile, her hair, her eyes, her waist. He thought about how he felt when he was around her. Was it all a lie? An act?

"No, she's definitely not like that," he said, but the statement fell flat.

"Are you sure?" Polyperchon asked. "Be careful Philip."

Philip stood and watched Arsinoe, now on the other side of the room; she had seemingly forgotten about the fight and was talking to a group of the nobles. He recognised the ones who were around his own age from the gym. Her back was to him, her hip was cocked the same way it was when she talked to him. He didn't know their names, but he was sure they were distant relatives. They would be claimants to the throne if his father didn't have them all under his boot.

He took a long sip of his wine and took a slow survey of the room. He had always known that there were competing lines, but not until this very moment, seeing all of them in the one place, had he realised just how many there were. He had only ever considered his half-brothers, sons of his own father.

The tension in his chest began to build, and he continued to drink. How did his father keep all of them in check? Surely at any given time, there would be several plotting against him. His father had mentioned Argeus a few times, the usurper, who was still on the run. The king had spies in full time employ looking for him. He suspected he was at the court of Bardylis, his great enemy, where he could not be reached.

The feast was served and Philip and most of the other youths were forced to stand and eat. Only the men who had earned their sword belts were allowed to sit. Philip stared at his brother Alexander's; he had long coveted earning his own. He hoped this would elevate his status enough to make his half-brothers leave him.

Chapter 6

The next day, the court travelled back to Pella and the Royal family finished the final day of the wedding drinking at the palace. For the whole journey, Philip's mind was occupied with thinking how he would earn his belt. He excused himself earlier than he would normally have done, saying that he was tired from the journey, which earned him some curious looks.

Darkness fell and he sat awake in his room. He had tried to drink as little as possible, but his cup had been constantly replenished and there had been many toasts to the newlyweds, so the room spun gently around him. After a while the sounds of the celebrations died down and the last of the guests retired for the night, leaving the palace grounds quiet and peaceful.

He put on the darkest cloak he could find, pulling its large hood over his head. He slid his hand down the side of his bed and pulled up the dagger that he had had by his side ever since the night when his half-brothers had first attacked him, heeding Alexander's advice.

Philip felt the tip of the blade with his thumb, as sharp as an eagle's talon, and even though the touch was light, it cut the skin. He raised the finger and sucked the wound, the metallic taste of the blood lingering in his mouth. He rubbed the tips of his thumb and forefinger together, inspecting the cut, a bright red orb of blood like a ruby, grew and rested on the wound, but did not flow any more than that.

He stared at the polished blade, which glinted in the moonlight. He gulped at the lump in his throat, then his focus turned to the white rabbit that he had taken. He took it out of its cage and clutched it in his arms. The animal had been bound, its front feet and back feet tied together. It wriggled and its head bobbed hard as it tried to get free, but it gave up after a few minutes.

He snuck out of the palace into the night with the animal under his cloak.

In the darkness the gravel path crunched under his feet. He was still quite drunk, and the sound felt amplified, making him step onto the grass. He moved as stealthily as possible but his head still swam with alcohol, making it difficult to tell if he was being quiet. He passed through the palace courtyards unnoticed and headed out towards his destination, the gymnasium.

If he was caught, there would be consequences, that he was sure of, but he was not sure what they would be. The stolen rabbit was most likely intended as a sacrifice for his sister's marriage to Ptolemy. If he were caught there would be questions; this would be viewed as a bad omen for the union and the subsequent alliances. The repercussions could be dire. Sentries with torches patrolled the palace grounds and he would have to avoid them.

Philip looked to the sky, the moon mostly covered by clouds. He squinted into the darkness and could vaguely make out the path he was on, and the wall that ran along it. There was a crunch of sandals on gravel on the path ahead, the click of buckles on armour, then the bright orange glow of a torchlight began to emerge from behind the end of the wall. He slunk behind a tree and stumbled, half falling against it. His breathing was loud in his head, for a moment it was all he could hear or concentrate on, so he held his breath and waited for them to pass, two of them.

He swallowed a belch which tasted of the wine from earlier, the sting in his throat almost making him sick and he pressed the back of his hand against his mouth.

One of the guards froze, "Did you hear something?" he said, and the other stopped to listen. His head turned slightly as if he was reaching out with his ear. The two stepped forward, scanning the darkness. By chance the tree cast a long shadow from the light of the torch, which shrouded Philip in blackness. The first guard's sandals crunched on the gravel as he turned a half step to look around. The one who had spoken stepped closer to Philip, almost standing over him. The other stood back with the torch, and gripped the handle of his short sword. Philip could not hold his breath any longer and drew in a breath as quietly as he could. "It was probably nothing," the guard said after a few moments of looking over Philip's head, and continued back to his comrade. The two of then resumed their patrol, their footsteps fading into the night.

The rabbit Philip was carrying struggled and wriggled under his cloak and it scratched his ribs, which hurt, but the sting of the claws ripping into his side was numbed by alcohol and because of the many beatings from his half-brothers he was able to ignore the pain. Once the sound of the footsteps diminished, he adjusted the animal so it could not claw him, and he continued on.

When he reached the walls of the gymnasium, he cursed because the door was locked. He walked around the outside and found somewhere where the wall was lowest and managed to scale it. It was not an easy task because he was still carrying the rabbit. He slunk down on the other side trying to land as quietly as possible, but lost his balance when his feet struck the floor, and he staggered and fell. Even though he was drunk he was able to fall and roll with the momentum, keeping his arms relaxed so as not to injure the rabbit. This was a result of training, repeated break falls in the gym to prevent being injured when thrown by an opponent. Regardless of this, it made a thud and he froze to the spot and listened for signs that he had alerted anyone. There should be nobody in there at this time of night, but his head was not clear. After a long pause, he decided the coast was clear.

The central field of the gymnasium stretched out into the darkness. It was flat and the walls were too far away to see, giving the place a surreal quality and he paused to take it in. Was this how it felt to be in the underworld? In the dark, surrounded by nothingness? He shook these thoughts, and focused on where he was going. He headed straight for the statue of Hermes at the opposite end.

The statue loomed over him in the moonlight, and seemed taller than it ever had in the daylight. He brought the rabbit out from under his cloak and presented it to the god.

"Great god Hermes, I am Philip of Macedon, I ask that you give me and my family the strength and cunning to overcome our enemies," And with that he drew his dagger, which had been tucked into the ankle of his sandal, and slashed the animal's throat. It thrashed hard. Warm blood ran between Philips fingers, its soft fur becoming matted. It thrashed again, trying to wriggle free. He gripped it harder, so much so that he could feel the animal's small, thin bones begin to crack under its soft flesh. A tear dripped from Philip's eye.

The animal slowly stopped thrashing as the life drained from it, and he placed it on the podium which the god stood on, alongside all the other trinkets and flowers that had been placed there by others. He wiped the tears from his eyes and sniffed. Philip had witnessed many animal sacrifices to the gods, but doing the killing himself was different; it was usually carried out by a priest or his father, whose role as king was also spiritual leader. Maybe I am weak, he thought, how am I to kill my enemies when I can't even kill an animal without crying.

"And why should a god grant you this wish young Prince of Macedonia?" Came a deep voice from behind. Philip jerked and turned to face whoever it was behind him.

A figure slowly emerged from the darkness, it was tall, over six feet, and wore the hooded cloak of a priest. This hood obscured the man's body, but in the moonlight, Philip could make out the man's face now that his eyes had adjusted. He was older than Philip, probably older than Alexander, but something about him was more youthful than he was, Philip thought; he was clean-shaven which was strange for a man of this age in Macedonia. The men would grow a beard after killing their first boar on a hunt, thus becoming a man and earning their belt. His face was handsome, with beautiful yet masculine features. Philip stood confused.

"Who are you? No one should be in here at night."

"Yet you are in here young Prince?" The man said, his voice was deep and masculine, but the sound of it soothed Philip's ears and relaxed him.

"I, came to see Hermes, to make him an offering, I could not do this during the daylight," he answered, and immediately wondered why he would say this to this stranger.

"Very well, but what do you offer the god in return?"

"Are you a priest?"

"No"

"Who are you then?"

70

"Answer the question," the man said, his voice still deep, but soft and patient. "What would you be prepared to sacrifice to the God for him to grant your request?"

Philip pondered the question. What would he be willing to sacrifice? In his drunken state, he could not think clearly.

"My life," he answered, "I would give my life to ensure the Argead dynasty survives."

The man was gone. Philip stood stunned. Had he ever been there?

"Hello?" He shouted, then remembered he was trying to be quiet. Nothing. Surely, he hadn't imagined it.

…..

In the morning Philip woke up groggy and tired, but sat up abruptly and excited. He was going to head back to the gymnasium and this was a day when there were no formal lessons on, so they could train freely.

Most of the court would be battling hangovers, so the gym would be quiet. He was still at that young age where he did not get much of a hangover, just a dry mouth and minor headache, much to the jealousy of the older boys at court. He stretched his arms out wide; as he went to have a wash he was reminded of the night before. There was dry blood caked on his hand, not only where he had cut himself, but in-between his fingers and under his nails from where he had held the rabbit. His thoughts went to the man he had spoken to, who had he been? What had been his purpose? I must not speak of him to anyone, they will think I have lost my mind, he thought.

He got something to eat, dressed and headed down to the gymnasium.

When he arrived, there were already a few youths warming up who must have had the same idea.

"Morning," some of them said and nodded to him.

"Morning," he replied politely. These were boys that he did not know by name, the sons of some of the nobles that were at court with their fathers, and Philip loved to train with them; he could pick up techniques from different parts of the kingdom where they might do things slightly differently, but he always felt a little discomfort at being given respect simply because of his royal status. He felt he had done nothing to earn this respect.

They started off by warming up, just some running and moving up and down the gym and doing crocodile crawls. Crocodile crawls, as they called them were great for warming up and stretching the muscles of the core. Philip had never seen a crocodile, but he had seen images of them and Antipater had described them from when he had travelled to Egypt in his youth. The crawl that they adopted to mimic the creature was low to the ground as if you were going to do push-ups. As you took a stride, you stretched the body down one side then switched to the other. Philip joined in; once their muscles were warm and beginning to sweat, they partnered up to stretch.

Once they had stretched, they started to practise techniques that they had had difficulty with during their formal lessons; Philip felt very relaxed in this environment. The tension that he felt when his half-brothers were in the class was gone and he could just focus on what he was doing. This anxiety quickly returned however when all the other youths had split into pairs, and as he looked around for a partner. The only one that was left was Antigonus, the boy who he had trained with before and had thought he had angered during slow sparring. He desperately looked for someone else to train with, but there was no one, so he nodded awkwardly at him. Antigonus nodded back, apparently the awkwardness was shared.

Antigonus was tall, taller than Philip, and despite his facial hair already starting to grow seemed about the same age; he remembered his strength from when they had last trained. Philip had been unable to move him for the most part. Yes, he was quite a bit stronger than him.

"Is there anything you want to work on?" Antigonus asked.

"We could just spar lightly and see how it goes," Philip answered.

"Sounds good to me."

They wrestled lightly, then Antigonus suggested some light boxing. He seemed to Philip to be far more relaxed than when they had first trained. He was opening up a little, even almost smiling when Philip made a joke.

They fell to the ground still wrestling and continued to try for a pin or submission on the ground, each trying to wrap the other's arm or leg and twist it until they surrendered.

This went on for a while and Philip was getting outmuscled in almost every situation. Antigonus was far too strong for him to handle and he took deep breaths, his chest heaving. His skin prickled as the sweat began to gather in beads and drip from him. Antigonus, on the other hand, didn't seem to be in the least bit challenged, and was even able to talk while they trained, offering Philip advice about his techniques, repositioning his grip and footing to make it more efficient.

Every time Philip almost had him in a position to throw, he would be outmuscled, but with each attempt he would get a little closer to a throw, then a pin. He

73

was becoming quite comfortable with Antigonus, and wondered what was different about the last time they had met; maybe he was distracted by something.

More boys trickled into the gym, some in groups and others on their own. Philip's heart sank into his stomach as he glanced up toward the door. Two of his half-brothers had entered to come and train.

"Something wrong?" Antigonus asked, turning to see.

"Nothing," he said, unable to look away.

"Ah, your brothers. Do you not get along?"

"They're not my brothers. I hate those bastards," he said, trying to hide the feeling of intimidation by sounding aggressive. They were both staring at him, both smirking. Menelaus whispered something into Arrhidaeus's ear.

Philip looked up and locked stares with Arrhidaeus, until after a moment the discomfort became too great and he had to look away, as his face began to feel warm. Philip could feel Antigonus watching him, probably noting how uncomfortable he was, his chest fluttering and he had to move and turn.

"I've heard rumours. Don't worry, surely they won't do anything in a place like this, with so many people around," Antigonus said.

"You don't know them like I do."

Their stares then locked again as they moved around the room to start their warmup, Philip keeping his whole body and head still and following them with his eyes. Once they started their warmup, they went for a run around outside the gymnasium and the staring lock was broken. Philip didn't move.

"Ahem," Antigonus coughed. "Will we get back to training?"

Philip gave a slow nod, but was distant, his mind on those two, what they had been whispering and what they would do next. They started wrestling again, trying to get a submission hold on each other and this continued for a while.

They stopped for a break and sat next to each other in the shade of the roof, backs against the wall, watching the others wrestle and box. They shared a skin of water, Philip gulping at it. The need to quench his thirst was addictive and he gulped harder, then they sat quietly.

"What was your name again?" Philip asked Antigonus, even though he remembered perfectly well, he wanted to break the silence. He lay back, his eyes lightly closed, taking slow deliberate breaths. Philip flicked a stone that was on the ground next to him.

"Antigonus."

The one-word answer did not break the silence for long, he tried again. "I'm Philip, I'm-"

"Yes, I remember, I know who you are," Antigonus said, "You're the son of the king."

"Yes," he said, not really knowing what to say to that. People always expected big things from a Prince, but in their house, it was all about Alexander. He was the one who was being groomed to be king; Philip didn't really seem to matter most of the time.

"I've always wondered what it would be like to be royalty."

"It isn't as great as you might think. In fact, it's - never mind."

"I know what you're thinking," Antigonus told him. That caught Philip's attention. "You aren't weak Philip. I've watched you. You're tough. I have just spent the morning beating you down, and you just keep coming back for more. No one wants to spar with me. They're afraid of me."

"They are afraid of you," Philip said. "When we trained last week, I was afraid of you."

"You *were* afraid of me." He put his hand on Philip's shoulder. "But you face your fear in plain sight, like one of the heroes of the myths, no hiding. Don't ever underestimate that."

Philip looked at him, stunned; he had not expected to ever get more than a few words out of Antigonus. He sat and thought about what he had said, the silence no longer feeling awkward.

They were approached by one of boys from the other groups that were training. "We're about to fight bouts like in the games. You boys want to come train with us?"

"Sure," Antigonus said, without checking with Philip.

"Sure," Philip repeated, unable to refuse.

The boys had drawn a large circle in the sand, and they drew lots to fight Pankration style, one versus one boxing and submission wrestling combined, with few rules, no eye gouging, and no biting. Each bout, a new boy was selected as referee, who would decide if a fight was over. The boys would keep going until there was a winner.

Philip's new acquaintance, Antigonus, was matched against Menelaus, Philip's half-brother.

The two stared each other down from opposite sides of the circle. The referee signalled them to enter. They both circled each other with their knees bent, sidestepping, their fists raised to protect their faces. The other boys stood around the outside the circle, shouting and cheering.

Antigonus shot forward and jabbed at Menelaus's face. He slipped the punch and came back with a hook to the ribs. Antigonus blocked this by tucking his bent arm in to cover it.

Antigonus then threw a false jab with his left and when Menelaus backed up and raised his hands to protect his face, Antigonus threw up his foot and front kicked him in the stomach. He bent forward and winced, but recovered quickly. A red mark the shape of a foot quickly emerged on his skin.

They closed in a chaotic flurry of punches, none of which landed cleanly, their heads bobbing and weaving to avoid each other's strikes. The sound of the other boys shouting and jeering built up like a storm into a roar. They were yelling support to their chosen man. Philip yelled in favour of Antigonus, shaking his fist furiously, willing him to hurt his half-brother badly, to at least wound his arrogance if nothing else.

The two locked in a clinch, palms around the back of each other's necks, Menelaus throwing up a knee to Antigonus abdomen. He grunted and responded by jabbing his forehead into the hinge of Menelaus's jaw, who lost his grip and staggered back, dazed.

Antigonus shot forward, straight like an arrow, and low to the ground. He lifted his opponent by the thighs, twisted him in the air and speared him into the sand. Still holding onto him and controlling him with his head, Antigonus pivoted his body around to his opponent's side and sprawled his weight on top of him. Menelaus regained some of his composure, and pivoted on his back, wrapping his legs around Antigonus's waist to control him. He pulled him forward and back to keep him off balance, while throwing punches up at him. The pace slowed as they ground against each other, both of their mouths wide open, chests heaving. Antigonus's nostrils flared, sucking in air.

After they had both paused for a moment to draw breath, all the youths started yelling again, and shaking their fists. They responded by both starting to throw lethargic punches at each other from their locked position, motivated by being egged on.

Antigonus began, to Philip's delight, to get the better of Menelaus. He was in a more dominant position, above his opponent, and so was not being physically taxed as much. He reached forward and landed a hard punch on his cheek and managed to escape the legs locked around his waist. He pinned Menelaus's thigh to the ground, and slipped past it into a superior position, controlling him from the side. He now rained hammer fists into his face, while keeping his body weight on him.

Menelaus flailed, trying to cover his face, but the fists kept hitting him; he tried to squirm and break free, but after a moment he yelled, "I yield. I yield!"

The strikes immediately stopped and Antigonus stood up; breathing hard, he offered his hand, and helped Menelaus to his feet.

The boy who was refereeing stood them next to each other, and signalled Antigonus the winner, raising his hand.

Antigonus turned to come out of the circle. Menelaus watched him walk away, then stepped over and picked up one of the hand weights that was lined up along the wall. He tested the weight of it in his hand, then rushed forward and swung it at the back of Antigonus's head.

"Look out!" one of the boys shouted. Antigonus dodged the swing, just quickly enough to not take the hit, the weight glancing off the top of his skull. There was a crunch that caused some of the youths to wince. Philip stood, but then realised the crunch was not Antigonus skull. Menelaus cradled his hand; he seemed to have jarred his wrist in the swing, white bone protruding through the skin.

Antigonus whipped around, furious. He went from being magnanimous to aggressive in an instant. He charged at Menelaus like a bull, throwing a flurry of punches. They were thrown in a pure animal rage. Not with the calm, relaxed technique they were taught. The strikes hit Menelaus in the face and stomach.

He pathetically backed away in a panic, still cradling his hand, and trying to cover his face. He partly tripped over his own foot and Antigonus swept his legs out from under him. When he fell to the ground hard, the beating continued. Antigonus stomped on his stomach and kicked him in the face, and when he tried to turn away, he rested his knee on his chest, pinning him on his back.

Menelaus threw his hands up and flailed erratically in a pathetic attempt to save himself. Antigonus gripped his throat in one hand and punched him repeatedly in the face with the other. Then he stopped himself.

The boys stood back, shocked.

Menelaus lay on his side, cradling his arm, looking up at Antigonus, "My father is going to have you crucified," he spat.

Antigonus got up, calmly wiping the blood off his knuckles onto Menelaus's chest. The boys parted to let him pass and he walked out of the gymnasium.

Philip, who at the initial attack had sniggered, was now stunned, as were most of the other boys. He now caught the attention of Arrhidaeus, who helped Menelaus up, and the two turned on him.

"What are you looking at, you bastard piece of shit?" Menelaus spat blood and bits of broken teeth. The two advanced on him rapidly.

Philip froze and was pushed up against the wall. Menelaus crushed his cheeks hard between the thumb and forefinger of his good hand, pinning his head to the wall. He snarled in his face, so close that Philip could smell the salt of his bloody breath. The other boys stood back; they didn't know what to do: what do you do when a prince attacks a prince? The two stomped on his feet with their heels trying to break his toes and then raked them down his shins, the pain shooting through his body like a lightning bolt, as his legs gave out from under him. He tried to claw away and use the wall to stand up, but they dragged him out into the middle of the gymnasium floor. He desperately looked around for help, but the other youths stood back, afraid. Not one would dare lay their hands on one of the King's sons.

Philip picked up a handful of sand and threw it at their eyes, trying to get up again, but he was repeatedly kicked and punched. He tried to protect his head as much as he could with his arms, but they threw kicks and punches with such haste that he could not block them all. In covering up his head, he could not see most of the strikes coming in.

After a short while, their pace began to slow, the hardness of the strikes lessened, and he could hear both of them panting for breath. Philip was curled up in a ball, stunned, but not really hurt. As he was coming back to his senses the strikes suddenly stopped. He could hear gasps all around him. He glanced at feet from his curled-up position, and saw that the circle of youths had parted.

He slowly got to his feet and looked up. Their father, King Amyntas stood in the doorway, his arms folded.

Philip was ashamed. He felt his cheeks start to burn; the last thing in the world he wanted was to look weak in front of his father. Menelaus and Arrhidaeus stared at their feet.

"Philip! Go back to your chambers, I will meet you there soon," he said.

Philip slunk past his father through the doorway, his head hung, unable to look him in the eye, as he made his way down the marble corridor.

"You two! Come with me!" He heard his father's voice bellowing like thunder down the corridor behind him. "Everybody out! I need to speak with my sons!" His voice echoed off the walls along with the footsteps of all the other boys scurrying out of the gymnasium.

Chapter 7

In a blind panic Philip dashed into his chambers. He was light headed and his sight began to go white. He half tripped over the couch at the end of his bed. Deciding he was not going to wait for his father's chastisement, or the wrath of his half-brothers. He picked up his riding cloak and ran down to the stables.

He rode hard out of the city along the banks of the Axios and past the vineyards where he knew he would come to a crossroads, just past Arsinoe's family estate. He was going to run, this much he knew, but was not sure where. He could head onto the Thracian Road, which followed the river north into the mountains, and eventually Thrace and Illyria, or he could head east to the Chalcidice, the three fingered peninsula, and cities like Olynthus or Amphipolis, from where he could get on a ship to Athens, where he could blend in and disappear.

This part of the Axios ran deep and wide, insects hovering above the surface in clouds. The hooves of his horse pounded on the dirt, and dust flew up in a mist around him. He coughed and tried his best to cover his mouth. The bounding of the horse's body battered the inside of his legs, and he tried to stay loose and breathe, but coughed more. He spat the dry mud out of his mouth, but the taste lingered on his lips.

His heart pounded so hard it felt as though it was going to burst out of his chest. His mind worked just as fast; this incident with his half-brothers was dangerous. It was one thing in private, but for half the nobility's sons to see how fragmented the royal family was, and what would happen when the sons go back and tell their fathers about it? Even perceived weakness could be very dangerous for his father.

He slowed to think. What would happen now? They might need him, but what use would he be? Would his father change who he favoured? Of course not! Although Arrhidaeus and Menelaus were more formidable than him, they were scared of Alexander, who was still the first born, and still the heir. Still though, what will *they* do to me? he thought.

As he got past the vineyards and out onto the open pastures where there were shepherds herding their goats, he realised he needed to find Antigonus, the boy who had ran as well. Where would he have gone? Would he have gone back to his family? Philip felt that in time, if he lived, this youth would be a valuable friend and ally.

He slowed more, bringing the horse to a trot. He had been riding for over an hour, his joints and muscles aching. He came over a grassy knoll at the edge of some woods, and chose to stop there, so that he was not visible from the road. There was a gravel beach on the inside of the meander of the river where the water was shallow. As his horse lapped up the cool water he squatted down, cupped his hands and drank. He looked up and noticed a hooded figure, standing further downstream from him, also with a horse, letting it drink. It was Antigonus, who looked up.

"By the gods, how did you find me?" Antigonus said, holding his horses' bridle and patting its neck. He tied the bridle to a low tree branch, and sat down throwing pebbles into the river.

"I don't know, I had not even decided to look for you until this very moment," Philip said. "It must have been the will of the Gods."

"I'm sorry for what I did to your brother, I didn't mean for it to go so far."

83

"Remember what I said to you about them?" Philip asked.

"Yes, I do. You said you hated those bastards."

"Exactly."

"I didn't realise until now that you meant it, we all say we hate family members from time to time," Antigonus said.

"I didn't think you were someone who would run?" Philip asked.

"I panicked. I won't do it again," he said, "My father hates me, I think, and I hated him, he still beats me, more occasionally now, but he is still my father. His name is Philip, just like you. If I ever have a son, I will do my very best not to treat him as I am treated."

"I hope he isn't too angry when you go back."

"I won't go back. I don't know what will happen."

"You have to go back. We have to go back. I'm sure your father will understand."

"What will happen with your brothers?"

Philip sat down next to him, first tying his horse next to Antigonus's. The two sat in silent contemplation. Philip felt his heart and breathing start to slow.

"They're not really my brothers, we have different mothers. They are rivals to my real brother, Alexander, although we were all friends as children. I wouldn't worry about that anyway. They are not in my father's favour. Probably nothing will come of it," Philip said. "Where will you go?"

"Far away; if I stay here, I think they might have me killed too," Antigonus said. "Thrace, maybe even as far as Persia".

"Persia? You'd never make it that far."

"And why not?" Antigonus asked.

"Do you know how far it is to Persia? It would take months of travelling, maybe years," Philip said, "Of course if you go, I will come with you."

"Why would you do that?" Antigonus asked, "You are a prince."

"Do you think my life has everything I want because I'm a prince? My father thinks I'm weak; he's right, I'm the runt of the litter. My death is more likely than yours now, I think, they've wanted it for years," he said.

"No, I've seen the way your half-brothers treat you. I knew even before we spoke," Antigonus said, "This tensing up and freezing like a Gorgon has caught you in her stare. That is your problem. Why does it happen?"

"I don't know, I can fight in training, but as soon as it becomes real, that happens." Philip said, picking at the grass and letting it go into the breeze. "I think it's the reason my father has not started my military training. He thinks I'm what the Spartans call a trembler."

Antigonus took a moment. Then he stood up and extended his arm out to help Philip to his feet. Philip sat up a bit and reached out, but instead of taking his hand, Antigonus screamed in his face from deep down in his guts. Philip tensed and fell back down. He stared up at Antigonus, stunned, his heart fluttering. He had to fight back, his hands shaking.

"No, remember what I said in the gymnasium? You aren't weak. You've just had those pieces of shit, like a splinter in your mind all the time, never giving you a moment to find yourself. We can train this out of you," he said with a smile. "All it will take is a bit of work."

Philip took a moment. "Okay, what do we do?"

"Practise."

They wrestled lightly and Antigonus shouted at him, or threatened him some more when he wasn't expecting it, causing him to lose his technique every time.

They continued on into the afternoon, Antigonus got right in Philip's face and snarled, bared his teeth, even struck him with his forehead. They wrestled more, and repeated this over and over. Eventually when Antigonus jumped up and screamed at him, he didn't react like before. Philip simply threw up his arms and grappled as he would in the gym, completely relaxed.

"That's it!" Antigonus said and smiled. Then when he realised he had broken character, he bared his teeth and tried to kick Philip in the shin. "What the fuck are you looking at runt?"

Philip stayed composed and dodged the blow. Sometime later, Philip was composed more times than not, and when he saw an attack coming, the freezing didn't happen. They then tried Philip standing with his eyes closed, Antigonus building the tension and stalking around him. He fought the urge to open his eyes, until it became almost unbearable. Antigonus would then strike him and yell insults at him. He did not flinch.

After a while they stopped and they sat by the river, the trickling of the water pleasant and relaxing compared to what they had done all day.

"Next time they come for you. You have to be ready for them," Antigonus said, "or maybe we could even, no…"

"Maybe we could what?" Philip raised an eyebrow.

"Maybe we should try and jump them, you know, when they least expect it. What do you think would happen if we killed one of them? Would the others back off?"

"Kill one of them?" Philip shook his head, startled at the very idea of it. "That is out of the question."

"Why?"

"Because…" Philip did not answer immediately. He had not known Antigonus for very long, but when he looked at him, he knew that he trusted him. "It could anger the furies."

"The furies? They didn't care about the furies."

"Okay." Philip stood up and shook his head again. "If not the furies, it would divide the nobility, which would weaken the kingdom. Since my father's return we have had stability like we haven't seen in decades. He is making Macedonia stronger and richer than ever before. If his sons from different wives started to murder each other their families might revolt against him. It could start a civil war."

Antigonus nodded, "Now I understand, but we have to do something. Why do they hate you? How did it start?"

"I can't remember. They're older than me. I think that it's me and my brothers that they hate, but they're like lions trying to pick off the weakest of the herd."

"Philip, you are not weak, you are far tougher than you think. When we box, I hit you hard as anyone; most boys won't spar with me after that, but you kept coming, you never back down."

Philip sat and pondered this. "I am the weakest of my brothers," he said. "Alexander is strong and Perdiccas is wise."

"Enough," Antigonus said firmly. "Let's see if we can stop this way of thinking."

They fought again, they practised and practised. It got rougher and rougher, with Antigonus shouting at Philip, hurling insults at him, punching him when he wasn't expecting it. By the end of the day Philip did not freeze at all, not once. He was like a statue of a god, head up and proud. They rode their horses back to the palace in the cool air of the dusk. The sun was low and red.

They said their goodbyes and agreed that they would meet in the next lesson, both ready for whatever faced them back at the court.

…

The following morning Philip woke up sore, his knees black and stiff, the skin scabbed and sticky from friction burns, sand from the gymnasium embedded in the wound. Every time he moved, he felt a new bruise, but nothing seemed to be broken.

He checked his eye in a looking glass; it was black and swollen. It was also half shut and the skin was tight. As he slowly closed it and opened it, it stung, the skin being cut around the bone of his eye socket; touching it with his fingertip hurt even more. The pain didn't bother him, but the shame that he had not fought back did.

He dressed and headed down the stairs to the dining area of the Royal apartments. Heavy black bruising down the outside of his left leg forced him to limp, although he tried to hide it as much as he could.

Sitting at the table for breakfast were his mother, sister and Perdiccas. His father and Alexander were nowhere to be seen; this was often the case, as they would rise early and attend to matters of the kingdom, and the son often shadowed the king to learn from him. Philip was greeted and he sat down at one end, keeping his distance and trying to keep his head turned so they would not see the condition of his face. However, this failed when he lifted a loaf of bread and ripped a piece off. He asked to be passed the olive oil by his mother to pour on it, and Eurynoe saw it as he turned. She gasped.

"Gods Philip! What happened to your face?" she asked, causing him to cough on the water he had just taken a sip of. Even though he was expecting to be asked, he hadn't prepared an answer.

Perdiccas, who had seen what had happened looked him in the eye, and subtly shook his head as if to tell him not to tell the truth.

Amyntas and Alexander arrived; Philip kept his head low, and ate. He could feel the unblinking stare of his father from across the table.

"Good morning husband," Eurydice greeted him and he kissed her on the cheek and sat down beside her.

"Just boxing, I stepped into a punch," Philip lied, keeping his eyes lowered.

"Boxing seems such a silly thing to do," Eurynoe said, "Punching each other for sport"
She had bought the lie. She was still young and naïve.
"It is not a game," their father said, "Competition will
        win the favour of the gods."
"Well, I don't understand it," she said and continued
        eating.

His mother kept her eyes on him as he ate, and carried on looking at him without breaking her stare. He could feel her eyes on him. She carried on eating. She knew this was no boxing injury, he thought.

"Who punched you? Was he bigger than you?" his mother finally asked. "Maybe only spar with boys your own size."

"No mother, it was my fault," he said. "I have to go."

He stood up.

"You've hardly eaten anything," she said as he got up to leave, but he ignored this.

"Will you leave the boy alone woman," His father said. "The boy was punched, it will heal; how will he ever be a man with this kind of talk around him?"

"Amyntas, perhaps the trainers are pushing them too hard? Perhaps I should talk to Antip-"

"Silence Eurydice. You will do nothing of the sort. We will not discuss the matter any further."

They all sat awkwardly for a moment; Amyntas seemed furious. He chewed noisily on his bread. After a few moments he calmed and returned to indifference, his breathing out of his nose slowed. The tension around the table began to lift.

Philip slowly walked away; as he did, the conversation between mother and daughter returned to what they were discussing previously. He once again felt his father's eyes on him. He was halfway down the hall when he was stopped.

"Philip!" His father's voice came from behind. Before, he would have completely frozen at the sound of his father shouting him back; but he felt nothing, and was completely relaxed. He smiled to himself and thought of his new friend Antigonus. He was ready to accept whatever punishment his father decided.

He turned to face his father, whose face was stern and serious as always. "We are going on a hunt in a few days. Ptolemy is home in Aloras to deliver a message to his father; we will leave when he returns. The time has come for you to kill your boar. You will become a man, and start your military training."

The mention of this again, should have caused Philip to tense, but he felt perfectly relaxed. He would go on a hunt with his father, and once he killed his boar, he would be considered a man, no longer a youth. He had long waited for this opportunity.

"Who will be coming?"

"Not Arrhidaeus, Archelaus or Menelaus if that is what
        you are concerned about."

"Father, they tried to kill me."

"I know."

"You know?" he asked, dumbfounded. "I have told
no one about it, well, apart from Perdiccas, and
Alexander."

"That I also know," Amyntas said.

"Why did you do nothing?"

"Do you think sibling rivalry is a new thing in
Macedonia? Do you think my brothers did not try and
kill me?"

Philip's mouth was wide open, listening to his
father, astonished. He did not know how to react, this is
the most his father had spoken to him in years, and the
first time ever about matters such as this.

"Listen Philip," he said, taking a step closer to him,
one corner of his lip starting to curl up. Scars on the
corner of his mouth drew the lip up, making it look like
he was snarling, but it was half a smile.

Philip resisted his reaction to lean away, stood his
ground and lifted his chest up, trying to look brave.

"I would love to help," his father said, "but if I try to
intervene, it will only make it worse. I have too much to
deal with at the moment; you will have to resolve it
yourself. Do you realise the full extent of the trouble we
are in?"

"Well I-"

"No, you don't. Macedonia feels-," he leaned to
look over Philip's shoulder. Philip turned his head to see
his mother and sister looking up from the dinner table to
see what the fuss was. Amyntas lowered his voice,
"Macedonia feels like a vassal to Athens, Sparta, and
Thebes all at the same time. They constantly interfere in
our affairs. We have to pay huge tribute to Illyria,

91

namely Bardylis, I'm sure you know that name. His tribe, the Dardanians are the dominant tribe of that region. We have to heavily bribe the Paeonians and the Thracians in the North, and the ones that call themselves our allies, the Paeonians, can be fickle, and raid our borders when it suits them. For trade we are almost completely reliant on the Chalcidians for the use of their ports, and they tax us massively for it. We are in debt paying for mercenaries…"

He paused for breath and pointed a finger, strong and solid, but it was crooked, with a lump on the side of the knuckle. Philip had never concentrated so much on his father's hand. The finger must have been broken at some point.

"So those cowardly little shits bothering you is the least of my worries," he said.

"Father I-"

"You kill your boar, and they'll back down."

"Father, thank-"

"That's all," Amyntas cut him off, turned and headed back toward the breakfast table.

"What will happen to Antigonus?" Philip shouted, then immediately regretted it, fearing his father's reaction.

Amyntas stopped and half turned his head. "Nothing."

"Nothing?"

"Nothing," he said again and returned to his seat.

Philip stood in amazement. Nothing would happen to Antigonus. He felt the corners of his mouth curl up a little into a smile. His father was trying to help him; it wasn't much, but Philip understood now that he would have to prove himself. He was also beginning to understand that his father was subtle, very subtle, never giving much away. His father knew far more than he

92

had ever let on; Philip's respect for him swelled, and the anger he felt toward him burned less brightly.

Now that he was on his own, he thought about having to kill his boar. His thoughts went to the men who had shown him their scars from when they had killed their first, and then he thought of the ones that hadn't come back. His stomach fluttered.

Chapter 8

After a few days Ptolemy returned and they left on the hunting trip. Philip's father told them they would be gone for a few days, and to pack enough food and provisions to last that long. Ptolemy was very excited to come, even though he had only just arrived back and was probably eager to see his wife, but was his usual boisterous self, and loved to be among the men on this kind of journey. They were also joined with a few of the generals and nobility, a company of the Royal Guards, and a group of servants who guided the pack animals, a total of around thirty men. They headed south on horseback along the foothills that led toward the mountains.

It was a crisp morning and the air was cool, birds tweeted in the trees. The plants were damp from the morning dew which had had not yet been dried by the sun, as it was cool in the shade of the trees.

The king rode his horse at the front of the party with Alexander next to him, apart from two of the Royal Guard, who had scouted ahead. The path they were on ran along the side of a low hill, and was only wide enough for two horses abreast. Amyntas had chosen this over the wide, busy road that the Persians had built years before, to easily move their armies into Greece. He said he wanted to get as close to the way their ancestors lived as possible, and get away from the capital. Perdiccas and Philip, rode side by side behind him, and the rest of the party followed behind in twos.

The leather of the reins creaked in Amyntas's hand as he turned to face Philip and Perdiccas. He took a long sniff of the air, "My sons, this is going to be a great journey, I am praying to the Gods that we make good enough time to take a detour to see Mount Olympus. That is a sight to behold. I haven't seen it since you were small children."

"It will be sight to behold Father," Perdiccas said.

He was humouring the man, Philip thought, certain Perdiccas had no interest in seeing the home of the gods. He was far more interested in Philosophy and Science, and matters of state, than religion. He didn't think he liked even being out in the wilderness, preferring to find a quiet corner of the palace to read his books undisturbed.

Philip did not share his father's excitement, but he was glad to see him unusually light hearted and even smiling. He liked the idea of seeing Olympus, but his thoughts were preoccupied with what they were out there to do. They were going to hunt and kill a boar each. It could not be held down or netted; he must spear it, in the open, by himself. This was the right of passage to become a man and earn his belt.

"We'll be fine," Perdiccas said, in a loud whisper, just loud enough for Philip to hear.

Only he and Perdiccas had to do this of course. Alexander, being the eldest, had already earned his a long time before, and wore it proudly. Philip was afraid that he would freeze as he had done before, and this was real, a wild animal that was two or perhaps even three times his size, that could kill him easily if he allowed it past his spear.

In his mind were also the thoughts of what was to come afterwards. This crept into the forefront of his mind as he tried to take in the scenery to distract him. He was being drawn into the royal business and starting his duties as a prince. Assuming he killed the boar and not the other way around, he would be trained in military school and have to go into battle, which he wanted to do, but still, self-doubt plagued him. He had heard stories from his father's generals about battles. His thoughts flashed to the corpses littering the road from Thessaly he had seen as a child, the smoke, and the clouds of flies. He had had nightmares for years. Whenever he had asked his father about it, he had told him he would speak of it when he was ready.

Ptolemy, as usual was talking himself up to Philip's father, shouting over Philip and Perdiccas, telling the tale of some fight he'd won. There used to be stories of women he'd bedded as well, but these had stopped after the wedding, at least to them.

The stories of the ancestors ran through Philip's mind, Heracles and all the beasts he had to slay during his labours, of Theseus and the Minotaur; and Odysseus and the Cyclops. He clutched his boar spear nervously by his side, the hard wood creaked in his grip; what would this creature do to him if he failed to kill it quickly? Even wounded, it would be dangerous.

He closed his eyes, imagined himself standing tall and brave, locking stares with the beast, its nostrils flared, breathing out hot air. It raked the ground with its front hoof, its head lowered. He stood his ground, bracing his spear, waiting for the charge. Then it came, charged forward, hooves pounded the ground, it squealed a high-pitched squeal that filled him with dread, he braced…

His thoughts were broken by a slap to the back.

"Ha! Is my story boring you Philip?" Ptolemy said boisterously, grinning at Philip, all his perfectly straight teeth on display. The road had widened and he was now alongside Philip and Perdiccas, talking away and swigging at his skin of wine.

His stories were always exaggerated to many times the reality of what had happened. Although Philip knew

96

the story was either exaggerated, or indeed a complete fabrication, he enjoyed listening to it. Ptolemy told his stories well, it was part of his charm, and he was universally liked. If he had not been a noble, he would make a fine bard. Amyntas nodded along and gave him the responses he always gave, praised him for his valour or wisdom and Ptolemy never seemed to realise that he was not being listened to fully. Philip found this amusing.

After a day's travelling the sun was starting to get low, and the sky was slowly becoming a deep blood red, their shadows stretching out long on the ground ahead of them. They set up camp. Amyntas and his sons built a fire, while the Royal Guards were split into shifts to patrol the perimeter. They drank into the night; the king and his officer's shadows danced as they told the tales of the day they killed their boar, and claimed their belt, and toasted to their friends in Hades who had failed.

Philip felt singled out, isolated, as he watched and listened carefully to each of them as they told their own story, hoping to find some insight into what he was about to face, not daring to ask if any of them had been afraid. Some opened their tunics and showed the scars they had received and thanked the gods that they had lived. He felt the tightness building in his chest and shoulders. The wood cracked and snapped in the flames. His father took a swig of his wine and stoked the flame, the brilliant orange light flickering on his face.

Philip awoke the following morning to the smoky aroma of the smouldering camp fire embers. A light breeze blew some of the ash and it floated away like snow. The men lay about in the open; the drinking had gone on long after Philip had fallen asleep. They took the camp apart and continued on their journey. The road became steeper and rockier, and as they began to climb the mountains, they had to dismount and guide the horses on foot. Further on, the well-trodden path changed to a narrow, winding one, and the ground became treacherous; some of the dirt was loose and they had to be careful of where their horses trod. They heard a crash and rubble fell as one of the generals lost his footing and nearly went over the edge. He stumbled and slipped down onto a knee, and was helped back to his feet by a comrade.

They climbed higher, and when they got over the difficult, rocky part of the road, the slope became shallower. As the party came over the crest of the hill, they came into sight of Mount Olympus. It stretched majestically up into the heavens; the summit obscured by the clouds.

Philip's smile grew, even though he did not always care for the gods, this *was* a sight to behold. The whole group stood in awe; they were overwhelmed at the beauty of the domain of the Olympian gods.

"Well?" Philip heard his father break the silence, "Did I not tell you boys? You understand why I was excited now?"

They nodded. "It is beautiful, Father," Perdiccas said.

Amyntas smiled. "I told you, I have longed to see it again. And look to the south there, Thessaly, Southern Greece herself. Do you see the road down there in the bottom of the valley? That's the road we came by years ago when we came back home to Pella. Do you remember? It was glorious."

Philip looked around at the others, who were nodding in agreement. He looked Perdiccas in the eye, who was clearly thinking the same as him. He did not remember the glory, he had only been small, but he remembered the bodies, and the fire and the stench of burning hair and rotting flesh.

"One day those bastards will think of Macedonia as part of Greece," Amyntas said to Alexander patting him on the back. "If not in my lifetime, in yours my son."

"It will happen," Alexander replied. "We will make them bow with respect for us. I promise you Father."

"And down there," Amyntas said, turning to Philip and Perdiccas, pointing to the dense woods in the valley floor, "there, you boys will find your boars."

Philip stared down at the dark, foreboding forest and swallowed a lump in his throat.

The party pushed on. Getting down the other side of the mountain may have been more treacherous than going up it, Philip thought, but did not say anything. They stopped just inside the edge of the woods. The Royal Guard stayed with the baggage and had the servants unpack some equipment, cooking pots and a spit, ready for when they returned with the boar. Amyntas led his sons deeper into the woods.

They walked as quietly as they could; the ground was strewn with pine needles. The trees were thick and with no low branches, looking like the pillars of some great natural temple that had grown from the ground. The trees populated the forest so far in every direction that you could not see an end to it, and the air was dead silent, giving it a surreal quality. It made Philip uneasy. He felt like they were being watched by some unknown spirits they couldn't see, nymphs, satyrs or something else. A twig snapped under his foot, earning him a look of annoyance from Alexander who raised a finger to his lips.

After a short while Philip looked at his father, who had squatted down to examine some marks in the dirt.

"There is boar nearby, these prints are fresh, Philip, come forward," he said.

Philip advanced, nodding to his father as he passed him, trying his very best to look calm and in control. He raised his spear and walked forward as softly and quietly as he could. His father and brothers followed closely behind.

He heard rustling in the bushes ahead. His heart pounded in his chest. For a moment he forgot to breathe. He waited, and waited, when suddenly he stepped forward, raised his spear above his head, ready to thrust it down as hard as he could into the throat of the boar that was sniffing around on the other side of the bushes.

Then he heard a cough. He paused and looked back over his shoulder to his father and Alexander, who motioned for him to go ahead. They had not heard it.

He burst through, ready to strike, and they followed behind. There was no boar. They all looked at each other in disbelief.

A man lay where they had been expecting the wild animal. He had a thick, unkempt beard and long hair, dark red, like the dying embers of a fire. He quickly raised both his arms in a gesture to not hurt him. Philip noticed they were covered in intricate blue tattoos that looked like tree branches that knotted and weaved about each other. The man spoke to them in a language none of them understood. Ptolemy hung back from them, and Alexander stepped forward, his hand on his sword.

"Who are you? What are you doing here?" Amyntas asked him calmly and stepped forward, although keeping a safe distance. His hand rested on the grip of his sheathed sword. The other hand was raised in an open gesture of peace.

He looked back to his sons. "He's Thracian," he said. "I wouldn't expect to see any this far south."

The man had calmed down; obviously realising they weren't going to attack and kill him. He spoke something back in his foreign tongue and they looked at each other. Philip stared at him, keeping his distance, as the breeze blew; he caught the man's scent, an earthy, peaty smell. "What are you doing out there?" he said. "Are you alone? What is your name?"

Alexander pushed past the man to examine where he had been lying; there was a crude shelter made of leaves and sticks that he had been hiding in.

"Could he be a runaway slave, Father?" Perdiccas asked.

"I doubt it, see those tattoos? That's the mark of a warrior, they aren't easy to take alive, and they're difficult to break in as a slave."

The man spoke again in his strange tongue, and beckoned them to come with him. He started to take a few steps away, holding his hand out to them. All of the Macedonians stayed put.

"I don't like this," Alexander said, "What is he doing out here? It doesn't seem right."

Then came the howls, from over the hills on three sides of them, howls and scampering feet. The Thracian drew a dagger from his boot and thrust it toward Amyntas's neck, who avoided the blow just enough that it only nicked his skin. The Thracian was immediately struck down by a massive downward blow from Alexander's sword. The blow penetrated deep into his neck, blood spraying into the air and some of the drops flecking onto Philip's face. The taste of iron and salt was on his lips, the same taste as when you were punched boxing, and your lip was burst. It was strange without the pain that came with it. Alexander stood on the Thracian's twitching corpse and pulled his sword out.

Philip stood in shock.

Alexander's face appeared in front of him, seeming to fill all his vision. He patted him hard on the cheek. "Philip, wake up," he said. "This is it."

Philip came to his senses as a group of men came over the hill, more Thracians, about twenty of them. They had dogs as big as wolves, which snarled and bit, pulling on their leads so hard their front feet were off the ground, and the skin of their necks stretched.

"By the Gods!" Amyntas shouted, wiping the blood from his face and drawing his sword.

The Macedonians backed up together, ready for the attack, but before they could the Royal Guard escort appeared quickly from behind to form a wall with their shields, their short swords drawn. Philip stood in the second rank, behind the shield wall, his face butting against the metal shoulder of the cuirass of the warrior in front. He held his spear high overhead, ready to thrust it. His gaze looked to the men on the hill. They wore light armour and thick furs, and carried swords and crescent shaped shields. They released their hounds and they snarled, tearing towards the Macedonians with blinding speed. The men charged behind them. The dogs leapt at the Macedonians, some bit and scratched at the men's feet, but they were stabbed and crushed with the bottoms of their shields.

The Thracian warriors then crashed into the shields and the formation immediately broke with the weight of so many bodies hitting it. Philip was knocked to the ground with the man he stood behind. He got up dazed. His head whipped around. All the men around him were fighting, swords clashing off shields and other swords. He saw his brother Alexander wringing a man's neck from behind. His father parried a blow and then thrust his sword into his opponent's stomach and drove it up, deep into his torso. The man fell to the ground, but he didn't scream, just curled up on his side holding onto the wound.

Philip looked down and saw his spear in the dirt. He reached down and grabbed it. An arrow whistled past his head. He heard a scream and turned to see a Thracian running at him, yelling a war cry at the top of his voice, a sword held in front of him, his eyes wild with rage.

Philip simply reacted, and gripping his spear in both hands, he parried the sword with the tip and drove it forward, towards the Thracian's torso, who ran onto the end of it and kept coming. Philip's feet slid back on the loose dirt under the man's weight. He tightened his grip and bent his knees to keep his balance. He drove forward with his legs, keeping his hips and torso stiff. The metal tip of the spear disappeared into his opponent's torso. Philip thrust forward hard. The Thracian dropped his sword and contorted on the end of the spear as he was driven to the ground. He wriggled and then looked Philip in the eye, and began to plead. Finally, he curled around the end of the spear like a foetus in the womb, then went still, his eyes still open, but blank.

The fighting died down and Philip stood over his dead opponent. He relaxed his grip and his knuckles started to get their colour back. His fingers tingled as the blood came back into them and he shook them. He looked at his palms, the skin where the fingers met the palms of his hands was blistered from gripping the spear.

He was not sure what to feel. Time stood still. He didn't care for this man, but his face, which had been fearsome, and had terrified him only a few moments before, was now contorted and pathetic. He did feel remorse, he thought, or something close to it.

Philip was dragged back to reality by Ptolemy grabbing his hand above his head. "Forget killing a fucking boar! Philip just killed his first man!"

He looked around and some of the Macedonians looked up and cheered. Most were too busy cutting the throats of the corpses to make sure they were dead. They had taken two crippled survivors and sat them on the thick exposed roots of a tree, and propped them up against the trunk. Philip stood a short distance away and watched his father approach them.

"Who sent you?" Amyntas asked the man calmly.

The man did not reply.

"Who fucking sent you?" he screamed in the man's face.

The Thracian's arms were then held apart behind his back by two burly Royal Guards. Still, he did not reply.

Amyntas drew a knife, and nodded to two of the Royal Guards, who locked the man's shoulder and elbow in a hold, forcing his arm out straight. He tried to get out of it, squirming from side to side, but was wounded and did not have the strength. Blood dripped from under his soaked furs onto the roots of the tree.

"Was it Bardylis?" There was a long pause and the man simply looked him in the eyes defiantly. He glanced at the blade, but still refused to answer. "Argeus?" He did not answer. Amyntas pressed the tip of his knife into the man's knuckle joint, deep in between the bones of his forefinger and palm and twisted it, then yanked the finger clean off with his other hand.

Philip stood and watched. He was numb. The man gritted his teeth, and told them he knew nothing, but Amyntas slapped him hard across the face and continued to remove fingers. When he fainted with the pain, cold water was fetched from the nearby stream and thrown in his face to wake him up.

After both men had had all their fingers, noses and ears removed, their throats were cut. With no information gained, the men took it in turns to go to the stream to wash the blood and dirt off themselves.

Philip had always had a distant relationship with his father, but had never until this moment been afraid of him.

Chapter 9

That night, Philip sat with his brothers and Ptolemy around their campfire. It crackled as Ptolemy placed a fresh log on it. His face was illuminated in a mixture of the orange light from the fire, and cold blue from the moon. The Royal Guards were out watching a perimeter, but were not in sight, nor could they be heard, giving the illusion that they were alone in the wilderness.

A wolf howled in the distance and Philip looked out into the night, putting his hand on his spear which he had kept by his side since the attack.

"Don't worry, it is far away," Alexander said, his wry, relaxed smile visible in the moonlight. "Sound carries at night. Especially when the air is so still."

They heard footsteps approaching, and their father emerged from the blackness into the light of the fire, wearing thick furs over his wide shoulders, looking like a bear. He walked around to Perdiccas and Philip and handed them each a beautifully made leather sword belt. "You have earned these," he said.

Philip felt the tension rise in him at the presence of his father; he swallowed.

He waited a long moment before taking the belt from him. Growing up he knew his father lived a violent life, but he had never imagined anything like what he had witnessed. What if he were ever accused of treachery, would he do the same to me or my brothers? Or my sister?

"What do you all think about what happened?" he asked his sons, carefully looking from one to the other to see who would answer first. Alexander had already been into battle with his father, and so was really there as the heir and didn't need to answer.

Perdiccas spoke first.

"I don't feel bad at all about what happened; they were going to kill us," he said. Philip thought this was probably a lie. He must be as confused as me, he thought. Their father, with a straight, hard expression, slowly nodded. He turned his gaze to Philip who could not look him in the eye, so stared into the fire. There was a long silence, aside from the popping and crackling of the embers.

"It was us or them father," he said eventually. Although in his heart he was incredibly torn, he had killed, with his own hand, and felt guilty for the loss of life, but on the other hand he was proud to kill an enemy of Macedonia and his family. When he closed his eyes, he could still see the Thracian's body contorting around the end of his spear, the empty stare of his eyes.

"Exactly," Amyntas said, nodding again. "That is it exactly Philip. I know you are going to be thinking about this for a while; I want you all to know that I was very proud of all of you today. You defended your father and your king against an assassin's blade."

"Do you think it was an assassination attempt? Surely they were just bandits after our silver?" Perdiccas asked, and Philip leant in and listened. Alexander stared at his father in silence; he was to take all the burden of the throne when his father died.

"Of course they were assassins," Amyntas said, "sent by either Bardylis or Olynthus maybe. Probably Bardylis."

"Bardylis?" Perdiccas asked. "We haven't been at war with Illyria for years."

"Not an actual war," Amyntas said, and leaned in to his two younger sons, "but there is always an invisible

107

war being fought in Macedonia; this I will share with you now that you are men. Do you know how many assassination attempts I have survived?"

Philip and Perdiccas looked at each other, and shook their heads. Philip looked at Alexander who sat with calm indifference. As he gently stoked the fire, it suddenly became obvious that he was already privy to this information.

"No? Nor do I," Amyntas said, taking a swig from his wine skin. "I have lost count. The war is being fought all the time, maybe since the beginning of time, between all the families, there are always pretenders trying to take my throne."

The two of them nodded along, taking in everything he said. Philip looked over to Ptolemy who was not his usual boisterous, boastful self. He sat a little bit away from them, just in the light of the campfire, looking nauseous. He must be shaken, Philip thought, maybe he has not fought as much as he made out.

"Who was it this time? I'm not sure. Bardylis will have sponsored one of these pretenders, some distant relative of ours to try to kill me, and not only that, the three of you. End our line and try to take the throne for himself."

"Why Thracians? Why out in the woods like this?" Perdiccas asked. "Why not have you poisoned?"

"And why didn't they talk? I've never seen a man take that kind of torture and not talk," Alexander said.

"These Thracians are tough Alexander," Ptolemy said, "but the barbarians probably just didn't understand us."

"No, it's not that, they feared the repercussions worse than the torture," Amyntas said.

"What's worse than getting cut up like that?" said Ptolemy.

108

"What would you value more than your own skin?" Alexander said.

"Family," Perdiccas said, joining in with the conversation standing on the edge of the circle.

"None of us even know who these Thracians were, Boy. How would we go after their families?" Ptolemy said.

"We'll never be able to know now anyway," Alexander said. "They didn't reveal a thing."

"Whoever it is must still be at court, they needed you away from Pella," Ptolemy said finally. "They may even have announced your death and be trying to convince the Macedonian Council to sponsor their place as king."

"I don't know, my spies did not make me aware of this; fortune was looking out for us though. The Royal Guard were close enough to get to us quick enough."

"We will find him, and when we do, he will pay for it," Alexander said.

"What can we do to help?" Philip asked. His father turned to him, surprised. He had probably expected that kind of question from Perdiccas. He still thinks of me as the wimp, even though I killed a man today, he thought.

"You don't need to do anything. When we return home, you will begin your military training. I was the target. I will get my spies to make enquiries and find out as much as they can," Amyntas said.

"Ptolemy?"

"Yes?"

"I want you to take half of the Royal Guards and ride back to Pella through the night. Make sure that there has not been a coup attempt while we have been away. I hope to the gods that they were waiting to hear of my death before trying anything."

109

"Yes, Your Majesty" Ptolemy said, and left to go and get his things together.

Philip and Perdiccas obviously looked concerned.

"Don't worry, everything will be fine. As I said, this happens a lot. At least it would have been a good death, by the sword. I can think of nothing worse than being poisoned and dying in my bed. No glory in it."

The conversation continued. When Ptolemy was prepared to leave, he came and said his farewells, then rode off with his entourage.

Once he was gone and the hoof beats faded to silence, Amyntas turned to his sons.

"This does not go beyond the four of us."

The three looked at each other, by their expressions Perdiccas and Alexander were just as confused as Philip. They also nodded their agreement.

"Your sister told me of something that Ptolemy said when he thought she wasn't listening," he said, his voice only a little louder than a whisper. "She thinks it sounded as though he was plotting to kill me."

"Kill you?" Perdiccas said, sounding sceptical. "Ptolemy?"

Philip felt his eyebrows come down into a frown, "Surely not Father, you've given him lands and titles."

Amyntas lips curled up into a slight smile and he exchanged a glance with Alexander who mimicked the look.

"And you have almost brought him into your inner circle," Perdiccas said.

There was a pause.

"Do you believe her?" Philip asked, unable to wait.

There was another pause.

"I believe that your sister believes she heard what she thought she heard. She may be mistaken, but of course, I would be a fool to not investigate. Of course, he was absolutely correct when he said any coup would mean that he would have to have people in Pella ready to move once they thought I was dead. Oh, and my three sons."

"So why did you let him go back? He could do that now that he'll be back before us," Philip asked. He looked at Perdiccas, whose raised eyebrow told him he was equally shocked.

"Don't worry, any plans he has set in motion would not come to be, I have made sure of that," Amyntas said. Looking perfectly relaxed he took another a sip of his wine. "I have him under close watch; the men who are with him are some of my most trusted soldiers. Any sign of treachery, he will have to answer to me when we get back. This was the best way to deal with a rumour, let them take their plan so far, and make sure you're prepared. But don't make it look like you're prepared."

Philip sat back, in total awe of his father. He knew all along that this was going to happen. Clearly Alexander knew as well. He would be privy to almost everything his father knew at this point. He was getting advanced in his years and would be looking to put forward Alexander as his heir and look for the approval of the council. It would be no surprise. He had baited this coup, put his head in the jaws of a lion to see if it had teeth, and he had discovered that it did. Whether it was Ptolemy or not was still unsure.

...

When they arrived back in Pella, Philip's father congratulated him again for killing his first man. He told him how proud he was, especially that he had managed to shake his fear when they were attacked.

111

However, as happy as he was at the recognition, he had mixed feelings; he had killed, but they were trying to kill him. Was this justified in the eyes of the gods? Yet, he still felt guilt. This man had been the enemy, but did he have a wife and children who would never know of his fate, stabbed and left to the crows far from home?

And he questioned his own bravery. He had not been alone, his confidence had been inflated by the presence of the Royal Guard, his father, his brothers and Ptolemy fighting all around him. Had that made him braver? Had he been alone, would he have been so brave? He did not know.

He briskly walked to his bedchamber, trying not to look in a hurry. He washed his hands and face in cold water. The smell of the wilderness still lingered about him, and the dead man's blood had dried into his clothes, the rich salty smell clinging to them.

Although he had washed, the stubborn, dry blood was also under his fingernails. The thought of his father torturing the captured men lingered in his mind, making him wretch, but he wasn't actually sick. Would he ever forget that? His hands shook as he reached for a towel to dry them.

He supped with his family, even though he had seen enough of them over the last few days, not including his mother and sister. He had missed them. He wore a clean, fresh chiton, but felt dirty.

"I hear you are a man now?" his mother asked, even though she had obviously been well informed, and she embraced him tightly. When she withdrew from the hug, she wiped tears from her eyes and blew her nose, even though she was smiling and seemed happy. "My youngest is now all grown up," she said.

He acknowledged it with a half-smile and an awkward nod. A mother losing her youngest child to manhood was a big event. It was hard for him to imagine. He tried his best not to betray what he was really thinking.

"I'm very proud of you my son," his father said while eating some bread he had dipped in oil. The food they had eaten while out in the wild had been basic, and they had not even managed to hunt and kill anything substantial because of the ambush. Philip stared at his father as he ate ravenously. He looked up with his eyes as he leant over his plate to save any drips. "You will now begin your military training. We will start first thing in the morning, and you can come with me and train with your brothers and the Royal Guard.

Once he finished his food, he excused himself and headed back up the stairs past the guards and into his chambers. He headed to the window and out onto the balcony. Leaning on the white stone banister he stared far across the rooftops of the city to the parade grounds, where he could see the men drilling. He sighed. This is it, he thought, the moment he'd been dreading, nothing to do but take it head on, like Antigonus would have done.

He kept seeing the expression on his man's face, contorting in pain, the life draining from his eyes while staring into Philip's. Then, staring into his eyes, those pleading eyes, he felt his hands get wet and looked down to see the warm blood rushing over them down the shaft of his spear.

His thoughts then went to his father hacking at the captured men's fingers, sawing them off one by one. He did not know how brave he would be under such torture; he doubted he would be as brave as the Thracians he had witnessed. He reached down and felt his own fingers. They hadn't said a word, not one word. Why? Were they brave, or did they fear worse than Amyntas?

113

Were they really sent by Ptolemy? Or was it Bardylis they feared? How bad did Bardylis have to be for them not to betray him? He shuddered thinking about it. Never, ever, let Bardylis capture you. He decided he would kill himself rather than be taken alive into Illyria.

Chapter 10

Ptolemy walked down the street, his eyes shifting from side to side, checking no one he recognised was around; why would there be? No one here knew him, and he wore a pauper's clothes, an old worn tunic and brown patched cloak. The hood was pulled up over his head, partially covering his face. Even if someone who could recognise him was there, they wouldn't expect to see him in this part of the city, an agora in one of the poorest of slums.

He stopped walking and paused to look through the crowd. The agora was bustling with people, but not like one in the uptown area where the nobility and the wealthy would do their shopping. They would sell jewellery and fine food, cured meat, spices and the like. He would have felt much more comfortable at such a place, but this meeting could not be held there. This market was under the cliff that the palace stood on, and the dwellings of the denizens that lived here surrounded the claustrophobic market square; it was a shanty town built on different levels, houses built on top of each other and overlapping. Presumably someone would simply build a house wherever there was space, with no respect made for whether it would fit. A woman tipped a bucket of shit and piss out of a window and it ran down the street, the stench floating past his nostrils. Ptolemy sneered with disgust as two children skipped across it.

The stalls sold basic things, simple food, clothes, carpets. A thief was being apprehended by some of the guards and begged to be let free, piss trickling down his leg.

A pack of stray dogs hovered around a butcher's stall, looking for scraps of meat, their fur mangy and balding, and their ribs showing. The butcher shooed them and flapped his hand at the flies that buzzed around his meat. An old man sat on a stool next to it staring vacantly at the passers-by, taking shallow breaths, not even reacting to the several mosquitoes that sat on his bare shoulder, their long, needle-like mouths biting into his flesh. Ptolemy scratched at his own shoulder, feeling a sudden itch. The idea of getting the mosquito plague scared him.

A troupe of actors were up on a small stage, miming out the triumphant King Amyntas killing his cowardly attackers. He was portrayed as a colossus; the actor was on stilts and towered above the attacking enemies, who were being acted by dwarfs with bright orange and red wigs and their faces painted bright blue, an exaggerated look of the Thracians for the peasants to understand what was going on. Ptolemy sneered in disgust and clenched his fist under his cloak as the crowd cheered and clapped, children standing at the front waving wooden swords above their heads.

He looked around to see if anyone who might recognise him was there, although was unlikely, he still checked. When he could not see anyone but peasants, and the guards had moved on with their prisoner, he slunk behind a market stall and down the alleyway hidden behind it.

The man he met there was sheepish and agitated, he too wearing the clothing of a pauper, but speaking in an aristocratic tone, his voice hushed.

"You're late," he whispered.

"Don't take that tone with me," Ptolemy said. "Want your head on a spike when I'm king?"

The man cowered "Sorry, I just..."

116

"Forget it. All this lurking in alleyways and sneaking around makes me uneasy too."

"He's still alive."

Ptolemy rolled his eyes up to the sky. He let out a sigh and brought them back down. He locked stares with the man. "Of course, he is still alive, obviously. Do you think we'd still have to meet like this if he was dead?"

The man continued to cower and could not keep the eye contact. "So what do we do now? I had everyone in place, ready," he said. "It was perfect. We had him away from the palace, with only a few of his guards; and his three sons were there to be killed along with him, maybe if-"

"Maybe if what?" Ptolemy began to raise his voice above the whisper it had been.

The man stared at his feet. He had clearly regretted what he had said, but Ptolemy was not willing to let him get away with the implied insult. "Well? Spit it out!" he said.

"Maybe if you had just killed him yourself instead of this elaborate plan with the Thracians," he said. "You could have got close to any of them. We could have taken care of the other three sons here, Arrhidaeus, Menelaus and the other one. Or we could have brought them in on it or something."

Ptolemy stared hard at the man, gritting his teeth. The man kept his eyes down. He slowly raised them up and their eyes met, but he quickly looked back down at his feet.

"How could we involve the other sons of Amyntas?" Ptolemy said. "They would either tell their father about us, or take the power for themselves once he was dead."

"It was just a thought. They have land and the name, but would soldiers follow them?"

117

"I doubt it, they're snivelling little cowards."

"So, what do you suggest?" the man asked.

Ptolemy gritted his teeth. "We need to keep the sons separated from him; Alexander and Perdiccas mostly. We also need to keep any of the companions away from him; they'll die for him. And Alexander is ferocious; I will not put myself in a position where I have to fight him. He'll kill me; but Philip is a wimp. He'd shit himself rather than fight me, and Perdiccas has too much sense; he will follow whoever shows they're in authority."

"Is Philip really a wimp, I heard he killed his man, and a Thracian brute no less?"

"Yes, he did kill his man, but I saw it, the man ran onto his spear, and he is torn up about it, all over the place, losing sleep, we will be able to pick him off easily. Trust me, it's Alexander that I'm concerned about."

"But what about that Antigonus boy? I heard Philip and he are becoming inseparable, and he seems like a big tough lad, how else are we going to..."

There was a chinking, a rattling of metal further down the alleyway. Both of them froze on the spot and looked to see what the sound came from. Ptolemy pushed his cloak to the side and rested his hand on the handle of the sword that had been concealed beneath.

A figure made its way towards them down the alleyway; head to toe in ragged cloth, even his face and hands were covered. He shook a small basket towards them, coins rattled inside. Both of them took a step away in disgust. "Anything to spare for a poor man my lord? The gods have afflicted me with leprosy."

"I'm no lord, and no, we don't have anything, now piss off!" Ptolemy said to the man. His body turned away from the leper and he tilted his head away, as if

118

this would in some way protect him from the man's disease. There was a hole in the cloth around the hand that held out the basket, exposing the skin, dry, flaking and swollen around the knuckles.

It looked agonising, but Ptolemy knew that lepers did not feel a thing. He could cut the man's hand off and he would probably not realise.

The man Ptolemy was meeting with dropped a few coins into the leper's basket, and gave an uncomfortable smile. The leper moved on. "Thank you, sir," he said and shambled away towards the open marketplace, where people parted to avoid him.

Ptolemy turned back to his man. "What kind of poison can you get your hands on?" he asked.

Chapter 11

The following morning Philip left for the parade grounds, the flat open area not far outside the palace. There were a few shallow potholes and some small patches of grass, but it had mostly been worn away to the bare, dusty earth by the number of soldiers drilling up and down on it. The king's soldiers always trained here. Philip had often watched them from his balcony, pining after the day when he would be able to join them; now that it was finally here, the idea did not seem so romantic.

The sky was grey, and there was a slight threat of a downpour in the air. It felt heavy and cool, as some splashes of fine rain fell lightly onto his skin. This was good, he thought, not wanting it to get too hot because of all the time they were about to spend out in the open marching and drilling. They would cook like a boar on a roast.

He was nervous at coming to train, remembering the first time he had trained at the gymnasium, knowing that everyone there must know each other, and he didn't know anyone. He glanced around to see if either of his brothers were visible. They were not.

He was greeted by an officer of the Royal Guard, whom he recognised immediately as the man from the hunting trip. He was in or around his mid-thirties, with a thick, black beard that was starting to get a few grey hairs in it. He wore an aged bronze cuirass that bore an Argead star on the chest. The officer carried the scars on his arms that most soldiers had acquired during their time fighting for Macedonia, and it made Philip wonder how many generations the fighting in Macedonia had touched.

He approached Philip unceremoniously, without any kind of bow or show of respect. Philip wondered if this was how he was with other members of the royal family; not that it bothered him. Philip welcomed not getting any special treatment. On the contrary, he preferred to be treated the same as the other men; he wanted to be one of them.

"Grab yourself a spear and shield Philip," the officer said to him as he arrived. "And armour if you can find any that fits. You'll be training with us to start off with, so fall in with the rest of the men and then once the peasants arrive, you can join in with their instruction. Never sure how many will show up for training, but you should get some experience; you'll be drilling them on your own when you're an officer."

"Thank you. What is your name? You have my gratitude for protecting my father. You know, on the hunt."

"Parmenion, but no thanks are necessary, I am a soldier. I'm here to do a job, and your father pays the wages."

"I thank you anyway," Philip said, and gave him a nod of respect.

As a royal boy in Macedonia, he was already used to training with a sword or spear. Along with the other sons of the nobility they been taught together in a formation against opponents, but this had always been fundamentals, more technique and nothing too hard, as they were far too valuable to risk sustaining a serious injury so young.

A bundle of spears, shields and a variety of cuirasses had been laid on the ground along a short wall that ran the length of the parade ground. He examined the equipment, most of it was in a poor state of repair. He picked up a shield, a round pelta; this was the shield most of the King's soldiers used, being smaller and lighter than the heavy Aspis, the shield that he knew the southern Greek infantry had used for generations. Why had his father not bought newer shields for his men? He flipped it in his hands; it felt light and flimsy, the wood was thin, surely a spear or arrow would puncture this with ease? He took hold of the leather strap on the inside; it was loose. He wiggled it and it came off in his hand. He let out a sigh and placed the shield on top of the wall so that no one else would pick it up and have the same issue. He found another, with a strap that was still intact after a good tug, but the bottom few inches of the wood had been split along the grain and was barely attached. He worked it looser and pulled it off.

"What are you doing? Fall in," Parmenion shouted over.

He quickly picked a spear up and felt the rough wood. There were two light spots where the wood had been worn so that the finish had gone, having been used many times, but it would do. It was only training.

He quickly ran over to a line of youths around his age who were standing in a line at attention; Parmenion gestured with his head for Philip to join the end of the line. He did so and stood up straight, his body stiff, looking straight ahead like the others; he resisted the urge to turn his head and look around.

For a moment his thoughts went to his first man, the Thracian, curled up like a foetus in the womb, praying to whatever gods he worshipped before he died. Will that image stay with me the rest of my days? he thought. Maybe the more you kill, the more you forget who you've killed. None of the soldiers seemed to be as conflicted as him; most likely they just didn't discuss it.

His father had delayed his training because of the jitters that he had witnessed involving his half-brothers.

He has always thought me weak, Philip thought. He has sent me here but obviously still has doubts. I will prove him wrong.

The King's Royal Guard arrived, marching double time into the parade ground in a column formation from the barracks, all in full armour, carrying spears and shields, dressed as hoplites, the heavy armoured infantry that made up the bulk of Greek battle formations. Their boots pounded the ground like hoof beats in a stampede of cattle. Their heads were high and proud.

They marched so that their column was halfway past where the drill instructors stood. The officer who led them shouted "Royal Guard! Halt!" They all stopped and stood to attention. He then yelled "Left turn!" and they all turned ninety degrees to their left in perfect synchronicity to face the officers. Their boots stomped the ground making a sound like a single crack of thunder. Philip stood proud of the men, a few more of the faces he recognised from the hunting trip. They had fought valiantly against his father's would-be assassins, and he was glad to be training with them.

Parmenion took control of the group and Philip and the youths were separated out and fell in with them; the men drilled up and down, marching in time. They drilled with their weapons and shields in pairs, repeating the same moves over and over to commit it to memory. It's just like in wrestling and boxing; train it until it becomes as natural as walking or breathing, he thought.

The youths were taken out and told to observe the next drills. The men arranged themselves into two opposing lines and made a shield wall with their aspis shields, overlapping in an unbroken chain. Then, as the two lines pushed against each other, training officers stalked up and down the line, shouting instructions to the men as they tried to dig their feet in and push. The damp ground was clearly making it difficult, and their sandals slid in the mud, churning up the ground. This continued until a gap was pushed open. The drill was then reset and repeated.

After this had been repeated many times over, the men collected spears with no heads. They then repeated the drill, but were allowed to strike at their opponents. Philip stood in awe at the display of how they stood their ground while being struck at. He observed some of the changes in their posture, the lines sliding off each other to the right. He wasn't sure why, but each step seemed to go to the right instead of just leaning forward now.

Their chests heaved as they panted for breath. The drill seemed exhausting, but Philip was excited for his turn to try.

The men were kept cool by the rain. It remained damp throughout the morning and the men's boots and calves were speckled with mud. They took a rest after a few hours and Philip stood with Parmenion while the soldiers had some bread and water that had been brought out to them by pages.

"I'm impressed Parmenion, the men are well trained and professional. I don't know why we bow to the Illyrians if this is the quality of our soldiers."

"Thank you, Prince, I appreciate the compliment about the men I train, but these are not the entire army," Parmenion said carefully, seeming unsure as to how Philip would react.

"Oh?" Philip asked curiously, his eyebrow raised.

"Forgive me, but these are just your father's guard, and are very few in number. The vast bulk of our infantry is made up of levies, peasants, farmers and the like. When there is a war, your father musters his men, and sends word to all the nobles he can trust, who all have their own soldiers, and they bring peasants as well, and mercenaries if needed. Most don't have this kind of discipline. Most Greek states are the same, there is a small elite and- "

"I see," Philip said, "even the Spartans? I'm sure all they do is train and fight?"

"Ah, the Spartans," he said, the corners of his lips stretched up into a smile. "I see your father's love of the Spartans has rubbed off on you? Only the Spartan homoioi, their citizens, train the way you think, and they only numbered around ten thousand even at their peak, and this was generations ago. Who knows how many they have now, after Leuctra."

"Leuctra?" Philip leaned in, listening intently. He liked Parmenion. The man didn't treat him like a prince, but talked to him like anyone else. Philip liked that.

"A great battle in Boeotia in central Greece, they-"

"I have heard of Leuctra. The Spartans lost to the Thebans."

"They didn't just lose, they were crushed by Thebes," he said "Anyway, never mind that. The point is that the majority of the Spartan army is made up of the perioikoi, it means those around. They live in the villages around Sparta herself, living normal lives and training to fight when they can, like our people. They also have vast, vast numbers of slaves. Only the homoioi train to fight all the time."

"How many slaves do they have?"

"I'm not really sure- Anyway, we must get back to training. Don't expect much from the peasants, and never rely on them."

"I'm sure they'll be great," Philip said, nodding slowly, confidently.

"You'll see soon Prince, apart from the Royal Guard, the levies make up most of the Macedonian army. These men are farmers, and potters, and other tradespeople, who rarely train. The Royal Guard are professionals, paid by the king from the royal purse."

The Royal Guard were dismissed from their own training to become instructors themselves. They split up into groups and separated out to train their designated levies when they arrived.

"This is something we have learned from the Spartan advisors that your father has here. There used to be a lot more of them when you were a boy."

"I remember."

"Yes, they train all of their *homoioi*, the ones I spoke about before, as officers, that way they are all able to be sent out to lead allied armies or advise, as they do with us. The Royal Guard can train their own groups of levies."

"I see," Philip said. He could see a clear picture in his head of the Spartan who used to advise his father, wearing his poor, patched cloak even though he was part of the nobility.

"We have been trying it for a few years now; it seems to be working well. They are improved greatly from before we did it like this. The levies will be here soon. We train them as much as we can, but can't tell how many will show. They can't come too often because their fields and animals need tending to. But we need to train them as often as we can now. Your father thinks war is coming."

"War?" Philip asked.

"Yes, war… I. Never mind for now, here they come."

As Parmenion finished speaking, the levies began to arrive; they trickled in, some on their own, some in small groups that walked in chatting and gossiping.

They shared skins of wine. Others came quietly, seeming apprehensive.

Philip was amazed to see that some even led livestock with them.

"Why have they brought animals?" he asked.

"Maybe they have nobody to tend to them. Maybe they don't trust their neighbours not to steal them. It's even worse when they bring them on the march to battle with them. Slows the whole fucking army down," Parmenion said. He sniffed back, and spat on the ground.

Philip shook his head. Then he noticed that some of the men carried good quality armour, a few even having helmets. Wealthy men? Or merchants? Maybe they were family heirlooms.

Most of them however, had no armour at all; only the most basic of equipment, a pelta shield, like the one Philip held, and a spear. A lot of it looked old and worn to him, although he did not see any up close. Barely half that were meant to be there were there on time, and the officers who were to train them shook their heads as the rest came in one or two at a time, unimpressed but not at all surprised. Philip stood and watched, deflated. Unfortunately it was just as Parmenion had described.

There was a mix of men who came; they all recognised their training groups. Some were still drinking, perhaps for courage, which horrified Philip. He stood in disbelief at how disorganised they were, standing around in bunched up groups, gathering around their Royal Guard trainers, while a register was taken, like a crowd that would gather around a boxing match.

Once they were all accounted for in their group they fell in, all lining up for an inspection.

127

They drilled the same drills that the Royal Guard had trained first, but this time it lacked the precision he had witnessed before; it was clumsy and disorganised.

They trained at the weapon exercises in formation, but for most groups this had to be regressed because the officers decided that they were trying to coordinate too many things at once. When the two lines pushed against each other, there were too many gaps left, and men were getting struck in the face and chest with alarming frequency, and with no helmets, they would lose teeth and maybe eyes. It was too much in training.

"How long have these men trained for?" Philip asked Parmenion in total disbelief at what he had witnessed.

Parmenion sighed, "It's not a matter of how long they have trained, a lot train as often as they can, but it's just not enough to get them to equal our enemies."

Philip pondered this. "I will speak to my father," he said.

Philip wondered how long it had been that Bardylis had dominated them on the battlefield. After witnessing the way they trained, he wondered how much longer they would be dominated by him. All eternity if nothing was done. These *are* all farmers, he thought, just as Parmenion had said. He went over in his head what he planned to say to his father. "They are training in their spare few hours while their goats are grazing or whatever else they were doing in their lives. They were not warriors."

After the training had finished and everyone had left Philip sat with his back against the wall that ran the length of the parade ground, picking small stones out of the now dry dirt. He was astonished. Surely the crown could afford better equipment for Macedonia's soldiers. They had enough money to pay for mercenaries, although he did not know amounts, but he knew soldiers got paid a fraction of what mercenaries did. He didn't want to be disrespectful to his father, but how could he not afford to train the men?

Chapter 12

Philip paced outside his father's study for what felt like hours, even though he had been there less than one. His father had summoned him, though he was not sure why. Now that he was beginning to train with the army, he wondered if he was also being brought into the politics of the kingdom. Politics was for snakes. This was not something that he wanted. He just wanted to be a soldier.

He paced up and down again, running his finger along the key pattern border that ran the length of the wall at about his chest height.

One of the two guards standing at the other end of the corridor, opposite his father's study yawned, then immediately swallowed it back and stood up straight when Philip looked up.

Philip yawned himself.

There was a muted clunk from the other side of the doors and they finally creaked opened. Amyntas stood on the other side.

"Philip, please come in." His father seemed different somehow. He was still stern and serious, his voice as dry as ever. What was it? Philip couldn't place it, but there was a tiny bit of cheer in his voice.

He followed him to the room, but stopped in the doorway, where there were two men that he did not recognise; his father took his seat behind the large wooden desk in the corner of the study. The first man sat opposite his father and had turned his chair to an angle where he could both talk to the king and see the door. A cautious man? The second stood behind him and to the side. He was much younger, about Philip's age he guessed, and wore a clean and well pressed tunic, which was made of very basic material. His servant? Maybe a slave? He kept his head slightly lowered and stayed quiet. The desk was strewn with papers and scrolls.

"Philip, this is Iphicrates. He is a prominent general from Athens."

Iphicrates raised his hand in a polite protest. "Now now Amyntas, I am simply a citizen doing a service for my city state."

Philip tried to hide the confused look on his face, but he knew they had seen it. Amyntas smiled in mild amusement. A smile. He *was* pleased, relaxed even. The first time in his life Philip has seen him like this.

"If there is nothing else to be discussed, I will be going," Iphicrates said, still looking amused. He gestured to his man. He must be a slave, Philip thought; he had been ignored and had not even been introduced. He was a ghost. The man collected up some papers and scrolls from the desk and placed them in a linen bag he wore over his shoulder.

Iphicrates threw a woollen cloak over his shoulders and said his farewells to Amyntas. On his way past he paused and lightly placed his hand on Philip's shoulder. "Good to meet you Philip, I will follow your career with keen interest."

He left and was followed by his slave.

Philip stood, awkward and confused, what was going on? Why was an Athenian meeting with his father in private like this? No more diplomats or ambassadors? And no scribes?

"Come, come, my son." He motioned to the chair that Iphicrates had been sitting in. Philip stood awkwardly, barely in the doorway.

"Why have I been summoned?"

"Come in and sit," his father said bluntly, his voice starting to lose its patience, "and close the door behind you."

Philip closed the heavy wooden door, entered the room and sat in the chair. It was still warm from Iphicrates sitting in it. He sat in a stiff upright posture, the chair being uncomfortable, and he shifted his weight from side to side, in a vain attempt to get comfortable.

There was a long silence as his father watched him, reading the expression; Philip glanced at the papers on the desk while he squirmed in the seat. He was starting to get aggravated. "How did that Iphicrates get comfortable in this chair? He looked so relaxed."

"He wasn't relaxed, or comfortable," Amyntas said, smiling at him.

Philip didn't want to ask why he seemed to find it amusing. "What do you mean?"

"These clever Greek politicians only show you what they want you to see, and you only hear what they want you to hear. "

Philip nodded, not really understanding what his father meant. "Father, why am I here?" he asked.

"My son, now that you have killed your man, I am going to be trusting you with more royal duties. You are training with the army, and now you are going to have to learn about the running of this kingdom."

"But father, I-"

"Listen!" he said, cutting Philip off. "I am proud of you. You have always shown intelligence, but I am ashamed to admit I was always concerned you were weak, that you may never be able to kill. It takes a man to kill. Now I see that you are not afraid to kill, now you know how it feels to take a life, you are ready. I have also observed that you are not keen to kill, you take no pleasure in it. This is a great quality for a soldier to

132

have. He does what he must. Now you must take your place with your brothers and…"

"Father," Philip said, "I will be a soldier for you, and Alexander when you pass to the house of death, but I do not want to get involved in the politics of the kingdom. I don't want to get involved with these petty Greeks; they never say what they mean. They look down on us."

"You are my son, so whether you want it or not, you are involved," Amyntas said, his eyebrows lowering with impatience. "You are now training with the army, and you will make a great general one day, of that I am certain. I have heard great things from your instructors. I need more from a son. Petty or not, these Greeks are the only thing stopping Bardylis from marching straight to the Pella and killing us all."

"Why, what are they doing for us?"

"I have agreed to send them all the timber they need for their fleet, and they are going to pay us well for it. I am prepared to ignore their condescending attitude for that."

"Do you trust them?"

"No," Amyntas said immediately, then paused and scratched his thick, greying beard. "I would trust Iphicrates himself, but because of their democracy I can never completely trust him. You see, he has to convince his peers, and they are fickle. Not like here in Macedonia. Only a fool would go completely against the Macedonian Council, but the final decision is mine. If we did this through the normal diplomatic channels, we would be as slow as them to react. We can assume they will be trustworthy as long as we keep supplying them with timber."

"Why do they need timber so badly?"

"Come Philip, have you not been listening to your tutors? Athens is dependent on its navy; their entire society depends upon it. Southern Greece has very few forests, and we have many. How was your training anyway? An eye opener?"

Philip paused. He tried to remember his practised speech, but couldn't.

"Father, our army is completely inadequate, we need to spend the money we spend on mercenaries on paying our own soldiers," Philip said, not trying in any way to hide his feelings.

Amyntas's relaxed demeanour melted away entirely. He sat upright in is chair and leaned in to Philip, pointing his finger. "Don't you think I know that? We can't afford to improve the army. If we stop paying the mercenaries we are done, and we can't pay for both. We rely on politics to keep our would-be conqueror's beaks wet."

"What do you mean?"

"We can't rely on our army; we can only hope to survive. My strategy is to keep Macedonia in the favour of these Greeks. Athens makes the most sense. We have what they want, and if their navy can protect our coast, we can open more trade from the sea and when that happens, we should have the funding to develop the army. And on that day, when our army is strong enough, I will kill Bardylis. He is the key."

He gritted his teeth and clenched his fist. Philip watched him for a few moments. He was in a daze, staring intensely into space, seeming lost in his thoughts. "Father?" he finally said.

His father came back to the present. "Yes Philip, sorry, so Athens… I have just secured a deal with Athens; we will sell them our timber exclusively. I am soon to attend a Pan Hellenic congress which they have

134

called, to settle many matters among all the Greeks and their allies. Iphicrates is a powerful, influential man, and he has promised to back our cause, if we support Athens in retaking Amphipolis to our east. They claim it as a territory, but it has been its own city for generations."

Philip nodded along, trying to keep up. This talk now had him engaged, but he was new to all of this. "What about your Spartan allies?"

"What about them?"

"What will they make of you becoming so close to Athens?"

"They don't know, and they will not know. Do you understand?" He stared intensely at Philip, who looked him in the eyes but was forced to nod and turn away. "Sparta will continue to be our friends, but they are no longer the great power they once were. We can't rely on them either, but for a different reason."

"Why not?"

"They were defeated in battle, near Leuctra in Boeotia by Thebes. Their power has been mostly crippled. They will no longer readily commit soldiers to war."

"Yes, one of the officers at training mentioned Leuctra, Parmenion was his name."

"Parmenion, yes, I know Parmenion, a good man, from a good family. He shows great loyalty. Did he train you well?"

"He did."

Amyntas smiled.

There was a pause in the conversation and Amyntas got up, walked around the desk to stand at one of the drapes that hung from the wall. A gold Argead star was embroidered into it. Philip knew how proud his father was of the family line. Amyntas brushed the dust off the drape and brushed his hands together.

135

"Do you remember when I left to war, to attack the city of Olynthus?"

"Vaguely," he lied. He remembered it well.

"We were supposed to be allies, but they knew we did not have the military might to assert ourselves. Olynthus helped us against Bardylis, but then they fucked us."

Philip leant in.

"I paid them for their help against Illyria by allowing them to take our timber in north Macedonia. Look." He beckoned Philip over to his desk, where a map of Macedonia and the surrounding territories was laid out. "They were supposed to give it back, but refused. Gradually the territory under their influence crept further south. Our resources up there in the north were no longer under our control. The timber we rely on was being logged from our land by the Olynthians. With Sparta's help we retook it. Athens backed Olynthus in this fight. Now that Olynthus has been reduced in power, Athens wants to deal with whoever has access to the timber. Us."

Philip nodded along. "Clever," he said.

"We will be wealthier from now on and the Spartans have advised me to hire mercenaries in the short term. In return for Athenian support, I have agreed to recognise Athens sovereignty over Amphipolis and will help them to retake it if necessary."

"Why do they need our help? Why don't they just take their timber and Amphipolis themselves?"

"We give them a foothold much closer to their goal of Amphipolis, a base to launch their attack from. With this new alliance, we are being backed by Athens and Sparta. I am going to stop paying the Illyrians their tribute and use the gold to strengthen our military, "

His gazed returned to his map.

136

"Listen, now this is important. I know that says North Macedonia on the map, but the reality is we have no real control over it. It is constantly raided by Thracians; the nobles there show loyalty to me only when it suits them. All these Greeks and Illyrians are always making their presence felt. I spend most of my time trying to keep them at each other's throats and not ours. Remember that."

"I won't forget that Father."

"Good, anyway, back to what I was saying… I am going to stop paying our tribute to Illyria. By the time they have tried to resolve it and bully us into paying up, with the help of our allies, we will be strong enough to oppose them and I will kill Bardylis,"

"Father?"

"Yes?"

Philip had always been curious what had happened to his father that has caused this hatred for Bardylis to be so strong; he had never asked about it. "Why do you want to kill Bardylis so badly? What did he do to you?"

Amyntas chewed his bottom lip, avoiding looking him in the eye, he stared into space. "You will learn soon enough," he eventually said.

…

After a few months of training with the infantry Philip was invited to train with the cavalry. This he was very excited about, as he loved horses and riding them. He loved the speed, and the wind rushing through his hair, the might of the beast itself, especially once it was at a full sprint and breathing hard, a mass of muscle and sinew.

He had never ridden one to attack another person, and was excited to learn about cavalry, and how they

137

trained and fought. His father and Alexander both trained with the cavalry, but they were not present today.

The training was led by a Thessalian. The greatest horses in Greece came from Thessaly, and by extension the best riders. The Thessalians had long been allies to Macedonia, and Amyntas had done a great job of cultivating that relationship. Horses were useful for everything.

"The greatest horses in the world come from my country, the most beautiful horses. These are the stallion. They are born black, and when they get old enough to ride, they change to white," the

Thessalian horse master said when Philip approached. He patted the horse's neck. It was a beautiful horse, just as he had been told.

"These are the horses we will be training with?" Philip asked and joined the Thessalian in patting the horse's neck, and the horse seemed to like it.

"Not yet my Prince, first we will train on lesser animals to see how you are at riding."

Philip was not too pleased with having his riding ability questioned, although he was thought of as a wimp by some, people also knew that because of his smaller stature he was a very fast rider. He looked across from the stables to the open field where you would train the horses. As his gaze moved across, he saw his half-brothers, and felt a lump in his throat; *not them*, he thought, why do they have to be here?

They had not seen him. They were readying their horses for training as well. Philip was caught staring over in their direction, when Menelaus looked up and saw him. He patted his brother Arrhidaeus on the back, who was kneeling over, inspecting his horse's hooves.

He stood and they both looked at Philip and grinned, the mocking grin bringing Philip back to being a child.

"Just ignore them," Perdiccas said. "That's what I've been doing and they don't seem to be too interested in us at the moment anyway"

"Oh, they're interested, trust me, they're just picking their moment, and when my back is turned..."

"I'm not so sure," Perdiccas said. "You're training with the cavalry now too. Your status has gone up considerably. I'm not sure if they would dare touch you now."

"You think?"

"Definitely," he said. "Do you think father would invest in your training if he was not sure of your potential? Trust me, they won't touch you."

Perdiccas and Philip spent the rest of the morning practising with the cavalrymen from Thessaly, and they were impressed with Philip's horsemanship, and speed of manoeuvre. This filled him with confidence that he was finally being recognised as someone useful, and not just the puny third brother.

They took a short break, and Philip sipped at a skin of water, and stood with Perdiccas, waiting for the next session of training. Arrhidaeus and Menelaus approached them.

They stalked over, as a predator approaches prey that it has crippled and let bleed out. Arrhidaeus led, a sneer on his face. He raised his finger, ready to prod or poke Philip in the chest, then inevitably a push would come and then worse.

He still stood almost a head taller, and when his hand got within arm's reach of Philip, Philip stood up casually and looked him in the eye. "What do you want?" he said.

Arrhidaeus turned to his brother and the two sniggered. "I want to see you beg for-"

"Well, you won't get any of that. Not today. Never again," Philip said.

Arrhidaeus slapped the skin out of Philip's hand and cool water flicked onto his face and it burst on the ground, making the dirt go dark. He could feel the eyes of everyone there watching them.

The memory of when he killed his man flashed into his mind, just before it happened, when the blood from the man Alexander killed had splashed him in the face. He licked his lips; he could almost taste the iron in that Thracian's blood, even though today, it was just water.

"What?" Arrhidaeus said, his eyebrows raised in disbelieve.

"I said, never again," Philip said, louder this time, so everyone who was around could hear, and he raised his head and stature up. He clenched his fists by his sides, ready for a fight this time. "Now fuck off, before I open your fucking throat."

Arrhidaeus' mouth was wide open. "Listen you little-"

Philip gritted his teeth and flung himself forward. His balled fist struck Arrhidaeus clean on the chin, and he staggered back, dazed. Philip clinched with him, pulled him in tight, turned, and threw him over his hip. He landed hard on his side, his head struck the ground, he went limp for a moment, but almost immediately rolled onto his back and started to blink hard, trying to regain his composure.

Philip walked over to one of the racks where the weapons were stored, and drew a kopis, a short sword from it. The forward curved blade caught the sunlight as he turned. Menelaus stepped back, half turning to run. As Philip walked past him, he backed right off.

Arrhidaeus, still on the ground, suddenly seemed to shrink. He crabbed back away from Philip, who stood over him, pointing the tip of the sword in his face. If he hadn't been crawling back, he would have been cut as Philip walked him down.

"No. You listen. If you ever come near me or my brothers again, I'll kill you. You understand? I'll fucking kill you," Philip said, staring him in the eye, his bottom lip quivering with rage.

Arrhidaeus, whose wide eyes were locked with Philip's, glanced to Menelaus, who was dumbfounded, frozen to the spot, speechless. He slowly backed away.

"Menelaus. You piece of shit!" Arrhidaeus spat. "Come back!"

"Philip," came a calming voice. Philip broke his stare and looked over. It was Perdiccas, placing his hand lightly on his shoulder. "That's enough. He's had enough."

They walked away together. No one rushed to help Arrhidaeus up.

"By the gods Philip," Perdiccas said. "Where did that come from?"

"It must have been the gods," Philip said, and lifted his hand to inspect it; it shook a little, but only a little.

Chapter 13

The stopping of the Illyrian tribute did not provoke the reaction Amyntas had expected. Instead of sending an embassy to discuss the matter, Bardylis had wasted no time, and sent one of his sons, with a full entourage of elite soldiers to tell Amyntas to immediately resume payments, or there would be war.

"The tribute has been sent my friends, like always. It must be the result of bandits intercepting it that it did not make it to your master in Illyria," Amyntas had said, trying to stall them.

They did not believe the lie.

Amyntas suspected a spy in his court, but was not sure who it could be. The scouts from the north of the kingdom, watching the passes, had reported that the Illyrians had sent a force to raid the farms and villages near the border as punishment. This made Amyntas furious, but by the time word had reached him, autumn had turned to winter, and the passes had begun to close with snow.

Amyntas stewed for the whole of the winter, grumbling about Bardylis. Philip grew concerned as his father had developed a cough that the physicians could not manage to settle, despite all their efforts. His worry grew and he feared the worst when, one night, he could not hear his father pacing and coughing. He was relieved when he discovered he had slept in the barracks that night.

In the spring, as soon as the news came that the snows were beginning to melt and the passes were open, the royal army was mustered. They marched north to oppose the Illyrians, who had reportedly been preparing to resume their raiding.

Amyntas had been informed that there was now an army coming, headed by Bardylis himself, so he marched his own army to face him. Philip travelled with them. He was concerned about his father's brashness; all his companions had advised against a battle, feeling that it could not be won. Alexander was left to act as regent, with Perdiccas to instruct. The two had also been charged with the task of finding the spy.

Philip felt his shoulders begin to tighten, and a sickness grow in the pit of his stomach as they crossed into the hills in the north west. They were now clearly in upper Macedonia, and beyond where his father could reliably control; it was bandit country. It reminded him of the time when he and Arsinoe had witnessed his father's return from their defeat at Olynthus, and now, looking at these hills unsettled him.

The land had become less and less populous the further they had got from Pella. Now it was sparse. There were fewer herders visible on the hillsides, which were becoming rocky and treacherous; there were almost no buildings in sight. The rivers that ran down the hillside were steep and flowed rapidly, spilling their banks in some cases; the snow had almost gone, only the peaks of the mountains were still covered in white. He breathed out, and watched his breath slowly float up in a cloud and disperse. He pulled up the neck of his cloak and tucked his chin into it to keep warm. The road was overgrown with long grass that was covered in frost.

"This road was well travelled decades ago," Amyntas told him, "but because of the fighting and raiding between Macedonia and Illyria, and all the backstabbing between the nobles who own these lands, trading has lessened over the years. It would take brave souls to live here with all the bandits in the hills."

143

After marching they reached their destination, a valley near the border. The king positioned the Macedonian army in the flattest, widest part of valley, opposite the woods that Bardylis's army was reportedly camped in. These woods were at the bottom of a shallow slope in the valley floor. "We will lure them out of the woods and they will have to fight us uphill," Amyntas said.

Philip sat on his horse behind the main line with his father; his Spartan advisor; and Ptolemy, who had brought his own levies. He looked nervously between Amyntas and his men, who were part of the centre. The main line was made up of these levies, who were armed with a spear, and a small round shield, just like the ones Philip had used in training. They were in a formation that resembled a Greek hoplite phalanx, but the looseness of the formation was obvious, even to Philip. Few had armour because it could not be afforded by them; some wore helmets, all were of varying quality and condition. They were also accompanied by Thracian mercenaries.

Amyntas had gone through the battle strategy with his generals in the camp that morning, based on the intelligence that his scouts had come back with; he knew their rough numbers and where they were positioned, so he had, correctly, predicted the time and place of the engagement.

"I want the Thracians on the flanks. The front line will be made up of our Macedonian infantry; if they hold long enough, the Thracians can then spread out and move around the Illyrian flanks and rear, if possible. I will lead the cavalry to chase any skirmishers," he said.

A few of the generals had not been confident the line would hold long enough; Philip had remained quiet;

144

he had known better than to question his father in front of his generals.

"Here they come," Ptolemy said.

Silhouettes appeared on the tree line, in a very loose formation, the men wearing small helmets, but no armour, carrying javelins, light bows or slings.

"Just skirmishers," Ptolemy said, relief in his voice.

"They're not my concern," Amyntas said. He casually turned his head and spoke to the officer on his right. "Signal our own to advance."

"Skirmish screen!" the officer yelled.

The Macedonian skirmishers that had been in amongst the loose phalanx for protection filtered out from in between the infantrymen and advanced towards their Illyrian counterparts, spaced out to shadow their opponents.

They began to launch their missiles toward the enemy, who returned fire. They dodged these for the most part, then launched their own volleys again. This back and forward went on for a while. Philip watched as one man, a Macedonian, was struck in the face by a sling ball. The distance made the blow and any scream silent. He collapsed face down on the spot, presumably dead. Philip's thoughts flashed back to his first man's face, his eyes staring into Philip's, until they glazed over. They looked in his direction, but didn't see him; they looked through him.

The skirmishers continued to jostle for control of the centre of the battlefield, while the main line continued to form up. They now stood in a straight line, almost the width of the valley, their shields poised and weapons raised at the ready.

Then the rest of the Illyrian army emerged from the tree line. Again the silhouettes appeared, but this was a more frightening sight to behold. The figures were

145

packed tightly together, their large round shields overlapped like the scales of a snake, locked together to form their phalanx. Their tall spear shafts bristled above them. Head to toe in bronze, and horse hair plumes tall on the top of their helmets, they looked like monstrous automatons from the workshops of Hephaestus, marching forward relentlessly. A chill ran down Philip's spine.

As more and more came into view and began to fall into formation, Amyntas's demeanour sank. This force was not only much larger, but far better equipped than they had been led to believe. He turned to one of the young officers on horseback next to him.

"Glaucous."

"Sire."

"Make sure the scouts that reported this raid are taken into custody; if we survive this, they will be questioned," he said. He chewed the inside of his cheek. He was trying to keep his composure, but Philip knew his father: he was brave, but not stupid, and although he did not show it, he was on the verge of panic.

"Sire," the officer nodded and ran back to the camp to make sure the orders were carried out.

Amyntas patted his horses' neck and it snorted. He looked up and down the line and shook his head. The Illyrian line was the same length as the Macedonian's, but it was deeper. Much deeper.

"Greek mercenaries," Amyntas said.

The Spartan officer looked to Amyntas and spoke slowly and calmly in his strange accent, his face showing no expression. "Your army is not equipped for this engagement. It will get heavily outflanked. We do not know what forces are concealed by the woods, and if they disperse their troops from the rear into the flanks this will be a terrible defeat. You should consider withdrawing."

Amyntas slowly nodded in agreement.

"I agree. Prepare to retire," Amyntas said.

No more infantry filed out. But behind them came cavalry, and in the centre emerged a silver haired man in white armour on a white horse, surrounded by men dressed similarly. He was too far away to make out his features, but a golden crown on his head glinted in the light.

"No," Amyntas said, "not today, today we will send *him* a message."

Philip stared at his father in disbelief, but closed his mouth when he realised his jaw was hanging wide open. He had not understood until this exact moment how deep his father's hatred for his enemy ran. He stared intensely at his enemy, his hands gripping the reins of his horse so hard they shook.

Philip looked around at the soldiers, and he thought of the days training with them. This army was mostly made up of farmers, not hardened soldiers like the ones that were forming up on the other side of the battlefield.

"Order the attack," Amyntas said to his officers, and they sent their orders down the line.

"Father I-"

"Silence boy," Amyntas ordered Philip furiously through gritted teeth. "We have made far too many retreats from this man. Today I will have him. We can beat them. He is here, with one or more of his sons. If we can kill them, great; if we can capture them, even better, we will finally have some leverage over Illyria. I want to hurt him."

Philip nodded in false approval. He did not want to press his father further; he looked at the Spartan, desperately hoping he would do it for him, but he stayed silent as a statue. He had already offered his council.

The Macedonian frontline was the same width as the Illyrian's; didn't that mean it was even? If they fought hard enough, they could win. His father certainly seemed to think they could. Their Thracian mercenaries would have to fight ferociously to take one of the flanks, but they could do it. The Spartan did not look impressed, although he barely let on, his expression blank, as it was with all Spartans he had met.

The trumpets blew and the line advanced. The army raised their shields and lowered their spears. The Macedonian line marched forward, but it was clumsy and disjointed. The officers had to keep stopping them to get them into a straight line. Philip looked across the battlefield at the Illyrians, who advanced far more smoothly and at a quicker pace. He wondered if the Illyrians were like their soldiers, farmers and the like, or if they were a professional army.

The two front lines met in the middle of the battlefield and the sound of metal hitting metal immediately began ringing in the air. Shields clashed and spears splintered. Philip was not as horrified or as frightened as he had expected to be. Having some training now, and from the hunting trip, had fought and killed up close. He could hear the screams and shouts and grunts of the pushing and shoving on the frontline, the sounds muted because of the distance they had travelled, but they were unmistakable. As the shields clashed together and men tried to stab over the top with their swords and spears the lines flexed and pulsed backward and forward.

Amyntas and Ptolemy had moved off with their cavalry to support the right flank and Philip was left to stay back with the Spartan advisor for safety. The

148

Spartan stared straight forward with his indifferent expression, observing the battle.

"Have you fought many battles?" Philip asked.

"Yes. Many," he answered. He did not turn his head; his eyes were narrow, watching the battle like a hawk. He did not change his expression or tone of voice.

"Have you killed many men?"

"Yes. Many," he answered, again maintaining his manner.

Philip gave up asking questions and there was a silence between them, only the sounds of the battle could be heard. The silence would have been awkward, if they were not observing the battle.

He could see his father and his cavalry riding out to the right flank and clash with light Illyrian cavalry. They were forced to back off when skirmishers emerged from the rear of the Illyrian army and pelted them with sling balls and arrows.

Philip's gaze went back to the centre of the battle and out to the tree line. More silhouettes appeared; they stepped out into the light.

More Illyrians.

Philip felt a lump in his throat. Lighter armed men with crescent shaped shields and swords were now pouring out of the forest and spreading to the flanks, just as the Spartan had predicted. In an out of character moment, the Spartan chewed his bottom lip.

"We have to warn my father," Philip said, becoming restless.

"There is no time for that, Prince. It is time for us to leave."

"No, we have to stay," he said, and stubbornly refused to move; the Spartan stayed with him.

Before long, the Macedonian army was being overwhelmed on both flanks, and the centre had been pushed back and back under the mass of the opposing soldiers. The line flexed into a bow shape. The men had started to peel off the back of the line and retreat, dropping their weapons and armour to get away quicker. It would not take much for the full army to break.

When this eventually came, more and more men ran, the whole frontline collapsed, many fell and the others fled. The Illyrians did not pursue and were left in a hollow crescent shape. They instead stayed to loot the bodies of the fallen Macedonians, who fortunately did not number many, most had run.

These were farmers and craftsmen, not professional soldiers. They broke and ran much more quickly than most professional armies would. The Thracians had fought fiercely on the flanks but were eventually overrun. They ended up trapped and surrounded. The enemy did not kill them. They would no doubt be given conditions to being left alive, possibly being recruited by Bardylis. Next time they saw them, they could well be on the other side.

"It is time to get you to safety young Prince," the Spartan advisor reiterated to Philip, who this time agreed, and they withdrew back to the camp.

Philip paced in Amyntas' tent, and his Spartan advisor stood like a statue, his arms folded, waiting for the various reports coming in.

Amyntas burst into the tent, accompanied by Ptolemy, both were sweaty and bloodied. His sword was caked in what was now drying blood, although some still ran down the handle and dripped off his forearm.

Philip stood mortified at the condition of his father, whose armour was caked in blood and gore, and was marked and scored from sword and spear strokes.

"Father are you okay?" he asked.

"Don't worry, most of it isn't my blood," Amyntas said between laboured breaths, in an attempt to reassure him. He then immediately turned to the Spartan.

"Illyrian bastards!" he shouted, nursing his forearm. He was wounded, but with the amount of blood on him it was impossible to tell how badly.

"Father, we should leave. It's too dangerous here," Philip said.

Amyntas shook his head, gulped a long swig of water from a skin and gasped a breath of air. He was handed a towel, which he used to wipe the blood from his face, hands and neck, but there was so much of it that the towel was saturated. It still left red streaks all over him. He looked up to the Spartan to explain.

"They will not pursue," he said, with his monotone voice.

"Why not?" Philip asked.

"They are not interested in killing their own workers. The Macedonian tribute to the Illyrian economy is important, they know that if they kill too many of your men, it will make Macedonia poorer, and thus make Illyria poorer. They have to keep you weak, but not too weak."

"Why draw us into a battle at all then?"

"It was a show of strength. Designed to intimidate."

Philip sat and pondered what he had observed, and what he had been told. Illyria was bleeding Macedonia dry. It needed to break away from them. Mercenaries cannot be relied on, they're too expensive, he thought. The core of the army must be our soldiers. We need to hold the centre ourselves.

He looked over at his father who was shouting at his officers; Philip had never seen his father like this. The physicians appeared to tend to his wounds, and he shrugged them off; the heat of battle was still fresh in his mind, Philip thought; the excitement could make you ignore almost any pain. Philip had experienced it many times boxing and wrestling.

His father hated Bardylis, really hated him. He wanted to kill his family. How had he wounded him? Not in the literal sense of the word, but what had he done to drive Amyntas mad with bitterness?

His thoughts were interrupted when his father broke into a coughing fit. He coughed harder and harder into his fist. He lowered his hand and looked at it; he had coughed up blood.

Chapter 14

After returning home from the battle humiliated, Amyntas took ill, and a few days after that he became too weak to walk, and had been put in his bed. A fever took a hold of him and vomiting and loss of bowel control followed. He had only taken minor cuts in the battle, but the doctors feared that the wounds had festered somehow, even though the wound itself showed no evidence of this. The priests were kept away so that if they thought the gods had cursed him, they could not spread the word.

After a day and night in bed, Philip and his brothers were called in because Amyntas's condition had worsened further; he was having episodes of delirium. When Philip and Perdiccas arrived at his bedchamber, he was asleep, taking shallow breaths. Sitting beside him was Eurydice, Eurynoe and Alexander. His second wife Gygaea had been to see him when he was awake, but had since left. The doctors sat in the corner of the room looking gaunt and drawn. Philip thought they must have been up most of the night.

They all sat closely around his bed, Eurynoe held his hand. Philip stared at him, his hair damp and messy, and matted to his forehead. He seemed small and frail, not like he had been only a few days before, when he had been strong as an ox and as ferocious as a lion. Even though the bedsheets had recently been changed, a dark patch of damp was growing around the king's neck and chest. His laboured breathing sounded ragged and painful. Eurydice dabbed at his head with a cloth.

He woke and coughed weakly. Talking made his struggle for air sound worse. "I think the Fates are close to cutting my thread," he said, slowly closed his eyes and fell back asleep. The doctors rushed over to check him, and the family stepped back to give them space.

"He still lives," the senior doctor said, trying to reassure everyone.

A few days prior, when he was still able to walk, he had still seemed strong and confident, like he had always been, despite the cough. Seeing him like this, Philip felt powerless, robbed of any control.

The family sat and made small talk around him, not knowing what to do. Alexander had visits from different nobles who were making their allegiance to him clear, and promised to sponsor his ascension. He thanked them and assured them their loyalty would be rewarded.

In the early evening, Amyntas's breaths became shallower and shallower, until they could almost not be heard, and then they stopped altogether.

Alexander lay his ear on his father's chest to listen for his heart. Time lingered before he stood up and shook his head.

The women wept and the men stood solemnly. Philip's eyes welled and he sniffed, wiping the tears from his eyes with his thumb and forefinger. A moment later his eyes welled again and a tear ran down his cheek. Perdiccas put his arm around him.

After a short time passed, Parmenion and Antipater, who had been waiting outside entered the room and paid their respects to their king. Parmenion then spoke directly to Alexander, whispering in his ear. He then quietly and politely asked the women to leave. "Tell no one of his passing. This is important," he told them as they left. He also sent away the doctor who was stood on the corner.

"Do you want Philip and Perdiccas here?" he then whispered to Alexander.

Alexander looked at both of his brothers, and paused for a moment. "I trust my brothers," he said, and allowed them to stay. He knew what this was about already.

"Alexander, I've been sent here by the Council of Macedonians. They want to know what the condition of the king is." Parmenion looked over at his old friend and comrade Antipater, who stepped closer in to the pair. He then lowered his voice, "We have secured favour for your ascension to the throne, gods forbid that the king is now passed to the underworld. We have made certain all institutions and guilds are with you."

He crouched beside his father and brushed his matted hair from his brow. He kissed him on the head and placed a coin in his hand for the ferry man. He rose and wiped tears from his eyes.

"Thank-" He coughed and cleared his throat. "Thank you Parmenion. We must secure any dissent and secure the throne before anyone knows he's dead. Start putting your arrangements in place, I will be with you shortly."

"Yes," Parmenion said and gave a short bow of his head "…Sire."

Parmenion and Antipater left, and the Doctor sheepishly approached Alexander. "I must speak with you," he whispered and beckoned him over to a corner away from earshot of the others. They moved over and he whispered something to him. He then motioned with his head for Philip and Perdiccas to join them.

"The doctor does not believe that Father's death was natural," he said, and the doctor nodded.

"You said before that his fever was brought on by wounds he sustained in battle?" Perdiccas said.

"That is what we believed. At first, we thought the blood being brought up was the result of a puncture to

155

the lung or stomach, however, he had no such wound, and he was recovering well."

"What are you saying?" Philip asked.

"I believe the king was poisoned."

Alexander gritted his teeth, and Philip scratched his chin.

"Thank you, doctor. I will come and speak with you soon," Alexander said and dismissed him. He immediately turned to Perdiccas and Philip. "Brothers, there will be time to mourn, but now we must secure our family's ascension. Go now and find those pieces of shit, Arrhidaeus, Menelaus and Archelaus. Arm yourselves and bring them in to custody for now. We will interrogate them later and make sure they were not behind this, and that they had no plans to challenge me."

They did as he said. As they passed Alexander, he stopped Philip by placing a hand on his chest. Philip looked his brother in the eyes, "If they did," Alexander said, "you will get your revenge."

They both nodded and left, stopping to touch their father's body on the way out of the room. They armed themselves, and took ten men from the Royal Guard with them, to the wing of the palace where their half-brothers resided with their mother.

They burst the doors open to the royal apartments to discover their half-brother's mother, Gygaea, stood on her own, sobbing.

"Please," she pleaded with them, "do what you must with me, but do not hurt my sons."

"Alexander has told us to simply find them, no harm will come to them," Philip said, assuring her of their intentions.

Gygaea clearly did not believe him and she took a hold of Philip's hands and threw herself to his feet, her head bowed low, almost kissing them. Philip felt awkward and embarrassed for her. He twisted a little to break free of her holding his hands. Up until a few moments ago she had been the proud wife of a king and a mother of three princes. He took a short step away from her and broke the grip She looked up at him through her red, tear-filled eyes.

"Please Philip, I beg you, I know they were not kind to you, I always chastised them for it."

"Where are they? What are their intentions?" Philip asked her, frowning; in the moment he had forgotten his sadness, and his father's passing, all his focus was on finding his half-brothers. The thought of getting revenge for the years of torment they had forced on him clouded every other consideration.

"Where are they?" Perdiccas asked, "Our father is dead and Alexander is king. If they have no ambitions for the throne, Alexander has no reason to hurt them. On the contrary, they could be useful to him."

"Amyntas is dead?" she asked, and sniffed. "I knew he was likely to die. When did he pass? Take me to him."

"We will. First, where are your sons?" Philip asked, trying to appear as calm as possible; in truth he could feel a murderous rage building in him. He had to catch his half-brothers. They could not be allowed to get away, or they would risk them raising their own supporters to try and claim the throne.

"They're hiding," she said. "They took their horses. I don't know where they went. I told them to flee, I knew you would come to kill them. They're not in the palace".

Philip ordered an officer from his retinue of the Royal Guard to take Gygaea to see her late husband. Perdiccas, Philip and the rest headed down to the stables. When they got there, he looked over the gates into the pens as they passed; some horses were missing.

He marched across the yard to the storeroom, where he could make out the stable master through the open doorway. He marched in to question him. He was a small, slight man and he was standing on his toes to lift a saddle cloth down from its hooks on the wall.

"Where are the Princes Arrhidaeus, Archelaus and Menelaus?" Philip asked sharply. The stable master dropped the saddle and turned, startled. He appeared dumbstruck when Perdiccas and the retinue of the Royal Guard filed in after Philip.

"Prince Philip, I… I…don't," he said.

"When did they leave?"

"I… I don't know young Prince, they left not an hour ago. Didn't say anything about where they were going," he said.

"Shit, the bastards evaded us." Philip said.

"I know. Alexander is going to be pissed," said Perdiccas. "Well, we still have their mother, they won't do anything while she is still in Pella."

Philip nodded and then looked over at the empty spaces in the stable. "How many of them came to get horses?"

"Two."

"Only two? And how many horses did they take?"

"Four Sire."

"Four?" He looked at Perdiccas. "Why take four horses? They didn't come back for their mother."

"Maybe they were going to come back for her, then lost the nerve? Maybe they found out we were coming for them?"

"Maybe." Philip scratched his chin and stared at the other horses. "No, I think only two left. They took the horses for themselves to travel faster. One of the

158

bastards is still here. And they're going to bring back help, someone who supports their claim, or maybe mercenaries."

"I think you might be right. It would have to be Arrhidaeus that stayed. He would be their heir. He would need to try and show his strength by staying."

"We must tell Alexander," Philip said.

The thought of Arrhidaeus still being there filled him with dread. What if he was able to get more support than Alexander? There would be a lot of blood spilled.

Perdiccas nodded in agreement and they headed back to the palace.

...

Philip stared up at the funeral pyre. Alexander stepped forward with the torch he was holding, and threw it onto the bales of hay at the base of the large wooden frame. It was two tiers high and the king lay on the top in his finest armour, clutching his sword to his chest; all of his other weapons and his shield were laid out around him for his journey to the afterlife.

It was early evening and there was a chill in the air that caused Philip to shiver. Rain began to spit. He stood with his family and they huddled together to keep warm; the mood was sombre. Alexander stepped back and took their place standing by their mother and sister, who wept quietly.

The flames took a hold of the pyre and began to build up and crackle, licking the bottom of the second tier just below his father's body; he felt the heat that emanated from it on his cheeks, but his ears and nose still hurt with the cold and his cloak was now beginning to get damp. He rubbed his hands together, cupped them and blew a hot breath into them.

159

Smoke rose up from the flames in a pillar that partially enveloped his father. Through the gaps in the black cloud, Philip could make out Gygaea, his father's second wife, now widow. She stood on the other side, sombre in her funeral robes, weeping. Philip watched her, as she stared forward, like a statue, not daring to look anywhere else, seeming afraid of meeting eyes with anyone. Philip chewed his cheek. Standing next to her was Arrhidaeus. When Philip and Perdiccas had returned to the palace, he had already been there. His mother had begged for his life, and he had bent the knee and pledged his loyalty to Alexander, who had accepted and spared him. Philip had never seen someone kneel to a king before, he had heard stories about how it had been done long ago. He tried to recall if anyone had even knelt to his father, but he couldn't remember. This was far from the show of strength they had expected, and this made him look incredibly weak in the eyes of the Macedonian nobility.

Philip stared at him across the other side of the pyre, the heat making the air ripple upward in waves. The light of the flames danced on his face, immediately evoking memories of the night they had tried to kill him. A tear ran down Arrhidaeus's cheek; he wiped it away and put his arm around his mother.

Philip wished no harm on Gygaea. The woman had always been kind to him, but he hated her sons. He ground his teeth at the sight of Arrhidaeus. He would pay, and so would his brothers when they were found. Now that their father was not the king, Alexander had to protect his throne. He might have said that they would be safe, but there could be no other sons of Amyntas outside of the three of them.

As the pyre burned down to hot embers, the mourners slowly began to leave.

160

Philip watched Arrhidaeus closely, not sure what he was expecting, some kind of trouble perhaps.

Two heavy set men from the Royal Guard appeared, flanked him, and placed their strong hands on his shoulders. Gygaea was brushed to the side. She looked aghast, her face confused, her eyes darted around, her gaze then finding Alexander, her eyes pleading with him. He did not acknowledge her.

Arrhidaeus' expression was blank, as though he did not believe what was happening.

Philip then felt something he did not expect, as he watched Arrhidaeus marched off. Pity. He actually felt remorse for what may happen to him.

"Do you really feel sorry for him?" a voice that Philip recognised whispered from behind. He turned and met the eyes of his friend Antigonus.

"I think so," Philip said.

Antigonus motioned with his head to come to the side, away from the crowds of mourners. They moved over to a quiet corner against one of the pillars of the temple.

"Where have you been my friend? I haven't seen-"

"I've been at my family home in Elimeia. But never mind that now," he whispered harshly, his eyes looking over Philip's shoulder at the crowd, darting from person to person. "Be careful not to feel pity. I think we need to get you out of here. There's going to be trouble."

"It's fine," Philip said. "As you can see, Alexander has my half-brother's family under his boot."

"I'm not talking about them. While I was home, I overheard my father. They were speaking about other pretenders preparing to stake their claim. There's going to be a lot of trouble here soon. I came back to Pella to warn you and Alexander."

"I thought you were done running?"

161

"I am, but we need to keep you safe; I will follow you wherever you go."

"We should stay, if there is trouble then my brother could use a man like yourself,"

Antigonus nodded. "Good. Good. I didn't want to go anyway. I hate to travel."

…..

Weeks passed since the funeral games and Alexander sat at the head of the table in the great banqueting hall of the palace. The table was not a normal part of the decor, and ran the length of the room; the many chairs that were around it had not been filled yet.

Alexander was flanked by Perdiccas and Philip. Behind them stood Parmenion, Antipater and Ptolemy. Antipater had now become a close advisor of Alexander's. He had been his teacher for many years, and so had seemed a natural choice for his mentor as King.

Many ambassadors now filed into the room, and took their seats around the negotiating table. They had travelled from every part of Greece; the North; and Asia Minor, to decide the fate of Macedonia.

Alexander had been crowned King in a short ceremony, and sacrifices had been made to the gods. This was done quickly, because if left too long many pretenders to the throne would have appeared like termites out of a rotten log, and it would cause chaos.

Philip also recognised many of the Macedonian nobles who had been at his sister's wedding. Most of these men had come to pledge their loyalty to Alexander, and had done so at the crowning, but some had not. If they supported the king, he would reward them with silver and military support if their lands were raided, but Philip knew that some of them would not be loyal for long if Alexander was not a strong king like his father.

Among the many others that were attending, there was the Spartan general who had helped Amyntas retake Pella from the Illyrians, and had been at the battle with Philip. He had brought several other men who looked like they may be officers or nobles from the way they carried themselves, but it was hard to tell with Spartans, they never wore any jewellery or anything else that might give a clue to their wealth or status, and it seemed that they wouldn't buy new clothes until they actually fell apart.

The General sat at the opposite end of the table from a group of politicians from Athens who had come to protect their trade interests. Among them, he recognised Iphicrates, the man who had met with his father. He had only met him briefly, but was sure it was him. The Spartan sat completely relaxed, casually looking at them. They stared back at him with venom, but this did not seem to bother him. There was great distrust between the two cities. In his lessons, Philip had been told that only twenty or so years before he was born, they had stopped fighting each other in a bitter war that had lasted a generation, and most of the Greek cities had been dragged into it. There had been many losses on both sides, and even though it was long over, the hatred clearly still ran deep and intense. Philip had never seen a Spartan and an Athenian in the same room; it was uncomfortable to say the least.

He remembered his grandfather telling him and his brothers the stories of Macedonia's involvement in the war. The old man had sat in his chair, and they had sat around him, hanging on his every word while he told

163

them about his uncle, King Perdiccas II, and battles he had fought; a warrior king. He remembered that Perdiccas had loved that he was named after the man. The war had pushed both sides almost to ruin, he had said, and this was good for Macedonia, for they had always meddled in Macedonian affairs. They had listened to the old man's stories until their mother had put them to bed bleary eyed.

Philip looked further along the table. Amyntas's lifelong enemy Bardylis had sent two of his eldest sons. These two had been fighting and raiding the North Western frontier of upper Macedonia. Philip ground his teeth; he knew how both the Spartans and the Athenians were feeling, having to tolerate being this close to their most bitter of enemies.

They were sat next to a general from Thebes named Pelopidas, who had arrived a few days before the rest. He had had business settling some dispute in Thessaly to the south. Pelopidas had been asked by the others to attend to arbitrate proceedings; they all seemed to know him. Philip noticed that his presence provoked a reaction from the Spartan. His eyes narrowed when he entered the room and he seemed to be grinding his teeth, but hid it well, his lips were closed and relaxed, but the muscles on the side of his jaw flexed. The Spartan and his officers spoke quietly among themselves while looking over at him.

Pelopidas was a tall, serious man, with a thick, long beard worn neatly trimmed in the Greek fashion. He was well-groomed, but in a practical, not an ostentatious way like some of the others, namely those from the city states on the East coast of the Aegean, in Asia minor. They sat with him, their look seeming almost Persian rather than Greek. Their eyes and beards were blackened with make-up, and they were covered in gold jewellery.

The chatter around the room died down as Alexander rose to his feet, and all eyes looked to him to start negotiations.

"Welcome friends, you are all here because of the passing of my father," Alexander said. "As his eldest son, I have been sponsored and made King in his place by the counsel of our nobility. I hope we can all work together to retain stability so we can all prosper."

Philip glanced across the table to the sons of Bardylis, the ones he had seen on the battlefield. Bastards, he thought, this is because of you, all of it is because of you and your father. They sat looking smug in their chairs. They spoke to each other loudly, in their own language. No-one could understand them, although the Theban Pelopidas appeared to be listening to them. Philip looked around to see if anyone else had noticed. Pelopidas was concentrating on what they were saying too much to not understand, but he kept it subtle, mostly looking straight ahead and not looking at them for too long at once.

Philip had to choke back his anger at these two; his thoughts immediately went to his half-brothers, yes, that's who these pieces of shit reminded him of. Why was the mighty Bardylis not here himself to look his brother in the eye? He had to send some of his spawn to do his bidding.

Each delegate took it in turns to say what they had to say, and laid out what their interests were. Alexander's biggest concern was the Illyrians or Thracians in the north trying their hands at a territory grab. Once they were dug in and had the mountain passes guarded, it would be extremely difficult to retake any of these territories. They then argued back and forward, between

165

the Athenians and the Spartans, the city states from the Chalcidice, including Olynthus, the city his father and the Spartans had done harm to. They wanted reparations. The Thebans tried to keep the talks orderly, and to an extent it worked. The General Pelopidas seemed to be a man who was very well thought of generally, especially among the northern tribes, but his speaking provoked the Spartans.

The talks went on for hours, and Philip had trouble keeping up with what was being said. Being so new to the world of politics, he felt completely out of his depth, like an imposter posing as a prince. Unfortunately, as he watched Alexander, the same seemed true of him; he was under pressure. It showed. He could barely get a word in.

All these politicians and nobles were creating complete confusion, obviously far more experienced in this kind of negotiating than Alexander, and they held back much of what they seemed to know and postured against each other. This posturing made negotiations last a lot longer than they needed to. They all spoke in Greek, apart from the Illyrians and the Thracians who spoke through interpreters. With the Thracians this seemed to Philip to be a necessity, but for the Illyrians it appeared to be out of choice, because every time something was asked that would not favour them, they miraculously didn't understand what was being said, and it had to be repeated over and over for them.

Philip felt sorry for his brother. He had never seen him flustered in his entire life. He had always been the strong one.

"And what assurances do we have that Alexander will not try and enact some kind of revenge against us?" came the voice of one of the Illyrian interpreters.

166

"You have my word as a soldier," Alexander said, which was met with some amusement around the room, and Alexander's face flushed a little red, confused. In Macedonia a king was as good as his word.

Philip glanced around at those that sniggered the loudest, politicians from Athens. He heard some of them whispering, making out the word "naive," and something about "he won't last long."

After some more arguing back and forward, this time just between Alexander and the Illyrians, with all the others listening and their scribes frantically taking notes, the elder of the two sons of Bardylis said something to the interpreter and grinned at Alexander cruelly.

"A marriage. Prince Perdiccas to a daughter of King Bardylis?" the Spartan General said. "Tie their houses together. This will prevent bad blood."

The Athenian Iphicrates stood and shook his head. "No," he said. "What my learned Spartan friend fails to recognise is that until King Alexander has a son, Prince Perdiccas is the heir to the throne. If he married an Illyrian Princess, and… if King Alexander was, say, killed in battle, we would have more of a crisis than we have now, over the succession itself. This would create a chaotic situation."

"Athenians talk too much. Always plotting. No honour," the Spartan said.

The Athenians all stood up sharply, and the room erupted into arguing. The Spartans mostly seemed amused that they had caused the Athenians to lose their composure. Philip knew the Spartans weren't as simple as they presented themselves to be.

Eventually Pelopidas of Thebes stood up and raised his hand. The voices slowly died down.

167

"If not a marriage, then I would suggest that if Illyria is concerned about revenge, they should be allowed to take a ward from the family of Amyntas. Perhaps the King's brother Perdiccas would be suitable?" he said.

Philip looked over at the General Pelopidas and ground his teeth before the Illyrian interpreter could speak. In that moment Philip's rage almost boiled over. What was Pelopidas suggesting? That his brother should be taken into Illyria to be Bardylis's pet? The general sat back down, and Philip looked around frantically at the others around the table.

The Spartans nodded.

The Athenian Iphicrates nodded. "That would be acceptable. If it will keep the peace."

The Illyrian brothers talked among themselves, then replied to their interpreter.

"No," the interpreter said. The room became silent. "The Princess, Eurynoe. She will return with us to Illyria, to be a hostage."

Alexander at first looked shocked, his mouth was wide open; he was nudged by Antipater, then he stood up and slammed his fist on the table. "That is out of the question," he shouted.

The Illyrian prince spoke to his interpreter and looked innocently over at Pelopidas.

"We're not leaving without a hostage as an assurance that these Macedonians keep their end up. They raid us constantly," the interpreter said.

"That is a lie!" Alexander shouted.

Philip felt a knot begin to form in his throat; he stared at the son of Bardylis. He had noticed him leering at their sister while they had been in Pella. The Illyrian caught him staring and winked to him. Philip then

168

looked to Ptolemy, who did nothing, simply stood, his head lowered slightly.

Alexander's anger began to fade, as he looked around the room for support it was turning to panic and desperation. "No, my sister will…"

Philip stood up, drawing the attention of the room. They all fell silent.

"I will go. Take me instead," he shouted. Immediately regretting it. He felt the flutter in his chest again and had to clench a fist to stop his hands from shaking.

"No," the son of Bardylis said, immediately, this time in Greek. "We want the girl."

Pelopidas looked over to Alexander whose mouth was open, staring at Philip. He then turned back and nodded. Pelopidas looked over at the Illyrians. "A brother of the king is a far more valuable hostage for Illyria than a girl who is already married. I can see no practical reason why you would turn down this offer," he said.

The Illyrian, opened his mouth to say something, but his advisor whispered in his ear and he became silent, he stared at Philip with a murderous rage.

It was settled. Bardylis's sons agreed on borders and that they would not take more territory than they had already, but Philip was to go as a hostage to Illyria as assurance that the Macedonians would not try and retake them. Philip retired to his rooms. He threw the furniture around, furious at Pelopidas for making the suggestion, and regretting his own, new-found impulsiveness.

Chapter 15

Philip was taken down to the stables by Alexander. Perdiccas, his mother, sister and their bodyguards followed like a funeral procession. There, they met with the sons of Bardylis and their entourage to take him to Illyria.

The Theban general Pelopidas was also there with his men, and a small troop of soldiers, readying themselves for the journey back south. They exchanged looks, but not words, Philip boiled with rage at the sight of him. He wanted to ask him why, and if he was proud of himself for being the cause of this. He fought back the urge to run at him; maybe if he was fast enough, he could throw him and dash his head off the hard ground.

Alexander cupped his hands and knelt for Philip to stand on to get onto the horse that was waiting for him. The reins were held by a heavy-set Illyrian soldier who had wrapped the leather around his hand several times. He sniffed back hard and spat the phlegm onto the ground. Philip looked to his family, their mood sombre, almost as if he was already dead.

His hands were bound by another Illyrian soldier. Alexander stood close to him; his face solemn.

"I'm sorry brother, I won't rest until I have you back," he said, glancing over his shoulder and shooting the sons of Bardylis a look. The look was met with a sly grin.

"It's okay, don't worry about me. You have to hold the kingdom together," Philip said. He turned, "Perdiccas, Mother, I-"

"That's enough of that," the heavy-set Illyrian said, and grabbed a fistful of Philip's tunic and pulled him forward, almost off his horse. The Illyrian produced a hood and pulled it hard over his head. His vision faded to black. The last thing Philip saw before he was blindfolded, was the look of concern on his brother's and his mother's faces. A string was drawn in to tighten it around his neck. This made it uncomfortable to breathe at first and he had to fight back the panic, but after he got used to it, it just became irritating, the strings rubbing against the skin of his neck. He felt his ears prick and listen; his hearing became more heightened in the absence of sight.

Alexander protested at the way Philip was being treated, and the Illyrians ignored him. Horses' hooves began to clomp all around him, then his moved. They were leaving.

The journey took them north west through the mountains. Philip knew where they were heading; they would follow the Axios river up into its valley, high in the mountains. He had travelled into the foothills before with an escort, but this would be the furthest from home that he had ever been, and he was completely at the mercy of these Illyrians. All he had were his thoughts due to the lack of vision, even his hearing was muffled. They dwelled on the memory of his father's army returning down this very road all those years ago. He thought of the wolves out in the wilderness whose howls in the night had scared him as a child, as he swallowed the lump in his throat.

He winked and flexed the muscles around his eyes, to try and work the blindfold loose, so he could at least tell if it was night or day, but it failed, it was too thick and it was tied too well.

After what seemed an eternity, he felt the horse begin to climb, after a while he could hear the boots of the soldier with the reins crunching on the loose dirt of the road. He was turning the horse. They then began to

171

climb again. The road was winding uphill, and it quickly felt as if it was getting steeper. Here the temperature started to drop, Philip shivered, the wind began to build up and howl through the trees, he could picture them clearly, their branches swaying.

He thought of leaping from the horse and making a run for it, but decided not to. He would be ridden down and killed no doubt. He was unsure of how much care they were going to show to the king of a failing kingdom's youngest brother. If anything happened to him, he doubted Alexander would have the strength to go to war for him.

He shivered from the cold again and his nose began to run. He tried to comfort himself by picturing Arsinoe, her smile and her lithe figure. This worked for a time, but then all he could imagine was the frost that probably surrounded him; they must be high up in the mountains now. Who knew how many days of this it would take to get to Illyria, then back down the other side of the mountains and nearer the sea, where it would be warmer.

He rubbed his hands together and tried to tuck them in under his thighs to get some feeling back into the tips of his fingers. He lowered his body, laying as low as he could to get some heat from the horse. The warmth and smell of the animal's fur was comforting.

He heard one of the soldiers grunting something to another in their strange tongue, and he felt a cloak being thrown over him. He was grateful that they weren't going to let him freeze.

After another eternity of being unable to see, they slowed down and stopped. He felt the soldier that was guiding his horse move away from him. They were all moving around. He heard the click of a flint being

172

struck. They were making a fire, maybe setting up a camp.

Philip's whole body ached, and the inside of his thighs were blistered. He had ridden horses a lot, but never for this this length of time, and because of the position he had to lie in to keep warm, blisters were also forming on his chest and the side of his neck, the skin raw and stinging.

He tried to listen in to the conversation; hopefully he could gain something, find a way to escape, anything. They said nothing important or even interesting to Philip. He was more interested that, unlike their comrades, they were speaking in Macedonian; he was curious why Illyrians would be talking in the old language, and not Illyrian or Greek.

"My wife should have had the baby by now," one of them said. "We've been out fighting for so long. I can't wait to get home".

"Don't worry. We're heading back now. In a few days we'll be home and you can see them, and hold the child." A second soldier said, "Do you think it's a boy or a girl?"

There was the crack of a stick being broken and thrown on the fire.

"I was hoping for a boy. I could teach him to hunt, and wrestle. One day maybe he could be an Olympic champion."

Philip was comforted a little, realising these were just men, like those in Macedonia, men with wives and children, following their king, not the crazed zealots he had been told they were as a small child. One simply wanted to be home in his own bed, and was sent out on campaign. Were they just as tired of this endless war as the Macedonians?

After the soldiers had eaten, they commenced their journey. One of the soldiers had lifted Philip's hood up over his mouth, and he had been given some bread and water, and even though it wasn't much, because he hadn't eaten in what he guessed was a day or maybe two, it tasted like ambrosia from the gods themselves.

...

Philip jarred upright, realising he must have fallen asleep. Now he wondered how long had he been asleep? How far had they travelled? They had stopped, that much was certain, but why? His vision was still black, so he slowed his breathing while he listened out for clues.

Around him he could hear the men talking to each other. Somebody just ahead of them was shouting something in Illyrian; his tone was not aggressive; it was more like he was bargaining with someone who was a distance away. Someone shouted something back in a similar tone; there was more talk, the person answering sounded high up, as if he was at the top of a hill.

This went on a little longer and then the talking stopped. Philip heard a horse trotting closer to them, the first soldier re-joining the party? There came the sound of something heavy and metallic, screeching and sliding. It stopped with a loud clunk. Then came a long slow creaking. A gate being opened. Had they got all the way to the capital of Illyria already? Surely not.

There was a loud crack as his horse's reins were whipped, and he nearly fell back as the animal started moving again. He could hear a lot going on; wherever he was, it was a beehive of activity and noise: groups of men marched past at a quick pace, their feet clomping in

174

time, the unmistakable ring of a smith hitting an anvil with a hammer, another grinding weapons on a whetstone, weapons clinking off each other. They travelled farther and he could hear animals, pigs and goats, sniffing and grunting, with them came the smell of dung. He could feel cold mud splashing his legs and feet.

They went further and the sounds faded; they stopped again. Philip was pulled from the horse and immediately pushed down onto his knees. The cold wetness of the ground soaked his lower legs and he shivered. The hood and blindfold were yanked from his head. The sun seared his eyes and he closed them tight, momentarily back into darkness. He slowly opened them as they adjusted to the daylight.

Standing over him, silhouetted by the sun, was a silver haired man, smiling down at him. Despite his advanced age, he appeared fit and healthy. He wore an ornately decorated bronze cuirass, well made and well-worn; at his side was an equally ornate sword on a fine leather belt. Over his shoulders was a black fur cloak, probably from a bear or wolf. Around him stood a group of hard looking men in similarly expensive looking armour.

Philip imagined that in his youth this man had probably been tall and good looking, but the years had taken their toll, and now his shoulders hunched and when he reached out to stroke his thinning beard Philip noticed the skin on his muscular arms was wrinkled.

But his eyes, his eyes were steel.

"So, you are the third son of Amyntas?" the man said in Greek, and as he did so, although his face did not change, his smile drained of all its perceived warmth and became as cold as ice. It filled Philip with dread.

175

Philip coughed and swallowed to try and wet his throat. "I am," he said, and quickly looked around at his surroundings; he was in a busy army camp. They appeared to be in a makeshift space that was being used for the cavalry to practice in. There were long deep trenches all over made up of crescent shapes from the horse's hoofs, and most were filled with muddy water. He was kneeling in one of them.

He took in the snow-covered mountain peaks stretching up in the distance above the rows of tents. He was relieved they were not in Illyria yet; there may still be a chance to run.

"Do not think about escaping," the man said bluntly, as if he were some kind of seer that could read Philip's thoughts; he then looked Philip up and down, seeming to see if he measured up to his expectations. He looked to his sons and said something in Illyrian. Philip did not understand what he said, but he distinctly made out the name "Amyntas". It got a snigger from the men who were stood around him.

"I-"

"If you behave well, you will be treated well. Behave badly and you will be treated badly," he said, reverting back to Greek.

"Who are-"

"You are my hostage. You do not ask questions," he said, "but as you are my enemy's son, I will extend you this one courtesy. I am Bardylis of the Dardanians, King of Illyria. I will-"

"I have questions," Philip said.

"If you interrupt me again, I will have you thrown in with the pigs. Now, kiss my feet for that insolence."

Philip froze for a moment, unsure what to do. Then his thoughts flashed to Antigonus in the gymnasium striking Menelaus back and giving him the beating of

176

his life. It gave him strength. He gathered what little moisture was left in his mouth and spat it onto Bardylis' foot.

"I hope you die screaming like a fucking-" he started to shout, but he was kicked hard in the face by Bardylis.

Seeing lightning bolts, he was dragged away by two heavy Illyrians. He was taken to the animal pens and thrown over the fence, landing on some muck covered hay. He lay staring up at the sky, spinning around and around. The smell of animal faeces invaded his nostrils, and when he gasped in a breath, he had to fight back the feeling that he was going to gag.

After a while of watching the spinning clouds, he fell asleep with exhaustion.

…

He woke up in the morning shivering, still in the pen; the ropes on his wrists were now stretched out and tied to the post in the corner, holding his arms up above his head, while he lay on his side. He thought he must have spent the whole night in that position. He sat up and tilted his head from side to side, trying to stretch the cramp in his neck and shoulders away. His hands tingled painfully, but this feeling went away after he flexed his fingers for a few moments.

A guard was asleep against a post in the opposite corner, on the outside of the pen, presumably so that Philip couldn't strangle him and use his weapon to cut himself free.

Soldiers in the camp were being woken up and pots of hot soup were being brought out to feed them for breakfast; the smell floated past and filled Philip's nostrils. He was almost able to see the scent in the steam rising from the pots, and his stomach rumbled. His guard woke up and looked at him. "Want something to eat?" he asked.

"Yes please," Philip said, seeing no reason to be discourteous. This man had done him no harm.

The guard brought him some soup and stale bread, but that didn't matter; he ate it like there would be no tomorrow; maybe there wouldn't.

Once he finished, he looked around at what was visible from where he was tied up. Not being able to stand fully upright, he couldn't see much, just more animal pens. Once the warmth of the soup was gone, he sat for a while; he started to become quite concerned about what was going to be done with him. If Bardylis was going to kill him, he would have done it already because of the insult yesterday. He thought today he would request somewhere better to sleep, deciding that he would argue that he was a valuable hostage, and that harming him would be bad for the treaty, and Illyria.

He looked over at his guard, waiting for him to look over. He ignored Philip.

"I request an audience with the king," he said.

He was ignored again.

He looked around the ground of the pen and found a stone about the size of a grape. He closed one eye to aim, and threw it at the guard. It bounced off the back of his cuirass and he whipped around furiously.

"Look pup, you are a prisoner, you don't request an audience with the king, he will speak to you when he sees fit," he said. After a moment the annoyance left his voice. "He'll come to get you soon anyway, after what you did yesterday. You've got balls boy, which he respects, but you probably shouldn't do anything like that again though, or he might cut them off."

…

178

Philip spent the next few weeks, although it could have been years, in the animal pen. Whatever it belonged to had been removed and presumably slaughtered for sacrifice or food. Bardylis clearly didn't have a plan for him other than keeping him imprisoned, and perhaps the camp didn't have anywhere to put prisoners.

After these few weeks he was allowed to get up and walk around for exercise, under heavy guard, of course. Everywhere he went in the camp he was stared at. The soldiers whispered about him.

He did however get to witness some of their training one morning, when on a walk. He stood at part of the camp that was wide open, and the wealthier Illyrians were training in full hoplite armour. Were these the men that were so easily able to beat Macedonian infantry on the battlefield? They even had blunt training spears and they were put up against men carrying peltas, the smaller shields that the Macedonians were using. They were drilling to use the size and weight of the aspis shield to deflect the lighter pelta downwards and stab over the top.

Philips eyes widened with astonishment. They were training for fighting *Macedonians*, and only Macedonians. This was the type of soldier they were expecting to fight. He stood with his mouth open, astounded at the revelation, before he was nudged along with the butt of his guard's spear.

He was taken daily to a narrow stream to wash, just outside the camp, which he assumed it was part of the Axios. While he was at the side of the stream, he always pondered running, glancing around to see where the guards were looking, but then his senses got the better of him. He had a much thicker skin now than even the

179

year before. He knew he could endure this humiliation for the time being, until his brother was able to negotiate for him to be freed. He had however, never felt more alone.

…

A few more weeks passed and Philip found himself being allowed to move around freely for exercise, but still followed by several guards. One of the sons of Bardylis came and spoke to him. "You know why you are here?" he asked.

Philip refused to answer.

"Running is no good, all it will do is jeopardise the peace, and hurt your people."

"I won't run," he said, and with that, he was moved to a tent to sleep in, but was still chained at night and kept under guard.

During his walks he always tried to catch a glimpse of their training. This had to be reported back to his brother Alexander, but he had no way of contacting him, so he tried to train his memory to remember what he saw. In his tent at night, he replayed the drills he witnessed during the day in his head, playing them over and over to commit them to memory.

The food he was given improved, and he was even snuck a little wine by one of his guards which he appreciated; the taste after dirty water for, what he guessed had been a month or more, was blissful. He realised how much he had taken it for granted.

The guard spoke to Philip in Macedonian. He was from a part of Illyria that was in dispute. It was right on the frontier between the two countries, and had been part of Macedonia when he was a child.

…

Philip was woken one morning to the noise of bustling around the camp. He sat up sharply and then stood up, the chains on his wrists rattling and the weight of them pulling his arms back. He stayed sitting.

He looked around. His Macedonian speaking guard was sitting in the doorway of the tent along with another. "We're going," he said.

"Going where? Are we going back to Macedonia?" he asked excitedly.

His guard opened his mouth to speak.

"Don't tell him shit," the second soldier said before he could speak. "Do you want to get yourself a lashing?"

"It won't make any difference, he's not going anywhere," he said to his comrade, then turned back to Philip. "No, we're going home, further north."

Deeper into Illyria.

Philip's heart sank. For a moment he had hoped that arrangements had been made for him to go back. He looked around, desperately looking for a way out. He thought about trying to rush the guards when his chains were undone, but no, that would never work. They would easily overpower him.

"We're going to help disassemble the camp. We'll be back soon. Don't think about trying to escape. Even if you got out of the camp, these mountains are teeming with bandits who'd love to get their hands on a boy like yourself."

"I'm a man."

The guard chuckled. "And how old are you?"

"Fifteen, and I've killed my first man."

"Doesn't matter, they'd still bugger you to death. Very well then, they'd love to get their hands on a fifteen-year-old man!"

With that they both left. He was ignored for most of the morning. Around midday his tent was taken apart and a few hours after that, most of the camp had been disassembled.

He was blindfolded and hooded again, strong hands grabbing his legs and he flinched, expecting to be struck, but he was hoisted onto a horse.

"We're heading north, back to Dardania, to my family's stronghold," a voice he recognised said. One of Bardylis' sons. "We no longer need to protect this frontier; your brother has started paying his tribute in full. What a bitch."

Philip clenched his fists under his cloak, and considered lashing out blindly at him, but resisted.

Chapter 16

"It was not in your control sire."

Alexander turned to look at his Spartan advisor, his daze broken. All morning he had gone into these daydreams, unable to concentrate. He did not even realise he had been called "sire" which Macedonian kings rejected, and would have if he had. His lack of speech was forcing the Spartan to talk.

"You must concentrate on the men's training; we must get them ready, and quickly. Your brother will be safe enough in Illyria. They will not risk upsetting the balance, and bringing down the wrath of the Greek states. Pelopidas of Thebes is a soldier, and an honourable man. I hate what the man did to my people, but he will keep his word and hold Bardylis accountable if anything happens to Philip."

Alexander had been staring into space, albeit in the direction of the new regiment that had been created. Some more of the peasants had been mixed with the Royal Guard, and this had doubled their number. They were now training with full hoplite equipment that he had funded out of the royal treasury. They were still few in number, but they were only the core of the army, and he hoped this would be enough of them to form a solid front line if and when he had to take them into battle.

He stared as they stood in their lines, trying to lock their shields together into a solid wall. They were still clumsy and slow at it. Between some of the shields were gaping holes, and others overlapped too far, and were upsetting their neighbours balance and spacing.

His thoughts were on Philip, wracked with guilt over what had happened to him. Would he ever see him again? Probably, but who knew. Bardylis might kill him. The thought did not sit well. Despite what the Spartan said, the stories of the Illyrians from his childhood haunted him. He was already thinking about a possible way to attack Illyria and rescue his brother. An invasion with an army would fail. Were any of the agents that he had inherited from his father reliable enough to try and sneak him out? They already had reports of the army camp where he was last seen. About two thirds of their number had left and were heading deeper into Illyria, in the direction of their capital.

"I don't know what you're talking about, I don't care if Philip is gone. It was the cheapest way for Thebes and Athens to back off," he said, turning away to hide his pained expression, but trying to make it look as though he was inspecting the troops. "Will we get going to inspect the cavalry?"

The Spartan looked at him for a long, silent period. Alexander could feel his eyes on him. He was not fooled, he knew, but he kept the pretence up anyway.

"Actually," Alexander said changing the subject, "we should let the men rest. They are not used to training in this equipment. The plate armour is far heavier than what they are used to."

"No." The Spartan looked to him with disapproval. "Spartan *children* train far longer than this in the same armour with the same weapons, we need to push them hard."

"We are not Spartans. A few weeks ago, half of these men were goat herders and farm hands and..." Alexander stopped as he was met by Parmenion's arrival.

"Parmenion," he said.

Parmenion nodded his head to the two men. "Alexander, we must speak in private."

"Don't worry old friend, you can speak in front of the Spartan. His honour would not allow him to break our trust."

The Spartan wore his usual expressionless face, but Alexander felt it had a subtext of gratitude and almost happiness, that he was being trusted so well; it was true that he had served their family well, and Alexander had no reason to distrust him. He did not think that he would repeat what he heard to anyone else outside of his inner circle of companions.

Parmenion spoke in a hushed tone, his eyes narrowing. He looked from side to side to make sure no one was nearby within earshot. "It has to do with your father, the doctors all agree now that he was poisoned. This was not an illness Alexander."

Alexander chewed the inside of his cheek, then scratched the stubble on his chin. "Who?" he asked.

"We're not sure, it could be any one of many people. I would suggest we speak to your brother Arrhidaeus. Your father had many enemies. He might know something."

"Could it have been him? Why would he kill our father?"

"Maybe not him, but we know he would profit from your father's death. If you had not acted quickly to suppress his supporters, his fortune and your own may have been in reverse."

"I agree," Alexander said, then turned to the Spartan. "Train the men a bit longer, but do not push them as hard as you would push Spartans. It will take time. Understood?"

The Spartan nodded in agreement and Alexander followed Parmenion back toward the palace.

….

The prison was dingy and dark, and the two of them walked by torchlight toward Arrhidaeus' cell. The darkness stretched on forever, and seemed to envelop them, like it had limbs that floated all around them, not like the soft moonlit darkness of the surface. As they descended the slippery steps he felt like Odysseus, or Heracles or any of the other heroes on their journey down into Hades. It was cool down here, the warm of the night air had departed. Parmenion led. Alexander could not see past the halo of light that Parmenion's torch revealed, and when he looked back over his shoulder, he could only see a few feet back with the light of his own torch. This made him feel unsettled, as if something was following them. The ground was damp, and things grew on it, slippery things, all around was the sound of dripping, the source of the damp; he concentrated on sure footing.

Something scampered around his feet, and there was faint squeaking. In the distance, he could hear coughing, deep coughing, as if someone was actually coughing their lungs out. Parmenion turned to check on him. He lifted his chest up and shoulders back, standing tall. He was not afraid, and did not want to appear so, although he had never been in a place such as this, this abode of the damned. It made him cautious, and he focused his senses.

They made their way past skeletal figures shrouded in the darkness, whose sunken eyes stared back coldly from behind bars. They reached the end of the corridor, and Alexander found himself face-to-face with his half-brother. As expected, he was not pleased to see him, and Alexander thought that the feeling was mutual.

"What the fuck do you want?" he asked. He was leaning with his arms through the bars. Although he had

186

only been here months, he was already thinner, his cheeks were drawn, but his eyes, those pale eyes still had so much hatred and aggression in them. "I said. What the fuck do you want?"

Alexander kept him at arm's length, not that he was afraid of being grabbed by his half-brother, quite the opposite. He was more concerned about losing what could be a valuable source of information, and didn't want to be forced to wring his neck.

Arrhidaeus' cell, by the standards of the rest of the dungeon was luxurious; he had furniture, and a torch that was kept lit, so he had heat and light. He was also not chained up and could move freely around the cell.

"We are keeping you are here for your own protection," Alexander said.

"My protection?" he said and let out a laugh, "and who do I need protection from, Brother?"

Alexander paused.

"Tell us where your brothers are," he said. "Have you remembered yet?"

"I've already told you, I have no idea," he sniffed back mucus, and casually spat it out at Alexander's feet. "Can't you see I'm starting to develop a lung condition? How are you going to keep my side of the family under control if I die in this shit hole? They'll come after you."

Alexander kept his bold expression. "Why don't you leave me to worry about that?" He then turned to Parmenion. "Parmenion, I believe you have some questions for my brother?"

Parmenion, stepping forward, switched places with Alexander.

"Yes I do. What hand did you have in the death of Amyntas?" he asked.

187

Arrhidaeus sneered at Parmenion. "My own father?
"

Parmenion kept his stern expression. "Parricide is not entirely unknown in Macedonia," he said sarcastically. He waited for a response. "If you won't answer, we could always bring your mother down here to stay with you."

Arrhidaeus could not hide the worry on his face, Alexander could see that. He was hard, even when he had been put down here, and threatened with torture and execution he was still defiant. But his mother was his weakness, always had been Alexander thought, ever since they were boys.

"You wouldn't," he said, still defiant.

"Did you kill our father?"

"No."

"No?" he asked, feeling the stretch of his eyebrows raising.

"No."

There was a pause "Care to elaborate?"

"Apart from not pissing off the furies, what would I have to gain? We are the second family, as you are so fond of reminding me. You are the heir and without men like Parmenion here on our side, how could I have hoped to secure the throne? I had nothing planned."

Alexander and Parmenion looked at each other, then looked back to Arrhidaeus.

"Very well then, now where are your brothers?" Alexander asked.

"I don't know. All I know is, that they are out of your reach."

"You do realise that if they hadn't run, I wouldn't have hurt any of you? As long as you accepted that I am the king. Now that they've run, I have to kill them, and possibly you."

Arrhidaeus sighed. "I'm sure your brother will be happy about that."

"I expect he would be, but if you bastards hadn't spent years tormenting him, maybe he wouldn't hate you so much. You'd better pray that he comes back safe or I'll imagine some horrible way for you to die, to keep the balance for the gods."

They turned to leave and as they started to walk away, Arrhidaeus shouted them back. "Alexander!"

"What is it?" he shouted back, becoming more aggravated.

"If you organise to get me out of here, then I can help you," he said.

Alexander glanced at Parmenion who raised his eyebrow.

Alexander spun around and marched back over to the cell. He grabbed Arrhidaeus by the throat and pulled him hard against the bars. Arrhidaeus clawed at Alexander's hands in a vain attempt to loosen his hold, but Alexander knew his own grip; it was iron like the bars, he had been told so many times.

Arrhidaeus gasped for air and twisted to try and get away.

"You just told me you knew nothing you piece of shit. You think ending up in here is the worst thing that can happen to you? I'll tell you how this is going to work. You're going to tell me everything you know, or I'm going to call the torturer down here and have him take you apart. Piece by piece."

He released his grip and Arrhidaeus slumped forward against the bars, clutching his throat and gasping for air. Alexander stood and watched him for a minute, waiting for him to get his breath back.

"Tell me what you know," he said.

Arrhidaeus breathed hard. "I didn't kill our father. Look at what's happened to my family as a result of his death. We didn't even have a chance to mourn before they had to run." There was a long pause and Alexander stared at him as intensely as he could, his teeth grinding and his hands shaking with the burst of aggression.

"What *do* you know then?" he asked, after he had calmed down. Parmenion stood at his side, ready to remember anything that was said.

"Have you thought about looking closer to home?" Arrhidaeus said, "to your own brothers? Perdiccas and Philip? They have more to gain than I ever would. Maybe you should watch your back, you might be next. Perdiccas is next in line after you, and why do you think Philip volunteered to go to Illyria so readily?"

....

Back in the King's study, the same room that had bcen Amyntas's, Alexander was glad to be out of the stench and the darkness of the dungeons. The words of Arrhidaeus plagued his mind. He scratched his chin. Parmenion and Alexander were joined by Antipater.

"He has a rotten soul that one, he was obviously lying," Parmenion said.

"Was he? He makes some valid points," Alexander said.

"He was trying to drive a wedge between you and your brothers; to sow discord," Parmenion said. "Nothing more."

Alexander thought about what Parmenion said, taking a few minutes, pacing up and down the room. He then settled, standing next to his father's desk, now his desk. He scratched his chin. Parmenion stood and watched him. "I agree," he said finally.

"I don't believe Perdiccas or Philip had anything to do with your father's death, but still..." Antipater said.

"But still?" Alexander asked.

"Still, I would suggest as a precaution we have the two of them followed. It would do no harm for you to know for sure."

"But Philip is all the way in Illyria. How are we supposed to watch him there?" Parmenion said.

"Don't worry about that, I can make the arrangements. My spy network is quite extensive as you know; I can find somebody who is able to get there and report back to us on his activities," Antipater said.

Alexander nodded along, but chewed his cheek. He was uncomfortable with the distrust he had to have, even in close family members; he had never really liked Philip, who was a wimp, and Perdiccas, whose obsession with the Greek philosophical nonsense he filled his head with he would never understand, but this was different. He was now having to make decisions that could lead somewhere he didn't want to go. What if either of them was behind it? There could only be one punishment.

"Do it," he said and gave a single nod.

Antipater nodded back and left the room. He closed the door behind him.

"Do you agree with him?" Alexander asked.

"No, but no reason not to be careful," Parmenion said.

......

Philip lay face down on the floor of his cell. It wasn't really a cell, just a bare room that he was kept in at all times, but he thought of it as if he was in prison. He was a prisoner after all. It was at least warm and

191

clean, and he did not need to worry about rats or other vermin, so he thought he may be in Bardylis' palace somewhere. It was definitely an improvement on the animal pens at the army camp.

He had begun doing push-ups and sit-ups to keep himself fit. In the time he had been there he had not been allowed to leave the cell for exercise. He was catching his breath back between sets. The aim was to get to a hundred press ups, but had already done five sets, and his strength was starting to wane; he had been getting fed enough, but not well.

Philip looked down at his muscles. The fat from around them was starting to disappear and they were becoming more defined. The veins in his arms were popping out. He continued the set. The floor got closer, then further away, then closer again. As his face got close to the ground, he felt his breath bounce back from it as he exhaled, and then extended his arms to heave his body back up.

His body prickled with the sweat that was starting to flow. Blood was rushing into his muscles; they felt taught and hard. He paused and put his knees on the ground, and sat up to get his breath back. He felt his bicep.

The sound of footsteps clomping down the hallway made him sit to attention, and he looked up as the cell door opened with a loud screech and banged against the stone wall. Philip looked up at the eyes of the man that came in accompanied by a group of five guards, all in military uniforms, each wearing a bronze cuirass and an open-faced helmet. They were accompanied by the jailer, who wheezed his way in and coughed up phlegm, which he spat on the cell floor.

"What's going on?" Philip asked.

He wasn't sure how long he'd been in the cell this time. They did let him out on occasion. It had been days maybe, the only way he had been able to mark time was by how many meals he was getting, and he suspected that they had been giving them to him at erratic times to make it harder for him to keep track. He had been marking a line on the wall for every day, but wasn't sure how accurate it was, as a few times he had fallen ill, and being bedridden had lost track of time. He supposed it had been about a year since he had left Macedonia.

"Someone wants to see you," the jailer said and wiped the saliva from the corner of his mouth with the back of his hand.

"Who?" Philip asked.

The jailer looked at him with a blank expression. A turned-up lip exposed black, broken teeth. "How the fuck should I know?" he grumbled "Some politician from Greece."

Politician from Greece?

"From Macedonia?" Philip asked, standing up.

"No, I said Greece, you dumb shit." The jailer shook his head, as if Philip were simple, and raised a set of heavy shackles, speckled with rust.

Philip saw no need to resist; his mind played more on who this politician from Greece was, and why he was here to see him.

The guards put the shackles on his wrists and marched him out of the cell. He was taken through the maze of corridors of the palace; these reminded him of the Palace at Pella, what had seemed like a labyrinth when he was a child; when he had been Theseus hunting for the Minotaur. The heavy chains pulled on his wrists. Now he felt more like a sacrifice to the minotaur.

Having spent most of his time in Illyria in the cell, he had not been able to explore the palace, so most of

193

the corridors were new to him; it made him uneasy as he looked from side to side. The walls were clean white, with a key border down the centre outlined in gold. It was like Pella, only the fixtures were far more lavish. Is this how they spend the wealth they bleed from Macedonia? he thought.

The guards stood in a square, and walked along with him and the jailer in the centre, leading him like a pack animal. They arrived just outside a closed double door at the end of a long corridor, and Philip recognised this as the entrance to Bardylis' main audience chamber and the King's throne room. He had been brought here when he first arrived. One of Bardylis' sons that Philip recognised waited outside, and met with them. He took a good look at Philip. "You idiots, why didn't you clean him up first? You know that Pelopidas is here to see him?" he said.

"We just got told to bring him up, Sire, no one said anything about cleaning him," the jailer said, lowering his eyes to the floor.

"Lucky for you I don't have time to deal with you right now," the son of Bardylis said. "Follow me."

Philip watched him open the large double doors, and they followed him in. *Pelopidas*, that name filled Philip with rage; it was his treaty that sent me here, he thought.

The vast audience chamber was empty, except for Bardylis half slouched up on his throne on a raised platform, surrounded by finely dressed men. Philip looked at each of them; they must be his family and the nobility, just like the Macedonian kings and their companions. They all ignored Philip, except one. They were more concerned about the Greeks that had been mentioned by the jailer. The one that did seem fixated on him was probably in his mid-twenties, and was dressed in a simple white tunic, unlike the others. When Philip looked back at him, he looked away.

A group of half a dozen Greeks wearing armour breastplates, but no greaves or helmets stood on the floor below, looking up at Bardylis. They had their backs to Philip, but he recognised the one at the front from his size and shape, *Pelopidas*. The very sight of him filled Philip with rage, he tensed his chest muscles and tightened his grip on the chains.

As Philip approached, Pelopidas turned his head, and his eyes widened as he looked Philip up and down. His head whipped round to face Bardylis. "Have you been starving him? The treaty did not include maltreatment. He is here as a hostage, under your protection."

"He's my prisoner, I will treat him as I wish," Bardylis said, raising his hand in a dismissive gesture.

Pelopidas took a step closer to the throne. "He is a prince of one of your great rivals, not a common thief that has been arrested in the Agora. If he dies because you haven't fed him or he gets a disease because of where you are keeping him, the treaty will be over."

Bardylis stared at Pelopidas hard, his eyes narrowing. Pelopidas stared right back, but he appeared as calm as if he was having a quiet drink with an old friend, but these men certainly had no love for each other. Philip looked from one to the other, each unwilling to break their stare.

Bardylis finally broke the silence. "Why don't you go back to Thebes, general? Leave our northern affairs to us, eh?"

Pelopidas continued staring at him unimpressed. One of his men whispered something into his ear. The Thebans all gathered a little closer and had a quiet discussion. Philip leant toward them to try and hear what was said, but could not make it out. Bardylis watched them talk and scratched his chin, he turned his head so that his ear faced them. He was also trying to hear what they were saying. His own Illyrian guards looked at each other.

The son of Bardylis who had brought Philip in had joined his father's side on the raised platform, upon which sat the throne. "We would prefer if you did not plot in our midst," he said.

The Thebans however, were undeterred and continued their conversation and after a few moments Pelopidas came forward a step and looked to Philip. "Do you want me to take you away from here?" he asked, loudly enough to be heard by Bardylis and his courtiers.

The man who had been staring at Philip stepped forward. "I will not allow you to take him, general, he has to be made-"

"Be quiet, it is not your decision to make," Bardylis said through his teeth. He stood up and placed his hand on the man's shoulder as he stepped by him. "Argeus is right though, and I will not allow you to take him."

Argeus. Philip looked at the man's face, then back at Pelopidas. *The Usurper.* The realisation suddenly hit him. Anywhere would be better than here. He was in great danger here.

"We're going to take him back to Thebes. You have no right to keep him locked in a dungeon like some common thief," Pelopidas said, his voice firm.

"This is outrageous!" Bardylis yelled, clenching his fist. His guards readied their shields and half unsheathed their swords. The Theban delegation all half unsheathed their swords except for Pelopidas, who gently raised his hand.

"This is not what I want. My government knows I am here. Are you going to risk violating this treaty and bring down the wrath of Thebes, Athens *and* Sparta, who all agreed on this settlement?" he said, his voice steadily lowering with every word. With his voice, the tension in the room also seemed to lift; everyone relaxed their sword arms.

Bardylis stood dumbfounded, his lower jaw wiggling from side to side, grinding his teeth. After a while he spoke. "And what is my guarantee that the Macedonians will keep up their end if I have no hostage?"

"I will take him back with me to Thebes, where I will make sure he is not mistreated. I have been to Pella and King Alexander has already agreed to give up more hostages in return for his brother's safety, sons from all the noble houses. I will agree to be responsible for Macedonia keeping up their end. We want stability. Argeus there will have to wait a bit longer if he wants the Macedonian throne."

Bardylis turned and looked at Argeus, then his head whipped back round to face Pelopidas.

"I will inform our ambassador in Thebes of this violation."

"You are welcome to make a complaint to the ambassador. He is sympathetic to the situation. I am changing the conditions of what was agreed to protect the stability of this whole region, so it does not come to war yet again. Your endless fighting is creating a deluge of refugees into southern Greece."

They made their way toward the door to leave.

"I am not interested in war, only making Macedonia mine," Bardylis shouted as they were leaving.

"I expected as much," Pelopidas shouted back.

Philip followed them out of the door. He shivered when he heard Argeus shout to Bardylis, "You can't let him leave here alive!"

Chapter 17

Philip stared at Pella in the distance, longing to go back and see his family. The Theban convoy travelled around the base of the mountains, just on the plains where the city was built. The flat, green land meant he could just make out its shape, far in the distance. Pelopidas had met with more of his men on the road, who had the other sons that had been mentioned at the meeting in Illyria, but Philip had not been allowed to return even for a short visit.

The convoy was more like a small army now; Philip looked back over his shoulder and guessed there were as many as a thousand hoplites, maybe more, as well as the cavalry and the many wagons pulled by mules, carrying the baggage. It was small wonder that the Illyrians let them leave with him, now that he had seen how many Thebans had come with their general.

They had passed through a few small towns after exiting the mountains, and the locals had flocked to the convoy; farmers to sell the rich Greeks their produce, and prostitutes looking to work their trade with the soldiers.

As his eyes traced along the army, they were drawn to the other boys that Pelopidas had collected from Pella. There appeared to be about thirty of them. Was there anyone he knew? There must be. They were too far away to see, but one boy stood taller than the rest; he hoped it was Antigonus.

Philip sat on a beautiful Thessalian horse that had been provided by the Theban Pelopidas, and they rode close to the front of the army side by side. The Theban cavalry rode in front of them, presumably for the safety of their leader.

"You will be safer with us than in Pella. It will be a very dangerous and unstable place for a while," Pelopidas said. "They are still in a period of unrest, and rivals are trying to take control of the throne; your brother has it under control for the moment, but-"

"How long will that be?" Philip asked, looking down. Unable to look Pelopidas in the eye, he clutched hard at the horse's reins. He knew that the man had saved him from almost certain death, yet he was still furious that he had sent him there in the first place.

"Don't worry Philip. My city is an incredible place. You most likely will not be there very long, just until things settle down in Pella."

"But do you know how long that will take?" Philip asked, looking over his shoulder, back at Pella shrinking into the distance. The city was still visible, but the palace at the top of the hill, built by his father's idol Archelaus, was disappearing into the haze of the heat and humidity in the air. It reminded him of the day they returned to Pella when he was a child. That day would be forever in his memory.

"Unfortunately, I don't. You heard first-hand what Bardylis is planning, and he is one of many," Pelopidas said. "Don't worry, Thebes is the greatest city in all of Greece. You're going to be our guest, a ward; it will not be the same as it was in Illyria. The gods favoured I was nearby in Macedonia and was close enough to come get you."

Philip looked at Pelopidas, his head still lowered. The Theban smiled at him.

Philip thought about the words he was using; he had been vague whenever he had been asked a question. Philip wanted to scream at him for answers, grab him by the throat like Alexander would. He had been taken within sight of his home, but had not been allowed to see his family. Pelopidas seemed unsure of everything, or at least wanted Philip to think that. Why did he keep saying he was going to be a guest? Was he, or was this a trick? Would he be thrown into prison when he got there? Too many questions and no real answers.

Philip looked around at the scenery to try to calm himself, to resist the urge to shout at Pelopidas, knowing this would achieve nothing, even if it might make him feel better. He watched the soldiers who rode ahead of them. These soldiers appeared to be veterans, and the armour they wore was uniformed, unusual for Greeks. Were these the Sacred Band, the famed elite of the Theban army? Pelopidas was not armoured like his men, and wore a loosely fitting tunic, and a wide brimmed sun hat.

Were these the ones who had defeated the Spartans at the battle of Leuctra? He looked at the pair that walked alongside the wagon in front of them. They were dressed as hoplites, both carrying a large round shield, and an eight-foot spear with an iron tip. Their armour was bronze, perfectly polished, and blinding when the light caught it, making him half close his eyes.

Philip had a closer look at the shields they were carrying; they were made of heavy wood and were reinforced with a full sheet of bronze, not like the ones his family's Royal Guard carried, which only had bronze around the rim. They must have been expensive, and they must have had some weight. He remembered once when the guard had let him and the other boys his age play fight with each other, only for an hour, but the muscles in his neck and shoulder had been tender for days after, and sore to the touch. His gaze was drawn to the necks and shoulders of these two soldiers. They were like tree trunks; they reminded him of Antipater.

He'd seen men with such muscles before, the blacksmith's who forged weapons and shoed horses, and the rowers they had seen getting off the triremes at the docks, had huge arms. These men were different, they did not just have muscles in the neck and shoulders, their arms were also extremely thick and lean. He realised he was squeezing his own bicep; it made him feel small and puny. These men had also scars, scars on their hands and arms. These muscles had been developed through years of fighting, of raising shield and spear above their heads, and thrusting it towards other men in a phalanx.

He glanced down to his side at the arms of Pelopidas. His arms and hands were also covered in scars, some were so faded that they were almost not visible, just a lighter shade of skin in a streak going from the front of his arm to the back. Philip imagined a spear being thrust and the tip grazing Pelopidas' arm, biting into the skin.

Some though, were fresh, not long healed, almost even a scab. They couldn't have been more than a week or two old. "Why did you come to Macedonia?" Philip asked. Pelopidas looked surprised at the question, his eyebrow raised.

"I was in Thessaly for a different reason, settling a local dispute much like here in Macedonia. I was asked to come here and sort out matters in Pella, knock on effects from when your father…"

He paused.

"I was then asked to settle a dispute in Macedonia, as I have said. Don't worry, you will be safe with us, safer than you would be in Macedonia, and definitely safer than you would have been in Illyria, especially if

Argeus had got his way. He was lobbying to have you killed."

"Are you a soldier?" Philip asked him. "I thought you were a politician, but your scars tell me otherwise."

"Not exactly."

Pelopidas scratched his beard, clawed his fingers through it, and twisted the ends between his thumb and index finger.

"We don't exactly have politicians as you would think of them, every city is different. Thebes is not Athens. Each has its own laws and structure," he said.

There was a silence. Philip looked at the mountains on the horizon to the south, remembering some of the sights from the hunting trip.

"I am a citizen," Pelopidas said. "I serve my city. I am a landowner, so I suppose if I were to compare myself to a Macedonian, I would be something close to a noble. I am also a general and have commanded armies in many battles, except the men I command are not my serfs."

Philip sat up straight; he wanted to ask about the battles, ask about where and who he had fought. He then remembered his anger at the Theban, lowered his eyes, and feigned disinterest.

"You say you were in Thessaly for another matter, but came to Macedonia to settle things? Does Thebes always meddle in the affairs of its neighbours?" he said.

"I was dealing with a dispute in Thessaly between two of the local chiefs. It was an important matter, but I came to Macedonia at Ptolemy's request, and your mother's to help Alexander. How much schooling in politics have you had, Philip?"

"None really," he said. He did not want to speak to the general anymore, but something about him drew Philip in, but he resisted saying more.

203

"None really. Well, you'll get an education in Thebes, if you want it of course," Pelopidas said. "And I was meddling in the affairs of our neighbours, as you put it, because civil war is no good for anyone. It makes people into refugees, some into slaves or whores. People starve. And with the absence of law, men turn to banditry. Please tell me, if you are the political genius you seem to think you are, what would you have done?"

"I… I…" Philip said.

"I didn't think you knew. Be careful not to criticize others when you yourself do not have the answers, Philip."

They rode in silence. Was it possible that Philip had got this man completely wrong? Maybe he was just trying to help.

"I'd never given much thought to why you were getting involved before today," Philip said finally. "In Macedonia, politics is usually done with a sword... and it's usually in the back. There's always one feud or another and the only reason is to make themself king."

"You're right, Philip, and these feuds go back centuries and cause never-ending fighting. Macedonia has so much potential, but it will never be realised if you don't stop fighting amongst yourselves."

"Surely the Greeks are the same?"

"What do you mean?"

"They have never stopped fighting amongst themselves."

"That's different."

"Why?"

"Because we are all different city states, with our own laws and customs. There is no law in Macedonia, only the king. We have no monarch who could unite us. And most would not stand for a king."

"But shouldn't the Greeks stop fighting and unite as well if war is so bad?"

Pelopidas smiled. "You may be right, perhaps we are more alike than we Greeks care to admit. Maybe one day the Greeks will be unified. I doubt if it will happen in my lifetime. Perhaps it will happen in yours."

"Perhaps," Philip said.

The army travelled further south and set up camp for the night. Philip lay awake for a long time, thinking about Pelopidas, and everything they had discussed, before falling asleep.

.....

"He's not as weak as you think he is," Perdiccas said. "He never has been."

"I don't think Philip is weak," Alexander said. "I believe if fear was not a factor, he would have won every fight he ever had. But he gives in to his fear, he lets it rule him, not the other way around."

He dipped his cup into the large crater bowl and dragged it through the dark red wine, filling it to the point where it would likely spill.

"You never gave him a chance," Perdiccas said.

"Chance? What chance-" he glanced around the room with agitated, narrow eyes. The other guests' conversations had lowered. Perdiccas had raised his hand slightly to his older brother. Alexander lowered his voice to almost a whisper, "What chance did I have brother? Those bastards from Greece took him away before I could do anything, I had only been king for a few hours. Father's corpse was barely cold."

Perdiccas had felt sympathy for his older brother, being helpless to stop Pelopidas and his Thebans take Philip away. He glanced around the room. The walls of the hall echoed with talking. The drinking was well under way. Present at the gathering were Alexander's closest companions, officers in the army and men whose council he valued. Perdiccas did not put the same amount of faith in some of these men as Alexander did. He found them to be too blunt an instrument, too willing to resort to violence before thinking.

"I know, but you could have been more forceful with Pelopidas when he said he was going to take Philip and the rest of them to Thebes, and now we have the fathers of these other thirty lads that they took to answer to."

"Don't test me brother," Alexander grumbled under his breath, as he swallowed a belch. "I'd rather he was in Thebes than with Bardylis."

Perdiccas took an exaggerated swig of his drink, tipping it back far, but keeping his mouth mostly closed, only taking the tiniest sip. He worried for Alexander; these symposiums had become more and more frequent, and more of the negotiating with the kingdom's nobles was getting done in a drunken state.

"I have taken care of the nobles who took issue with their sons going to Thebes. They have been generously compensated. They understand the position I was put in."

"Compensated?" Perdiccas asked. "Generously?"

He watched Alexander, his brother clearly troubled, as he stared into the room vacantly. He wiped his mouth with the back of his hand. "To be truthful, I'm glad they took the other lads as well as Philip. This way he isn't alone, and the thirty families of the nobility have a reason to back me as king, since we're all in it together."

"Or they have a reason to supplant you if they think they can do a better job negotiating for them back."

"Ptolemy has asked if he can marry mother," Alexander said. Changing the subject.

"What?" Perdiccas said in a mix of shock and disgust. "How can he?"

"He asked for a divorce from Eurynoe on the grounds that she is barren. A few years with no child. He would then marry our mother to keep his strong ties to our family. Eurynoe can remarry or become a temple priestess to whichever god or goddess she prefers."

"It's outrageous," Perdiccas said. "Does she know?"

"Who? Mother or Eurynoe?"

"Well, either?"

"Our sister doesn't know, although she may suspect." He took another swig of his wine. "I think our mother might be already bedding Ptolemy."

"How do you know this?"

"I have had them followed. I need to keep watch on them. Ever since father died."

Perdiccas thought for a moment, scratched his chin, then took another shallow sip of his wine disguised as a deep swig as he looked around the room. The men were in good spirits, some laughed, a group were singing some war song he did not recognise. He met eyes with Parmenion, who had been recently promoted to one of Alexander's generals, raised his drink to him.

"What did you say to Ptolemy?" he asked.

"Say? I was ready to strangle the bastard," Alexander said, "but I told him I would consider it."

"I don't think that would be wise," Perdiccas said.

"I was exaggerating. Of course, I wouldn't actually strangle the fucker," he said. "Not while his soldiers are loyal to me. He knows he's indispensable; he was not shy about making his request."

Perdiccas thought about this. What would it mean for Ptolemy to marry his mother? The queen mother. What did he have to gain? She held no office. He didn't believe that it was to do with Eurynoe being barren. It was true, they had had no children, and under normal circumstances this may have made sense, but immediately asking to marry the mother of the king after the divorce, this was most unorthodox. What was he up to? He surely didn't plan to take the crown. No-one had been able to prove that their father's death was anything more than old age, but the suddenness of it, so shortly after the attempt on his life during the hunt had never sat well.

When the fighting had broken out on the hunting trip, Ptolemy had been nowhere to be seen, but had reappeared when it was over. No-one else had noticed, or at least had not mentioned it publicly, but Perdiccas had, and he had been suspicious of the man ever since, but had been careful to try to not make his mistrust show.

The noise in the room continued to build like a storm, then came to an abrupt quiet. Perdiccas followed the gaze of the men. Ptolemy had entered the room along with five other nobles and two heavy looking men that Perdiccas didn't recognise, although he suspected they were hired thugs. This entourage had become a permanent accompaniment of Ptolemy. He had started mingling with people as he made his way casually towards Perdiccas and Alexander. What rumours have been spreading? How does everyone here seem to know? Perdiccas thought.

"Greetings my brothers," he said. His confident smile was different, the playfulness that was normally there was gone. It left only an undertone of arrogance in the way he carried himself now; his chest was high.

Alexander now looked visibly drunk. He swayed a little, his eyes were narrow slits, and they stared at Ptolemy hard. In that moment it felt like every eye in the world watched them to see what Alexander would do. Perdiccas swallowed at the knot in his throat.

Chapter 18

The convoy was brought to a halt because of a fallen tree across the middle of the road. Pelopidas dismounted and beckoned Philip to come with him. Several of the guards came with them as they approached the tree to investigate. Pelopidas whispered something to one of the guards and he ran back. The message was passed on down the line and the soldiers formed up alongside the convoy, raising their shields, facing outwards towards the wilderness.

They were nearing the bottom of a deep v shaped valley, and although it was still rocky, there were now trees around them, getting denser towards the forest further down. Pelopidas approached the tree; it clearly aroused his suspicion as he had now drawn his sword from its belt and was looking up into the cliffs above.

"Look here Philip," he said.

"What is it?" Philip asked; surely trees fell down all the time here.

"Do you think this tree fell on its own?" Pelopidas asked him as if he had read his mind.

Philip looked at the lower end of the trunk. The broken part of it was flat about halfway into the trunk, and the rest was jagged, bristled and snapped. It was too far away from the stump to have merely fallen. This had been brought down with an axe or a saw, then moved here.

"No, I think it was cut down and placed." He looked up at Pelopidas, confused.

"And why would somebody cut down a tree, and place it in the middle-of-the-road?" Pelopidas asked, his tone suggesting that he knew the answer.

Philip scanned around with his eyes. His gaze moved along the fallen tree, and up the sides of the valley, then down onto the woods ahead. He suddenly remembered the battle with the Illyrians, how they had held his father's army in place before more of them had come pouring out of the woods and surrounded the Macedonians on three sides.

"Are we going to be ambushed?" he asked, feeling the panic begin to rise.

Pelopidas was a picture of perfect calm.

"Maybe. That's what this was intended for, and we are a long way from Pella now, out in the wilderness," Pelopidas said, keeping his calm tone. This started to make Philip feel his apprehension lifting. "This is bandit country".

Philip's eyes darted to all the dark, shaded spots of the forest; they seemed so much darker because of the brightness of the sun surrounding them. The sound of every snapping twig and bird taking flight seemed amplified. They waited a while with the soldiers and guards still standing in their defensive positions.

Pelopidas organised a few of them to come forward with axes. They formed a line and worked in shifts chopping at the tree; after fifty or so swings, the axe would be passed to a fresh man. Before long they broke the tree into two parts, ropes were attached and it was pulled off the road by horses.

Skirmishers with slings had been sent up the cliffs to search for any bandits, but returned finding none.

The soldiers stood braced, waiting. When no attack came, the convoy started moving again. Philip released his grip on his tunic, realising his knuckles were white and that he had been holding his breath. As he held his

211

hand out flat to look at it, it shook a little and he quickly lowered it to his side.

He looked up to see Pelopidas watching. He must have seen it.

"I don't understand," Philip said. "What happened? Were there bandits? Why was there no attack?"

"What do you think? Were there bandits out there?" Pelopidas asked. He glanced at the road ahead, then back to look Philip directly in the eye.

"There weren't any bandits?" Philip said.

"Is that a question or an answer?"

"I don't think there were bandits," Philip said, unsure, not knowing what to think. "Maybe someone was cutting down the tree for some other purpose, building or firewood, and was scared off by us?"

"Oh no, they're out there alright. This is bandit country. How many do you suppose there are?"

A few moments passed while Philip pondered the question. How many are there out there? Twenty? Maybe fifty? Surely not as many as a hundred? No, that many could never stay out in this part of the wilderness. He looked over his shoulder at the convoy once again.

"There was an ambush set," he said, "but not for us."

Pelopidas's lips curled up into a smile; he looked pleased. "Excellent Philip," he said and gave a small satisfied nod. "They weren't intending to take on an army, maybe some merchants or travellers."

Philip felt a smile growing, then immediately straightened his face; this was the most comfortable around someone in as long as he could remember. He thought of Antipater and his lessons, how it made him feel when he was praised by him. He thought about the possibilities of what Thebes might bring since he had

212

only been with the man for a few days and felt himself learning.

Pelopidas felt less like a stranger. Philip was starting to warm to him greatly, but then he quickly remembered the anger he felt to the man for taking him from his home and sending him to Illyria for the benefit of his own city.

Further down the road they set up camp, and Philip lay in his tent listening to the wolves howling in the hills, but the sound no longer scared him as it had done once.

. . .

Days later the convoy arrived at Thebes, the city visible from miles away as they came over the crest of a hill on the inland road.

The white stone temples, the Acropolis, and the citadel towered high above the pristine city walls. Their pillars had the slightest curve which made them seem like muscles flexing to hold up the white marble roofs of the buildings. The whole city was reflected in the freshwater lake around the base of the walls, making it look as if it was suspended in the air. Philip thought it looked how he imagined the dwelling of the gods on Mount Olympus.

This was like nothing Philip had ever seen before. He was speechless, never realising a city could look so beautiful. It made Pella look like a village.

Pelopidas smiled warmly at the view of his home city, and watched Philip's reactions. The young prince's reaction was one of marvel. His smile grew.

"This is the best road to travel to see Thebes for the first time," he said.

"It's incredible," Philip said, in awe. "This is all one city? I can't believe how big it is."

213

Philip looked at him, the man smiling warmly at the view as well, transfixed, as if he was seeing it for the first time himself.

"When were you last here?" Philip asked.

"I have not been back in over a year," Pelopidas said, and sighed. "I have the honour of being the man who represents Thebes in the north. With the endless trouble, I'm rarely home for long. The gods have a sense of humour; they make you good at something until it becomes a curse."

"Welcome to your new home Prince of Macedonia," Pelopidas said. Philip looked at him sharply, and when he noticed his alarm, he raised his hand to calm him. "For now," he said, "only for now."

They continued along the road and approached the gates, which were wide open, guards standing at either side scanning the people who came and went freely. In fact, the place was bustling with people from all walks of life coming and going. Tradespeople brought full wagons in and empty ones out. People carried all sorts of things from all over Greece and from the north; the wealth of the city was obvious.

Most of the army left them outside the city. Pelopidas and his bodyguard of around fifty men stayed with Philip, and the thirty other Macedonian youth hostages followed. Philip looked around to check for Antigonus. The tall boy he had seen in the distance was him. He seemed well. They met eyes in the crowd and he nodded to Philip, looking perfectly relaxed. Philip hoped he looked so calm himself. His heart was thumping. The exhilaration he had felt had gone now that they were within the walls, and thoughts of a prison or dungeon or even torture were now beginning to creep into his mind.

They moved on down the main road towards the centre of the city, where the acropolis rose above the other buildings. The traders that were with them left one by one to go about their business, no longer requiring the protection of the army. Nobody even glanced up as they moved through the streets; everybody was far too busy going about their business.

They made their way through a bustling agora, as they passed the owners of the stalls shouted and held up their wares, trying to sell them whatever they had. The smell of spices filled Philip's nostrils, his eyes following the smell to a stand surrounded by sacks full of exotic foods that he had never seen before.

They passed a smith banging a hammer on an anvil next to a furnace, the heat it gave felt like a solid wall, even over the heat of the sun. The smith wiped his soot-covered brow with his leather apron. His apprentice held an iron sword on the anvil for him to strike. It glowed red hot. His stand was stacked with weapons and armour, shields and helmets. Philip wanted to stay and watch the weapon take shape but they moved past. There was a loud hiss as the blade was placed in a trough of water.

A beggar shook a cup at them, and to Philip's astonishment, Pelopidas dismounted, placed a bronze coin into the man's cup, patted him on the shoulder, and even gave him water from his skin.

Pelopidas climbed back onto his horse and they left the agora. After a while the streets opened up into a large square surrounded by pillared buildings. This place was quiet and tranquil compared to the agora. Men who were well dressed in pristine white tunics came and went between the buildings, carrying scrolls and stacks of papers; their sandals could be heard pattering on the stone ground. Some sat out in the square on wooden chairs, leaning back, sipping from cups and talking.

"Where are we now? Who are these men?" Philip asked.

"This is the government district, the heart of our democracy. These men all work for the city. Law makers, accountants, politicians."

The boys were brought to one corner of the square, where a group of men stood. They were wealthy, that was obvious; they were well groomed and wore high quality, but not extravagant tunics. The boys all dismounted and followed Pelopidas. One of the men, about the same age as Pelopidas, came out of the group, his arms outstretched to embrace him.

"Welcome home Pelopidas," he said.

"Pammenes, I hope you and your family are healthy."

"They are. You have been in the north too long my friend."

"I know, I'm glad to be home," Pelopidas replied warmly. He turned and reached to beckon Philip forward, stepping toward him and he placed the outstretched hand on Philip's shoulder. "Allow me to introduce Prince Philip of Macedonia. He is going to be your guest I understand?"

"Yes, yes, of course," he said and smiled a weak smile at Philip, clearly apprehensive at his presence. "Greetings Prince, welcome to Thebes."

Philip looked around awkwardly. The two then stepped away and discussed matters in Thessaly and Macedonia, and he lost interest in listening once they started talking about financial matters.

He felt as though he was invisible to Pammenes; he would rather stay with Pelopidas.

Their conversation moved to his father's death, and they talked as if he was not there; although his relationship with Pelopidas had grown this conversation was making him uneasy.

The feeling of wonder at the great city had evaporated and his thoughts returned to home, his brothers and his sister and mother.

"Excellent work my friend. Anyway, you must be tired from travelling, go home and rest and we will discuss these matters at length later," Pammenes said.

Pammenes beckoned Philip over to him, "Come young Prince, we will go to my estate; you will be living with me for now, just while you get settled."

Philip looked to Pelopidas. He looked at him with an expression that said he would have preferred Philip to stay with himself. For a moment Philip felt a connection with the man. However, it had already been arranged that he was to live with Pammenes, and he did feel relief that he was not going to a prison.

Pelopidas patted him on the back. "I will say what I have said many times since we met. Don't worry. We will see each other a lot while you are here. Pammenes is a good man, an old friend of mine, he will look after you. Get settled in and you will hear from me soon," he said.

"Good," Philip said, feeling comfortable that he was staying with one of Pelopidas's friends at least.

"What do you think of our city so far then, Philip?"

"It's very beautiful. Will I be free to move around and explore?" he asked. He wanted to see more of the city.

"We will see in time. First, I must offer my condolences for the loss of your father; if you need anything from me let me know, one does not know what to say in these situations," Pammenes said.

217

"Thanks for your concern, but I am well for now," Philip said, trying his best to hide his true feelings on the matter. He hoped that Pammenes had not noticed the welling up of his eyes at the mention of his father. He resisted the urge to turn away; it would be too obvious.

Pammenes guided Philip over to what looked like a wagon, but with no wheels, and covered in white curtains, it had four men, one standing at each corner holding poles to lift it. He looked at it, unsure what to do.

"It's called a litter. These men will carry us to my estate. Please get in."

Philip leaned down and parted the curtains. The inside was lavishly decorated, containing two couches facing each other. They were scattered with white cushions with a gold rope trim.

"I can walk," Philip said.

"Nonsense, in you get," Pammenes said, nudging him toward the opening.

Philip climbed in and sank into one of the couches. He had never felt so comfortable, the cloth was softer than he thought possible. Pammenes sat opposite him and smiled. Philip squirmed a little, and looked away. He looked out through the thin linen curtains. Pammenes guards marched in a box around it. Were they there to protect him? Or to protect them from him? The litter was hoisted up and they were carried along; the ride was smooth, the men who carried it must be well practiced to make it so.

"Your Greek is excellent, although your accent will take getting used to," Pammenes said. "Do all boys speak it in Macedonia?"

"Yes," Philip said, while watching the streets go by. Then he turned to Pammenes. "In court, we all get taught Greek from a young age. Peasants mostly only speak old Macedonian though."

"Ah," Pammenes said, lifting his head.

The customs in this city were strange. How did it work having no king to give them leadership? Were the men who carried a litter slaves? Philip wondered. He knew the Greeks kept slaves but in Macedonia, the people worked the land with their own hands, even the king did not have slaves. A man of Pammenes apparent wealth could surely afford as many slaves as he wanted.

They were carried out along the streets, back through the agora and the city to Pammenes estate, which had its own walls and a private army of guards that patrolled them.

They got out after being lowered to the ground. Pammenes stretched his arms and hips. He was obviously of a high status, and particularly wealthy, because of the clothes he wore and the way he spoke. The cloth looked very expensive, and he wore gold jewellery.

Philip looked around at the grounds. This place was more extravagant than the Palace at Pella, and must, in Philip's imagination, be what the Great King of Persia's palace was like. The garden stretched as far as he could see, a statue of a god standing in a small shrine between flower beds. It was too far away to make out who, and there were reflecting pools everywhere; gardeners and servants milled about. There were large birds with huge fanned tails of beautiful colours, peacocks he thought they were; he had never seen one, but had heard them described.

They walked up a gravel path to the house; it was a white marble pillared building, with another large reflecting pool and fountain opposite the large double doors at the entrance. They creaked open and two heavy set guards stepped out. Their chests were high and they looked down their noses at Philip. He glanced down at their hands; they had scars on their knuckles. Was this a ruse? He clenched his fists by his sides, ready to raise them and throw a flurry of punches before making a run for it.

But they stepped out of the way and put their backs against the wall, standing to attention. One of Pammenes staff, presumably the men who managed his estate, emerged from in-between them. "Welcome home master," he said and lowered his head to Pammenes, "and welcome Prince Philip."

Philip followed him into the house. He stepped past Pammenes and his servant into a vast atrium, containing many colourful plants and flowers perfectly arranged. Servants quietly pottered about their business attending the plants.

An unseen musician was playing relaxing music from a lyre. Exotic birds in a large wooden cage sang. The amber-coloured walls were painted with a mural depicting a forest hunting scene. The woman who was the focus appeared to be the Goddess Artemis, whom he recognised by her short tunic, above the knee, unusual for a woman; she carried a bow, and was accompanied by hunting dogs.

The place made him think of the palace at Pella, or rather how it must have been generations ago under Archelaus, and how it could have looked if his father had succeeded in emulating his predecessor and returned it to all its glory.

"Beautiful isn't it?" Pammenes said. "It was painted by some of the finest artists in Greece. It shows-"

"Artemis?"

"Yes, that's right," Pammenes said, and smiled. "My servants here will take care of anything you need. Please stay within the walls of the estate for now. I have matters to attend to. I will see you when I get back."

Pammenes left, and the servant who had welcomed Philip into the house approached him silently. He wore velvet shoes and his feet glided on the tiles.

"Shall we get you cleaned up, Prince?" he asked in his soft voice.

Philip was taken to guest chambers, a beautiful set of apartments with a balcony overlooking the lake. Incense burned, giving the room a scent of flowers.

After a short while Philip was taken for a bath. The servants took off his dirty travelling clothes and laid out a fresh, clean chiton in his size on the bed for when he came out. Flower petals floated on the surface of the water; he took a long sniff; the scent was like the room.

He lowered himself in. The bath water was warm, and he had never felt anything like it. In Macedonia, washing with warm water was prohibited. He remembered being told once that the only exception was for a mother who had just given birth. He felt all of his troubles wash away, and his mind and body felt light, as if a great weight had been lifted from him.

The servants allowed him to relax for a short while, then he was washed, his hair was trimmed and combed and they shaved the soft hair on his chin that was starting to grow in thicker and tougher.

They brought him a large silver plate of fresh fruit. His mouth watered with anticipation, and he helped himself to some grapes, an apple, and some others he didn't recognise.

The house of Pammenes was paradise. It felt as though he was on Olympus itself.

Chapter 19

Philip spent some time living on the estate of Pammenes. He relaxed, ate and exercised. Although Pella and his family were always on his mind, he did not feel the pressure that he had felt living there. The estate was a safe haven, and he felt as though no harm could come to him within the walls.

He was shown the stables after the servants learned of his love for horses, and was permitted to help feed and groom them, but not to ride them until Pammenes was present. He was mostly away during the day attending to "matters of the state" as he called them.

So, when after a few weeks, Pammenes and his retainers arranged to go on a horse ride and invited Philip to come along it filled him with excitement.

However, once they embarked, he felt like a shade, invisible. They all acknowledged him when the group first met, but none engaged in anything other than polite small talk.

It was a beautiful summer day, and the sun was already climbing high before they left, so the party all wore loose fitting clothes and wide brimmed hats to prevent burning their skin.

As they passed through the gate and left the estate, Philip breathed a little harder, feeling like he was leaving safety behind. He felt exposed, naked even. The last time he had been on a journey like this they had been attacked.

They followed the road south, not far from the city. The landscape around them was made of low, rocky mountains rolling in all directions; it was much drier than Macedonia and because of this, less plants and certainly no forests, only tall slender cypress trees that dotted the hillside. A slight breeze cooled Philip's skin and carried the sweet scent of Pammenes' gardens. Although Philip's knowledge of the area was limited, he guessed they could not be more than a quarter mile away from the house. After a while, Pammenes had tired of the political discussion and beckoned Philip to come and join him at the front, and Philip rode his mare up alongside him.

"How do you like the horse?" Pammenes asked.

"She's a beautiful animal, she must have cost a fortune," Philip said, and he patted and stroked his mare's neck, and the horse snorted, enjoying the affection.

"It was a gift from Pelopidas. He brought me her from Thessaly, a fine animal," he said. "He told me you love horses, so I thought you would like to ride her."

"Are you and Pelopidas close friends?" Philip asked.

"I have known him for many years. We fought the Spartans together when we were younger. I hope everything you want is being catered for?" he asked.

Philip was unsure why he was being asked this. Had Pammenes forgotten that he had lost his father and his home? There was a long silence. Both of them looked around at the scenery. It was dryer here than Macedonia, the ground was cracked and the trees were sparser, but it was still beautiful, especially the lake, which stretched out like a clear icicle between the mountains.

Maybe he was just being a good host, he thought, and the truth was that he was being treated extremely well. It was a little unsettling to not have to look over his shoulder all the time for his half-brothers.

"Yes, thank you for your hospitality," he said to avoid the awkward silence.

"I'm still getting used to listening to your accent, Philip. Pelopidas has spent much time up in the north, not just in Macedonia but much further north dealing with Barbarians, Paeonians and Thracians mostly. He understands you quite well." He smiled.

"I will try and speak more slowly," Philip said.

"Don't worry, I understand you well enough. What do you want to get out of being here?" Pammenes asked.

Philip was caught off guard at being asked this question. He was expecting to be a hostage and thus treated as such, as he was in Illyria. Pelopidas had told him that he was more like a guest. "I... hadn't given it much thought. My understanding was that I was a prisoner."

Pammenes gently nodded, seeming a little amused. "Ah, you don't have to answer right now, have a think about it and let me know. I'll see if any arrangements can be made for whatever you want. Within reason of course."

"There was one thing," Philip said, suddenly realising that he had an opportunity.

"What can I do for you?"

"I would like to train as a soldier. I want to train with your soldiers."

Pammenes sniffed, amused. He stroked his horse's mane.

"A soldier? Why by the gods would you want to do that? We have every comfort ready for you."

"I want to make our army stronger."

"Why?" Pammenes asked, frowning.

"So we can protect ourselves. From-"

Pammenes paused, waiting for Philip to continue. He didn't.

"My dear boy, Macedonia's problem is not with its army. Mostly," Pammenes said, raised an eyebrow and tilted his head. "Wars cost a fortune, and they are to be avoided. You should always try the diplomatic route first. Macedonia has lots of resources that simply aren't utilised."

"What do you mean?" Philip asked, leaning in.

"Never mind that for now," Pammenes said. "So you want to be a soldier? I'm sure we can arrange for you to train with the army, but if it's exercise you want, you could- "

"With the Sacred Band."

Pammenes sat upright, both eyebrows raised. He let out a small laugh, then paused for a moment. Philip kept his face straight, trying to make himself look as serious as possible. When Pammenes realised he wasn't joking, he looked around to see who else heard what had been said. "The Sacred Band?"

"Please. I want to train with the Sacred Band."

"My boy…" he said. "You can't be…" His expression grew serious to match the mood Philip was trying to create. "And what will you do with your new-found ability to soldier? Having trained with the Sacred Band?"

"I have been training with the Macedonian army. I want to keep the skills and improve them, when I return home, I'll…" Philip stopped abruptly, realising he didn't want to give too much information. However, he realised that Pammenes saw right through it.

"Bardylis?" he asked.

"How do you know about him?" Philip said.

"Philip, I know everything about your stay in Illyria, and I have been well informed of your family's blood feud."

225

"I'm going to kill him," he said, clenching the reins of his horse in his fists, gripping so hard that it hurt his hands. "The way he treats us, the way he treated me."

"I understand, but be careful, Philip. If you hate all of your enemies with this intensity, you're going to have trouble dealing with them all."

"I just want to kill him."

Pammenes sighed, as though he was bored with the conversation; it was almost as if he did not understand revenge. "When you have many enemies, you have to keep them all in check but you will very rarely have the strength to take them all head-on."

"What would you suggest? I can't do anything while I'm here anyway."

"All in good time Philip, you just arrived," he said.

"No please, I want to know," Philip said, now desperate to hear it.

"No, you will have formal lessons on politics; this is going to teach you exactly what I'm talking about. For now, it just isn't appropriate Philip. Let's just enjoy the day."

One of Pammenes' slaves handed them some wine, and they drank. Philip took a drink but could barely taste the wine because it had been so heavily watered down. He remembered hearing about how the Greeks only drank their wine watered down, and this confirmed it. It tasted so weak, he would rather have just drunk water.

They spent the rest of the day with the horses. When they got back Pammenes took him on a tour of his stables and showed him some magnificent horses. He also kept birds of prey, and he held some of these birds. "Soon I will take you out to hunt with a bird," Pammenes told him.

They retired back to the house. Philip spent the rest of the evening planning in his head when he could next bring up the training and to find out what Pammenes was going to tell him about. He would ask him at the gathering that was arranged for the next night.

.....

The night came and the house of Pammenes was being prepared for the party. The entrance where Philip had first entered the house had been filled with couches and benches, and small tables were placed all around for drinks to be left on.

Once again Philip felt like a ghost; everything seemed to be going on around him. Servants and slaves were buzzing about like bees around a hive to get the house ready for the gathering. There were some incredible smells drifting through the house from the kitchen. Philip found himself loitering about outside the doors that the servants came in and out of for a good part of the morning, just taking in the smells and trying to guess what food was being prepared. His stomach rumbled.

After a while boredom set in. He had not seen Pammenes much that day. They had eaten breakfast together, but since then he was preoccupied with managing the preparations for the party. They had not exchanged more than a few words. Whenever Philip had asked questions, Pammenes had shushed him away in the politest way possible and got back to choosing the dishes and wine to be served, and what he should wear among other things. He chased the servants when he noticed something was not quite to his exacting standards. "I am hosting the finest of a Greek city, not some barbaric Thracian revelry!"

These things seemed trivial to Philip; what would these men care if a couch was a few inches one way or the other, or if one of the dishes was slightly burned? If these Greeks were as tough as they made out they were, these luxuries surely made them soft.

In the forefront of his mind was always what may be happening in Macedonia. In his boredom he had a lot of time for thinking, mostly about his family, and Bardylis, feeling a great rage every time he thought of *him*. The anger was starting to consume him. His thoughts were always about what could be done about him, and he felt helpless that he could come up with nothing, and that he was stuck in Thebes, unable to help Alexander.

When the guests started to arrive, Philip was sitting on a couch in the hall, and he stood up as Pammenes appeared to greet them. He introduced Philip to everyone who arrived as they came in. Many were friends of Pammenes and his family, all wealthy, high standing citizens. He wasn't sure what their actual titles were. They were a southern Greek democracy, but were they the aristocracy of Thebes, in practice if not in name? He didn't feel confident asking.

Some of them had a curiosity about Philip, making polite conversation with him, but asking the same questions about Macedonia. One or two mentioned his father; he felt that he hid the hurt from his face well. There did seem to be a fascination with him, but from a safe distance; he was, after all, a barbarian from an archaic tribe to the north, not a Greek. He soon came to the realisation that they saw him as his people look down on the Thracians or Illyrians; as an inferior culture. Some mentioned his accent, how different it was from their own and how they had not heard it before. Some said how much they liked his voice; and some simply didn't bring it up.

228

The house quickly filled up, and before long there were guests in every room on the ground floor and some even met in the hallways. They all talked and drank.

Philip filled his cup from the large krater of wine and slowly pressed it to his lips. The tang of the wine was a little stronger than before, but still the plain taste of too much water was there.

"I had the servants add more wine to the mix than normal. We wouldn't normally drink before dinner," Pammenes said in a voice raised so he could be heard over the chatter of the room. He patted Philip on the back. "I hope the flavour is more what you're used to."

The volume of the conversation had steadily climbed, but quietened down when Pelopidas arrived. Philip was standing quietly in a circle with Pammenes and some of his guests, listening to their conversation.

Pelopidas came into the main room with another man about the same size and build; the two were talking and looking around the room from the entrance. They removed their cloaks and handed them to servants. They then made their way across the crowded room while Philip was listening to one of the guests in the circle talk politics, about the state of the relationship with the Athenians. He was trying his best to keep up, but a lot of the talk was about legal matters and treaties.

Every guest, Philip noticed, moved to give Pelopidas and his friend space, and nodded to them as they passed. Pelopidas spotted Philip across the crowd and raised his hand in a static wave; he spoke something into his friend's ear, who immediately looked up and smiled at Philip. They then changed the direction they were going, and walked towards Philip. The room parted to let them through.

"Philip! My young friend! Greetings! I hope you are well," he said. The circle of guests Philip stood with parted to allow him and his friend to join them.

"I am well, and hope you are too," Philip replied warmly, softening his accent; he had been a little careful with it since someone commented on it; even though they said it had been a compliment, he thought it might be wise to make it less strong in case any of the guests were unfriendly to his country.

"I am," Pelopidas replied. "I trust you have been settling in well?"

"Yes, I have been made to feel welcome," Philip said, a half-truth. Although he not been treated badly by anyone, he felt like a stray dog in the house for most of the day; no one really knew what to do or say around him. It was however a paradise in comparison with the time he had spent in Illyria.

"I am glad to hear it. I want to introduce you to my friend. This is Epaminondas, one of our greatest citizens."

"One of?..." Epaminondas said with a look of anger, his face contorted, fierce.

"Calm down, you don't want to injure yourself," Pelopidas said.

There was a moment's pause, then Epaminondas' scowl melted away and grew into a smile. Pelopidas grinned back. The two clearly knew each other very well.

"This is Prince Philip of Macedonia," Pelopidas said, although Epaminondas clearly knew who he was anyway. It was also clear that they had been talking about him before they arrived.

"I'm very pleased to meet you," Epaminondas said. He seemed much more sincere than some of the other guests. "I've been hearing good things. Please accept

230

my condolences for your father. I hear he was a brave man, and that he died trying to rid you of a bitter enemy, something I have always had a lot of respect for. We had a similar situation here in Thebes not too long ago."

He was talking to him on equal terms; there was not the patronising dipping of the head that had come from almost everyone else.

"Not exactly, he died in his…" Philip started to say, but then decided not to tell him that he had actually died in his bed, probably poisoned. Death in battle gained his father's memory much more respect.
Philip nodded his head solemnly.

"Thank you for your sympathy," he said. "My father was brave. I miss him, although we weren't close, we didn't…"

"Philip," Pelopidas cut him off, "I'm sorry my young friend. We can talk more about this in private later. If you want to that is."
"Of course," he replied.

Pelopidas and Epaminondas excused themselves, and walked over to a more secluded area of the room. Pelopidas beckoned Philip to come with them.
"Excuse me," he said to the guests he was talking to and headed over to them.
"So? How are you really being treated?" Pelopidas asked.

Pammenes was standing talking to his guests; a servant came and whispered something in his ear. He then clapped his hands high above his head. "Okay everyone. Dinner is about to be served."
"Really, I'm being treated well," Philip said.

The guests all strolled into a vast dining room, were there were low tables laid out, and feasting couches arranged in a large square. Philip stayed close to Epaminondas and Pelopidas and they sat either side of him on one of the couches. The guests filed into the room, carrying their drinks with them. They spread out, and slouched back, helping themselves to cheeses that the servants offered around. The musician playing the lyre sat down on a chair in the corner, and continued to play.

Philip felt relaxed for the first time in as long as he could remember. Food was being served and servants were always milling about, ready to top up anyone's wine cup.

One of the servants, a girl about Philip's age caught his eye. Although her body was concealed by her dress, he could make out its outline, firm and toned; he immediately thought of Arsinoe.

As the meal went on, the wine flowed and the volume of the conversations got louder. Philip could not take his eyes off this girl; his eyes searched the room whenever she went out of his view. Pelopidas noticed and winked at him, and he felt his cheeks going red.

Philip talked a great deal with Pelopidas and Epaminondas about Macedonia and its culture, and in turn they told him about the culture of Thebes; their rivalries with other city states and their politics.

This was the most welcome he had felt anywhere. That made him uneasy, unsettled, suspicious. He constantly scanned the guests for any looks that might betray someone's true feelings towards him.

Even at home when he wasn't being attacked by his half-brothers, he was being lectured by one of his tutors or his father, always under pressure. Everyone here seemed to be getting along fine; he didn't feel there was going to be a brawl, or that daggers would come out at any moment.

When the main meal had been served, the musician bowed and left. He was replaced by a bard who had come to entertain with some of the stories of the myths. He told the tale of Theseus and his ordeal with the Minotaur in the labyrinth, and of the adventures of Jason and his Argonauts.

Everyone hung on his every word, including Philip, and when he was finished, he stood and took a bow. He was met with tremendous applause.

Pammenes stood up from his couch and continued to clap. Once the bard had left the applause continued for a minute or so, and then died down. Pammenes then held out his open palm to Epaminondas.

"Epaminondas! I would love to hear a great deal more of your bravery and adventures! Tell us the story of your victory at Leuctra.".

Epaminondas having, a mouthful of goat's cheese, held his hand up and covered his mouth with the other hand while he finished eating what was in his mouth. "No, I've had far too much to drink! You host a great party Pammenes my friend."

"Please! I insist," Pammenes smiled, and a few of the other guests quickly and quietly started to whisper, "tell us," and things to that effect. This built-up in a crescendo until he started to nod, and the noise and chatter in the room died down. All fell silent in anticipation.

"Okay, okay, but it is not that great a tale," he said, feigning modesty. "I will keep it brief."

Philip's jaw had dropped; he was *that* Epaminondas, who had won a great victory over the Spartans. How had he not realised? He did not know what to think. He was mingling with the men who had caused so much damage to the people his father had admired, and allied himself with. The men who had helped them return home. He was angry at what this man had done, but when his teeth ground, the pressure of his closed jaw eased off as he realised how much he actually admired Epaminondas as well.

Philip sat and drank, and missed the first part of Epaminondas's story. His eyes looked around the room; all the guests were hanging on his every word, and drinking cup after cup of wine. He then began to join the rest of the guests and listen to Epaminondas.

"So, we get to Leuctra, and find the Spartans did actually want to fight, and they've completely blocked the valley with their phalanx; ten thousand of them! As we know, the Spartans all follow the strict rules of war," He stood bolt upright, his expression completely straight and stiffly pretended to march, this was met with laughter and a small amount of applause from some who were pleased at the mockery of the city, which had once been their great rival.

"All the best fighting troops were on the right, of course; always on the right flank; phalanx in a perfect straight line. Now, we needed a way to beat this; our men, apart from the Sacred Band, could not take the Spartans on one-on-one, so..." There was a long pause while he took a long swig of his wine from his silver cup, and wiped his mouth with the back of his hand. "Instead of using this." He flexed his right bicep, placed his cup on the table and patted the muscle with his now free hand. "We had to use this." He tapped his index finger on the side of his forehead. He took another quick swig of his wine. "So, what we did was reverse our formation, put all our best troops on the left, their right. Our best against their best; but not wanting to take any chances we doubled the depth of the ranks. The rest of our phalanx deployed slanting back, away from theirs. The idea was to completely overrun their right flank where all their generals would be. Cut the head off the snake."

234

"The two lines engaged, and the Sacred Band, led by our courageous General Pelopidas." He patted his friend on the back, who looked up at him and smiled. "Completely stormed around their flank, crushed them and killed the Spartan king. This caused the whole flank to roll over and many more were killed; their army collapsed. We sent them running!" he shouted, his voice having grown progressively louder throughout the story. The party guests all applauded loudly and stood up, giving him a standing ovation.

Philip was now in awe. He was careful not to react, when his mouth nearly fell open. These men could not only fight, but they really understood how the army functioned on the battlefield, really understood, and they had warmed to him. He decided at that moment he would learn as much as he could from them, and if he ever returned home, he would be a great general for his brother.

The evening carried on, and more wine was brought in, this time three large kraters, and the level of drunkenness continued to build. The musicians returned; Philip heard them, the soothing sound of the aulos, but when he turned to look it was not the same ones. Philip closed his eyes hard and when he opened them, he tried to straighten himself, his vision was blurred, and he could see two of each of them; women; women as lovely as nymphs. They played the double reeded instruments beautifully, as they pranced around the room on feet as light as feathers. He was transfixed.

Philip relaxed on the couch and talked with Pelopidas and Epaminondas. Time lost all meaning as he drank more and more wine. It seemed to get stronger as the first and then the second krater was drunk dry by the guests. "They get stronger from the first to the second. By the time the third is finished a wise man

235

should have called it a night," Pelopidas said, speaking more slowly than usual. He laughed. "But even wise men do not always do wise things."

The three then talked about a whole manner of things, his family and how he was fitting in in Thebes. He opened up to them more than he had intended to because of the wine. He felt he should restrain himself on certain topics, like which city his brother Alexander favoured, but he did not keep his control.
He lay back and blew out a slow breath through his pursed lips; the ceiling was spinning.

He sat up and slowly looked around the room, realising there were women everywhere; he had not noticed them before. Had they been there before the meal? No. How long had he been talking? He couldn't recall.

He looked over at the other couches, a few were sitting talking to the male guests, but most were either kissing or performing various sexual acts with the guests.

"Is this normal?" he asked Pelopidas.

"Whores are normal at a symposium here," Pelopidas said. He leaned in and half fell against Philip. "Feel free to partake. You are welcome."

Philip looked up and down the figure of one of the women. The man she was with was someone he had spoken to earlier, one of Pammenes lawyers. He was leaning back on the adjacent couch while the woman kneeled in front of him, her head bobbed up and down below his waist. Another was being bent over one of the couches. At first, he just watched, then he thought of Arsinoe, and how he was going to keep his word to her; he told her he would wait for her, and they would be together when he got back to Pella. She had promised the same.

"I'm too drunk," Philip said. "I couldn't satisfy a woman in my current state."

Epaminondas just laughed. "It's the girl from earlier? The one you were watching? I saw you," he said, slurring his words. "You like her? I can have her brought here for you?"

"I don't know who you mean," Philip said, knowing that they didn't believe his denial.

"Come now Philip," he said. "She was gorgeous, I would have had her too."

"I have a girl at home, she's waiting for me to return," Philip said. "I thought Greeks only drank watered down wine?"

"This isn't Athens," Pelopidas said. He laughed, and then swallowed a burp behind his fist. "In Thebes we drink a lot. I hear you enjoy a drink in Macedonia?"

"We do," Philip said, relieved that he had successfully changed the subject.

The three drank into the early hours of the morning before Philip slipped into a stupefied sleep.

Chapter 20

Philip woke the next morning and immediately bent over the side of the bed. He stared down at the floor, nauseous; his face and head throbbed. Then suddenly the sick feeling rose from the pit of his stomach and he retched, throwing up onto the floor. He stared for a moment at what was left of the previous night's refreshments, then slumped back onto the bed before the smell made him roll over and throw up again. He lay back down after dry heaving a few times.

He tried to relax, despite the agonising pain in his head. He had never drunk that much wine in his life, and vowed he would never again.

He opened his eyes and stared at the ceiling; beautiful artwork was painted on it, a scene from Homer, the death of Patroclus. He had not remembered going back to bed, or most of the evening after the meal. What had he done? He tried to recall if he had embarrassed himself. The sickly-sweet smell of the vomit at the side of the bed drifted past his nostrils.

Lying flat on his back he turned his head to the side and almost fell out with the fright he received.

His face flushed, and his cheeks burned; the servant girl that he had been looking at the night before was standing at the side of the bed the whole time.

"I am sorry Prince Philip. I didn't mean to scare you. You look like you have seen a gorgon," she said softly, staring at her feet. "I have brought you some water. Please drink, it will help the pain in your head."

She poured some water into a cup from the small urn she carried, knelt beside him and held it up to his lips. The water was cold and it washed the stinging taste of vomit from his mouth and throat. Even in the state he was in, he could not help taking a glance at her chest as she leant to pour, her scent making him ignore the way he was feeling for a moment.

He coughed.

"Thank you," he managed to say after an awkward silence. He buried his face in his pillow, embarrassed at the state he was in; what must she think of me? he thought. He was definitely living up to the reputation of being a northern barbarian. "I'm sorry for the mess, I'll clean it," he said, taking shallow breaths, the pain in his head becoming apparent again.

"No Prince... I..." The girl stammered, "a slave has to do whatever she is told."

She knelt down and began to clean up the sick; the stink of sour wine rose from it, making Philip almost retch again. He thought she must share this feeling.

"A slave? I thought you were a servant. I've never met a slave before," he said, his head thumped with the effort of talking.

She continued to clean. Her head down, the comment clearly made her uncomfortable.

"Leave it," he said. "I will clean it myself soon, when I'm up to it."

"No, I'll be whipped."

"I'll see to it you aren't." He lay flat on his back, staring at the ceiling, still too embarrassed to look at her. He closed his eyes and could still see her; he wanted her badly, but not if she didn't want him. She was beautiful, and reminded him so much of Arsinoe. He wished he was home. "I promise."

She nodded and stood up.

"Leave me… please," he finally said, after a moment of silence.

"Yes Prince," the girl replied shyly. She backed away from him with her head down, turned and left once she reached the door.

Philip sat up sharply. "Wait," he shouted, and she came back into the doorway. "What is your name?"

"Briseis, Prince."

"Thank you Briseis. Please call me Philip," he said gently, holding his forehead with his thumb and forefinger. She lowered her head again and left down the hall.

He slumped back onto the bed, unable to get her out of his head, and fell back asleep.

. . . . . .

Later, when Philip had rested a while longer, and drank more water, he got up and dressed himself. The vomit on the floor was gone. He shook his head and headed down into the main living area, where Pammenes sat at the table having breakfast with his wife.

The air was warm to breathe, thick and moist, the sunlight shone in beams through smoke from incense burners. The servants must have set up the incense burners all around the room to help clear the smells of the night before, wine, sweat, sex and vomit, that still lingered through the jasmine scent.

Pammenes beckoned Philip over, and he sat with them to have something to eat. A little bread, and some sips of water; his stomach was still sensitive. When he was finished, he excused himself and headed to the stables. He took a horse out for a ride round the estate; he thought the fresh air would help his head. He took in a breath through his nostrils; it was good to get out of the stuffy air of the house.

He thought about the night before and the men he had spent most of his time with. Pelopidas, the man who he had thought nothing of, and then hated after he had brought him here, was a great general, who had fought and defeated the Spartans.

He was a member of the Sacred Band. The Spartans were the men who his father had always held in high regard, until the day of Leuctra where they had been crushed by the Sacred Band. Philip had always held the Spartans in high regard as well, never once questioning that they were the greatest warriors who had ever lived. In Macedonia, the boys were taught to be tough and resilient, just like the Spartans. He had been taught that they were descended from Heracles, the same as the Spartans, but with Epaminondas making his speech last night in a half drunken state, made Philip question everything he had been told. The Thebans had used strategy, and tactics, to win over brute force. This was far beyond what even the Spartans with all their experience and strength had anticipated on the battlefield. And by the Gods these Thebans could fight.

Pelopidas had been up in the north sorting a dispute in Thessaly before he had come to Macedonia. How far did their influence reach? He wondered how well Thebes now measured up against Athens and Sparta given the damage that they had now suffered.

For a time, all the questions running through his head made him forget about Macedonia. In that moment he told himself, I will learn everything I can from these Thebans, beyond just soldiering. If he ever saw home again, he would kill Bardylis, and Alexander would rule Macedonia without the sword of the Illyrians constantly at his throat.

....

A few weeks past, and Philip was excited to receive an invitation to meet with Pelopidas at his house. He

241

had been several times since the symposium and they had drunk together and talked. They had played a game the general called Petteia, which they played on a wooden board on a tabletop. The board was marked with a grid, and each player would have a line of coloured stones which started opposite each other. The aim was to capture or surround your opponent's stones. Philip had been thinking over his strategy from the last game, and was eager to have another attempt to win.

He arrived at dusk in a litter, accompanied by guards that Pammenes had arranged. "You do not want to walk the streets at this time of night," he had said. "Any thug or low life would surely take your life for your purse."

The estate was large, similar to Pammenes and as well guarded, but nowhere near as lavishly furnished or decorated. He had nowhere near as many servants, and the gardens were not as elaborate. They were more open, like a field; in the dark Philip could make out the silhouettes of shrines to the gods, but could not make out who they were for.

Philip was ushered in by Pelopidas' body slave.

"Come in young Philip," he said and bowed, smiling. "My master has been looking forward to your visit."

Pelopidas welcomed him in and the two embraced. Philip was a little unsettled by this greeting. He still harboured anger toward the man, but every time they had met, it became harder and harder to maintain ill feeling; he felt a synergy with the man he could not explain, and had to make a conscious effort to keep up the hostile thoughts.

They sat out on the veranda overlooking the gardens and played Petteia, the board having been already set up when he had arrived.

242

Pelopidas' slaves brought them wine and bread, far more basic than what he was served at Pammenes house. He did not think to object, and this was all that Pelopidas ate; Philip realised that he had never seen him eat or drink anything too extravagant.

Philip surrounded Pelopidas' last few pieces to win the game.

"Excellent move Philip," Pelopidas said. "Your strategy has improved greatly. I didn't see that coming; you set it up like we talked about."

"I'm enjoying our games," Philip said. "I... Can I ask... "

He could not find the words. Pelopidas lounged back on his couch, raised an eyebrow and made a small nod to Philip. He smiled warmly.

"Yes?" he said.

"Can I ask you a question?"

"Of course, what is it?" Pelopidas asked. "I'm intrigued."

"When you first brought me here you said it might be possible to learn and train in military matters?"

"I did?" he said, feigning ignorance. Philip had seen this in him before and saw through the facade.

"Well, I was wondering if it was something I could do. I want to learn anything you have to teach. Pammenes always avoids the question."

Pelopidas sat up straight on the couch, putting his feet on the floor, leaning toward Philip. His expression was hard and serious. He made a series of small nods with his head, and clawed at his beard. Philip understood that he was very careful about what words he chose, and wondered what he would say next. He tried to gauge what he was thinking.

"You are a prisoner. We don't train prisoners," he said, giving a look as serious as death.

243

Philip's heart went into his mouth. He felt that he had crossed a line, then Pelopidas smiled warmly.

"Don't worry, it is already a topic of debate among our equals," he said and paused looking at Philip.

"Equals?"

"Our government is like a council. We have to debate everything. Unfortunately, democracy can sometimes mean that making a decision takes a terribly long time."

"I see," Philip said.

"Some are reluctant to teach you our methods; they fear that one day you may be a threat."

"To Thebes?" Philip said in disbelief.

"Not necessarily," Pelopidas said, and scratched his beard. "It could upset the balance in the north."

"The balance?" Philip said, "All I want is to be able to defend Macedonia against Bardylis."

"You see, I know you a little better now Philip, but they fear you would not show restraint, and kill him and anyone else who got in your way."

Philip frowned. "How could I possibly do that? Macedonia is weaker than all its neighbours; I understand that now."

"It is. For now."

"For now?"

"Yes, for now."

He stared at Pelopidas, feeling his eyebrows frowning deeper. "I don't understand," he finally said.

"Don't worry; I am confident they will train you, in time. I will keep pressing for it. Now, let's get back to our game."

Philip dropped the matter, and believed Pelopidas could convince the rest of them it would be okay.

They played a few more games, then drank more wine; this carried on well into the evening. As the alcohol began to loosen Pelopidas' tongue, the conversation moved on from hard matters, such as military logistics and war, to more philosophical and theoretical questions about subjects like the gods.

After their hands brushed by mistake, Pelopidas looked him in the eyes and they kissed.

They went to bed together and fell asleep in each other's arms.

...

The following morning Philip woke up groggy. He sat up and tilted his head side to side; the bones in his neck cracked; it had not been a restful sleep. The sheets were damp with his sweat. Now that he was sober, but hung over, the acid taste of the wine lingered in his throat.

Pelopidas was still asleep. What would be made of this? What problems may this cause among Pelopidas friends and the Theban elite? He tiptoed over to his clothes, which were in a pile on the floor, got dressed and snuck out, closing the door to the bedroom as carefully as he could.

He returned to Pammenes estate and had breakfast with him and his wife, who did not question where he had been.

He went out for a ride on one of Pammenes horses to try to clear his head; his thoughts went to his father in the afterlife, then of his brothers. All news of home came from the Thebans, so now he was unsure how much was being kept from him.

He had not heard anything about Alexander for a few weeks, or what state the kingdom was in. Philip had been told everything was going well and that Macedonia was stable, but he could not be sure. If all seemed to be well, would he ever return? If he did return would Alexander accept him? He was over the fury that he had

245

felt when he was first told he was being sent to Thebes, but Alexander was not aware of this, and regardless, had always thought him weak. Would he want him back? And how did Perdiccas fit into all this? He hoped he was well.

When he returned to the estate, he was met outside the house by Pammenes who led Antigonus and a group of the Macedonian boys.

"We have decided that you can now meet in small groups, as long as you all behave," Pammenes said.

Philip jumped down from his horse and embraced his friend. Antigonus bumped him on the shoulder with the bottom of his fist.

"How are you my friend? I thought you were here. Are they treating you well?" Philip asked.

"Very well, I have been living with a few others. Although our lodgings are nothing like this," he said and looked around the gardens, then up and down the villa building itself, he smiled. "Is Pammenes a Persian King?"

Pammenes smiled at the jest and he took them to a circle of stone benches in his gardens and they sat out in the sun for a short lesson.

They spoke much about the world, the politics of the Greeks; Macedonia; and Persia, the greatest and most powerful empire the world had ever seen. Thebes was on good terms with Persia, which did not help with their relations with Athens or Sparta, and many of the other Greek cities.

They then talked about economics, a subject that Philip had never been interested in, but Pammenes pointed out that a country's military was only as powerful as the economy that was backing it. "Much like an army in the field without good logistics and supplies is unsustainable," he said.

Philip had not realised about all the natural resources Macedonia contained: iron, copper, tin and most importantly to the Greeks, timber.

"The timber is the main reason that Macedonia is in the predicament it is in," he said. "The forests are vast, and the high quality of the wood makes it much sought after. This, combined with Macedonia's position in the north, on the Persian road, makes it so important; also, you do a terrible job of defending it."

Philip had never realised why there was so much fighting in his homeland. He always knew there was fighting, but he had never really thought what caused it. Men fight, he thought, it was that simple.

Pammenes lessons made him realise that all the Greek city states meddle in the affairs of Macedonia and that of their neighbours, like the gods meddling in the affairs of mortals. They would sow discord to keep Macedonia weak, and take advantage of that weakness to gain access to its resources. Of course, Pammenes only accused the other cities such as Athens and Sparta of this, never mentioning Thebes' part in it.

Philip found himself gritting his teeth behind his lips, staring at Pammenes giving his lecture, but he didn't hear the words; the Theban's lips moved silently.

"Are you alright Philip? Antigonus whispered to him, bringing him back to reality.

"I'm fine, never better," he lied.

Philip decided in that moment that Macedonia would not be second-tier to these Greeks forever; as much as he admired, and was even growing to like, the Thebans he was with, he would not allow this to continue any longer. The more he was taught, the more determined he became.

Chapter 21

After a few days, a messenger arrived at the estate while Philip was listening to a lecture from Pammenes about logistics. They sat at the circle of stone benches in the garden. The messenger approached carrying a sealed scroll. He stood about ten paces away, escorted by one of Pammenes private bodyguards, waiting to be acknowledged. "I have orders for the prince's eyes only," he said, maintaining his distance.

"Very well," Pammenes said, waving his hand, allowing the messenger to come closer.

Philip took the scroll from him. The messenger nodded and left. Philip broke the seal and scanned through the document, a set of orders as if he was in the army. He skipped to the end; it was signed by Pelopidas and Epaminondas. He felt a smile begin to grow.

"What is it, Philip?" Pammenes asked.

Philip looked back and read form the start. "It's an order to allow me to train with the army."

"Excellent," Pammenes said. He also smiled, "It has been a topic of hot debate since you arrived. I wasn't sure if it would ever be agreed to allow you to train. Pelopidas and Epaminondas pushed for it, and their voices carry a lot of weight."

"It says my training will commence tomorrow if my schedule allows? I don't want to miss our lecture."

"We can move our lecture to later in the day. I know how keen you are to get started."

Philip nodded.

……

True to their word, he was collected the following morning by one of the officers who was under

Pelopidas's command. "Join your friends," he said with total indifference, as if he had drawn a bad lot to look after the Macedonian babies. He already had some of the Macedonian youths with him.

Philip was a little alarmed when he recognised three who were friends with his half-brothers. He awkwardly approached them, and then his eyes met with Antigonus' who smiled and nodded to him. Unbreakable Antigonus. He never seemed phased. To his surprise, his half-brother's friends also nodded to him with respect. "Philip," one of them even said, leaving him wary. He half nodded back and joined them, making sure they were in front of him.

"I'd keep a watch on them," Antigonus whispered to him.

"I know. I won't turn my back on them, or I may end up with a knife in it."

They were taken to the training grounds by the men that had guarded Philip at Pammenes estate. It was inside the city walls. When he saw it, he let out a sigh of disappointment. He wasn't sure what he was expecting; it was an open patch of dirt, the same as the training ground at Pella. Apart from a few birds cawing, they were the only living souls there; the early morning sounds of the city waking up were quietened by the distance. Training grounds must be the same everywhere Philip presumed after thinking about it.

There was a wall at one end, which looked like it may have been part of a building at one point, but was now crumbling and only about the height of Philip's waist. The youths sat on this wall, with their guards standing like statues in the distance, keeping a watch on them. Philip felt a speck of rain on his cheek and looked up, the sky was cloudy. Perfect, he thought, no need to worry about getting burned if we're out in the open all day.

"Here they come," Antigonus said, nodding his head in the direction of the richer part of town, the direction from which the Theban hoplites now filed down the road. Hoplite warfare was the domain of the wealthy of the city, Pammenes had told them. Thebes was not yet at the stage Athens was at, where they had a navy and they could put hundreds of men on triremes rowing, but they had very strong infantry. A powerful navy, he had told them, was something Epaminondas was very keen to build.

Philip expected much the same as when he had been training at home, but the first thing that struck him, was the orderly fashion in which they filed in. There were no drunks or animals brought like there had been in Macedonia, and not a pauper in sight. They were far more professional, standing tall and proud, most of them already wearing their own equipment, full bronze cuirasses, helmets, greaves and carrying their aspis shields, broad and dome-shaped, along with spears and short swords.

They confidently passed the group of Macedonian youths with their heads held high. Philip felt exposed like he had at that first party at Pammenes' house; none of them said anything, but almost all of them turned their heads in curiosity, not shy at having a glance at these Macedonian youths who must have been alien to them.

"Look at their equipment," Philip whispered to Antigonus in astonishment. "It's all in a perfect state of repair, and there are hundreds of them. We could never afford to raise an army this well-equipped."

"You see the houses these people live in here Philip? Is it any wonder they can pay for it all?" Antigonus said.

"You know the Greeks though. They still shit themselves at the first sign of trouble."

Philip shook his head. "Not these Greeks," he said. "Our guards here, I'm sure they're the Sacred Band. A few years ago, their generals Pelopidas and Epaminondas-"

"The ones you've been spending time with?" he said, and had a glance at them over Philip's shoulder.

"That's right, well, Pelopidas anyway, I've only met Epaminondas once," he said." Anyway, they defeated a Spartan army at Leuctra only a few years ago, and I mean crushed it."

Antigonus sat back and scratched his chin. "Leuctra? I've heard of it. It was them? Really?"

The Thebans began to drill; they all stood in a vast square, precisely spaced out, facing forward. The drummers would keep the beat, and the officers would yell an order. The officer's voice was almost as percussive as the drums themselves. The soldiers would all follow it, almost perfectly synchronised. Sidestep left, sidestep right, step forward, and step back. Close ranks. Lock shields. It was like a dance.

"And what happened to the Spartans?" Antigonus asked.

"If they're telling the truth, Sparta isn't the power it used to be. They were allies in the Peloponnesian league when they fought Athens, but Sparta has since been crippled beyond repair. They have very few men now, and spend most of their time trying to stop slave revolts. According to Pammenes anyway. Maybe Macedonia needs Theban advisors instead of Spartan ones."

Philip sat in awe of what he was witnessing. Orders were shouted and they lowered their spears in harmony, as if to attack an imaginary enemy force. Another yell and they raised them, spear tips pointing to the sky,

251

turned on the spot and lowered them again, changing the direction of the formation in a matter of seconds. He tried to count them, but it was difficult because of all the movement.

"It would take years to get our soldiers to drill like that," he said.

"No," Antigonus said. "Remember when you used to freeze when someone attacked you? We trained that out of you in a day."

Philip looked at his friend. He was much wiser than people knew. "Look at them Antigonus, we need to learn as much as we can from them while we are here."

Antigonus nodded slowly. "I agree."

The Thebans drilled for a few hours and Philip and Antigonus watched carefully, trying to take in every drill they were practising. The Thebans all stopped and went for water, a short stretch and massaged each other's muscles. Philip looked at Antigonus and let out a slow breath. Antigonus' eyebrows both raised. "They're good, very good," he said.

One of the officers who had been shouting at the Theban hoplites approached the group of Macedonians; a stocky man with a limp. "Alright lads," he said. "Up you get, come join in the next drill."

Spears with blunt tips and shields were brought out and dumped on the ground in front of them, and they were all herded into what in Macedonia would have been an acceptable, but here seemed a disjointed formation. They were kept separate from the Thebans, who had fallen back, ready to train. They started the drill that the Thebans had started with. The Macedonians tried to keep up with the signals, which became increasingly fast, but they became more and more fragmented as they stepped forward and back, side to side. Philip breathed hard; they quickly started tiring and stepped into each other. All tension between himself and his half-brothers' friends had melted away; they were all in it together. The officer stalked among them, barking out his commands. He carried a short, hardwood stick, and poked and prodded at them to keep them right. This man reminded Philip of Antipater who used to train them in the gymnasium, both in appearance and the rasp of his voice.

After struggling for a while, they stopped for a stretch and a sip of water from their skins.

They were then shouted over to mix in with the Thebans. They were separated out into two columns, and they locked themselves into opposing shield walls. They began a sort of game or competition of wrestling, of pushing and shoving against their opposing man, trying to sweep their feet from underneath or strike the helmeted head over the top of the shield, while they were off balance.

Philip found this very difficult, and the weight of the shield was far heavier than he ever remembered, although he had held an aspis before. He felt the front of the dome shape. It was fully sheeted in smooth bronze, with a few imperfections where weapons had struck it. The shield he had practised with in his youth had only had a bronze rim; the difference in weight was huge, even though he was now bigger and stronger than he had been. The veins in his shoulder protruded, and the chords of his neck tensed. He could feel his pulse rushing blood into the muscle and after a short while it burned and began to shake. Even though the day was cool, the close formation quickly became stifling; he tilted his head up to breathe the cool air he could feel floating above them, and he was struck hard on his exposed neck.

The blow was only a glancing one, but pain shot through his neck and down his back and arms as if he had been struck by lightning, the skin felt grazed, but in the tight ranks, he could not check, it felt like warm blood was running down his chin and onto his chest, but it may have just been sweat. He ignored it and focused on the man who had struck him, staring him in the eyes, all he could see of the man's face. He imagined he was his half-brother Arrhidaeus, and fought back, grinding his teeth and gripping the ground with his toes. He carried on until they were told to stop, but didn't manage to return the blow, which was parried or avoided every time.

They took a break for bread and water, and the Macedonians went back to the wall to sit. Philip watched them intently, excited, wanting to train more. He couldn't wait for the break to be over. He leaned over to Antigonus who was ravenously eating some bread.

"This is unbelievable, isn't it? I can't believe how much better than our soldiers they are."

"Shit Philip, you're bleeding," he said.

"I know, it's okay, it's only a light cut. I got clipped by a spear," he said, and felt his neck. He took his hand away and rubbed the red crust which crumbled between his thumb and forefinger. "I'm fine. We need to remember as much of this as we can for when we go home. No matter how hard it is to breathe, keep your head down."

"Maybe you're right, we should be hiring them as advisers instead of the Spartans. If we ever get out of this god forsaken place, we should tell Alexander," Antigonus said.

The two watched the Thebans eat. They sat in small groups. A few looked up towards them. "I'm going over," Philip said.

"I wouldn't, you don't know them," Antigonus said, but Philip was already making his way towards them.

He approached the man who he recognised as the one who had struck him in the throat, sitting in a circle of about ten other men. He looked up at Philip and squinted, shielding his eyes from the sun. Philip stepped to the side, so that his shadow shaded the man's eyes, and his squint disappeared.

"Can I sit with you? I'm very impressed with all of you," Philip asked.

"Of course, please," the man said, and stood up, beckoning Philip to a space next to him. Philip sat in the circle with the Thebans and looked from man to man. "I hope there's no grudge for the…"

The man gestured to Philip's neck, which Philip touched with his fingertips; it stung a little.

"No, I'm grateful, I'm here to learn, I should have been stronger of heart and not exposed my throat for cool air."

"You kept your composure well once you'd been hit," the man said. "Came straight back at us."

This made Philip begin to smile, but he stopped when he felt his cheeks begin to rise, trying to keep a conservative manner. "Your equipment is all beautifully made and maintained. Are they gifts from the nobles?"

The man smiled, and the Thebans all looked at each other smiling as well. Philip smiled back at them, looking from man-to-man. He didn't understand the joke.

The man must have read his confused expression. "We don't have nobles here in Thebes, Prince, we are... citizens. Do you know this word?"

255

"Citizens? I do know the word, but what does it meant to be a citizen? Is it like a peasant?"

A few of the smiles turned down."

"I mean no offence, I want to understand your society. How it is structured," Philip said, holding his hands up. He noted that he must be careful of using the word peasant in future.

"Not exactly, Thebes is a democracy, we don't have nobility. There are still rich and poor, but there is no royal family, the citizens vote to make the decisions of our government."

"So, you aren't professional soldiers?"

The man smiled and shook his head "No, Prince, Thebes is our mother, and we all have a duty to protect her. If we don't, who will? We are paid a little to do this, but we must train for when we have to fight to protect Thebes."

Philip scratched his chin and looked around. "How often do you train?"

"As much as we can. Thebes is the most powerful Greek city. We have many enemies."

"We have enemies all around us in Macedonia as well. Have you fought often?" Philip said.

"How old are you, Prince?" another man asked. He was older, had a long white beard, but had good muscle tone.

"Fifteen."

"Then you were probably only a few years old when we overthrew the Spartan garrison that occupied Thebes."

"The Spartans occupied Thebes?"

"That's right, they took over after the war against Athens. Once Athens was defeated, the Spartans didn't stop there. They made us, their former ally, a vassal. They left a garrison and made us pay a large tribute."

"Macedonia is in that situation now. Although there is no garrison, we have to pay tribute to Illyria."

"Then we are the same. After many years, our general Epaminondas led a revolt against them," the older man said. "If we don't train, the Spartans could try take Thebes back, or another enemy could try to occupy us. We will never allow that to happen."

All the Thebans nodded.

We are the same. The words echoed in Philip's head; these men *were* in the same situation as him. A country or a city in a constant, never-ending state of war. He had so many more questions to ask.

"Are you men provided with equipment? What do you do for a living? For work?" he asked.

"I'm a-"

"Back to training!" the officers boomed, standing with their hands cupped over their mouths.

"Thank you," Philip said and ran back towards the others.

Antigonus had been standing behind him and now they ran side by side back to the others.

The training lasted the rest of the day, and he returned to the estate exhausted. It seemed every part of his body hurt, but at the same time, he felt invigorated, his muscles felt relaxed, light even. He sat on the bench outside Pammenes villa, where they had their lessons, and thought of home.

Democracy was a strange concept for him, as for any of the Macedonians. These people all took responsibility for their city, without a king or nobleman forcing them to. Everything seemed so stable here, there was no struggle, the people were all well fed, and educated. Are we really barbarians as some of them believe? The soldiers were wealthy, certainly compared to any Macedonian infantrymen.

257

He went inside and was greeted by the aroma of jasmine. Briseis had filled a bath for him.

He got cleaned up and then spent the rest of the evening with Pelopidas, playing his game. The two relaxed on the balcony, drinking some wine, the gameboard between them.

"I am keen to hear your thoughts on the training?" Pelopidas asked.

"It was incredible," he said. "I spoke to some of the soldiers today. They told me all about citizenship, and how they all want to fight for a common cause, to protect Thebes. It's nothing like Macedonia. We have a king who gives orders, and has to keep the nobility in line."

"I'm glad you're learning, and you're seeing the differences between our states. The idea of the citizen is different from what you are used to; everyone in Thebes is happy for now, we are hegemon of the Greeks, the battle of Leuctra put us in that position. But it gets better."

"Better?" Philip leaned in, intrigued.

"Yes, hoplites are wealthy men, not necessarily as wealthy as nobles in your country, but still, being a hoplite is a wealthy man's pursuit. We plan to build a navy."

"A navy?" he asked, then took a moment to think about it. "I see, you beat Sparta on the land and now you want to beat Athens at sea?"

Pelopidas smiled and sat back. "Yes," he pointed his finger and then sat back forward, leaning close to Philip, "but not just that, we do it so that even more of the people will feel the way the men you spoke to today feel."

"What do you mean?"

"Athens is the best example; to earn your citizenship there, you don't need to fight as a hoplite, you can row in the Navy aboard a trireme. This requires no equipment at all, so any man can do it, not just the wealthy ones. We are on the cusp of something very big."

Philip sat pondering this, empowering all the people the way the soldiers had spoken today would be a very powerful thing.

"But of course, we also want to rival Athens for control of the trade routes in the Aegean, and our part of the Mediterranean."

"I see why you want Macedonia on your side now. But we would still be no more than a vassal."

"Not at all Philip; you have something we want, and we have something you want. Do you know what that makes us? Partners. Allies."

Chapter 22

In Pella the sun had almost gone down, and the moon already hung in the sky as a perfect silver disc. Perdiccas thought of Philip. A full year had passed since they had been informed of him being moved to Thebes, and he missed his brother. He strolled amongst the crowds of people who had gathered to celebrate the coming of spring. Perdiccas had been there every previous year as far back as when they were boys and had been allowed to attend. Philip's absence was felt. When they were very small, they were not allowed because of the animal sacrifices; now he was older and had witnessed many.

Festivities were already underway, and a large number of the women had left to perform their own rituals out in the forest; what this entailed he could only imagine as no men were allowed to witness this.

He was in the open reception area of the theatre outside the palace. The nobility and other people pottered about, enjoying the cool of the evening; he could make out smiling faces in the soft glow of the torchlight and two young boys ran past giggling, playing chase. The air was warm but was beginning to cool down, the night would be frosty as was normal for the time of year, but the snows in the mountains had melted, and the rivers were flowing again. Farmers rejoiced at being able to water their crops once again. Alongside him walked Polyperchon whom he had met up with outside the gate.

"Have you heard from Philip?" Polyperchon asked him.

"Nothing for a while, since being moved to Thebes. He's living with some politician there; I think his name is Pammenes."

"Aaahh," Polyperchon said, "I've heard of him. He is a very successful general, supposedly he's a generous man, very charitable, but he also likes to show off his wealth."

This news made Perdiccas feel better, having not heard from Philip in months and knowing he had been mistreated at the hands of Bardylis in Illyria, he feared for his brother's safety. The attendees filed into the theatre, a tiered semicircle with stone seats which was built into a hollow in the side of the hill. The two were directed up the stairs that flanked the seating on both sides, and were ushered into the row about ten rows back from the front. Others that were seated already stood up and tucked themselves back to allow them to pass. They sidestepped along, facing the front, and took a couple of empty seats in the middle near the royal seats.

After a short while, when all the guests were seated, an actor appeared wearing a long flowing chiton in white, and a mask depicting a large, exaggerated face of Hades, God of the underworld, his features gaunt and twisted. The chatter of the crowd died down.

The actor moved on to a spot in the centre of the floor and stood on the circular stone platform that was there for delivering monologues. He raised one arm and although he was far away, he could be heard clearly. He began talking about his lust for the goddess Persephone, and how he would have her. The acoustics of the theatre had always amazed Perdiccas since he was a small boy, how the shape had been determined by mathematics to project sound so far.

"It's good to hear. I don't know anything about the man, and Thebes is so much further away than Illyria," Perdiccas said.

"Don't worry yourself, he is much safer there than in Illyria."

"I suppose, but it would be better if he was home now. Spring is here, the war will resume."

"Don't worry, soon that bastard Ptolemy will be dead, his rebellion will be put down, his accomplices stoned, and Alexander will be hailed a hero."

The two paused to watch the actors on the stage. Hades had abducted Persephone, he carried her down into the underworld, and so the over world had become a cold and frozen wasteland. The other gods, especially her mother Demeter, became concerned that winter seemed to have become permanent, for it was Persephone that brought the spring. The other gods frantically searched for her.

"I hope so, he betrayed all of us," Perdiccas said "I can't believe what he did to us, he was like a brother to Alexander and I."

On the stage Apollo and Hermes had found Persephone and brought her back, but she had been tricked by Hades; any food or drink that he had given her would cause her to be trapped there forever. He had offered her a pomegranate of which she had eaten six of the twelve seeds.

The narrator now moved out onto the acoustic spot. "The goddess Persephone must return to her husband Hades for six months of the year; now winter is gone, and we welcome her back, she brings with her the spring," he said.

There was a storm of applause, and a standing ovation from all around. Perdiccas' ears twitched at the deafening noise. Polyperchon and he also rose to their feet and clapped until their hands stung. After a few moments, all the actors came back out, removed their masks, linked arms and bowed. The whole stage was then cleared, the applause died down and the audience retook their seats.

"Is it time for Alexander's dance?" Polyperchon asked.

"Yes," Perdiccas said, "Now that he is King, he must assume his role as head priest."

"What does he do? I have never attended before."

"He is going to make a tribute to the gods, and tell them that the war is back on. His troops are still in Thessaly. He is going to leave for Delphi in the morning to consult the Oracle. If the omens are good, then he will join his men and march."

A formation of warriors filed out wearing white cloaks, and stood where the actors had been, Alexander led them. They stripped naked; their bodies were covered in war paint. Priests in white cloaks followed them out and stood behind them.

They began chanting, stomping their feet in the dry dirt. They banged their hands against their forearms.

Drums began to beat, Perdiccas could feel the vibrations in his chest and his heart seemed to fall into harmony with the sound.

"I myself am not one for these old superstitions," Polyperchon said.

"Nor am I," Perdiccas said, "but it does no harm."

Alexander and his men fell to the floor at the climax of the dance; Perdiccas could see that he was panting for breath, his chest rising and falling rapidly. They stood up and put their cloaks back on.

Perdiccas heard the droning of a cow, and looked over to the entrance to the theatre; a huge white bull that was to be sacrificed was led in by a group of priests wearing laurel wreaths and carrying staffs. The beast was chained around the neck; it too wore a golden laurel wreath on its head, its back covered in rose petals, and its horns had been painted gold.

The bull was held in place as the priests now chanted; one stood alongside it and stroked its neck. They banged their staffs on the ground, the crowd watching in anticipation. The chants grew faster and louder, building and building. Then they stopped.

Alexander stood opposite the great beast, as his sword bearer approached him with his head bowed, holding the sword above his head in its sheath, the handle pointing towards the king.

Perdiccas fought the urge to look away; he never enjoyed sacrifices, but understood that it was necessary to please the gods. He focused his vision on the sword. Alexander reached out for it. As his arm stretched out, the hooded priest next to his sword bearer stepped forward and grabbed him by the wrist. With his free hand he drew a dagger and plunged it up and sideways into Alexander's armpit. He turned the handle in and drove it hard, so the blade penetrated deep into his torso.

People in the crowd screamed.

Perdiccas felt his jaw drop. He rose to his feet in a daze, watched Alexander push forward and place his hands on his attacker's throat, but he simply took a step back away from him. The sword bearer had unsheathed the weapon and had it trained on Alexander.

Alexander lurched forward as if he was going to fight back, fists raised, then took a few lumbering steps to the side. He felt his armpit. A stream of blood now gushed out from under his arm. He staggered for a moment then fell face down in the dust, a pool of blood widening around him.

Panic had taken hold of the audience. People screamed and ran in all directions. Perdiccas tried to make his way along the stand to get to his brother, but Parmenion and a group of the Royal Guard closed in around him. He tried to run by climbing back over the seats but they were blocking his escape.

As he turned back, Polyperchon put his arms around him, then held him at arm's length and looked him in the eye. "It's okay, they're here to protect you."

Perdiccas felt himself being shaken. Polyperchon's words seemed muffled and far away. The screams all around him also seemed distant. He felt as though he was going to vomit. The Royal Guard had formed the perimeter around him, and then the realisation struck him, that he was now the heir to the throne.

"We need to get him out of here," Parmenion shouted in the ear of Polyperchon over the noise of the crowd. "There could be more of them, he could be a target as well."

Polyperchon nodded, and the men in their hoplite armour and helmets stayed close with him. They started to make their exit down the end of the aisle, ushering Perdiccas with them.

They got down onto the ground and started to move away towards the palace. Perdiccas pushed the burly soldiers apart. "No, I need to see my brother," he shouted.

"No, it's too dangerous," Parmenion said. "We don't know what's happened. We don't know who hired the assassin. They could be looking for you too."

Perdiccas looked over toward Alexander's body, a crowd of the nobility standing around him. His arm protruded out from the sea of legs, the fingers hanging limp. The men had their backs turned away so he could not tell who they were. He stepped away from his

265

protectors, but they stayed in a tight semicircle around him to protect his back and sides. He approached the body slowly

"What happened? Why did no one…" he asked the men who stood around the body.

They separated to let him in, none made eye contact. He felt lightheaded at the sight of his brother. They had rolled him over, his face calm and placid, his eyes stared up at nothing. Perdiccas' mind flashed back to only a few moments ago when it was in a tight grimace. His skin was already pale from the bleeding. His eyes seemed sunken in their sockets.

His cloak had been pure white before, but was now crimson red like a Spartan's. It was torn under the arm that had been stabbed, exposing the wound that had killed him. The threads that had been cut splayed out loosely, unraveled like the strings of the muscle that had been ripped underneath.

He was nauseated, and placed the top of his fist over his mouth. His head still pointed down towards Alexander's body. He glanced up at the nobles and recognised a face he did not expect to see. He stood upright in shock.

"Ptolemy?"

…..

Philip was at Pelopidas' house again. His visits there had become more frequent. He had spent the autumn and winter mostly studying under Pammenes during the day, but had spent fewer and fewer nights at his estate, choosing instead to stay with Pelopidas.

The army had disbanded when the winter had arrived. The grain supplies were low even though, compared to Macedonia in winter, Philip had found the weather mild. Since spring had arrived, the soldiers had reconvened and he trained more and more with them.

266

The evening started with another game of Potteia.

"Your instructors all sing your praises Philip," he said, sitting back and taking a sip of his wine. "They say you never give up, and that your skill has vastly improved."

"I have learned so much from the hoplites, but I want more, I want to learn how to command an army like you and Epaminondas do," he said.

Pelopidas mouth curled up at the corners in a subtle smile. "Why do you think we play this game so often? Why do you think Pammenes takes you riding? Do think it was an accident that you are living with him? Or that you have already been introduced to Epaminondas? The man practically owns Thebes. If we weren't a democracy, he would be our king."

Philip was confused. He didn't understand and made a few stammering attempts at an answer, and he finally said, "I hadn't given it any thought."

"I know," Pelopidas said nodding again. "This game teaches you basic strategy, flanking, pincering, we needed to know if you could pick these things up, Philip. These are skills you'll need." He paused and took a sip of wine. "Politics is a snake pit, even here within Thebes, where we are all supposed to be on the same side. You pay attention, you take in everything you see and hear. I know this, but you are still very young. You seek a war. War should only be used when politics fails. Good men have been defeated without even reaching the battlefield. A knife in the back can end it all."

Philip's thoughts went to his father; he had fought many battles and had been betrayed by people close to him. He nodded, taking in every word.

"You will be trained with the army, but we'll also tutor you in politics and matters of state," Pelopidas said, "and not just the general things you have been learning here. We want to teach you some of our most closely guarded secrets."

Philip was overjoyed, although he did his best to hide it. He smiled. "Thank you."

Pelopidas face was deadly serious now. "Philip, the others do not know that you know this, you cannot let on that I have told you."

"Why? Why wouldn't they want me to know?"

Then the reality of it struck Philip; he had been caught up in the emotion that they were going to give him everything he had wanted. He looked Pelopidas in the eye. He didn't move. Philip was very familiar with this look; he was frozen, unable to respond. "You want to make me a vassal? A puppet king? Another pretender?"

"No," Pelopidas said softly, raising a hand to calm Philip down.

Philip stood up, enraged and flipped the table with the food and wine over, the playing pieces scattering all over the floor. "You think you can act like the gods moving the mortals around in their games! Or Bardylis?"

"You can trust me Philip," Pelopidas pleaded with him. "You're going to be a great man, even if you never return to Macedonia. I will speak to Epaminondas soon to accelerate your lessons."

"Then what? Would you have me stab my brothers in the back?"

"Philip!" Pelopidas shouted.

But Philip had already stormed out. The shouts were behind him. He ran out of the house into the streets. His sandals pattered on the cobblestones as he ran.

Even if you never return to Macedonia. These words echoed in his mind the whole way back to Pammenes estate.

The next morning Antigonus came to the estate to join Philip for another lecture.

After they broke for a short recess, Pammenes returned to his house. The moment he was out of earshot he turned to Antigonus.

"Their plan is to make me a puppet king in Macedonia," he said.

"What? How can they do that? Alexander is our king. Would they not be better to favour him?"

"I don't know, I suppose so; they are probably either bribing him or bullying him, but I'm here," Philip said, he scratched his chin. "They have all of us, most of the first generation of Macedonia's nobles. If they teach us their ways, bend us to think like them-"

"Then what?"

"They're not planning for right now, they're thinking ahead. They may be plotting to kill my brothers, then put me in their place."

"We have to warn them," Antigonus said. "Should we try and escape?"

"No," Philip said. "Not yet anyway, I'm going to go along with it, learn everything I can from them until I need to. Use them like they're using me."

"Okay, but what if they do kill Alexander to put you in his place?"

"I've thought about that. I don't think they would kill him; it goes against everything that they've been trying to achieve. To have a stable, strong Macedonia that could be their vassal state, another dead king in less than a year would be counterproductive."

Antigonus stayed silent. Philip looked him in the eye, he looked as though he wanted to ask something.

269

"What is it?" he said.

"That's not what I meant."

"What did you mean?"

"Would you *want* to be king?"

Philip had never considered whether he would want to be king for a moment, all his life had been spent trying to be a soldier for his brother. Would he be a good king? He had plans to improve the army, and now he had been getting all these lectures from Pammenes about politics. After a year here, he would probably be more ready than Alexander to rule.

"Definitely not," he said. "I would never conspire against my brothers."

"But what if he and Perdiccas died, and these Thebans decided to send you home to be king?"

"Food is on the table!" Pammenes voice interrupted them.

"Coming," Philip shouted back. "We need to stop talking about this now."

The conversation changed as they headed into the house.

Chapter 23

Philip played in the heat with the other Macedonian youths; it was now almost summer, and the days had started to become extremely hot around midday. Since the fight with Pelopidas, he had not been back to visit him.

The youths laughed and joked with each other around the pond in Pammenes strolling garden, diving in and swimming to cool off in the midday heat. He was joined by Antigonus and several of the other Macedonians who had travelled with them to Thebes. The day was hot, and they dived in and splashed each other, wrestling and laughing. They were watched by ever present guards who were always there to keep an eye on the young Macedonians; today they had moved to sit under the shade of the trees; the sun was high, and to stand in the direct light of it for long would cause the skin to burn, even for the southern Greeks who were used to it.

A group of the servant girls, who were having a rest from their duties, came and sat on a grassy knoll to watch the boys play, and before long they noticed them as well.

"Girls!" Antigonus shouted to them, and climbed out of the water, swaggering toward them, his muscular body glistening. He shook the water out of his hair like a dog. "Come join us."

The girls followed him back down the hill and they joined in the fun.

Among all the splashing and pushing, Philip looked through the group which seemed to part, and his eyes met with those of Briseis. Her eyes were low and she smiled a playful smile at him, then lowered her hand and splashed him in the face with a huge spray of water.

He gasped and coughed, shocked at what she had done, and he chased her, scooped her up and threw her into the water. She screamed and laughed as she regained her footing. She splashed at him as she tried to run away and lifted her knees high in an attempt to get through the waist high water faster, but he caught up with her, and grabbed her from behind and pulled her in close to him. She flicked water in his eyes and he wiped them, pulled her in close, leant in and kissed her; she kissed him back and, when it ended, they stared into each other's eyes. The sounds of the others melted away and they seemed to be the only two people in the world.

"Philip!" a man's voice shouted. They were dragged back to reality; the moment was broken.

"Philip!" The voice came again; Philip stared into Briseis eyes for another second, then looked around to see who the shouts had come from. He saw Pelopidas standing a short distance from the edge of the pond, he wore his travelling clothes. He was dismounted, but his body guard of about twenty men sat behind him on their horses, one held his horse by the bridle; the animals were fully laden with supplies. His expression was serious, no, sombre.

"By the gods, what has happened?" Philip said, under his breath. Briseis was the only one close enough to hear it, and she must have, because she pulled him a little closer trying to comfort him.

He pulled away from her and ran to Pelopidas.

"What has happened?" he asked, breathing hard from the sprint.

Pelopidas beckoned Philip to step close to him, looking over his shoulder at the Macedonian youths;

Philip turned to look at them, and they had stopped what they were doing to watch. Briseis looked concerned.

"Philip, I'm so sorry. There is no easy way to tell you this," Pelopidas said awkwardly, flexing his jaw from side to side, and clawing his beard. "Reports are your brother... Alexander."

Philip felt the dread rise in him. His throat was a knot.

"What happened?" he asked, but he already knew the answer.

"Philip, he's dead."

Philip was not sure how to react. He fidgeted, and he could not muster any words, so he stood in silence. He looked at the ground and twisted his foot in the dirt.

"Are you okay?" Pelopidas asked. "I am going north with my men to secure the kingdom, keep the peace and protect Perdiccas. I will see you when I return."

"How did he die?" Philip regained his senses and bared his teeth. "What did you do?"

"We did nothing," Pelopidas said. "We're not sure what happened, the rumour is that he was assassinated by Ptolemy."

"What?"

"Yes, Ptolemy."

"Why? I can't believe it. Why would Ptolemy? He was like a brother to Alexander. They had their differences, but-"

"He must have his eyes on the throne. I'm going to head there as quickly as I can to investigate. We don't know anything for certain yet. Ptolemy is married to your sister, and so, if it's true, he may have been planning this for a long time, to take the throne."

"I have to come with you. I need to see my- "

"No," Pelopidas said, "I will have to tread carefully. You will be safer here."

"I don't care if I'm safe, I have to see them."

"I have arranged for you to be guarded all day every day by the Sacred Band. You will sleep in the barracks with them. Pammenes' estate is no longer safe enough, until we establish what has happened. I promise I will return soon. We have bridges to mend, but right now Macedonia is more important."

With that, Pelopidas and his entourage left.

They left behind ten men from the Sacred Band that shadowed Philip's every move; they slept in shifts and guarded him day and night.

With Pelopidas gone, Philip drifted around the estate for days, not knowing what to do with himself. He walked around the gardens. The men who had been sent to protect him did not interact with him at all; they kept their distance, and when he did try and approach and talk to them, they moved away or ignored him.

He wanted to cry. He had not done this since he was a small child; but he could not, he didn't want to show weakness in front of the Sacred Band.

He was alone at night, left in privacy. The guards sat out on the balcony and outside the door. They slept in shifts in the room adjacent to Philip's. His thoughts went back to the hunting trip in the woods, when he had killed his man. He clawed his mind for a memory, even a fragment of a memory of Ptolemy. Father had been suspicious of him. Had he fought with them? Had he killed any of the would-be assassins?

He couldn't remember if he had even been present when they were attacked. Had he protected my father, or had he fled? He needed to remember.

He thought of his father, and now Alexander, in the underworld. His eyes began to well, his cheeks squeezed out tears that stung his eyes as they ran, and dripped onto his bed linen.

….

The following morning Philip sat out at the stone benches where he was normally lectured by Pammenes.

He waited for his tutor to arrive, but there was no sign of him; this had happened more and more frequently of late.

Pammenes spent almost the whole day, every day, in the city, dealing with governing with his peers, leaving Philip with nothing to do. He spent most of his time exercising or down at the stables with the horses, grooming them and riding the ones he was permitted to. Even when he went for a stroll, his Sacred Band bodyguard were there. He watched their routine.

There were usually ten of them, five older men and five younger men; Philip thought of the rumoured tradition of the Sacred Band, that they were all pairs of lovers. In battle this would encourage them to fight harder, so as not to embarrass themselves or let their partner come to harm if they were defeated. He wondered if this really made a difference. The same was true of Sparta, but all of their male citizens over a certain age would be part of this, some ten thousand. In Thebes, the Sacred Band reportedly only numbered three hundred.

The idea that they were couples certainly seemed true from what he had observed of the guards. He had caught two that were off duty bickering as lovers would, the older man lecturing his younger peer. As soon as they had noticed him, they stopped.

When Pammenes didn't show he sighed, took the beautiful Thessalian mare and met with Antigonus. He was being well treated, even though he was not close to the inner circle of the rulers of Thebes as Philip was.

"I love it here, but it's becoming very difficult to distract myself and not think about home," he said.

"No, we should never forget; we will return, mark my words," Antigonus said, his eyes narrowed and his head made small nods.

"I don't think we'll ever go back, it's too dangerous," Philip said, his demeanour low and sorrowful. "Now there will be a lot of pretenders aside from the ones we know about, ready to kill me and Perdiccas. Now that I think about it, I don't know whether I want to go back."

Antigonus did not hide his disapproval.

"Philip, we will go back. Do not forget who you are, we are not Thebans. You can't abandon Perdiccas? We have to do what we can," he said firmly. Philip looked at his friend, thinking how unbending and unbreakable he was, a rock.

"But what am I supposed to do from here? I don't want to abandon my brother, but I'm a fucking prisoner here," he said, raising his voice. "If Ptolemy has taken the throne, then we're fucked, Perdiccas will already be dead, my mother is most likely dead. All our allies have probably been threatened or bribed-"

Antigonus put his hands on Philip's shoulders. Even though he was not trying to hurt Philip, just trying to help him gain control of himself, his hands felt heavy, his grip iron. "Then we learn everything we need to learn here, and when we're ready…" he said, and paused, looking over at the Sacred Band guards, who were far away enough not to hear, then he whispered, "then we run home, we kill Ptolemy, and you will be King."

….

There was another gathering at Pammenes' house a few weeks later. Many guests milled around drinking,

276

talking, and laughing. They were all familiar to Philip now, their faces at least, but he didn't really talk to them as they went about getting stupefied with drink. His thoughts dwelled on his family. He leaned against the wall in the corner of the guest receiving-area of the house. As the attendees mingled, Philip kept his head low and tried to avoid any eye contact, so he would not be drawn into any conversations.

A tall handsome man stood talking to a beautiful woman; she was feigning disinterest, but he spoke softly into her ear while she was turned away. She was smiling a teasing smile; she reminded Philip of Arsinoe.

A group of men who looked like soldiers, having the build and swagger about them, laughed boisterously and slapped each other's backs. They were playing a game where one man would bang his cup on the top of the others, trying to cause him to spill it. One of their cups was struck and wine lapped up, soaking his hand; they erupted with laughter as he shook it off, then licked the back of his hand.

Pammenes and his closest friends stood together, and although Philip could not hear what they were saying over the ambient hubbub of the room, the topic of conversation was no doubt politics or history. Philip now had a great interest in these, but did not feel like joining in. The absence of Pelopidas and Epaminondas made the crowded room seem empty somehow. Pammenes noticed him and beckoned him over. "Philip, come join us, young man, we are discussing your ancestor Heracles."

Philip waved and shook his head, smiling with just his mouth. He leaned against the wall at the back of the room where no one looked directly at him. The atmosphere of the place was cheery and relaxed, but he did not feel like talking to anyone. As his eyes moved across the room, he spotted Briseis making sure the guests' cups were filled. He downed his drink and wiped his mouth with the back of his hand.

He stumbled as he stepped down to get more wine, and stared into the bottom of his cup, the metal rim swayed, everything felt slowed down. Even people's voices and laughter around him, felt muffled. Servants passed him and filled his cup, and he returned to his spot against the wall.

A lot of the faces around were familiar to him now, but he missed Macedonia. When would he be able to go home? His thoughts inevitably went back to Arsinoe, the shape of her waist, the softness of her lips, and the deep pools of her eyes. He would have to keep his relationship with Pelopidas a secret, if it was still a relationship. How would anyone find out anyway? Nobody knew about it here, never mind in Macedonia.

"-And how are you getting on, young Prince?"

His thoughts were interrupted by one of the guests. Philip recognised the man, but could not place him; he was about the age of Pelopidas, maybe a little younger. He wore a pristine white tunic; Philip could tell from his physique that he had been athletic when he was younger, the muscle tone was there, if a little softer than it had been, but he now had a little bit of a stomach that his tunic draped over. Probably from too much wine and food at these parties Philip thought. The man had a gorgeous young woman hanging on one arm and a handsome youth on the other, neither were much older than Philip, and they were both clearly very drunk. The youth was having trouble standing upright and hung on the man's arm for balance. The woman seemed more balanced, but her eyes were glazed. She stared Philip in the eye; her look alone made Philip begin to feel aroused.

278

The man smiled a wide warm smile, and patted Philip on the shoulder.

"I'm very well, and yourself?" Philip replied politely, trying to place him. However, he clearly saw through his attempts.

"You're having trouble placing me, aren't you?" he said, again with the warm grin spreading from cheek to cheek.

"I- "

"Oh, don't worry about it," he said. "You must have met many people while you've been here; impossible to remember all of them, I expect."

"You're right, my apologies, who are you again?"

"Pagondas, I'm a statesman, much like Pelopidas and Pammenes here," he said. "You know your accent is starting to be a little less strong, not coming through as much."

"Oh? I hadn't given it much thought," Philip said, pausing to ponder it. "Pelopidas hasn't- "

"Yes, now that Pelopidas is going to be away for a while, if you want to... You know..." he said, taking a pause and pointing to the girl and youth with the side of his head, "we're going to be going somewhere a little more private soon, and would love it if you would join us."

"No thanks," Philip said.

"Come with us," said the girl, her voice softer than Aphrodite's. Philip watched her full red lips move as she spoke, time slowed by the wine. She stroked the back of Philip's hand, so gently, his breath murmured, the back of his neck tingled, and he moved below the waist. "You'll enjoy it, I always wanted a Macedonian."

"Really, I'm flattered, but I'll wait for Pelopidas for when he gets back."

"Very well young man, the offer's always there if you change your mind," he said, winked, turned and left with the two on his arms.

Philip stood, thinking about whether he should take the man up on his offer, and then it struck him like a lightning bolt. He knows about me and Pelopidas. The thought was sobering. If he knows, how many other people know? And *who* knows? How did he find out? He shrunk back against the wall, looking side to side at the guests. They continued to laugh and joke, and talk and drink and kiss. No one so much as looked up at him.

Among the crowd he picked out Briseis pouring drinks for the guests. He headed at pace across the room towards her, almost tripping on a couch and then a plant pot. His vision was a bit blurry now that he had moved. He took her by the hand and led her to his chambers.

Chapter 24

Several weeks passed. Philip and Briseis had been meeting regularly; she spent a lot of her nights in his chambers.

The two lay in bed together after she had spent the night. Philip rolled over toward her warmth and smelled her hair, that scent of jasmine reminded him of Arsinoe, and he immediately felt guilty. He had tried to stay faithful to her, but then he had taken a second, and now a third lover.

There was a bang at the door that jarred them both awake. "Urgent message for you Prince!" a muffled voice shouted through the heavy oak door.

They covered themselves up with the bedsheet.

"You can come in," Philip shouted back.

Pammenes' head slave entered the room and gave a bow. He headed for the curtains and threw them open. Light burst into the room and both Philip and Briseis flinched, covering their eyes and groaning. He handed Philip a sealed scroll. He reached up and took it, still squinting.

"The General's own man dropped this off at the gate," Pammenes' slave said, bowed again, and left.

"Thank you," Philip said. He examined the scroll; the wax seal was red as blood, and it did belong to Pelopidas. Philip's shoulders grew tense, anxious to hear of home. His heart raced as he broke the seal. The paper tried to curl back up as he unravelled it, as if the scroll did not want to be read. He read it regardless.

Hail Philip,
I trust this letter finds you well. I write to you with the deepest sadness and regret at having to leave you so

*abruptly and with our unsettled business. Your brother's
murder was a cowardly act.*

*After hearing of the death of Alexander, Pausanias,
a son of Archelaus, a distant relative of yours has
started an invasion of Macedonia, staking his claim to
the throne. He has captured the cities of Anthemis,
Strepsa and Therme in the Chalcidice with an army of
Greek mercenaries. This puts him within easy striking
distance of Pella.*

*My spies inform me that he is sponsored by
Athenian gold. I am yet to establish if this is true, as you
know, tensions between Thebes and Athens are high, but
we will not risk our friendship with your country and
allow Athens to become master of Macedonia.*

*I have taken command of the northern Theban army
and have hired a number of mercenaries from Thrace to
meet with this Pausanias and get the measure of him. I
will write to you when the outcome is known.*

*That is not the worst of it, because Perdiccas, who
in all other respects is capable of ruling the country, is
not backed by your Macedonian council; they say he is
not old enough. The reality I feel is that he does not
have the connections. To this end, I have had to appoint
Ptolemy of Aloras as regent over your brother. I know
there will be a lot of bad blood between the two of you,
though I have his assurance that your brother is safe.
Ptolemy will not dare cross me.*

*I beg you not to think less of me, this was the only
way to prevent a full-scale war; your brother, sister and
mother would have been murdered, and Macedonia
would be torn apart.*

*I know that you can be trusted and as such
Epaminondas and I have agreed to start your military
training with the Sacred Band.*

We will make you a great general and when you return to Macedonia it will be stronger than ever before, and we will become great allies.

We will talk when I return to Thebes.

Yours
Pelopidas

Philip let out a long breath, crushed the note into his fist and let it fall to the ground.

"What is it?" Briseis asked him. She sat up and put her arms around his waist and began kissing the back of his shoulder.

He shrugged her off.

"I'm not in the mood," he said. "My brother, he…"

"It's okay," she said, "You can tell me."

"I need to leave. I'm going to go back home"

He got up and started to get dressed. Briseis slid out and picked up the scroll from the floor. She unraveled it and began to read. She smiled still looking down at the paper.

"But Pelopidas," she said. "He wants you to train with the Sacred Band."

"I didn't think slaves could read?" Philip asked, surprised.

She smiled again and looked him in the eye. "My master taught me," she said. "Pammenes likes us all to be able to-"

"Okay," Philip said, and thought nothing else of it. It did sound like educating his slaves was something Pammenes would do.

"Philip, you have to stay, I'll miss you so much," she said. She got up and moved over to him seductively, the bed cover falling away revealing her naked body. She strolled over and put her hands on his hips.

"No, I have to go," he said, shrugging her off again and continuing to get dressed. "My brother will need me. I hope I will see you again."

"And what do you plan to do when you get there?"

"I don't know, I'll think of something."

"You will be violating the treaty with Thebes. You're supposed to be here as a ward."

Philip felt himself starting to breathe harder, his anger starting to build. "I have to go now. I don't care about the treaty," he lied. He didn't think it was a good plan either.

He was now fully dressed, and made for the door. He swung it open, but only managed to get it half-way when Briseis darted after him, swift as a cat, and pulled him back by the arm, her nails cut into his skin and he squeezed his lips in pain.

"Ptolemy will have you killed. It will do your family no good if you go there to die. You have to stay. Training with the Sacred Band is the only chance you'll have to defend Macedonia when you go home."

"Why do you care so much about it?" Philip asked.

She lowered her head and smiled, stroking his hand.

"I just worry about you," she said. And started to lead him back to the bed.

Philip sighed, and looked her in the eye.

"Okay," he said. "Okay."

That night a messenger arrived who had been sent by Epaminondas, telling Philip that the next day he was invited to come and train with him. He was torn. After Briseis had left he had again fought the urge to run back to Macedonia, but then he regained his senses, and he knew that what she had said made perfect sense. He would stay, train, and gain the favour of Epaminondas, and learn how to command. Then he would hopefully return home with an army of Thebans at his back.

Pelopidas was true to his word. The next morning one of Epaminondas' officers arrived just before dawn to get Philip out of bed. Philip was not prepared for a man to march into his room and tell him to get up before the sun had even begun to rise. The officer stood at the end of his bed and coughed, with a deliberate loudness. Philip yawned and rubbed his eyes, Epaminondas's officer stood over him, becoming less patient. He coughed again, even louder. In the limited light Philip caught a glimpse of the officer; his hair was dark, but a hint of grey shone in the moonlight. On his cheek was a long, ragged scar that ran along it from the corner of his mouth to his ear. It looked as though the weapon that had done it had been dull, and had taken a large piece of flesh with it. A veteran.

"Is it still night?" Philip asked.

"Hurry Philip! Let's get going!" he barked. Philip jumped out of bed and hopped as his feet touched the cold tiles of the floor. The officer sighed impatiently, and Philip hurried to pull some clothes on. Before he was even fully dressed, the officer was halfway out the door.

They travelled out to the parade grounds, which Philip was very familiar with after all the time he had spent there training. The vast space was mostly empty, save for the three hundred men of the Sacred Band who were training at one end. Philip wondered where everyone else was. It was still dark outside, but the brilliant orange light of the dawn was beginning to creep over the horizon.

"The citizens will arrive later, only the Sacred Band train for so long," the officer said. "And the cavalry."

"What training will I be doing?" Philip asked. He was ignored.

Tension arose in him again, his stomach fluttered. He would be judged, not just on himself, but Macedonia would be judged. They would size him up. Before, a simple rejection would simply have been an embarrassment, but now the stakes were much higher, he had to be trained in the ways of the Sacred Band. If they did not think he was up to it he would be sent back to Pammenes to simply be a hostage.

They had already been judging him, watching him from the moment he got there. He had been afraid of making himself and his people look weak, but this didn't matter anymore.

He would work his way up, and when he returned home, he would be the greatest general Macedonia had ever seen. I must not fail, he thought.

They were all out in groups of about thirty men; one group was being marched around the perimeter of the parade ground in full armour at a double time pace, carrying a weighted sack in each hand.

Another two groups were doing some kind of endurance exercise. They were arranged into two small phalanxes with no spears, simply armour and shields. The two formations faced each other as if on the battlefield. They pushed and shoved against each other, their muscles flexed and their feet dug into the ground. Instructors walking round the perimeter of the clash of flesh and metal, shouting their orders to different men inside the shield wall.

The others were involved in various drills like parrying shields and stabbing underneath, carried out with wooden swords.

This training put the Macedonians to shame, Philip thought, doing his very best to commit the drills to memory.

"I will find the General Epaminondas," the officer said, and left Philip standing alone.

He stood for a while watching the Sacred Band drill up and down their corner of the parade grounds. Their movements were so fluid as a group that it was as if they all had the one mind, as if they were being controlled by a god. They're so disciplined, he thought. His nerves quickly returned. He suddenly felt alone, and isolated, the absence of the other Macedonians, especially Antigonus, was uncomfortable, now it was just him and the Thebans.

A moment later his thoughts were interrupted when the ground began to shake, the dust on the ground became unsettled, and the small pebbles in it began to dance.

The cavalry arrived over the crest of the hill, fifty or so he guessed. When they rode into the open space of the parade ground they did not move in a straight line, they were arranged in a rhombus shape with an officer at each corner. When the formation turned, the officer that was now at the front took command. The formation changed direction quickly; they moved like a flock of birds weaving through the air. Philip stood in awe at how elegant it was.

He imagined he was with them, riding one of Pammenes' best horses, the Thessalian mare he loved, weaving and gliding, the wind rushing through-

"Come on Philip." His daydream was broken by the bark of the scarred veteran, who had returned. He then noticed one group of officers stood around in a circle while one drew in the sand with a stick; he looked up at Philip. The officer who had come to get him in the morning was present there as well. As Philip approached, he saw that the man with the stick was Epaminondas, and he beckoned Philip to approach. "Hail Philip," he shouted and held his hand up in a static wave.

"Hail Epaminondas," Philip shouted back, and all his tension melted away; he took a breath, something about Epaminondas's presence lifted his confidence; he raised his head and his chest. The rest of the group stopped what they were doing, all eyes on him. They all stared at him, studying him, but none made a sound, or smiled, or said anything. Philip gave them a nod of respect and then his eyes darted around, hoping for any kind of reaction out of any of them, but they just continued to stare.

Philip felt totally exposed, folding his arms in discomfort.

"Join us please, you're just in time. We were just about to head out for a forced march."

Epaminondas beckoned him into the group. The other officers parted to make space for him. A march? Good, he thought, that could have been far worse, he was fresh apart from the slight tenderness in his muscles from training the day before yesterday. The good kind of tenderness that comes from exercise, and makes the muscle feel stronger once it is gone.

The Sacred Band officers broke off from their circle, and went out to their separate commands, not one looked at him, he might as well have been invisible.

Philip stood dumbfounded; he swallowed a lump in his throat, his stomach fluttered. He then felt Epaminondas place his hand on his shoulder.

"Don't worry about them," he said. "They just feel respect should be earned. Here, take these."

He was handed a shield, spear, and helmet. They felt as if they were made of rock. The weight was unnaturally heavy.

"Training equipment weighs double that of what we use in battle. Training with this will make you twice as strong and fast," Epaminondas told him, then walked off to join his men.

Philip watched him leave, then followed him like a stray dog.

On the road outside the city, the Sacred Band marched with all their equipment. Philip ran with them; at first this was just a jog, his feet pounding on the ground; this was okay, he thought. He looked around a little and took in the scenery. The land around Thebes was dryer than Macedonia and there were less trees and other vegetation. The roads were much better constructed in this region than further north, and were flatter.

They ran in tight formation, shoulders brushing off each other, so he was enclosed, with men all around him. They were clad in bronze plate, eyes peering out from deep inside their Corinthian style helmets. Philip felt his breath coming back off the inside of his helmet into his face, and he only had a narrow view directly in front of him. They had not been out long, and it was already becoming stifling and claustrophobic.

He could hear the pounding of the men's feet all around him, the clicking of buckles in rhythm. He looked down. His shield had become burdensome and awkward already, the strap dug into his forearm and he shrugged it up, trying to rest the inside of the dome on his shoulder so that it would not drop; he would have liked to have held it in both hands, but carrying a spear in the other made this impossible.

The march was around the outside perimeter of the city walls, so the wall loomed over him to his right-hand side the whole way round; it provided welcome shade on the west side of the city, and reflected the sun on the east side, shining blinding light in his eyes.

Philip could tell that he had almost completed a circuit as the gate came back into view. His shoulders now felt as if they were being pulled apart, and he used his strength to keep them together; the straps of the cuirass dug into his flexed shoulders. He gulped for breath and his heart pounded as if it was a fist thumping inside his chest. His legs started to give up. He could taste metal in his mouth.

Some children sat on a grassy knoll opposite the gates and watched the Sacred Band run past, they waved to them, and some of them waved back.

Philip pushed harder and breathed deeper, relieved that it would soon be over.

As they approached the gate, to Philip's dismay, they ran straight past it. The Band then started to jog harder, and broke more into a run, not sprinting, but a very fast jog. He kept up with them for about half again, on sheer willpower and his ability to withstand pain. The men behind slowly began to pass him and pull away. He felt nauseated and had to stop. He bent over with his hands on his thighs gasping for breath. His heart felt as though it would punch its way out of his chest. He glanced up, not one of them looked back.

As quickly as he could, he moved to the side of the road and ripped his helmet off, the cool air rushing into his face. It felt glorious, but then the nausea came on much stronger and he lurched forward and vomited on the side of the road. He could hear the children laughing and kept his head down.

Wiping his mouth with the back of his hand, he walked along the wall back toward the gate. Once he was almost there, the Sacred Band ran past him and continued on their forced march, ignoring him.

Philip drifted along, through the gate and onto the parade ground, ashamed of his failure.

He walked to the far end of the dusty parade ground, and into the offices at the barracks, where he met Epaminondas. The general sat hunched over his desk, scribbling onto parchment with a feather pen. He paused and looked up as Philip entered.

"They left me behind," Philip said. His breathing and his heartbeat had almost returned to normal, but his skin was sticky with dry sweat and his body felt completely sapped of energy.

In the corner of the room, stood a dummy which was wearing Epaminondas's cuirass. Above the wooden shoulders supporting its weight, protruded a half sphere of wood in place of a head. Philip limped over and placed the helmet on it, and carefully leant the shield on the floor against it. He did the same with the spear and took a step back to admire the ornate armour of the general.

"Have a seat," Epaminondas said to him softly, dipping his pen in the ink pot and leaving it there.

Philip slumped down, barely able to stand. "I thought I was in good shape," he said.

"Don't worry young man, you did just fine. We know how much potential you possess."

Chapter 25

In Pella, darkness had fallen, the days getting shorter now that autumn was here. The air was heavy and thick, there been a thunderstorm earlier in the day, and the atmosphere felt as though another might be on its way. Perdiccas stood on his balcony under the cover of one of the drapes, and watched; occasional heavy raindrops fell from the sky and landed on the marble banister. He stared into the darkness, waiting. Father and Alexander would have taken this as a good omen from Zeus, he thought, but he did not have the same love for the gods that they had had.

There were lights from torches all around the palace grounds, and the lights of the city twinkled below and stretched out into the distance like the stars on a clear night. The chatter of the taverns and inns carried on the air. He could not see any movement, so waited a little longer. The torch above the gatehouse, the light from which had been stationary suddenly moved from side to side rapidly. Then it paused, and then the same again.

The signal.

He pulled the hood of his thick winter cloak up over his head, and went to one end of the balcony; he picked up the coil of rope that he had left there earlier. He looked at the knot already tied to the stone pillars of the banister and bit his lip, then threw the rope over the balcony. He sat up on the hard-stone banister, and swung his legs over.

Leaning over the edge he took a gulp, his heart in his mouth. It's only one floor, he thought, even if I fall it isn't that far, but the darkness shrouded the ground. He squinted down into the blackness in an attempt to see the grass below, but couldn't. He swung his feet back over into the room, and headed for the door. He stretched out his hand to pull on the handle; as he placed his hand on it, he stopped. There was a muffled cough from the other side and he froze. The guards were standing right outside.

Climbing off the balcony would be far less trouble than trying to avoid the guards outside the door, or try and explain to them why he was going out in the night. There was no way to tell who they would be loyal to. Even guards that were in principle loyal to the king could be bought for the right price, and Ptolemy was now in control of the palace treasury; he paid their wages, and could see to it that any "bonuses" might be paid, quietly of course, if he were to suffer a mishap.

He went back over to the balcony, swung his legs over, gripped the rope hard and gave it a quick tug. He took a deep breath, then stepped over the edge before he could give it too much thought. The rope creaked in his hands as he slid down.

He hit the bottom and fell hard. He waved his hands around in the dark to try and find something to orientate himself, his elbow throbbing from the fall, and he became aware that the callouses on the inside of his knuckles, the ones that he had built up from training with the spear and sword, had split on the rope. He picked them off and shook away the excess skin.

The hood of his cloak had fallen back; he lifted it up over his head again and made his way along in the dark, sticking close to the wall; the wet grass soaked through his shoes, and sent a chill through his toes. One of Parmenion's men met him at the gatehouse, the one who signaled with the torch. "Got a horse ready for you on the other side sire, the door's open," he said.

"Thank you. Your loyalty will be rewarded soldier," Perdiccas said and headed through the gate, took the horse's reins and climbed onto the animals back.

He rode out into the town, and made his way to the house of Parmenion,

The man had been doing very well for himself, amassing quite a lot of wealth and was well respected by most of the soldiers and the nobility alike. His house was in a modest walled estate in one of the better parts of Pella. Guards patrolled on top of the walls; looking up, he could see the tops of their heads, and their spears were visible against the pale moonlight.

Two of Parmenion's private guards were standing outside in the rain, at the main gate; one held his torch up to Perdiccas as he approached. As soon as he recognised him, he gestured for Perdiccas to follow him toward the house. Their feet splashed in the puddles as they crossed the paved courtyard. He knocked on the heavy wooden door. There was the screech of a heavy latch being opened from the inside.

There was a loud clunk, and the door creaked open, a streak of warm light spilling out into the courtyard. Another guard stood silhouetted on the inside.

"Welcome sire," the guard said and ushered him in with an open palm, stepping to the side to welcome him in. "The General is waiting for you in the main living area."

Perdiccas stepped into the hallway and brushed the rain off his cloak, and handed it to the guard. It dripped onto the tiled floor.

A small group of Parmenion's officers were gathered around the fireplace in the room. Parmenion was crouched in front of it, thrusting a poker into the coals which cracked and popped, the orange glow becoming brighter. He looked up when Perdiccas entered.

"Perdiccas," he said, and lowered his head.

"Parmenion," Perdiccas said. "Thank you for meeting with me, I know it isn't safe for you."

"I don't fear Ptolemy," he said. "I presume this is why we are meeting like this, to discuss Ptolemy?"

Perdiccas looked at the faces of the men that were in the room, illuminated in the glow of the fire.

"You can trust these men my King. Each and every one I would trust with my life. We are but a few of many that are unhappy with Ptolemy and stay loyal to the Argead line."

"Very well," he said, "that is why I am here."

They sat around on the couches that surrounded the fireplace.

"Well, I won't play games," he said, "I want him dead. When I am deemed old enough by the council there will be no need for a regent. I do not think he will let me see that day."

They all looked at each other.

"We all agree, Perdiccas."

"Good. I have a plan," he said. "I also know of someone who is unhappy under Ptolemy's thumb, someone who has been playing him for a while."

....

Philip sat in the main living area of the house with Pammenes, some of the other boys and Antigonus. Although winter was almost here, none of the Macedonians felt cold, but Pammenes insisted his slaves had the fires lit to keep the house warm. They had spent the morning revising economics, a subject that Philip had loathed at first, but had come to realise under Pammenes tuition that it was important for his desire to

295

be a soldier and a general; a strong army came out of having a strong economy. He talked about their own economy, and compared it to that of Athens.

"So, you see their fleet was built out of wood, but this would all come from your own country in Macedonia, purchased with the silver from the mines. Fleets cost a fortune," Pammenes said. Philip listened intently. "But if it's a fortune you seek, you have to look to East across the Aegean Sea, to Persia; rumour is they have wealth a thousand times what Athens has. Only accountants in the employ of the Great King will know for certain."

"A thousand times?" Philip asked. "There can't even be that much money in the entire world."

"But you see Philip, Persia is most of the world; we Hellenes, and you in Macedonia." Philip hid his disdain for Pammenes not including Macedonia as Greek, "are, in terms of land, tiny by comparison."

"How do you know this?"

"Because we were allied to the Persians during some of the Persian wars."

"What?" Philip said, "Thebes was allied to the Persians? And fought against other Greeks? Why would they do that?"

"Philip, please, it is not black and white, many Greek polis allied themselves to the Great King, as did your ancestors, Alexander, the first of course, not your brother."

"They what? I don't believe it." Philip rose from his bench.

"Believe me, the Macedonians under Alexander sided with Persia. It was the pragmatic thing to do. Look at the roads from along the coastal path from the Hellespont in the north to here. Who do you think built the roads? Persian engineers. The Macedonians would have been paid handsomely for their cooperation," he said, and looked around at the other boys to make sure they were paying attention. "Persians like to use bribery, remember that. If they have the funds to avoid a conflict, they will simply buy their opponent's submission, and that has proven most effective for them."

There was a long silence. Philip was angry and confused; he wanted to disprove what he was being told, but couldn't. Pammenes softened his voice and continued to speak.

"Anyway, we have strayed off the topic at hand. The wealth of Persia…"

Philip slumped back down onto his bench, and although he was listening to Pammenes, he did not take in any of the words being said. Did the Macedonians really sell out Greece to the Persians? He swore he would never make such a betrayal.

….

Queen Eurydice paced around the royal bedchamber, lighting the candles around the room. It was a cold night and the servants had lit a vast, roaring fire. It set the room in a beautiful orange glow.

She spread petals across the bed and took care to space them just right.

She poured wine in to two golden cups, and set them down on the bedside table. It was the finest vintage, and had been brought in from Kos at great cost, but it was Ptolemy's favourite.

She sat at the dressing table in front of the looking glass, and ran her hand through her hair. The servants had pinned it up to show her neck and shoulders, and she wore one of her silk nightgowns that draped over her figure, and showed just enough to drive him wild.

She opened the drawer and moved the contents to one side, and lifted out the small vial of hemlock she kept there. She stared at it in the palm of her hand, her heart beat harder.

She glanced over at the cups of wine. It had to be tonight. She walked over and tipped the contents into Ptolemy's cup, and sat staring at it.

She waited, but he did not show, so she paced around, scrutinising every detail of how she had set up the room and herself.

After a longer while, she sat on the bed and stared at her nails, and let out a sigh. Some of the candles had burnt down and needed replacing. Where could he be?

She opened the door. There were two guards standing outside.

"Sorry my Queen," one of them turned and said. "You know you are not allowed to leave without an escort, on Regent Ptolemy's orders."

She smiled softly at the guard. "I am not trying to leave. Do you know as to the whereabouts of the Regent?"

"I-"

There was a bang as the heavy doors at the end of the hall were thrown open and Ptolemy marched through them towards the bedchamber.

"Thank you," Eurydice said to the guard.

Ptolemy wore full armour, minus a helmet, and he marched straight past them into the bedchamber, frowning at the guards as he approached. They stood to attention. Eurydice followed him in and closed the door behind her.

He put his foot up on the chair of the dressing table and began to unbuckle his greaves.

"And where did you think you were going?" he asked, not looking at her.

"Nowhere. I was asking the guard if he knew when you would be back. I... have prepared..."

She paused as he looked around the room.

"I have to go back out. I need to meet with some members of the council."

"Why?"

"More tedious matters, got to sort out some loyalty issues with some of the nobles," he said.

She moved over and helped him take of his sword belt and placed it on the ground, and took his cuirass as he unbuckled it. She then started to massage his shoulders and neck while he unlaced his boot.

"I rather thought you would want to spend the night here," she said. "Your wine finally arrived from Kos. And I..."

She stopped as he took a long sniff of her perfume. She kissed the back of his neck and he stood up to face her.

Eurydice lowered her head, pouted her lips and batted her eyelashes.

Ptolemy paused and took a look around the room and another long sniff of her perfume.

"You haven't tried to seduce me like this since Alexander died," he said.

"Well," she said, pressing her body against his. "You have always protested your innocence; I believe you now."

He nodded slowly. "Like I told you, I had nothing to do with it. The assassin must have had a grudge for some reason."

"I know," she said, stroking his hand lightly with the tips of her fingers. She pressed her lips gently against his and he kissed her back. She took his hand and lifted it so that it cupped her breast, she felt her nipple start to harden.

He unbuckled his cuirass and his sword and placed them on the floor. They moved over to the bed and sat down side by side, and continued to kiss. Eurydice gently moved away, and picked up the wine cups. "Have a drink," she said.

She tried not to stare at the cup as he lifted it to his lips.

Good, she thought, die screaming, and when Thanatos drags you to Hades, you will spend all eternity paying for betraying my family and murdering my son.

He had only raised the cup slightly before he stopped, then lowered it. "No," he said, "I need a clear head for when I talk to these council members. We can continue this later."

He started to get up, so she squeezed his knee and started to kiss down his neck. She slid down to the floor so she was on her knees, and gently clawed the tops of his thighs with her finger tips.

"Please stay," she said, softening her voice. "I've been lonely. Can't it wait until tomorrow?"

She could see that he was looking down at her chest as he took a pause to ponder her question.

He sighed, "I suppose it could wait." He leant down and kissed her with his hands on her face.

"Thank you," she said. "Can you pass my cup? I'm thirsty."

He nodded and leant back, he passed her her cup, then raised his. She watched as he took a mouthful in. It is done, she felt herself smile.

Ptolemy's face changed. He frowned and spat the mouthful back into the cup.

Eurydice's heart thumped, she held her breath.

Ptolemy calmly sniffed the wine, slowly ran his finger around the rim of the cup, then rubbed the tips of his thumb and forefinger together. He stared at her hard.

"What is this?" he asked.

"What is what?" Eurydice said.

"Don't play stupid, woman. What is this? Smells like piss!"

"I hadn't noticed, the bottle must have leaked and it's mixed with the air."

He frowned and snatched her cup out of her hand. He smelled her wine.

"So why does yours smell fine?"

He stood up and pushed her to the side. He marched over to get his cloak which was draped over the chair by the dressing table.

She got up and followed him. "Ptolemy, I'm telling you, it must just be off."

As he placed his hands on the cloak, she noticed his sword on the ground. She snatched it up, unsheathed it as he turned, and slashed the tip across his neck.

He gargled and fell to his knees. He grabbed at his throat, blood gushing from the wound and splashing her, soaking her face and her night dress.

She stared into his shocked eyes until they became blank, and he slumped down and stopped moving apart from an outstretched hand twitching.

Eurydice was frozen still, in disbelief at what had happened. Her hands shook. Her eyes darted around the room. Then she came to her senses.

She wiped the sword blade with a dry part of her night dress and placed it in Ptolemy's hand.

She moved over to the balcony doors and opened them ajar.

She sat down on the floor at the foot of the bed, holding her knees to her chest. She blinked her eyes hard, and flexed her eyelids until tears began to flow. She took a deep breath.

"Help! Help! Guards!" she screamed at the top of her voice.

The two guards from outside the door burst into the room with their swords drawn, and both stopped immediately, stunned at the sight of Ptolemy face down in blood. One went to check Ptolemy, the other crouched down next to her.

"My Queen. What happened?" he asked.

"An… An… An assassin just killed Ptolemy," she said, making herself shake. "He stabbed him and made off out the balcony."

Chapter 26

Winter was over, the snows began to melt, and once the passes were safe enough to travel through, Pelopidas returned. He had spent the whole previous summer and autumn in the north fighting in Thessaly, and had had to winter in Macedonia, unable to make it back across dangerous territory to Thebes on his army's limited supplies.

Philip lay on the bed beside him. He had been regularly spending his nights with him since his return. They had become comfortable around each other again almost immediately, and had become very close in a short amount of time. Pammenes had queried this as Philip was there under his care. He knew about their quarrel before the general had left, but did not know what it had been about.

Philip got up and washed his face, a slave handed him a cup of water, he sloshed it around between his teeth; this washed out of his mouth the taste of the wine from the night before.

He looked down at Pelopidas, still asleep, and realised how content he was in Thebes. The pace of his life had slowed. He no longer went to sleep wondering if he would not wake. Macedonia was far from his mind.

Pelopidas opened his eyes slowly, he yawned and rubbed them, blinking away the sleep. He rolled over a little and stretched, and looked up at Philip.

"Morning," he said.

"Morning," Philip said. "Did you sleep well? I was just about to leave for training."

"Ah, another forced march? I do think you're the most determined man to crack your personal best that I have ever met."

Philip pulled on his tunic, and fastened his sandals.

"I just want to impress them."

"I can't believe the difference in you now and before I left," he said and smiled. "Trust me, they're impressed."

"But they still won't show it to a Barbarian from the north."

Pelopidas sighed. "Hardly anyone sees you that way anymore," he said.

"How long will it be before I am made an officer? I want to command."

"There's no rush."

"What if I have to go home at any time?"

"I wouldn't worry about that, any danger that your brother Perdiccas was in seems to have subsided; Ptolemy has them all under the thumb, and he needs to keep him safe or it makes his own position weaker. Macedonia is stable, probably the most stable it's been in your lifetime. Unless there is a change in the treaties, you're going to be here a while."

Philip stood up. He was glad that his brother was safe. He remembered that he wanted to go home, but only when he was ready. "I'm glad you want me to stay, but we can talk about it later, after the march," he said.

He made his way out into the darkness of the predawn gloom.

......

Philip's heart pounded. He ran with his own stifling breath coming back off the inside of his helmet; the narrow view from the inside was now familiar, safe, like a tortoise in its shell.

All he could really see was the backs of the men in front but he refrained from turning his head, and just listened to his body.

Keep tall. Body upright. Chin parallel to the ground. Squeeze shoulder blades together. Tense the stomach. Slight lean forward at the hips. Lift the knees. Keep tall. Body upright…

He controlled his breathing, in and out, in and out, feeling the slow expansion of his lungs and then the releasing of air from them. He became serene as his limbs continued to push at pace but at the same time felt loose and relaxed. His memory flashed back to that first forced march in which the shield had pulled his shoulders, his back, neck, and arms. His whole body had ached for more than a week afterwards, and not the usual pain that he got from exercising; this was different. He felt like he had done irreparable damage, and that it would be with him for the rest of his life.

However, this had not been so, and once the pain had gone, the muscles had all felt stronger, and tighter. Now he had done the run many times, his legs did not tire so easily, and although the feeling of his heart pounding hard in his chest was still there, his mind overcame the pain. The shield and the spear felt as though they were a part of his own body, and his bronze cuirass was another layer of his skin.

Sweat trickled down the back of his neck.

The sound of the officers yelling around him, egging on their troops was not only muted through the helmet, but drifted almost into silence in his mind as a faint echo. All he listened to was the sound of his own breath. He kept up with them for the full run without slowing.

He rejoiced, and as they returned through the gate, onto the parade ground, all the members he had been running with took it in turns to embrace him; some

305

patted him on the back, others clasped hands with him as they did with each other. He no longer felt like an outsider.

Back at the barracks, the Sacred Band ate. Philip was in the mess with the rest of them.

It was a long stone hall, and they all sat at their long tables in rows on benches. They laughed and joked, tucking into bread and steaming bowls of broth. It was a simple meal, but they ate it with gusto, as if it was a lavish Persian feast.

Philip stood on the edge of this near the door. This was the first time he had been invited into the mess. He had been through the room once, at night, and it had been empty; it had seemed so cold and hollow, but now the room lived and breathed, as if they were in the belly of some great creature. It was warm with the heat from all the men who had just returned from their training; he could smell the humidity in the air.

He wanted to run in and sit down, join in with all the joking and laughing, but was suddenly very aware of how much he stank, the dry sweat from the run still on him, and he hung back in the doorway. Never mind, he thought, they are all the same from the run and are slick with sweat too.

"Philip! Come sit with us," one of the men shouted and gestured for him to come over. He banged the chair next to him with the palm of his hand.

Philip edged his way over to the table and sat down next to the man, who was young and lean, and grinning from ear to ear; his dark brown eyes stared into Philip's, and he placed his hand on his shoulder.

"Congratulations," he said.

"For what?"

"You're one of us now."

"Thank you," Philip said sheepishly, squirming in his seat; feeling weary, the man's arm suddenly felt very heavy. All of these men had shown complete disinterest to him the entire time he had been in Thebes. Now he felt uncomfortable that they were being warm to him, too warm; it was unsettling.

They offered some bread and he ate it, not sure what they would talk about in the mess.

He wanted to ask them so many questions, about Leuctra, the Spartans. About Epaminondas and Pelopidas, what did they really think? He would have to be extremely careful when mentioning Pelopidas. Did they know about his relationship with the General? - His line of thought was interrupted.

"Tell us what Macedonia is like. How does it compare to Thebes?" another man shouted.

Familiar images raced to Philip's mind; at first the land itself, the Palace at Pella which had been built by his ancestor Archelaus, the fields stretching out to the vineyards on the hills, Arsinoe's family estate, the lush green vegetation that grew along the river, to the dry patchy grass of the lower land. He then thought of his family; pictured the faces of his mother and father and sister. It had been so long, he felt as though what he thought they looked like might not be true. Then brave Alexander, and the look of dread on his face when Philip was taken away; he had never seen Alexander look so vulnerable; he had always been the tough older brother, and that was the last time he had seen him, and the last time he ever would. Philip regretted that he had not been able to be there for his funeral games. He knew that he would regret that for the rest of his life.

His thoughts went to Perdiccas, his wise brother; and then to Ptolemy. Ptolemy. That lying, betraying, pretender piece of shit. Philip's fists slowly clenched under the table and his teeth began to grind. The moment he realised he was doing it, he stopped and relaxed the muscles of his face.

"Philip? Are you okay?" the man he was sitting next to asked.

Philip shook his head. "It's okay. Not that much different from Thebes really. I was- "

The doors flung open, and a cool breeze blew into the warm, stale air of the hall. The men stopped what they were doing as Epaminondas entered. They raised their drinks to him, and he raised his hand to salute them, then signalled them to return to what they were doing. He patted Philip on the shoulder as he passed. Philip felt himself smile; he was being publicly acknowledged by the general. Epaminondas' cloak billowed as he walked to his table at the top corner of the room.

The men looked impressed. Philip thought there was not one who had realised Epaminondas had taken so much interest in him; the gods had smiled on him in this respect if nothing else. He was grateful that his time had been spend in Thebes and not in Illyria. He could be dead, or worse.

The chatter quietened down.

A messenger had arrived. He stood at the door talking to a man who had turned and pointed to Philip. Philip stared, frozen as if he had looked into a gorgon's eyes, a lump in his throat, his hand started to shake. He put his cup down and pressed it into the table to conceal the involuntary movement. He glanced around. No one had seen it.

Not Perdiccas now.

The courier marched straight over to Philip, smiling and half bowing. Philip twisted in his seat.

"Philip," he said. The man spoke in Greek, but with a thick Macedonian accent, which now seemed unusual. "I need to speak to you immediately."

Philip stood up "You can tell me in front of these men," he said. All eyes were on the two of them.

"Philip, I think somewhere more private-"

"You can speak here."

The courier paused.

"Very well."

"My brother?" He asked, afraid of the answer.

"King Perdiccas requests your return, I was sent here to ask. I have just left the office of Epaminondas and he has agreed to release you."

"King?" Philip asked, stunned, feeling his smile grow. He looked at Epaminondas at the other end of the hall who smiled at him. "What happened?"

"Ptolemy has been killed. You're coming home," the Macedonian said.

"But I-" Philip tried to say something coherent, but realised the courier now looked at him in disbelief. It was his turn to be stunned. "What about the treaty?"

Philip had not realised until this moment that he did not want to go.

Why? Was he afraid? No. He wanted to stay in Thebes, and become part of the Sacred Band; become the great soldier and general he always wanted to be. That dream now turned to ash in his mouth. This would likely never happen in Macedonia. He was happy in Thebes.

"An arrangement has been reached," the courier said.

There was a long pause.

"I will get my things ready," he said finally.

Chapter 27

Philip was on the road between Macedonia and Thebes, with Pammenes and the other Macedonian youths, and their bodyguard. They had military escorts provided by Epaminondas to take them home, hundreds of hoplites in shining bronze armour, their officers mounted on beautiful Thessalian horses.

They were still in Thessaly, which fell under the influence of Thebes, but were not far from the Macedonian border. The road was swarming with refugees heading the opposite way. His brother taking over had apparently created a power vacuum, and some of the tribes to the north and northwest had taken advantage; they had been raiding over their borders already. Thebes had once again mediated proceedings to prevent complete chaos on their own northern border.

There was an exodus of people heading south. There were many families among them. Philip thought of his own family, and how it had been decimated by Ptolemy, his father and brother both killed, and how many men in the fighting that followed? Macedonia must be suffering with the loss of so many people, and how much had been raided and burned? He remembered when as a child the road had been strewn with the dead.

They were met by soldiers on horses from Epirus, the land west of Macedonia. They seemed peaceful, but were surveying the refugees as they passed.

"I believe you men are on the wrong side of the border," Pammenes said to them.

The rugged looking Epirote officer picked his top teeth with his tongue and spat.

"Sorry boss, but we're here on the business of our King Neoptolemus, He asked us to find out what was happening in Macedonia, lot of peasants crossing into Epirus. We heard the regent has been assassinated?" he said.

"Tell him everything is in order and that Thebes is mediating the situation," Pammenes said.

The Epirote officer took a long curious look at Philip. "Very well," he said. "Who can I tell him we spoke to?"

"Pammenes of Thebes."

"Good. I know the name. I'll return to my king and report back," he said.

"Gentlemen," Pammenes said. He gave a slight bow, and they rode off west. He turned to Philip. "I wouldn't be surprised if the Epirote border moves east. Do you still seek war? Even those who are not normally enemies will look to see what they can get out of your weakness."

"I don't," Philip said, and chewed the inside of his lip.

He would need to know the level of destruction when he spoke to his brother. Had there been much fighting? How much control did Perdiccas have? Had his removal of Ptolemy split the loyalty of the court?

The people they passed on the road were beaten, some were broken. Many begged for food and water. By their clothing, some were wealthy, or at least had been; they had the look of merchants or traders, but they walked alongside the poor. Mothers cradled crying babies in their arms. The sound cut through Philip like a knife.

They only had what they could carry, but some had clearly overestimated how much they could manage, and the side of the road was littered with possessions that had been abandoned.

Opportunists scavenged through what had been left and carried them away, their arms loaded with whatever they could claim. It pained Philip to see what was happening to his country and people.

They came across a couple being robbed by a group of five vagabonds; the woman was being held with her arm twisted behind her back, and a rusty knife at her throat.

"Let go of her! Please, I'll give you whatever you ask," the husband shouted at them.

The skinny, rat featured man who appeared to be their leader sneered at him. He looked the wife up and down and licked his lips.

"Maybe we could come to an arrangement," he said.

"I command you to stop," Philip shouted to the men, looking down from his horse. When they did nothing but casually look up and then continue, he dismounted his horse and drew his sword.

"Mind your business, they're fair game on the road," the leader said, shaking his head and turning away. "Theban cunt."

"Philip, you can't risk yourself for these scum," his guard said.

"No, I want this stopped. On me!" he ordered them.

His guards dismounted and looked at each other, unsure whether they should take orders from Philip. Then they looked to Pammenes, who had stayed on his horse, and had kept a distance, he shrugged and nodded.

The vagabonds formed a protective semicircle around their prey.

"Now!" Philip shouted.

The Thebans drew their swords and formed up in a line with Philip. They advanced, sidestepping toward the vagabonds, swords pointed forward. The vagabonds fled, and the husband and wife rushed together to embrace.

"Thank you, thank you," they said and fell at the feet of Philip. "We will sacrifice to Zeus for your safe return, Philip."

He helped them to their feet.

"Get up, get up. And how do you know who I am?"

"Everyone knows of your return. Prince. The King spread the word. Seems he was overjoyed by your return."

Philip wished to the gods that he had not, all of their enemies now knew he was on the road. Philip thought, looking around at the other refugees, could there be assassins?

"Why are you fleeing?"

The man looked at his wife, she looked away, then he turned back to Philip, and opened his mouth to speak, but no words came; he looked at his feet.

"It's just that," he paused. "We don't think that your brother will last long. He is a boy, and not known to be strong. We are fleeing to Greece, maybe Thebes or even as far as Athens."

"No" Philip said. He softened his voice, "It's something else. You are more troubled than just regarding the king. What happened?"

The man's bottom lip trembled. "We were out herding the goats. Thracian brutes with their Illyrian masters came down from the mountains. They burned our farm down; they…" the man stopped; his eyes welled with tears.

Philip placed a hand on the man's shoulder.

"Be strong my friend, what happened?"

"They killed our children. Slaughtered them with the goats. We ran." He fell to his knees and wept.

Philip embraced him; his shoulder wet with his tears.

"There is nothing left for us in Macedonia."

Philip felt his own eyes begin to tear up.

"By Mother Hera and all the gods, I promise you, I will kill them all." He whispered into the man's ear, "I promise you."

…

The rest of the journey went without incident. When they arrived back in Pella, the others left and were taken to their homes by their Theban guards, and Pammenes walked Philip to the Palace. No-one was there to greet them.

"I will be fine from here," Philip said.

"Very well. Goodbye Philip," Pammenes said. "I trust you will become a great man one day. I hope our paths cross again."

"Thank you Pammenes, for everything you have taught me."

The two embraced and Pammenes left.

At the palace courtyard there were four men outside the main gate. They were of the Royal Guard, and wore the armour and uniform of such, but they were not guarding.

One casually leant on his spear watching, while the other three stood behind a line they had marked in the dirt, and threw coins against the wall. The one who managed to get the coin closest to the wall cheered and triumphantly raised his hands in the air; the other two groaned as he stepped forward to collect his winnings.

He turned to them to gloat, and met eyes with Philip, who he clearly recognised instantly, and suddenly stood to attention. The others turned and did the same. "Philip, sorry, we-"

"You men have work?" Philip said, just glad to be home, although he did not show it; he kept his face as serious as he could. "You three, get back to your patrol, and you, take me to the king."

"Of course," the winner said, grabbing his helmet from the ground and fumbling it on top of his head, fastening the chin strap as he tried to catch up with Philip. "Follow me" he said, getting ahead.

The winner escorted him into the palace. They passed other guards, their boots clomping down the corridors; it was strange to be back, it was all so familiar, but somehow, he did not feel like it was his home anymore. It would take some time to settle back in.

They passed different messengers and officers all frantically going about their business. Some paused when they recognized him, and others either didn't recognize him or didn't feel the need to acknowledge him.

He was led to one of the council chambers and the King's office, the one that had been his father's. Perdiccas and some of the nobles stood around a large table that had been placed in the centre of the room; maps and scrolls were scattered all over it. The desk that had been his father's was clear and perfectly tidy, with its scrolls neatly stacked; all but one of the walls now had floor to ceiling shelves filled with scrolls. Probably Philosophy texts, he thought and smiled. Perdiccas had always loved the Greek Philosophers.

Among the group he recognized Parmenion, Polyperchon and a few others, but there were some he didn't know.

They were arguing, all talking over each other. Each of them was trying to get Perdiccas to listen to what he had to say. The king tried to hush them and get each to talk in turn, motioning with his hand. His efforts were unsuccessful, and they continued to shout, and drown him and each other out.

Philip stood in the doorway watching the arguing; this is pathetic, he thought, we must hear what each man has to say. After a moment he grew impatient. He slammed the door shut, causing the guard who had accompanied him to jump. All those around the table abruptly stopped and looked up. They stared at him in shock.

"Philip," Parmenion said, his expression quickly changing, a smile forming on his lips, "You're back."

Perdiccas said nothing, but strode over to his younger brother, extended his arms out and embraced him tightly,

"Welcome home brother," he said. "I'm glad to have you here."

"I'm glad to be home," Philip said. It felt strange that he was back. He had yearned to come home for years, and now that he was here, he could not think of anything profound to say for such an event. The whole reunion was underwhelming, incomplete somehow, like they had never been apart.

"What has happened?" Philip asked, taking a small step back and glancing over Perdiccas' shoulder to the table.

"I have restored our family back to the throne," Perdiccas said. "We have the kingdom in order, mostly, but a number of pretenders have tried to take advantage of our situation."

"And Ptolemy?"

"Ptolemy is dead."

"Good; how? What happened?"

"I had him killed. It's complicated."

"And is there any news of the whereabouts of Archelaus, Arrhidaeus and Menelaus? Are they contesting the throne?"

"Gods Philip, you've only been back a few moments," Perdiccas said; he sighed. "Arrhidaeus is still rotting in our dungeon, the other two are still on the run, my agents have not found them yet, although they have many leads to follow."

"Where did they flee to? We can't have those little bastards coming back with an army," Philip said.

"It's fine, they have no influence anymore, not since father died; no one of importance would take them in and risk provoking us."

Philip scratched his newly growing beard and then clawed his fingers through it while he thought, a habit he had picked up from Pelopidas. He took a few more moments to ponder the situation, then strolled over to the table and looked over the large map that was laid out. It was held down at the corners by heavy candlesticks and took up almost the whole table. The room watched in silence. Coins had been placed in a number of positions, along the upper Macedonian borders with Thrace and Illyria, areas which had always been difficult to keep under control.

"Each one represents a raid," Perdiccas said. "I am trying to buy off whoever I can, and not provoke any others into action."

"It seems you don't need to provoke anyone. They are already raiding," Philip said.

"They will be dealt with in due time. I have already dispatched mercenaries to support our levies and contain the raiders."

"What have you been buying these mercenaries with? Is the treasury as empty as when I left?"

Perdiccas opened his mouth to answer, but another spoke before he had a chance.

"Philip, we have the situation under control. You have only just got back. Why don't you eat and rest?"

Philip looked around to meet the eyes of a man he did not recognize. He was tall and lean, and he wore a beard that was neatly trimmed; his accent was not Macedonian.

"I don't require rest. My brother requires my help to keep his throne," Philip said. "What is your name? I don't know you."

There was a long silence, while the man looked as if he had forgotten his name. He looked to Perdiccas.

"I am -"

"Philip, this is Euphraeus, he is one of my most trusted advisors," Perdiccas said.

"Euphraeus?" Philip asked, looking Euphraeus in the eyes carefully. "Euphraeus of Athens?"

He said the word Athens not trying to hide his obvious distain. Philip stared at him, and he stared back, unblinking, neither wanting to break the eye contact.

"He is a student of Plato. He has proven a great asset," Perdiccas said.

"You are correct, my home is in Oreus, but I would consider myself of Athens," Euphraeus said. "I am not sure what you are implying?"

"I'm implying that-"

Perdiccas stepped between them. "Please, please. This will accomplish nothing; I know you both only want to serve Macedonia. Philip you must be tired. It must have been a long journey here. The throne is safe, for now; we have already removed anyone who may try to rival me; the generals and the council are with us, and

318

we are starting to plan attacking back in the north and secure our borders."

"The borders are not safe. Epirus seem to be trying to take some of our land. You should have seen the number of people I saw fleeing on the road south; Macedonia is bleeding its manpower."

"I will have the border with Epirus checked. Rest brother. We can talk when you've rested." Perdiccas' voice was beginning to lose its patience.

"Very well, I will retire for now," he said. He did not want to make his brother look weak. "When do you reconvene?"

"Tomorrow morning."

"Very well," Philip said.

As he left, he locked gazes with Euphraeus, who returned the look of dislike. Once he left the room, he shook his head, disappointed that his return had not gone better, and regretted that he had already made an enemy.

.....

Philip was quick to assert his knowledge of military matters, and over the next few weeks Perdiccas allowed him to train the army in the new methods he had learned from the Thebans.

When the morning to begin training finally came, Philip headed down towards the parade ground with Antigonus. Improving the army had been so firmly in his mind the whole time he had been in Thebes.

This was it. This was the chance that he had been building up to in his mind. Time to get the Macedonians trained as well as the Thebans.

319

On his arrival he was greeted by Parmenion, who had been through rapid promotion while he had been gone, and was now the general of a large portion of the royal army. The sun shone, and the dust blew in the breeze.

"Dry and not too hot," Philip said, "great conditions to train in."

"Better than the summer days in Thebes," Antigonus nodded in agreement. "You remember? It was too hot."

Parmenion had all the equipment brought out that they had for the men to train with, spears and shields. Philip stopped to look at the pile of weapons that had been placed on the ground. He picked up a spear and ran the wood through his fingers; the finish on the shaft was worn off where it had been held. This spear had been used many, many times. He dropped it, shook his head, and picked up a shield. It was a pelta, smaller and much lighter than the aspis shields that he had been using in Thebes; he almost struck himself in the face, expecting it to have more weight. He thrust his arm through the central strap and grabbed the leather thong on the inside of the shield.

This was not good enough, sufficient to train with, but was this what was being taken to war? Are the armies that are up and down the border fending off raiders using this kind of armament? It was so long ago he couldn't remember.

The Macedonian peasants began to arrive in their shambolic and casual way; some had their own spears shields and helmets, but many didn't. Philip's memories of this flooded back into his mind.

"Parmenion?"

"Philip?"

"Are we still reliant on the old equipment that was being brought out for training before I left?"

Parmenion nodded.

"For the most part, yes."

Philip stood up straight with his feet apart, toes pointing outward, hands clasped behind his back, and watched the men coming in. He looked over at the training officers, who were arranging all of the men into the groups they would be training with. He had spent the last few days briefing them on the new training exercises they would be doing, much more in line with how the Thebans trained.

Their warmup began; the men were separated and arranged into groups of about eighty men, with shields and spears at the ready all facing forward. He had instructed them to overlap their shields like hoplites, but the smaller shields did not allow for this, leaving large gaps between each man.

Flute players would signal when they were to step left, right, forward and back, close ranks or strike.

The men began their drill. As soon as the signals were blown to march forward, many of the men hesitated, looking from side to side to see what their comrades were doing; others, who had been paying attention when they were briefed took the steps forward, but the men in front didn't move and walked into the back of them. Then some backed away, and then looked around. Utter confusion spread through the formation.

The officers started yelling, and running out into the formation, pressing individuals, pushing them back to where they should have been. Philip took a step forward, ready to go in and start shouting himself, but was stopped abruptly by Antigonus's hand on his chest, holding him back. "Give them a moment Philip," he said.

After a while, Parmenion raised his hand, and called off the drill. The men were instructed to take a short break. He came over to Philip and Antigonus,

"I'm sorry Philip."

Frustrated, Philip opened his mouth to shout. It was far worse than he ever imagined. No wonder Macedonia had lost so badly in almost every engagement for as long as he or anyone could remember. He stopped himself, and took a slow breath.

"Don't worry Parmenion; this is the first time they have tried anything like this. We'll get them there. You begin again when you're ready."

Parmenion bowed his head and returned to the men. Philip glanced up and down the army. He turned to speak to Antigonus when his gaze was immediately drawn to a figure sitting on the brow of the hill, watching them train. Antigonus turned to see what he was looking at.

"Euphraeus," Philip said.

"What does that prick want?" Antigonus asked.

"I don't know. Just spying I guess, so he has something to undermine me with in the next council meeting."

The drill resumed, but the same thing happened again. Philip gritted his teeth, and again went to take a step forward but stopped himself this time.

After a short while, he marched over to Parmenion, who was frantically trying to communicate with individual officers. Philip glanced up to see if Euphraeus was still there, trying his best not to appear that he was looking. He was.

"Stop the exercise; we have to give them time to let this settle in," Philip shouted to Parmenion over the commotion.

"Are you sure?" Parmenion asked. "We could go over the commands with them again and give it another try."

"No, this is too different from what they were doing before. We're going to go for a march."

"A march?"

"Yes, get the men into a column; we're going to go out along the road towards the north, carrying full equipment."

"Can I have a word with you?" Antigonus whispered in his ear.

Philip nodded and the two stepped away out of earshot. He watched Parmenion head off to speak to the other officers. "What is it?" Philip asked, looking his friend in the eye.

"Are you sure you want to do this? A forced march? These aren't professional soldiers like the Sacred Band. You push them too hard. They may not come back to train."

There was the sound of the officers all shouting out their orders, getting the men into their column formation. They all shuffled around in a disorderly way, wanting to be with their mates.

"I'm not going to push them too hard, just hard enough. They've had it too easy, and I can't have him telling Perdiccas that we aren't doing a good job with them," Philip said.

"Forget about him, what does he expect in one day? And too easy? These people fight every time they're asked to by their king. They get beaten and killed and-"

"Exactly, they don't train hard enough; they don't get pushed hard enough. So, when they have to go to war, they're not ready. We need to get them in the best condition they have ever been in."

Antigonus nodded. "Okay, okay, I agree. But remember, this is only the first day. Remember what our first forced march felt like in Thebes?"

"Yes, I do. We both vomited, as if we'd been drinking all night. I didn't even know that was possible from exercise."

"Exactly, you don't want them to think of you as a tyrant. It won't help anything."

Philip nodded, always keen to listen to Antigonus opinion; he always told him exactly what he was thinking; he never tried to deceive him or break things easily to him. He always told it like it was.

The head of the column stood at the ready, at the entrance to the parade grounds, and the formation stretched back all the way to the other end. The men were standing with their spears resting on their shoulders, pointing up, and shields in the other arm. Some looked anxious, not sure what to expect. Philip and Antigonus moved to the head of the column as Parmenion joined him. The officers were dispersed evenly down the line.

"With me!" Philip yelled, and started marching out onto the road at a normal walking pace.

Philip got them at a slow pace to begin with, but once they had cleared the city, he looked at Antigonus who looked back, and gave a slight nod.

"Pick up the pace," he yelled, and drew his sword, pointing it high above his head, then lowered it forward, the shining metal catching the glint of the sun. He doubled his marching pace. He listened as the pounding of the feet behind him became more harmonious, synchronizing to make a steady beat like a drum.

Philip was now incredibly fit from his training in Thebes; they had been running for a while now, and he was barely breaking a sweat. His breathing had increased, but he was in complete control of it. He glanced back over his shoulder. The men were looking weary, their movements becoming more laboured, and the spring had gone from their step. Their weapons and shields would be a burden now, he thought, they would be readjusting their grip on them, but it wouldn't help. He remembered well from when he first trained in Thebes; the weight of the shield had felt like it was going to pull his arm off.

A wall followed one side of the road they were running on, and a memory flashed into Philip's mind as they passed the gate of the walled estate. It was Arsinoe's family home. He used to ride here on a horse, and here he was now, running past it on foot, barely out of breath. He must get his men to this level.

He looked back at the men once more; they had had enough. He did not want to make them think of him as a tyrant. He wanted their trust, so he stopped them. Many coughed and spluttered; some stood bent over, hands on thighs breathing hard; some looked ready to throw up, but there was an overall feeling of relief that he could sense from them.

He smiled and walked among them, patted some on the back and helped up those who were bent over, breathing hard.

"Well done! You all did well! Showed heart. Tomorrow we will get further!"

They turned about face, they chatted and joked, and walked back to the city with their heads held high.

Chapter 28

Philip strode across the square courtyard of the palace towards the royal apartments. He wore a bronze cuirass and carried his Corinthian style helmet under his arm.

He marched ahead of a group of bodyguards chosen from the Royal Guard, the clomping sound of their boots drowning out the soft trickle of the fountains and the courtiers' hushed voices. The courtiers pottered about back and forward, coming and going. A few nodded to him as he passed, but none looked him in the eye. There were a lot of new faces around since he had been away, mostly Greeks from what Philip had observed; his brother had been patronising philosophers, mathematicians, engineers and anyone he thought of value. Where he was able to get the funds for this was a mystery only Perdiccas and the gods knew. He hoped that Euphraeus was not privy to this information; Philip found his closeness to his brother unsettling.

His eyes scanned from side to side as he walked, suspicious now of anyone around him. It was unlikely that someone would try to have him killed in such an open public place, but it had happened to previous kings and claimants to the throne. His education in Thebes made him think this way, and he remembered well that few Macedonian royals died of old age.

His boots clomped on the marble as he crossed, and he froze as his eyes met Arsinoe's. She was sat on a bench with a group of her friends that Philip recognised, but he couldn't remember their names. His gaze immediately lowered to her belly, swollen and round, she was heavily pregnant. She gasped at the sight of him.

"You're alive?" she said.

"You're pregnant," he said.

She smiled a radiant smile and rubbed her hand across her stomach. "Yes, and due any day now."

"I can't believe you made it back alive, Philip,"

"You said you would wait for me."

"I waited for a long time. Because our relationship was secret, I could never find out reports from the palace of what was happening. Alexander and then Perdiccas took the throne; it was commonly thought you were not coming back."

"You should have waited longer-"

"I waited a very long time, Philip. You were gone for years."

"You could have waited a bit longer; I was always going to be coming back for you."

"Did you wait for me?" she asked. She stood up with her hands on her hips.

"Yes," he lied without a moment's hesitation. "Who's the father?"

Arsinoe looked from side to side at Philip's bodyguards, and then turned to look at her own friends who were stood back gossiping and whispering behind them.

"Can we take this conversation somewhere private?"

"Of course, let's walk," he said and nodded, content at how comfortable he was around her so quickly.

The two strolled side by side back towards the royal apartments, the direction he was heading originally, and through a gate into a secluded courtyard. They sat on a bench looking at the statues of the Olympian Gods that Philip had always loved as a boy. He remembered the condition they had been in when his family had returned from being supplanted; the paint had been flaked and cracked, exposing the white stone beneath; now they had been beautifully restored to their former glory, probably not by Perdiccas, he thought, most likely Alexander. He was always the most pious.

The guards hovered back, staying out of earshot.

She smiled and felt his chin. "You suit a beard."

Philip felt it himself, "It has not long started to grow in."

"When did you get back from Thebes?"

"Only a few weeks ago. My brother asked for me back. The Thebans thought it time for me to return."

"What have you been doing since you've been back? Have you seen your mother yet? I was so worried about her when she, you know…"

"When what?"

"She was with Ptolemy," she said. "I was worried she was getting too involved."

"Well, you do what you need to survive. She is a wise woman. She did what she had to protect her family. Like you."

"What is that supposed to mean?" she asked. Philip could tell she was hiding a lot of anger and hurt that his statement had caused. He instantly regretted saying it.

"I will never forgive Ptolemy though, fortunately he is being tormented in Hades," he said.

"Ptolemy was always kind to me though."

Philip ignored the comment about Ptolemy.

"Who is the father?"

"His name is Lagus, he's from Eordaea. He's a good man, brave. He loves horses, you'd like him."

"I think I remember him, I travelled through his land on my way to Illyria, although I was blindfolded." He let out a humourless laugh. "Seems a lifetime ago."

"Did they treat you badly?" she said, reaching over and taking his hand.

"Not really, the Illyrians weren't kind, but it could have been worse. It made me stronger."

"I'm sorry that happened to you."

"It's okay. The Illyrians were bastards, but I was treated well in Thebes."

"I heard," she said.

They sat in quiet contemplation for a moment. He realised that he had missed her, and that he wanted her back.

He lightly stroked her belly with his fingertips and felt a sudden streak of jealousy.

"It should have been my child," he said.

That struck a nerve. Arsinoe stood up, her lips pursed together hard, her eyebrows rolled down in anger, "Look. You'd been gone for three years. Did you really wait for me this whole time?"

Philip swallowed and looked up at her

"Yes."

"You're lying!" she shouted. "I heard rumours that you have been in a relationship with some Theban general or ambassador who was here before. And the gods only know how many slave girls you fucked!"

Philip stood up and looked down and pointing a finger at her. "You said you thought I was dead!" Philip said, raising his voice.

"Is it true then? Did you have sex with all these people while you were in Thebes?" she said, shouting back at him.

"Keep your voice down," he said, pointing a finger in her face, the strong thick index finger from his years of hoplite training.

"Why?" she said defiantly. "Do you not want anyone in the court to hear about you being in bed with Theban generals?"

"I'm warning you!"

329

"Warning me? What can you do?"

"I'll-"

"You'll what? Or is it that you don't-"

She was immediately silenced as his open hand struck her in the mouth, and she fell. She stared up at him in shock and disbelief, a red welt already starting to appear on her cheek. Philip shook his hand in a futile attempt to take away the sting. He turned and started to walk away; as he left, he looked over his shoulder. She stared at him. Her stare was like a scorpion's sting. Philip regretted striking her, and he had likely made another enemy.

.....

Over the next few months Philip had trouble settling back in. The way they did politics in Macedonia was so crude compared to Thebes. He did not sleep well most nights, concerned for the future of Macedon and for his brother. Perdiccas had many enemies, and either he didn't see it, was in denial about it, or was very good at not showing it in front of Philip. This sent Philip down a thought process he didn't like much. Either Perdiccas did not trust him enough to speak about who he was suspicious of, or worse, he did not know who these enemies were, which was dangerous. The absolute worst thought that entered his mind was that Perdiccas considered Philip himself an enemy, although he did not truly believe that, but Euphraeus was always there, whispering in Perdiccas' ear.

These men were going to try and outmanoeuvre Perdiccas, as had happened to Alexander before him.

Ptolemy was dead, but who else had been lying in wait? Which of them would be loyal to Perdiccas but would not have dared plot against Ptolemy?

He was making it his business to find out who these people were; those closest to Perdiccas would be watched, discretely. He had spoken to a few of the Macedonian council, officers and nobles who he was confident were loyal to the king, and was beginning to set up a network of spies to keep watch.

A meeting was held by Perdiccas with his advisors, and Philip was invited. He arrived with the usual awkwardness that all the new faces brought; all eyes watched him as he entered the room.

They all kept quiet until they saw the opportunity to undermine someone else. Philip hated this about them. The devious Athenian advisors in court plotted and schemed, but he had learned since being back that so did the Macedonians; but the Athenians were far better at it. He remembered one of Pammenes' lessons about the Thebans and their form of democracy. Until they had a common cause against the Spartans, he had said, they all schemed against each other, each jealous of the others' power. They were still in the honeymoon of victory, and were all friends, behind a common cause, but the old ways were beginning to creep back into their society.

The King's council convened in Perdiccas' office and started by looking over the maps of the territory that they had under control. These maps had become as permanent a feature of the room as the floor and the

331

ceiling. They discussed where there was fighting, the movement of soldiers, and considered anyone who was likely to take advantage of the perceived power vacuum, which had opened due to the death of Ptolemy.

They looked at the various resources they had available

"Thebes want to buy as much timber from us as possible. They are working hard to assemble their fleet so that they can control the Aegean Sea and protect themselves against... Persia" Philip said. He was careful not say Athens, being selective with what he said, maybe even misleading, and suddenly realised that he was being drawn into the political games he despised. The members of the council stayed quiet and listened, none seemingly wanting to anger the king, or make an enemy of Euphraeus.

"I am not sure if I want to stoke that fire yet, we do not want to side with anyone at this point," Perdiccas said.

"Exactly, and by selling to both Athens and Thebes, we are staying neutral. And doubling Macedonia's income," Philip said. A few of the council nodded.

As expected, Euphraeus leaned in and spoke very quietly, close to Perdiccas' ear so Philip could not hear.

"Persia?" Perdiccas said "Are they not allies of Thebes?"

Philips eyes narrowed towards Euphraeus and he shook his head slowly

"Not exactly, but they want to be prepared against any potential aggressor."

"Sounds risky, Philip. I don't want to disappoint our Athenian friends," Perdiccas said, looking to Euphraeus, who lowered his head humbly to the king.

Philip bit his lip in disgust. He swallowed the desire to strike him.

"Has he told you about how his friends in Athens are sponsoring Argeus the pretender?" Philip said. There were gasps around the room, and the council started whispering to each other. "Who at this very moment is raising an army in the east to come west and take Pella?"

"Is this true?" Perdiccas asked.

"What lies have your Theban friends been feeding you, my boy?" Euphraeus said to Philip, "Why would we assist your brother, then sponsor another?"

"I-" Philip hesitated; he was unsure of the answer. There was a long pause.

"Will you two stop bickering?" Perdiccas said. "I will start an investigation and we will soon learn the truth of it."

After much debate, Perdiccas decided that they would be working with Thebes, but would still send timber to Athens for as long as possible to bring in as much revenue as they could, until such a time as Thebes and Athens came to blows, and he was forced to take a side. Although Philip had won a small victory over Euphraeus, it did not sit well; the man was clever. Envoys were sent to Thebes to invite them to Macedonia.

. . .

A month later Perdiccas and Philip waited for the Theban's arrival, just the two of them. Perdiccas nervously paced up and down his office. Many secret meetings had been held in this office. They were to keep as low a profile as possible. The meeting would have no pomp or circumstance. Philip stood still, legs loose, and his hands behind his back as Perdiccas paced from left to right in front of him. He took a sip of wine from his cup.

"Calm yourself down. The men who are coming are very reasonable. I know them well," Philip said.

"It's not that," Perdiccas said. "If these negotiations go badly, they could pick us apart. We don't have the strength to repel either of them, never mind both. I feel nauseous."

"Don't worry, no one's going to war with anyone here," he said, "except Thebes and Athens fighting each other; we're the ones with the timber. We have what they want, both of them. They'll fight and weaken each other, and we'll get rich."

"What if they turn on us?"

"Neither of them has the reach to hold upper Macedonia and remove the timber themselves. If they did, we could maintain a guerrilla war there and make it far too disruptive for them. That's why both of them want us on their side."

Perdiccas nodded and stopped his pacing. Philip stood face-to-face with him and put his hands on his shoulders, and looked him straight in the eye. "We are the ones who are in control of this meeting brother, you'll see."

There was a knock on the door, and Perdiccas shouted to come in. The door creaked open and two tall muscular men of the Royal Guard entered, bowed their

334

heads to Perdiccas and stepped to the side. The two men behind them both wore long riding cloaks, with their hoods up. They both removed them, revealing their faces.

"Pelopidas! Epaminondas!" Philip said and stepped forward. They both smiled at him and in turn embraced him. "Welcome to Macedonia. I apologise for the lack of reception."

"We understand the need for keeping this meeting secret," Epaminondas said.

"We do not want the Athenians causing trouble for you," Pelopidas said. "I hope you're well my young friend."

"Extremely. I'm happy to see both of you. May I introduce my brother, Perdiccas the third of Macedonia," Philip said and extended his hand out towards his brother.

"Your Majesty," they both said in perfect harmony.

"Welcome to both of you. Pelopidas I've met of course, and it is a pleasure to meet you Epaminondas," Perdiccas said. "My brother speaks very highly of both of you. I hope this will be the beginning of a very special relationship between our two nations."

"Likewise, likewise," Epaminondas said.

Perdiccas beckoned them over to the desk

"Please, have a seat," he said.

The two men pulled out the chairs and sat. Philip stood at one end of the desk with his arms folded, and Perdiccas walked around to the other side and took a seat at the large wooden chair, a slight slouch to his posture.

"So," he said and opened his hands towards them. "You asked my brother to arrange this meeting? What can I do for you?"

"Simple," Epaminondas said. "We want you to sell us your timber."

"I already sell you our timber."

"Of course. But we want to buy more."

"How much more?"

"We want to buy it in much, much larger quantities. Around twenty times as much," Pelopidas said.

"Twenty times?" Perdiccas said. "We don't have enough lumberjacks to cut down that many trees and we don't have enough guards to protect them while they're out in the wilderness."

"We can provide protection. We can also help with the cutting down of the trees themselves. Trust us, this will be to your benefit."

Perdiccas looked up at Philip. He was clearly uneasy with what was going on. He looked back at Epaminondas.

"Very well, how much are you prepared to pay?"

Philip watched Pelopidas as Epaminondas and Perdiccas had their discussion. He was scratching his beard. His nervous tick. What was he thinking? What was about to be asked?

"Before we get to that, we have one more stipulation," Epaminondas said.

"One more stipulation? Is Thebes so powerful that they can simply come around and start making demands? -Suppose I-" Perdiccas said, sitting up sharply.

"I'm sorry, Perdiccas if we have come across as rude. That's not our intention," Epaminondas said. "We simply want to be as open and honest as possible with you, and tell you exactly what we want. No games. No tricks. We are partners."

Perdiccas sunk back into his relaxed position. He looked up at Philip, then back at the two Thebans.

"My brother trusts you. I trust my brother."

"Implicitly," Philip said, getting to nods of respect from both of them.

"What is this stipulation? I will consider it."

There was a long pause. "We want Macedonia to stop selling timber to Athens." Epaminondas said.

There was an even longer pause. Perdiccas stood up, the chair screeching out from under his legs. He paced up and down for a moment, then stopped and stood opposite them. He swallowed.

"That is absolutely out of the question," he said. "We have been trading with Athens for decades, with men who were great friends of my father. I am not prepared to break with them for gold and silver."

Epaminondas paused. Philip watched him, and then realised they had never actually seen any of them negotiate apart from Pelopidas, and he had hated the man then. This had blinded his judgement of them. They discussed the request for a while, neither side willing to budge. Philip observed the two Thebans staying incredibly calm, showing no aggression at all. His brother Perdiccas, who he had always thought of as being incredibly calm, never surrendering his logic to his passion, was becoming more and more agitated. How are they doing this? What negotiating technique were they using? He could not tell.

"Athens will attack us, simply take over the territory themselves," Perdiccas said. "They have always looked for an excuse to retake old colonies near our borders."

"Perdiccas," Epaminondas said, taking a step closer to the king, "They may have the Navy, but they don't have the ability to project their power that far inland. Do you know of the city of Amphipolis? It's not too far from here. It used to be part of Athens' empire, well, the Delian League on paper. They have tried to retake it for a century, with no success. And it's on the coast; we can make an arrangement with them."

"We are your friends King Perdiccas," Pelopidas said. "As Athens gets weaker, Thebes gets stronger. We are a far better ally to have. And we have friends and mercenaries in Thrace that can help you protect your northern border. We are on far better terms with Persia than Athens. Believe me when I say this is a great thing and it will benefit Macedonia."

"Why do you need so much?" Perdiccas asked.

"I'm building a fleet, one that will rival Athens, maybe even Persia when it is complete. We are natural allies here. Macedonia lies to our north. We both have friends in Thessaly. It makes perfect sense. My fleet can also protect your coast."

"You have been clearly heard. I will consider it for the future, but not today," Perdiccas said, standing tall. "I will increase timber sales, but not refuse Athens. That is my answer."

They all calmed down and relaxed. They then split; the Thebans returned to their lodgings for a few hours to give both sides time to think, and come back with fresh arguments. Perdiccas and Philip took a short break, and Perdiccas left to discuss the matter with different advisors individually, leaving out Euphraeus, to Philip's relief. He told Philip that he wanted an honest answer from them, and that any answer would be diluted if they were in a group.

Philip and Perdiccas met again in the study before the Thebans came back.

"Well, have you come to a decision?" Philip asked him.

"I think so. You trust them?"

"Yes, I do. I think…" He took a long pause, and looked his brother in the eye. "I think, if you had not

338

taken the throne back, and I had been trapped there. I would be one of them."

There was a long pause, Philip waited on Perdiccas processing this.

"Okay, okay," he said.

There was a knock at the door, the Thebans had returned. They entered the room.

"Welcome back," Perdiccas said. "Please have a seat."

Epaminondas and Pelopidas both sat back in their original seats.

"Good evening King Perdiccas. Have you reached a decision?" Epaminondas asked.

"I have," he said, and waited. Philip waited with bated breath. The silence seemed to last an eternity. He glanced at the Thebans who exchanged subtle looks. Pelopidas scratched his beard and then looked up to Philip, a pleading expression on his face. Philip shrugged his shoulders ever so slightly and Pelopidas gaze returned to Perdiccas.

"I'm sorry," he said, both of them let out their breath hard, sighing in disappointment, breaking their until now perfect masks. "The answer is still no. I am prepared to sell you as much as you need, but I am not prepared to break with Athens."

Epaminondas and Pelopidas shared a look, and turned back to Perdiccas.

"Okay, okay" Pelopidas said, "It's a start."

Chapter 29

"Faster!... faster!" Philip shouted, "but remember to breathe!"

The men looked exhausted already, their faces were red and their chests heaved. They were arranged in rows and squatted in unison. "Forty-nine!... Fifty!... Fifty-one!" they shouted as each repetition was completed.

Philip had begun to train the army more, and with the help of Antigonus and Polyperchon. He did not want to waste any time at all. He felt wiser and more confident in all things military, and this was his chance to prove that he was no longer the weak third son, a perception that seemed to have lingered while he had been in Thebes. The men had all stood to attention as he arrived.

He had decided on focusing on improving their strength and stamina, so that when it came to drills, they would keep good technique for longer, and this should carry over onto the battlefield. Although the gymnasiums would have been useful to train, they were not available to the number of men he had, who now numbered in the hundreds. They had made a makeshift gym. They had gathered rocks that they could hold while squatting and lunging. He had them carrying a partner across their shoulders and running up and down the parade grounds. This would then be repeated in full equipment until they could no longer do it and would collapse to the ground exhausted.

Perdiccas had requested to inspect the drills; Philip welcomed this, as the men would train harder than ever in the presence of their king. It was dawn and the sun began to peak over the mountains, flooding the parade grounds with a perfect orange glow.

Euphraeus accompanied Perdiccas. Upon seeing him, the hairs on the back of Philip's neck rose; he sensed there would be a clash, as happened almost every time they met.

"Morning Philip," Perdiccas said, his posture and demeanour so much more regal than when Philip had left, his head was high, and his back straight. Philip's strongest memories of him were when he was hunched over a desk reading scrolls. He had grown up as well. "I trust my presence is welcome."

Perdiccas had been spending most of his time with the philosophers, especially Euphraeus. Philip was not keen on this, but some of the new revenue that was coming in from Thebes was being used to fund the training, equipping and expansion of the royal army that he had requested, and since Euphraeus did not challenge this, Philip tried to tolerate his presence. Still, he mistrusted the Athenian.

"Of course, Your Majesty," Philip said. He turned to Polyperchon. "Tell them to take a breather and get some water."

"You are training them well I see," Perdiccas said.

"They are improving?" Euphraeus said.

"Thank you," Philip said. Could this be a gesture to begin improving their relationship? He was tired of it.

"No," Euphraeus quickly corrected. "It was a question. *Are* they improving?"

"Yes. They are," Philip said, trying not to grind his teeth. The muscles in his jaw flexed.

"I am curious. Where are these men from?"

"Some are the king's personal guard. The majority are levies. I have brought them in from the countryside."

"And who is working the farms while they are here?"

"Their families. I am only keeping them here for a short time, but it needs to be done. With the king's permission I will do this regularly."

"Why?" Euphraeus said. "Are you planning on starting a war with someone? Why do we need such a large number of soldiers?"

"To be ready."

"Ready? Ready for wh-"

"Ready for next time any of those bastards from the north come down and try to raid us again. Or if any fucking Greeks tr-"

Euphraeus looked at Philip with condescension. "My boy, when the farms are not being worked, you are damaging Macedonia's economy."

"Damaging the econo- Are you serious? And how much does our economy suffer when the Illyrians and Thracians raid the border and kill those farmers, burn the crops and steal the animals?"

"They-"

"Philip," Perdiccas said, "Euphraeus is right, we cannot afford to train the men as often as you have been doing. It's too expensive."

"But you can afford to pay for men like him?" he said, gesturing to Euphraeus. "Our army is not good enough. We-"

"Philip," Perdiccas said, adjusting the collar of his armour. "You will send them home now. Tell them to return to their farms. I want you to train our cavalry. They are made up of nobles, and can afford it."

"Perdiccas," Philip said. He glanced to the side and realised they were being watched by the men.

"No," he said. "Tell them to go home."

He gestured for Philip to walk with him, out of earshot of everyone else. Polyperchon shouted to them, and they resumed their training. They were now being trained in a phalanx in the Greek style, albeit with the lighter shields and no armour.

"You're right, the nobles can afford horses, good equipment and time to train. But our cavalry is not the problem. We cannot field a strong infantry force. This is what we must improve, the weakest link in the chain. I remember the day father was beaten by Bardylis. The centre-"

"No, I have begun talks of a new treaty with Thessaly to keep our southern border safe. This will include buying horses from them, and there is a possibility of a union between yourself and one of the noble ladies of the Aleudae, the most dominant of the political families in Thessaly."

"Perdiccas I am telling you."

"No Philip," he said, "I am telling *you*. I am your king. You will obey me."

Philip bit the side of his cheek

"Very well," he said.

The conversation was over, the men were dismissed and Perdiccas left with Euphraeus following behind him like a shadow.

.....

Perdiccas marched into his office, took a long deep breath, and slumped in the chair at his desk. After a few moments, he sat up straight to resume his work for the day, looking over tax documents and supply rosters. He dipped the nib of a pen in ink and began to scratch figures onto the paper.

Euphraeus had followed him into the room and since then had not moved; he was like a statue frozen to the spot, as if a gorgon had turned him to stone. "If I may sire," he said.

Perdiccas glanced up at him, raising his eyes, but keeping his head lowered.

"But what are you going to do about… him?"

"Excuse me?" Perdiccas asked calmly. "Him?"

"Yes sire, your brother."

"Oh. Philip," Perdiccas said. He lowered his eyes back to his work. "Nothing."

The philosophers jaw gaped open. "Nothing sire? You must do something, that sort of insolence can't be tolerated; in Athens he would be..." He hesitated to go on, but came around the desk and kneeled down next to Perdiccas, so that he was slightly lower than him.

Perdiccas sighed, put down his pen and sat back in his chair.

"We're not in Athens. He's my brother, I want him to speak his mind, no damage was done."

"But Sire..."

"Please stop calling me sire, I've told you to call me Perdiccas."

"Small opportunities make way for great enterprises. He will only get bolder if you don't nip this in the bud. My concern is that he has a huge amount of influence among the men, the soldiers. He is becoming quite popular."

"Having a popular general can only be a good thing."

"Perhaps, unless…"

"Please just make your point, you don't need to play games here."

"Very well. He is dangerous to your claim to the throne. The strength of the Macedonian crown is so

344

dependent on the loyalty of the soldiers and the nobles. Something needs to be done about him, you could make arrangements to have him…. removed. If he becomes too much trouble."

Perdiccas raised an eyebrow.

"Removed?"

"Well."

"Do you mean have him assassinated?"

"Perhaps, if necessary, it would be wise to prepare."

Perdiccas put his pen down, he felt a sudden rage boil up in him.

"Have you lost your fucking mind? I'm not going to kill my own brother. This is how we do things in Macedonia. We can talk straight to the eye. I am only the first among equals as king. I told him no, and he lost his temper, but he will respect my decision."

"If you will forgive me, the history of your family line says otherwise. Who was the last King of Macedonia to die of natural causes?" Euphraeus asked softly, almost in a whisper.

Perdiccas mulled over what he had said. He was right, could Philip be trusted? He didn't know.

"I'm not going to have my brother killed, end of conversation," he said, then looked back down to his papers to continue his work.

"Very well, but you should consider..."

Perdiccas sighed, and placed his pen down slowly, but hard and firm as if pressing a seal into wax. He slowly lifted his head up to the philosopher.

"I am about as patient as they come, and I value your teachings, but you are now starting to test my limits; this is a man I have trusted my entire life. Even if he were not my brother, he is trained effectively in matters military. His expertise is invaluable."

"Of course, of course, but consider this then; Philip is a military man, this much is clear since his return. Why not send him away to a province somewhere to protect one of your borders? So that he is away from the Capital, and there is distance between you and him. His skills will be getting put to good use, rather than him antagonising you here. Just a precaution. You have to be careful."

"Exile?"

"No. Not exactly. An assignment."

"I'll consider it," Perdiccas said and sat back again, and scratched his chin.

…..

Philip stormed through the entrance hall of his chambers and into his office. He threw his helmet onto the table, knocking over all the paper and stationery. It clattered to the floor. Antigonus followed close behind.

"Calm down Philip," he said.

"I can't believe that he would take the advice of that fucking snake over me! We need to make our army stronger, the only way we can do that is by building a professional army."

"We know that, but he won't listen. If you're going to get in an argument with him, you need to find another way to convince him, when that little sycophant isn't around."

Philip looked to the stone bust of his brother Alexander which stood on a plinth against one wall. He motioned with his hand.

"Alexander knew what had to be done. If he was not in Hades, he would have built up the army, but Perdiccas seems content to keep us a client state, a vassal."

"Philip, calm down, you shouldn't talk this way. People might start to talk," Antigonus said.

346

"Talk about what?" Philip asked, his voice starting to calm.

Antigonus sighed.

"Rivals to the throne, don't make Perdiccas look weak."

"He is weak," Philip snapped back into his rage. "I..."

"Remember what happened to Alexander?" Antigonus said. "Ptolemy saw a weakness and he took it. Alexander was the strongest man we knew, but he was not able to avoid a pretender taking his crown."

Philip began to calm down and think about it, when Perdiccas came into the room with two of his Royal Guard.

"Can you leave us?" he said.

Antigonus and the guards left.

"Brother. I'm sorry," Perdiccas said. He held his hands up.

Philip was still furious, he had not had time to calm himself, his blood still boiled. After a moment he took a deep breath. "No, I'm sorry. I didn't mean to lose my temper, but we have to do something."

"I heard you clearly, so I am going to send you north to Amphaxitis, to protect our northern borders. If any attack will come, that is where it will come from."

"Amphaxitis?" Philip asked. "It's practically in Thrace."

"Yes, and I want you to govern the province and train the army up there."

"Did *he* put you up to this?"

"No."

"Brother, are you trying to get me killed?"

"Of course not."

"So, it's just exile then?"

347

Perdiccas turned and walked around the room in silence; he looked through Philip's bedchamber and onto the balcony.

"Remember the night our half-brothers tried to take you away and kill you in here?"

Philip did, well. The painful memory of it flashed into his head. The muscles around his eyes flexed as a tear tried to squeeze out, but he fought it back.

"Yes, I do. Every day," he said.

"Alexander protected you, but he's dead now; father is dead, Ptolemy is dead; Arrhidaeus is still rotting in the dungeon; only the gods know where his two brothers are. It's just the two of us now Philip."

Philip looked at him, what he was going to say next, where he was going with this?

"Even though everyone said you were weak, we know now that you aren't. I remember standing in the doorway with Alexander, just a moment before we made our presence known. They beat you up really badly Philip, you didn't shout, you didn't scream, you didn't try and get away. You have a toughness, there's a strength in you, to stay put, to not waver, to stand your ground. Even when we first met Antigonus the unbreakable, he got in a fight with Arrhidaeus, remember? Even his impulse was to run, but you brought him back. You have never run." He paused. "I am looking to arrange a marriage with Philinna, daughter of the King of Thessaly, I hear she is gorgeous by the way. That keeps us safe from the South. And the way you are training these men to fight, we will be safe from the North."

Chapter 30

The scout charged through the stockade gate on horseback, so quickly that he only made it through by a hair as it was opened. The full length of the cloak he wore was splattered with mud which had frozen stiff, so it did not billow in the icy breeze, and small icicles had begun to form along the bottom.

 He jumped down from the horse, breathing hard. Philip was standing with Antigonus. They warmed their hands over an iron brazier, watching the men drill in the yard of the Macedonian camp. Steam rose from the shoulders and heads of the men as they clashed blunt training spears with shields. As the scout approached, stumbling and gasping for breath, his footsteps crunched in the snow. He was stopped by two soldiers who had been guarding Philip, shadowing his steps a few moments behind.

The scout unwrapped the scarf that was covering his face. Philip cringed; the skin around his eyes was red and blistered, and the cloth took some away with it as he peeled it off, his breath floated out of his wide-open mouth and rose as it met the air

"Looks like bad news," Antigonus said.

"It's okay, let him through," Philip shouted and waved the men to let him past. "I know this man. What news do you bring boy?"

The scout approached, his legs shaking from the hard ride through the mountains. He had probably not eaten, or slowed down to draw breath. Philip felt nothing but respect for the youth.

"Philip, a Thracian raiding party is moving through the passes to the north. They jumped our outpost, and are heading for the town. They will be there in a day."

He leant forward and rested his hands on his thighs for support. His chest heaved.

"How many?" Philip asked.

"More than before, maybe a thousand."

"Those bastards, they don't give a shit if it's winter or not, but they know we do," Antigonus said.

Philip nodded and placed his hand on the scout's shoulder. His horse appeared equally unwell, and Philip took the reins from the scout, winding the creaking leather around his hand as he patted the horse's neck.

"Get to the mess and get some heat in your bones," he said. "Get yourself fed and watered."

He then turned to Antigonus. "Get the men ready to march. It's good timing that they are all armed and armoured, and warmed up. We leave in an hour."

Antigonus nodded and clicked his fingers at the two members of the Royal Guard, and beckoned them with a tilt of his head to follow. He marched off and they trailed behind him; he took long strides because of his height, and the men had to walk quickly. The scout headed for the mess hall.

"So," Philip said, stroking the horse's neck; its skin was scorching. He ran his fingers through its mane. The animal snorted and steam shot out of its nostrils like flames from a chimera's mouth. Its flanks moved in and out like the bellows on a giant's forge. "You made it all the way from the northern outpost in a day. That was fast. You must have had Poseidon himself looking after you."

He patted its neck and kept talking to it softly. Two of his servants arrived looking for instructions.

"One of you take this horse to the stables, and make sure it is well looked after. Tell them I will come for

350

him after I am back from this fight, assuming I come back. The other needs to get a fresh horse and let Polyperchon know I am heading north to chase off another Thracian raid. I will likely be away for a week or more."

The servants nodded and led the horse away.

All around, shouts and the rapid crunching of footsteps could be heard while the men assembled. Philip quickly walked back to his quarters, trudging through the snow. He stood next to his fire and stoked the coals with a poker, rubbed his hands together in front of it, and squeezed his fingers into fists. He changed into his armour, keeping himself as close as he could to the heat. His hands were still not completely warm and fastening the buckles was difficult. He fed the chain of his sword belt around his waist and fastened it. He threw his black, bear pelt cloak back over his shoulders, then headed out into the frosty air.

....

Half a day later, the men made a double-quick march up to the pass where the Thracians had attacked. They passed their scouts' camp; the wood from the campfire had blown into the tents and they had burned down; the whole place was now covered in a thin layer of snow. The air was still. It was eerily quiet.

"It must have been abandoned days ago," Antigonus said.

"But where did our scouts go?" Philip said.

They both surveyed the mountains all around them; any footprints in the snow had been covered.

They moved on, and marched around toward the next outpost, the pass opened up into a vast horse-shoe shaped hollow on the north slope of the mountain, and at the bottom of this hollow was a frozen lake. Grip underfoot was surprisingly good; Philip stomped his foot in and twisted it side to side. The snow had compacted on top of the sheet of ice and had formed a flat surface as hard as stone.

The Thracians filled the opposite side of the valley in a semi-circle, with their backs to the inside of the horseshoe.

"They have fallen back here to wait for us," Philip said, as he glanced around the surrounding slopes. "There must be an ambush waiting."

The army of Thracians now assembled on the far side, in front of a frozen waterfall. The massive icicles hung like fangs, and behind them was a dark hollow, making the mountainside look like the gaping mouth of a Titan, or maybe Hades himself.

"Is that a bad omen? Are we walking toward an entrance to the underworld?" Philip said.

"No. These bastards just know their terrain," Antigonus said, shaking his head.

Philip's troops spread out to form a phalanx on their side of the valley, where it became wide enough.

The men were now all competent in a standard hoplite formation, an eight-man deep shield wall, commanded by Antigonus on the right flank. They stood fast, awaiting orders; the men had fought many battles like this in the years they had been there; most had been small skirmishes. Hit and runs were common, and the Thracians had proven to be excellent light troops. At times they had managed to gather a larger force and a battle would ensue in one of these valleys. They were choke points through the mountains and thus often fought over.

Philip turned to one of his young officers. "Watch their left flank. We are in the thin end of a wedge. When we advance and the valley gets wider our flanks will become exposed," he said, and looked to their right. Visibility was good, he could see far, and there was no sign of any enemies there. "They will have skirmishers, or maybe infantry waiting over the brow of the hill where we can't see them. I want the skirmishers ready to move and return fire when they show themselves. We must make it appear to them that we don't expect it."

The officer nodded, kicked his heels into his horse's flanks and rode off to his command on the opposing side.

"Five years in this shit hole," Antigonus said. "It's only the hundredth time they've done this; you'd think they would learn."

"Well, this will be the hundred and first time we beat them," Philip said.

He surveyed the battlefield, his companion cavalry on the right flank. In the coldness of the air every breath hurt his throat, his nose ran. He sniffed and wiped it with the back of his hand.

"How can people live in such a land?" he said. He hated it. He wished he was further south, back in Amphaxitis where it would still be cold, but he would be able to at least sit next to a fire, or take a shit without dying of frostbite.

"Pelopidas and Epaminondas thought we Macedonians were hardy, but these Thracians don't seem to feel the cold at all," he said. He stared at the frontline of these warriors; one stepped out from the frontline; Philip was unsure, but the man appeared to be completely naked, his whole body covered in blue swirls; he wasn't sure if it was the war paint that they wore or if it was tattooed onto his skin; he yelled something, his arms wide, his eyes rolled up in their sockets and only the whites showed.

Philip did not understand what he was chanting, but it echoed off the ice, sending a chill down his spine. It reminded him of how cold it was and he shivered. It felt like they were at the ends of the world, and that these were not men but some strange beasts from the myths. Every time he fought them, he felt the same way.

Philip had spoken to one of his Thracian mercenary generals the year before, and asked about it. He said that when not in battle they were perfectly courteous and polite. These men would frenzy themselves on a type of mushroom that they would pick in the hills and boil into a drink, they believed the paint would protect them like armour, a blessing from their gods.

Philip thought he must remember how uncomfortable this environment was for those not used to it, namely the Athenians, whom he felt Macedonia would soon be at war with. He was already very suspicious, for they had much to gain by sponsoring these raids into Macedonian land, without risking their own citizens. If they ever fight us up here, we will be more prepared than them.

"Join your men and signal the advance," he said to Antigonus, who rode off to join his men on the right flank of the Phalanx. Philip watched him dismount in the distance and walk to the front of the shield wall.

He did not want to waste time, and he was afraid that if the men stood still for too long, they would freeze. Once in the fury and chaos of battle, their bodies would heat up quickly and they would forget the cold.

The trumpeters blew down the line and the phalanx advanced, their spears lowered toward the enemy. The Thracians covered in their blue tattoos and warpaint began to chant and beat their chests and weapons against their shields.

Philip rode out to the extreme of the right flank with his cavalry ready to protect the gap that was widening from the advance.

The Thracian skirmishers emerged from the main line, screaming and shouting and launching sling balls, javelins and arrows. Philip watched his mainline still steadily advancing, their feet stomping the ground in harmony. As the missiles flew toward the line, the ranks tightened up, the men standing closer together and tucked behind each other's large hoplite shields.

The skirmishers continued to launch them. "Look out!" One of the cavalrymen shouted, as a sling ball completely cleared the top of the phalanx and whistled towards them. One of the cavalry men sitting next to Philip raised his shield and it bounced off the metal with a dull thud. The man lowered his shield and smiled. "Close!" he said.

"Yes. They're close now, we will go," Philip said turning to his men; he tugged on his horse's reins and took off. He guided his cavalry out round the right flank of the phalanx. When they were clear of his infantry, they wheeled back in toward the centre of the battlefield where the skirmishers moved around loosely.

The skirmishers saw this coming and ran. The cavalry chased them off behind their own lines. Philip then withdrew them, and they headed back out to extreme of the right flank. This game of cat and mouse continued as the two advancing infantry lines closed the gap.

Philip turned his head and looked over his shoulder. He had to stretch to see because of the stiffness of his cuirass. The two main lines had clashed; there was shouting and screaming, blood being spilt.

355

Philip and his cavalry managed to wheel around, ready to charge the Thracian front line in the rear. The skirmishers who were protecting the rear of the line broke off and headed for them in a loose formation. In a split second, he noted the unusual weapons the skirmishers carried. They had extremely long spears, longer than he'd seen before.

Philip's cavalry approached them. They sped up, building and building until their hooves thundered. Philip felt one with his horse, in rhythm together. They lowered their weapons ready to ride these skirmishers into the ground. He felt as if his heart was in time with his horses.

The skirmishers closed up into a tight formation and dug the butt spikes of their long spears into the ground and angled them down toward them. The cavalry crashed into them; many were crushed, the spears were split and most of the cavalry rode through the gaps and killed many of the Thracians. He glanced around; many of his own men had been unhorsed, and there was a whine of horses that had been impaled.

In the ensuing chaos Philip struck a man with his sword in backward thrust as he rode past him. It slashed deep down into the man's neck and blood sprayed into the air. He tugged on the reins of his horse and moved to find another man.

Any sense of formation was gone. There were men running and fighting frantically in all directions, hacking and stabbing their weapons at any enemy.

He spotted a man running towards him and dug his heels into his horse's flanks. It reared high and he held on tight as it bucked. The horse's front feet landed on the ground and the animal broke into a gallop. Philip lowered his sword to match the Thracian, who had braced and lowered his spear. Philip raised his sword ready to ride around the man and strike. His horse's hoofs thundered, and he braced.

Another Thracian emerged from behind a melee and came at Philip from the opposite side, armed with a spear; Philip tried to parry, but the Thracian swung it two-handed at him like a club. It struck him hard in the face, and he fell back off his horse.

He stared up at the spinning sky. He was trying to sit up, but couldn't. It was like he was not in his body any longer, floating off the ground, his limbs limp, heavy, but light at the same time. All around he could hear the ringing of metal on metal, and screams, horses whining. Everything seemed muffled and distant. His skin felt warm. He struggled to keep his eyes open.

All faded to black.

Chapter 31

Philip woke on a bed looking up at a spinning ceiling, unaware of where he was. He moved to sit up and was immediately forced back down by a shooting pain in his abdomen. Keeping his eyes open hurt and he immediately closed them.

"Philip, best you don't move," said a voice, through the fog in his vision and hearing. He didn't recognise it. "You took quite a blow to the head."

"Where am I? Who is that?" he asked; his head spun. All he could make out was light all around him. The man who was talking was an indistinct dark patch in a sea of light; his voice seemed to echo all around.

"He's awake! He's awake!" the voice called. "Fetch the Physician!"

There was some commotion around him; chair legs screeched across a tiled floor, and scurrying footsteps.

More dark patches stood up and flowed around the room like shades.

"Am I dead?" he asked. "Is this Hades?"

A calmer, older voice spoke now, in Macedonian, but with a Greek accent, "No, no, my boy, you're very much alive, but you did take a very hard knock to the head. It cleaved your helmet nearly in two."

"Father?"

There was silence.

"No Philip." The voice said, "Your father-"

"What?"

"King Amyntas died some time ago."

There was a pause.

"Can you see? Does the light hurt?" the voice asked

"Yes."

"Do you know who I am?"

He heard the scrape of curtains being closed, and the room darkened. As he gradually opened his eyes, he could make out who he was speaking to. The man was sitting next to him and dabbing his forehead with a cloth. He was an older man, his thick beard almost entirely grey; the hair on his head, although the same colour, was much thinner.

"No. Who are you?" Philip asked, sliding away up the bed.

"Don't worry, I'm a doctor," he said.

The room was dimly lit, with a shaft of light coming from between the two curtains. It looked like one in his villa in Amphaxitis, but he could not be sure. He had spent so little time there that he did not recognise all the rooms.

"Where am I?" Philip asked.

"You are in Amphaxitis, in Polyperchon's villa."

"Did we win the battle?"

"I think you best discuss that with-"

"I'm afraid you lost a lot of men, Philip," said a voice that he did recognize: Polyperchon. His old friend was standing by the closed curtains. "How are you feeling my friend?"

"My head feels like Zeus has struck it with a thunderbolt. And my nose…"

He sniffed and found he could not breathe through his nostrils. He took a deep breath in through his mouth.

"The physician says it was broken when they found you. They reset it while you were unconscious. Don't strain until it heals. We thought the gods were going to take you, but thank them, you are awake," Polyperchon said. "You've been asleep for almost two weeks."

"Two weeks. What happened?"

"The flank fell apart, and Thracians swarmed behind your line. Antigonus managed to escape with most of the army. He is unharmed apart from a few minor cuts, but angry and restless, ready to hit back, you know him."

"We need to study what happened. Find out exactly what went wrong, to avoid -" He tried to sit up again, but his head felt as though it was being clenched in a titan's fist and he lay back down rubbing his temples with his fingertips.

"Not until you've recovered. You need rest; you've had nothing but sips of water the whole time you've been out. I will bring you a little food to start off with, not too much, or you'll likely vomit it back up," the Greek doctor said, and left the room.

Polyperchon came over and sat at the side of the bed, and held a cup to his lips. He sipped; the water was cool and fresh.

"Who died? We need to find out what went wrong, in detail," Philip said, staying laid down this time.

"You heard the doctor."

"Forget the doctor, we need to-"

"Philip, you would not be alive if it weren't for him," Polyperchon said, with an expression that made Philip think about when they used to get a scolding from their tutors as boys.

Philip sighed, "You're right, I'm sorry. My head."

"Studying the errors will come, in time. Your brother sends word that he is on his way. You almost died Philip," Polyperchon said. "Have you considered…"

"Considered what?"

"Marrying this Thessalian girl that your brother is intending for you? I know you've been avoiding coming back to Pella."

"I haven't given it any thought. We have been fighting here for years."

"I know, but perhaps you should have the arrangements made. You need an heir"

"An heir? I'm not the king."

"Not now, but maybe in time. Have you considered what would happen if Perdiccas falls?"

Philip considered this. "Not now. Polyperchon, I feel like-"

"Yes now," Polyperchon said.

"Polyperchon. I'm not even sure I-"

"It will take time. You are mortal, as is your brother."

"Very well," he said, always trusting Polyperchon's advice. "Send word to my brother to make the arrangements."

…..

In the spring the lady Philinna arrived from Thessaly with the whole entourage of servants. She was given a full welcome. Philip gave up his quarters for her, and his staff to look after her.

Philip arrived for the wedding ceremony. He had still not seen her. The wedding was to take place in the gardens of his governor's mansion. He welcomed his guests as they filed in; it was early evening, just as it had been at his sister's wedding. That seemed like a lifetime ago to now.

He thought about Perdiccas' wedding, and how he had not been able to attend as he was a hostage in Thebes. The wedding had been a big affair that many of the people had talked about; Philip regretted having not been able to attend. Ptolemy had arranged the whole thing to benefit himself, eventually aiming to take the throne; now that he was dead, these alliances belonged to Perdiccas.

He had very mixed feelings about this wedding. He was excited, but nervous, his hands shaking ever so

361

slightly, which felt strange; he had been in battle many times now beyond count against monstrous Thracian tribes in the North, but he had never experienced this kind of nerves because of a girl, especially one he had never met.

He now stood with his whole male entourage behind him, which included the King himself. They had spent the previous day drinking, while Philinna would have been bathed and groomed by her closest female companions and family.

The wedding ceremony was functional and understated, no cheering crowds of people, and only a small number of the nobles in attendance to witness before the gods. He was only the prince and Perdiccas did not want it to be extravagant, which Philip was more comfortable with. He looked to Perdiccas, and his closest friends, Antigonus and Polyperchon. You would not have been able to tell Perdiccas was a King; he was dressed in the same simple clothes as the rest of them. This was true of him at all times. He barely wore his crown, had never been one to boast or pose, and when in victory at the games he was always humble.

They arrived together, and had spent the previous day separate from the females, as was traditional and still commonly practised.

"Are you nervous?" Perdiccas whispered in his ear as he waited at the altar.

"Not at all," he said and took a gulp at the knot in his throat. Perdiccas just smiled; he knew his brother could see right through the facade he was trying to put on. He was about to marry a girl who had never met or even seen in the distance. Would she be pretty? Would they have anything to talk about? In the end he thought, it didn't matter, it was a political wedding. This girl was from Thessaly, and it would be great for Perdiccas' throne, strengthened by having a union with her house.

He stood at the altar, next to the Shrine of Hera which had been set up; it was made of beautifully carved wood; two priestesses of the Goddess stood either side of it.

The females all arrived and took up their side of the aisle, his mother and sister among them. He smiled at them and gave them a small wave, only raising his hand from by his hip. They loved weddings; they must be excited for today, he thought, a day for them to forget all of their troubles.

"Here she comes," Perdiccas said.

Philip turned his head and looked over his shoulder; she arrived on a mule-drawn carriage with her father, a veil covering her face.

He stared hard to try and get a glimpse of what she looked like. But he could not tell. He swallowed again; the lump in his throat would not go away; instead, it seemed to grow.

"Is this what it was like for you?" he asked his brother.

"Yes," he said, and then laughed.

"What?" Philip asked.

"Except that I had the whole kingdom watching."

Philinna held hands with her father; they were raised high up towards the ceiling and walked down the central aisle that formed as the room separated into two groups. She was brought alongside Philip, and they stood next to each other; they then turned to be face-to-face.

Philip stared at the blank veil, trying to imagine the face underneath; he knew this marriage was political, but he prayed to the gods that she was beautiful. He smiled at the veil, and although he could not see her face, he thought she may have smiled back. The priests came out from next to the altar and said some words, her hand was transferred from her father's to Philip's, and he lifted her veil.

Philip felt his smile grow and his body relax. All the tension melted away; she was beautiful, her face thin with small delicate features. She smelled as fresh as the newly blossomed flowers outside. He turned to his brother, and he smiled back.

He smiled at her, but she stared straight ahead, through him, her shoulders stiff, as if she was scared to look him in the eye.

Philip felt his smile fade. He raised his hand up and felt his face, his crooked nose from being broken in Thrace, the scars on his cheeks where the skin had become blistered from endless fighting over one mountain pass or another every winter. In Thebes they called him a barbarian, was the same true of Thessaly? Surely not, the Thessalians knew him, knew his family.

He had spent all this time hoping she would be attractive. He had never given a moment's thought to whether she would find him attractive. The sudden thought that she might actually even fear him was difficult.

The two stepped up to the Goddess and made their offerings, then made their way back through the guests, who parted to let them through and threw flower petals over them.

Philip led her by the hand and helped her onto the mule-drawn carriage that was being held by servants, and made their way back to the house.

They spent the evening together, having a quiet drink; Philip tried to make polite conversation. He wanted to get to know her, make her feel at ease, but she was not for talking.

"Was the journey to Macedonia pleasant?" he asked.

"Yes," she said, not turning to face him.

There was a long pause.

He sighed.

"What is your home like? Is it similar to here?"

"Yes," she said.

Philip looked around the room.

"More wine?" he asked.

"Yes please," she said. He poured it and tried to think of something to say that might start the conversation. He thought about Arsinoe. She had never been difficult to talk to. He hoped the wine would make her more talkative.

Maybe she was just shy, in an unusual place, far from home; she didn't seem to be scared.

That night they consummated the marriage; however, it was purely functional, their movements were awkward, there was no affection or lust. He lay on top of her and was as gentle as he could be; he knew she would be a virgin. They lay side-by-side in silence for a short time after; Philip wanted to talk to her but could not think of anything to say; he pulled a sheet over them and went to sleep.

....

Philinna spent the next day in Philip's villa with her ladies, who had come with her from Thessaly. They all sat in the gardens under the shade of the trees, eating grapes and laughing and joking with each other. Philip was happy as he watched her relaxed with her friends; her smile was beautiful.

She played music on a lyre and was clearly well practised. She played every note beautifully as if she had drawn them from the air. Music was not something Philip had ever been interested in, but as he watched her, her fingers gliding over the strings elegantly, he became entranced, like a sailor drawn in by a siren's

365

song. He moved around the edge of the garden, trying to keep out of sight. He stood behind a pillar and listened. He did not approach her, knowing if his presence was known, it would kill the moment.

….

That evening Philip and Philinna hosted Perdiccas and his wife at their villa. Their mother and sister also attended. Perdiccas and his wife had brought their son, Philip's nephew, Amyntas who was now two. The villa grounds teamed with more guards and soldiers, but inside the house there were none, apart from the immediate royal family there were only servants serving food and drinks.

Philip waited for the family to arrive seated on a couch with Philinna; they barely said a word to each other. The king and queen entered, and her eyes lit up when she saw Amyntas in his tiny tunic, being carried by Perdiccas. He kneeled down and placed the boy on the floor, letting him get his balance. "Release the Titan," he said.

The infant plodded straight to Philinna, his footsteps clumsy, his body rocking from side to side as if he was a drunk outside a tavern. Philinna squatted down and stopped him from falling; he flopped onto her leg and embraced it, giggling. She turned and looked Philip in the eyes, smiling ear to ear. His heart fluttered at the sudden attention.

Perdiccas stood in the doorway with his wife. Philinna smiled and kneeled to him as they approached.

"Up you get, please. Hasn't Philip told you, we don't kneel or bow in Macedonia, especially not to family," Perdiccas said to her, and helped her up. The way she looked at him made Philip's warm feelings disappear, and his cheeks immediately flushed. She was his wife. He resisted the urge to put himself between them.

"I'm sorry," she said. "I was told to treat you as a king."

"I am a king, but it's just not how we do things in Macedonia"

Their mother and sister arrived, but as they had all spent the previous day together, they needed no introduction. Eurydice embraced Perdiccas first, and then Philip. He not seen her for some time. Her smile had a few more wrinkles, but her eyes still shone. She ran her finger down the bridge of his nose, and tilted her face down, followed by her eyebrows in a mock scolding, as she would have done when playing with them as children.

"What happened?" she asked.

"I don't want to talk about such things with you mother."

"Come Philip," she said, "you think I don't know what happens in a battle?"

"I think you can imagine," he said, and he sat in silence for a moment. His mother was now twice a widow, and had lost a son to a murderer's blade; even the women of Macedonia had to taste the violence of this land. "Very well, a Thracian swung a spear into my face and unhorsed me."

She nodded, and tsked, "Do try to be more careful."

"Mother!" he said impatiently, then resisted the urge to tell her he was not a child anymore, but this was always the way of it with mothers he supposed. He calmed himself down. "Very well, I will try."

They took a seat on one of the couches; his mother relaxed into the cushions of one the couches and listened to the lyre that was being played by a servant in the corner of the room. Perdiccas and Philinna sat and played with Amyntas on the floor, Philip watching, chewing his lip.

He glanced across at Perdiccas' wife, who sat with an expression that, he imagined, mirrored his own. When she turned, he looked away.

"How are things with your new wife so far?" his mother asked.

"Things are going just fine, Mother."

She sat back and took a sip. "That's good, so warming to each other then?"

"I wouldn't say that."

"It takes time Philip. With me and your father, it was years before we loved each other."

"No, we have barely spoken, but it will get better; she loves horses, that should give us something to talk about. I'm going to take her out to the stables soon."

"You should. Do it tomorrow." She smiled.

"I'm afraid we may be more like my father and his second wife; he spent almost no time at all with her, and her sons-"

He stopped when his mother placed her hand on his. His fist was clenched so hard that his knuckles cracked at the very thought of Archelaus and the others. She looked him in the eye.

"If you don't want that to happen, you need to go and speak to her." She pointed at Philinna with her head.

Philip nodded and got up; strode across the room and sat down on the hard tiles next to Philinna, who was tickling the baby. She looked at him and smiled. "Hello, Husband," she said.

"-Yes, I can get you all the best horses in Greece," she said to Perdiccas.

"Excellent, excellent, I will have to speak with your father sometime very soon, but don't let that trouble you; I will speak to my Thessalian ambassador in the morning. Relax and enjoy the rest of the evening," Perdiccas said. "Your husband here is quite the cavalryman; you two should go for a ride together."

He winked at Philip, then got up using his shoulder as a prop, and let out a groan, pretending he was older than he was. When fully upright, he gave Philip several pats on the shoulder.

"Can we talk?" he asked.

"Of course," Philip said. He smiled awkwardly at Philinna, then he and Perdiccas moved a few steps back, away from everyone else. He looked around the room at them. They were all mingling. Philip frowned, no one was listening to them, where was the need to be so discreet?

"I have spoken with the Athenian ambassador; Athens has said that they are unhappy at our current arrangement with Thebes."

"Can't this wait?" Philip asked. "I thought we were going to have a relaxing evening?"

"I don't want to speak about it now either," Perdiccas said, "but I need to talk to you now, where there is no one else to hear us, well, no one outside our immediate family."

Philip nodded.

"Okay, what have they asked us to do?"

"That's the problem, nothing."

"Nothing?"

"Nothing. They made no demands or requests. They have simply stated that they are aware of our arrangement, and that they are unhappy."

"So, what are you going to do?"

"I don't know," Perdiccas said. "Trading with both of them is making Macedonia wealthy; our debts to

Athens are almost paid. Perhaps they are unhappy that it is with Theban coin."

"That must be it," Philip said. "Not that it's Thebes, but that we will no longer be in their debt, we will be harder to control."

"I think you're right," Perdiccas said, chewing his cheek.

"Why don't you get your philosopher pet to talk to the Athenians? Isn't that where the prick is from?" Philip said.

"Keep your voice down," Perdiccas said. "Euphraeus is not my pet; he is my advisor, same as you. You know well enough that their democracy is slow; they have to discuss and argue, then have a recess, then discuss and argue again, until they agree on something that none of them is completely happy with. That is how Euphraeus describes it."

"Excellent," Philip said.

"Excellent?"

"Yes. If they take so long to come to any sort of agreement, then we can take advantage of that. Send them a message that will cause them to disagree and debate as much as possible. Slow them down, give us time."

"What will we say to them?" Perdiccas said. He scratched his chin and watched his son playing. Philinna had brought him a gift of a small wooden horse; he was chewing on it. His mother took it off him and told him not to put it in his mouth.

"I need to think," Philip said.

They spent the evening drinking and socialising with their family. Philinna was made to feel welcome. She played more with baby Amyntas, and after a time, he was taken to bed by his nanny. The adults stayed late into the night. The women were led out into the gardens by Eurydice who wanted to look at the flowers, and Philinna and Perdiccas' wife followed, taking their wine with them.

When they were out the door, and their drunken chatter became muted by the closed door, Philip turned to Perdiccas.

"I know what to do. Bring them here, both the Athenians and the Thebans. Put them in the same room," he said, "and we will stoke the fire between them."

Perdiccas nodded.

"Guard!" Philip shouted, and one of the guards who was standing to attention outside in the doorway came in.

"Philip?" he asked.

"Can you find Antigonus for me and bring him here?"

"Yes, Sir," the guard said and headed off into the night.

Chapter 32

When Perdiccas invited the Thebans and Athenians to talks, it was to be an official visit, attended by high-ranking delegates from both cities and Macedonia. Perdiccas and Philip had discussed it previously, and the accelerated sale of the resources from upper Macedonia.

The Thebans had been paying upfront for things, and had lent Macedonia many talents to fund Perdiccas' various projects, education and engineers, among other things. They regularly came to blows over this, however, as Perdiccas had continued to spend most of the military budget on mercenaries which Philip felt was terrible in terms of how poorly cost-effective it was.

They stood in the throne room, Perdiccas paced. Philip stood just behind the king, to the side of the throne. On his other side hovered Euphraeus.

"You'll be fine," Philip said, low enough so Euphraeus couldn't hear.

"I know, and I know your insight into how the Thebans think will be invaluable, stay focused."

Euphraeus had become one of Perdiccas' most trusted advisers. He and Philip still never saw eye to eye, and would clash even over the most basic of issues, mostly because the Theban money was being ploughed into his education and philosophical programs, rather than Philip's military training.

The Theban delegation arrived, and Philip's thoughts went back to when, in this very room, he was first sent to Bardylis and then to Thebes. The Macedonians had been helpless, or at least that is how it felt at the time. Now they were far richer than before, but the Treasury was in massive debt to Thebes; it was becoming a strong alliance, and they shared intelligence from the spy networks. However, Philip worried about how large the debt was getting.

The delegation filed in as the heavy wooden doors were opened, and their sandals clomped on the tiles.

At the head, as expected, was Epaminondas. He paced out in front of the rest, his head held high and confident. Philip had been expecting Pelopidas to attend as well. The increasing tension between Athens and Thebes had meant that he had spent a lot of time away, and Philip had not heard from him in a long time. His heart sank that his old mentor had not come, but he was happy to see Epaminondas. He turned to Perdiccas. "Be careful, he is a good man, but he is very persuasive; don't worry, I know all his tricks, I will not be fooled."

"Remember Philip, I have met him before."

"I know, but that was years ago, and we were at their mercy."

The general now walked with a limp, which he could almost hide, but his right foot turned in and he seemingly could not put all of his weight on it. Philip wondered if this was a recent injury that would heal or if he was now permanently crippled. He also noted new scars on the man's arms.

Epaminondas smiled widely as he approached, and now that he was closer, the crow's feet in the corners of his eyes and the greying of his hair were visible. Had it really been this long?

"Hail King Perdiccas! It has been too long since I have been in your beautiful country!" Epaminondas said. He lent forward at the waist in a half bow, his arms wide; Philip thought the Thebans were well aware we do not bow, and although he dismissed it, it made him cautious of the over the top courtesy.

"You are most welcome, General. I trust that your trip was safe and without incident?" Perdiccas said, and stepped down from the platform the throne was on, and the two embraced.

Epaminondas looked up at Philip over Perdiccas' shoulder, and nodded his head toward him, a warm smile on his lips. Perdiccas turned his head, his body followed, leaving one arm around the Theban's back. He motioned to Philip with his other hand. "Have you missed my brother?" he asked.

"Of course, by the gods, Philip. A man now." His eyebrows lowered. "How many years has it been?"

"Too many, Sir, too many," Philip said. He stepped forward and embraced the general. Epaminondas tilted his head, looking at the scars on Philip's face. His hand came up and felt the bridge of Philip's nose. It made him think of how his mother had done the same thing. He thinks of himself as a father to me, he thought.

"How many times have you fought, Philip?"

"Too many to count Sir," he said. "Mostly Thracians on our north-eastern border."

"Ahh!" Epaminondas raised his eyebrows. "Thracians, ferocious people; I remember when I was younger-"

"Pardon me, General," Perdiccas interrupted him. "We must get on with negotiations, you will have time to catch up with my brother later."

They talked for a while and Philip listened. After a time, his concentration lapsed and he found himself looking at the faces of the servants who attended Epaminondas. His heart fluttered when he recognised Briseis. He tried to make eye contact with her, but she either didn't remember him or she was avoiding it, and he could hardly start a conversation with her during the negotiations.

After watching her for a while, he realised she was whispering in Epaminondas's ear between him

374

speaking, and scribbling notes. She was also too well dressed to be a slave. He thought back to when he knew her, remembering a moment when he found it unusual that a slave could read and write. At the time, she had said Pammenes liked them to be able to do this. Now that he was older and wiser, he knew how dangerous it would be for slaves to be able to communicate so effectively. Was she an agent for Epaminondas the whole time? Or had she become one after he had left? A bead of sweat ran down his neck.

The talks broke for a short recess, and they split up into their two groups. When the Thebans returned, before they could start talking again, Philip caught Epaminondas's eye. The old general smiled at him.

"General, may I ask where is Pelopidas? I understood he would be attending."

Epaminondas's smile faded. He tongued the inside of his cheek. Philip understood perfectly what had happened, but did not want to believe it; his heart was in his mouth, he forgot to breathe, then gasped a deep breath.

"I'm sorry, you have been misinformed. Pelopidas was killed nearly a year ago. I'm sorry Philip, I thought you would have heard."

Dead? Philip was speechless. He breathed shallowly now, trying to hide his breathlessness, his eyes darting around the room, not sure at who or where to look. Despair took him. He felt his eyes begin to well, and his cheeks stretched out to the sides as he fought the tears, trying desperately to keep his composure in front of the Thebans.

"I'm sorry Philip, I know he was dear to you. He was a great friend of mine. There was no easy way to tell you. He was killed in battle, the hero that he was,"

Epaminondas said, his face showing his discomfort. "I have made peace with it. In time, so will you."

Philip felt a tear run down his cheek and it dripped to the floor; he stood on it in a vain attempt to hide his feelings. He sniffed and wiped the corners of his eyes with his thumb and forefinger. He felt Perdiccas' hand on his shoulder.

"Do you want to be excused? We can negotiate without you."

"No, I'll be fine, I just wasn't expecting this."

They took their seats; the negotiations went on for a while. Philip spent most of this time far away, thinking about Pelopidas and the time they spent together. He could not believe he was dead; he had not seen him for years, but this burned deep into him. When he had been in Thebes, it had seemed as if they were immortal like the gods themselves.

The voices around him seemed distant, and quiet. Every now and then he would be asked his opinion, and he would not give much of an answer, mostly just agree with what was being said. It would be fine, Perdiccas knew what to say and do, he thought.

His daze was broken when the final arrangements were made, and parchments were signed, new treaties were made.

"Do you agree Philip?" Perdiccas asked, looking into Philips eyes. Perdiccas looked concerned, but there was something else there. Irritation? Philip had never told him the full extent of his relationship with Pelopidas, concerned he would have thought it a liability. He also thought it could push him more towards Euphraeus.

"Yes, yes, I agree," he said finally.

Perdiccas stood up from his seat around the negotiating table, walked round and raised his arms wide in front of general Epaminondas. "Very well, Thebes and Macedonia will be closer than ever." The two embraced, and both delegations applauded.

Philip suddenly realised that he had not paid any attention during any of these negotiations What had been signed? How much had been given up? What had the Thebans offered? How much had Euphraeus influenced things? He found himself regretting what had been done. He caught Epaminondas looking at him, his eyes narrow. Had this had been part of a manipulation? Would he really use his friend's death in such a way? Philip never realised how naive he must have been in Thebes. He had been just a young boy.

They said their farewells, and as the Theban delegation left and filed out into the corridor, Perdiccas grabbed Philip by the shoulder and turned him, so they were face to face. "You should have told me you were lovers," he said furiously. "I was relying on you. They got far more than we intended to give them."

"I'm sorry I-"

"Perhaps you should return to Amphaxitis Philip," Euphraeus said.

Philip whipped round, "You'd love that wouldn't you? Send me away agai-"

They were silenced by noises erupting from the hallway, a lot of shouting. They quickly walked through the doors to see the Thebans being separated from the Athenian ambassadors, who were coming down the hallway for their meeting. It was clear that insults had been exchanged on the way past; an Athenian stood back holding his cheek, the others raised fists, trying to strike them over the burly guards.

Perdiccas looked at Philip. "Perfect timing," he said, the corners of his cheeks turning up.

He immediately stepped forward, his open palms to both sides.

"Gentleman, gentleman!" he said in a soft tone, but loud enough to be heard. They stopped momentarily to listen. "You are in Macedonia. This is neutral territory for both of you. I demand you be peaceable."

The pushing and shouting ceased.

"They insult us Perdiccas, be careful what company you keep," shouted one of the Athenians.

Then a punch was thrown and the whole situation erupted into a melee, kicks and punches were thrown from both sides. Perdiccas allowed this to go on. Someone was slammed to the floor in a hip throw, a few noses were bloodied, and one of the Theban's eyes was gouged with a thumb; he dabbed the blood from it with his tunic.

"Stop this now!" Euphraeus bellowed, his hands in the air.

Perdiccas stepped towards the melee, backed up by four of his armoured guards, and put his hand on one of the Athenian's shoulders, and they all began to calm down.

"We are sorry, but these Theban thugs attacked us, we must defend ourselves," the man said to Perdiccas.

Epaminondas caught Perdiccas eye, and both groups separated away from the guards, who straightened up and adjusted their clothes.

"Is this true Epaminondas? Did you start this?"

Epaminondas stiffened and stood upright, glancing over at the Athenians, panting slightly, regaining his breath from the fight.

"I apologise to you for doing this in your palace. But not to them, they are our enemies, and they insulted us as we passed. We had to defend our honour," he said.

"You lie Epaminondas!" one of the Athenians shouted. "It was one of yours who threw the first insult. Tall, young bastard. Although I can't see him now. He was clearly too cowardly to stay and fight."

"What is done is done," Perdiccas said, "but I want no more fighting. Our business is done. Please go, you and your men, and take any supplies you need for your journey back to Thebes."

Epaminondas pointed his finger toward the Athenians.

"Mark my words. There will be consequences for what has happened here," he said. The Thebans nodded to Perdiccas respectfully and backed out, down the corridor, not breaking their stare with the Athenians and not showing their backs to them.

"If the Athenian delegation would come with me, please," Perdiccas said once the Thebans had left.

Philip was amazed at the calming effect that Perdiccas had had on the two groups; his brother was no warrior, but his voice commanded the respect of even these seasoned politicians.

The Athenians followed them into the throne room. They sat down at the same seats that the Thebans had used; they had brought their own scribes to write down everything that was said.

"I'm sorry Perdiccas, about what happened back there. The Thebans are warmongers, they fancy themselves Spartans, always trying to fight before they talk," the Athenian ambassador said.

"It's true, the Thebans have always been like that, they would sell out all of Greece to save themselves," Euphraeus said. Philip tutted loudly, trying to make his disagreement obvious; he stared at the man, clenching his fist by his side. In his current state he was ready to

379

strangle someone, his vision focused on this man's puny neck, and he fought the urge to grab it.

His hands hurt, gripping so hard that his nails dug into the palms. He took slow breath through his nose, trying to quell his rage.

"Maybe if you Athenians didn't play so many games, they would not feel the need to go to war with you?" Philip said.

Some of the Athenians mouths were open, and Philip realised he had lost his composure.

"To what games to you refer?" the ambassador asked.

Perdiccas stared at Philip, his expression furious now. There was nothing he could do but continue with what he had said.

"Gentlemen please forgive my brother; he's just received some very bad news. A friend of his was killed in battle," Perdiccas said.

The men nodded their heads, all understanding this. Philip felt embarrassed, not for thinking what he had said, but because he let others know what he was thinking. He also wanted to maintain the tough image of Macedonia.

"My sympathies," the Athenian ambassador said, then immediately turned to Perdiccas. "Very well, we shall continue with our negotiations, Majesty?"

"Of course, follow me." Perdiccas beckoned them to start with open palm. He then turned to Philip and whispered harshly, "You are excused, we will talk later."

"I just-"

"No," he said in a hushed voice. He glanced over Philip's shoulder at the Athenians, some of whom were nosily looking over. "Go, and I will see you later."

Philip stood in the hallway as the heavy wooden double door was slammed shut; he looked around, not knowing what he was looking for, anything to take his mind off what had happened.

He spent the afternoon trying to keep himself occupied, nervous about what was being decided by Perdiccas and the Athenians, and Euphraeus.

He headed down to the gymnasium to take his mind elsewhere. He lifted weights for an hour or two. When he had done enough repetitions that it burned his muscles and he felt as though his lungs would burst, he pushed through. The punishment that he put his body through was not enough to satiate his desire to harm himself. The thought of falling on his sword crossed his mind, but he quickly dismissed it to the back of his consciousness.

When he finished, he washed and returned to his chambers to rest. Philip lay on the couch at the foot of his bed, staring into space. He looked up when there was a knock at the door. He ignored it.

The door opened regardless, and two Royal Guards entered. They separated and stood either side of the door. Perdiccas immediately followed. "Leave us so we can have some privacy," he said.

Two men lowered their heads and left the room, closing the door behind them. There was a muffled bump through the door, as they both put their backs up against it on the other side.

Philip swung his legs around and sat up and Perdiccas sat next to him. Philip opened his mouth to speak and Perdiccas raised his hand to silence him. "You don't need to say anything, it's probably best if we just put it behind us."

"How did the negotiations with the Athenians go?" Philip asked.

Perdiccas let out a long breath through pursed lips and looked up to the ceiling.

"That well? What happened?"

"Well, they're definitely not happy with us."

"I assume that's an understatement?"

"Obviously. They want us to stop dealing with the Thebans, and the Thebans want us to stop dealing with them. I'm an impossible situation. We need at least one of them. It's a risky game, Philip."

The two sat staring into space. Philip recalled his father trying to play both sides of the Spartans and the Athenians off each other; it mostly worked. He had been a very cunning man.

"I think your idea may have worked though. They confirmed that they are going to withdraw their ambassadors from Thebes, and they expect the Thebans to reciprocate. Us putting them in the same place and them brawling couldn't have been more perfect. They will both return to their cities with the angry tale of what happened. It will sow more hatred between them, and they will be too preoccupied by each other to do anything about us."

"Good," Philip said. "It will, at least, buy us more time."

"I did not realise you were so close to Pelopidas, you getting so emotional, and our argument..."

"I'm sorry about that, I think it was on purpose that he brought it up at that moment. I barely took in what was being said. I think he was being deliberately manipulative. I trusted him, I won't again."

"It made us look weak."

"It's fine, let them think we are. If they think we have turned on each other we can use it to our advantage," Philip said.

"Who does know about you and Pelopidas? The Athenians certainly seem to, even if they don't say it. The Thebans obviously do. Why am I the only one that doesn't?"

"You didn't have any spies watch me while I was in Thebes?"

Perdiccas chewed his cheek, not joining in with the joke. He took a long slow breath.

"My spies have had better things to do than to watch who my brother was lying with. I'm trying to hold the kingdom together here, and it's being torn apart. Everything was going fine up until now; these Greeks were fighting each other without Macedonia becoming a direct part of it. Pretenders will always come, and we can kill them, but this pretender Argeus seems to be gathering momentum; the Thracians are raiding as they always have, and the Illyrians are trying to form an alliance with Athens," he said.

"So, what are the Athenians going to do?"

"They have said they are not going to form an alliance with Illyria, but they kept avoiding the subject," he said, but his eyebrows were up, his face contorted. "I don't know if I can trust them though; there are certain Athenians that I trust but, like Father used to say, in Athens they make a promise, and then a year later they change government and break it."

"It's all about what motivates them, Perdiccas. The only reason that they have to ally with Illyria is if they will be a better partner than us. Illyria is a lot further than Macedonia, without a coast on the Aegean; they would have to sail all the way around the Peloponnese to get to their ports," Philip said. Perdiccas leaned in. "Their motivation is the timber, and to get to the timber without an ally in the region means they need to take somewhere to give them a foothold."

383

"Amphipolis," Perdiccas said.

"Amphipolis," Philip said. "They have tried and failed to take it back for maybe a hundred years. It is within our means to take it. Promise it to them. Even though you have no intention of helping them take it back."

"What if they don't believe me?"

"It doesn't matter if they believe you. It's an offer so tempting that they will be unable to refuse. In Amphipolis is not just the timber, it's the mines. Those mines have got both silver and gold in abundance. Pammenes, my tutor in Thebes told me. In the wars with the Persians, those mines built the entire Athenian navy, two hundred triremes if I remember right. Can you imagine? Two hundred! Losing Amphipolis to them was like when Father lost Pella, he had to have it back. It's their obsession."

"Okay," Perdiccas said, placing his hand on Philip's shoulder. "We will promise them Amphipolis."

"They will buy it, I promise you, Brother, and if we do ever take it, the silver and gold will be ours."

"Of course. I will leave for Delphi soon and consult the oracle on the matter," Perdiccas said.

"The oracle? You?"

"Yes," Perdiccas said. "I know, but it looks ill if I don't."

Perdiccas left the room, and Philip let out a huge sigh of relief. He had been expecting to be punished for damaging the relations with the Athenians.

Chapter 33

A year passed since the meeting with the Athenians; they had returned to Athens and Perdiccas' spies had kept a close watch on the political unrest on the Pynx where the Athenian citizens carried out their debates. One returned in the spring and told him that there were a lot of people furious that Macedonia was still dealing with Thebes, and that his offer to retake Amphipolis had tempted some, but enraged others, seeing it as an insult that Macedonia thought they could accomplish something Athens could not.

Philip, still in Amphaxitis, received a messenger telling him that the Athenian fleet was on the move, sailing up into the north of the Aegean. Letters from Perdiccas in Pella had become increasingly impatient. Trade ships were not getting through, revenue was dropping, and they could not do anything.

They had been told that Athens had blockaded the sea to allow only the ships headed for Athens through. Philip felt it important to see the blockade for himself.

When Philip's scouts reported that they had discovered where the Athenians were landing to replenish their supplies, he rode out to the coast to investigate; He took his cavalry and a number of his men from Amphaxitis.

As always, he brought Antigonus with him, who as commander of the infantry, marched with them. Polyperchon was left to govern. He was becoming very skilled at this during Philip's absence. Philip saw big things in his future, and always told Perdiccas how impressed he was with him.

….

Philip and his men approached the sea from the south and dismounted their horses. The land stretched out and came to a sudden stop in the distance. They could not see the sea, but they could hear it, the waves gently lapping the sand, and the smell of salt was in the breeze. The bulk of his force stayed back and set up camp.

Philip, Antigonus and some of the officers approached. They climbed down a rocky gorge and onto the beach; there was no sign of any ships. He looked out to sea; it was a perfect sapphire blue, and so was the sky. It was difficult to see the horizon where they met. He wiped sweat from his brow.

Around the cove, they came to a rocky outcrop that jutted out into the perfectly clear water. They splashed into the water knee deep, their sandals filling with cool water. They hugged the rocks and walked around; tiny fish swam about their feet.

Philip led, and emerged the other side. There were tufts of grass that led to a lightly wooded area that overlooked the sea. The beach itself was obscured from sight by a sand dune on the other side of the trees. They lay prone on the brow of the dune and surveyed the beach.

The triremes bobbed in the calm waves and stretched for as far as he could see. They disappeared over the horizon, into the heat haze. It was a thin line of ships, but it didn't matter, he felt his heart sink.

"We don't have anywhere near enough ships to stop this blockade," he said to Antigonus.

"I don't think even the Thebans do."

Macedonia had some ships, but not a powerful navy; they certainly didn't have enough to break through this blockade, or guard the trade route from this many Athenian ships.

386

Philip watched the end trireme, it had beached, and a gang plank had been lowered onto the sand; there was a steady stream of sailors carrying supplies onto the ship, like ants carrying leaves to their nest.

When they were all back on board, the ship lowered its oars and sailed away along the blockade. The next ship then beached, and the men all walked ashore to go and get supplies and the cycle repeated. Local merchants and fishermen had gathered to sell to them.

"Do you think the Thebans have built enough of a navy to break through this yet?" Antigonus asked.

"I don't think so," Philip said. He sighed. "If we can't get them their timber, we're going have to do something about it. This blockade will strangle Macedonia before too long."

"What are we going to do? Ask the Persians for help? Or mercenaries?"

"I'm not sure about the Persians." Philip scratched his brow, and dabbed sweat from it. He squinted up at the sun, "and we could never afford a mercenary fleet strong enough to stop this blockade."

They paused for a while, all of them thinking.

"I think I'll go and talk to them," Philip said.

"Talk to them? I would advise against that Philip," one of the officers said. "What if you're taken hostage?"

"Or killed," another said.

Philip shook his head.

"No, it's baking hot, we're in the middle of summer, the men on those ships must be dehydrated and hungry; we don't have enough ships, but we do have enough men to control the coast. We could cut off their resupply. See how they're rotating their ships? It's very clever, but we have them outnumbered on the land. A day without fresh water and they'll start to waiver."

"Okay," Antigonus nodded, "but I'm coming with you."

Philip got up and walked out in the open across the sand toward the trireme. He felt very exposed.

A few men followed as they walked out onto the beach toward the men who were loading baskets of fresh fruit and skins of water onto the ship. Some looked up and stopped what they were doing, one patted another on the back, and he turned around. He looked shocked to see this armed group of Macedonians approach, but they were already too close to react and he seemed too stunned to raise an alarm.

"Are you in charge?" Philip asked.

"No, em, you want to see the Admiral," the man said in a thick Athenian accent. Philip had never heard an Athenian that was not an aristocrat, and the man's voice was strange to him.

He led them toward the ship and hailed some marines who were guarding the beached ship. They wore strange white armour and short swords on their hips. The marines silently obeyed the man. A rowing boat that belonged to one of the fishermen was lashed to the side of the trireme. The man didn't object, although he looked as if he wanted to, as they climbed aboard the boat and took the ropes, and they pulled it in to the shore. One of the marines beckoned the Macedonians to come aboard. He seemed completely aloof and unconcerned about who they were, or what they wanted. They walked into the shallow water; it was cool, and it lapped around their ankles. They waded out to the boat; it was knee deep when they climbed into it. The wood seemed stained with the scent of fish.

The marines rowed them out along the blockade; they passed maybe five triremes before they reached the admiral's trireme.

388

Philip shielded his eyes and looked up at the ship as they approached. It was a huge vessel, and it dwarfed their tiny rowing boat. Three decks of rowers were open to the air. The huge iron tipped ram jutted out of the bow and was visible below the surface; a huge eye was painted on the side of the bow, making the ship resemble some monstrous sea creature.

Most of the crew lay about, doing their best to stay in the shade or keep cool; they were all stripped down as much as they could and were lazily fanning themselves with their clothes. They looked down at Philip and his party as they approached; their faces wore curious expressions.

A net was lowered, and they followed the Athenian marine, who climbed up it like a ladder onto the main deck of the trireme. His sandals clomped on the wooden deck, and left dark, wet footprints which dried out almost as quickly as they were left. The vessel bobbed in the waves; Philip was not much of a sailor and the movement made his stomach uneasy. The Athenian rowers found this amusing but when he glanced over at them, they looked down at their feet. Philip already had a reputation as "the barbarian" with the democrats in Athens, and they seemed afraid of how he might react.

He was taken to meet with the Commander of the trireme and Admiral of the blockade. He was a tall man of lean build and wore the white linen armour of the marines that were on the shore. He immediately seemed familiar to Philip who frowned, trying to place him.

"Ah, young Philip," the Admiral said, and welcomed him aboard. He spoke in an aristocratic voice, unlike his men. When he spoke Philip instantly recalled the man.

"I know you," he said, unable to hide his surprise. "Iphicrates? My Father's study. I remember you."

"Correct," Iphicrates said, a warm smile spread across his face. "What can I do for you, Prince?"

"These blockades are damaging our trade. I want you to remove them now and head to a port that is not near the Macedonian coast."

The corners of Iphicrates lips turned up in a smug smile. Although he seemed amused, Philip was not.

"Making demands of an Athenian Admiral on his flagship? You are not the timid, confused boy that I met before."

"I am not," Philip said. "I have suffered since we last met, but steel sharpens steel. I have also lost people close to me."

Iphicrates smile faded.

"I had a great relationship with your father, he was a good man to deal with, reliable, I trusted him. But your brother is not like him, not a military man. He relies too much on advice from philosophers, he does not want to make the hard decisions."

Philip was in complete agreement, but would not give that away. "Well. My father is dead, and my brother Alexander is dead. Perdiccas rules now; he is also a good man to deal with. Perhaps you should try to build a relationship with him," he said.

"I did try."

"Not hard enough. This alliance is deteriorating, to no one's benefit. I can make things very difficult for you. You will remove the blockade, or we will make you leave."

"Your fleet does not have the strength to send us home."

"I do not need a fleet. I have more than enough soldiers on the land. I will shadow you on the coast and stop anyone from coming ashore to collect fresh water and food," Philip said. "How long can you stay out there without fresh water?"

They both looked up and squinted at the sun. Iphicrates smile returned.

"You are a man now Philip," he said. "And a strategic one, managing what resources you have well. I have no desire to fight with you, Philip, or Macedonia, but we cannot allow this trade with Thebes to continue, you know they are our enemies. We once had great ties to your house; this ship you are standing on and the oars that propel it are built with Macedonian timber. For this reason, I will tell you straight, no tricks, you do not want to cross Athens; we are the only city with the navy to repel Persia in the Aegean."

"Persians? This is about Thebes; you don't want us trading with Thebes," Philip said, surprised at what he was hearing.

"Thebes yes, for now. We don't want Thebes to build a navy that could rival us. It will weaken all of Greece. Persia is interested in our land and sea."

"They have no interest in Macedonia."

"Are you sure?" Iphicrates leaned in, his eyes narrowed. Philip listened intently.

"Does your philosopher brother have spies in Persia?"

"I don't know."

"Well, we do. The new Great King Artaxerxes is young and ambitious. Rumour has it that his eyes already look west. A new king has to flex his muscles. He will look to expand his territory, and he will have to take Macedonia before he can march into Greece, just like Darius and Xerxes did a century ago. A storm is coming from the East."

"You lie."

"Why would I lie?"

"Many reasons," Philip said, dismissing him, yet he felt tension rise in his chest. If this was true then they were in far more danger than he or Perdiccas had ever imagined. Bardylis and his Illyrians were nothing compared to the Persian Empire. "If what you say is true, we are stronger together than apart."

Iphicrates walked to the side of the ship and Philip joined him. They looked over into the blue water, clear as glass. Small fish swam around the ship below them, perhaps hoping to get fed from anything thrown overboard.

"That may be true, we have done it before, but your friends in Thebes consort with Persia, even your Macedonian Kings did only a few generations ago," he said, "but there is always a bigger fish, Philip. Did you think that Athens, Thebes and Sparta were the greatest powers in this world? What is it you want?"

"What do I want?" Philip asked.

"Yes, what do you desire?"

"For myself or Macedonia?"

"Either."

"I don't care about myself. I want Macedonia to survive, that's all I care about," Philip said, seeing no harm in telling him this.

"Athens could put you on the throne," Iphicrates said. There was an awkward pause. "Choose us over Thebes and we can make it happen."

Philip stared at Iphicrates. His hand rested on the hilt of his sword, and he took a half step toward the Athenian; a few of the marines reached for weapons. Some of their archers gripped the feathers of their arrows, ready to knock them. Iphicrates didn't react. He appeared completely relaxed.

"You think I would usurp my brother?"

Iphicrates raised his hand to signal his men not to do anything. His tone stayed constant, steady and calm, a master politician, Philip thought; manipulative.

"Think about it, Prince, would you make a better king than Perdiccas? How long do you think Macedonia will last with a philosopher for a king? Don't tell me you've never thought it?"

"I thought you were already sponsoring a pretender?"

"I don't know what you mean."

"Don't lie, I know all about Argeus. I saw him in Illyria years ago, and I doubt he's changed his mind about wanting to be king."

"Ah, yes, Argeus. I see nothing gets by you now. He will do, for now, but to have a true Argead, no one could question your lineage."

"I will never betray my brother," Philip said.

Iphicrates looked at him long and hard. Philip felt as though the man was reaching into his mind to hear what he was thinking.

"Lie to yourself if you must, but not to me," he said. "If you want to talk, you can come back here. For now, please leave this ship before there is bloodshed."

Philip stared back at him again for another moment, then turned and climbed back down onto the boat, Antigonus and the others following him. The marines gripping weapons all relaxed.

Back on the beach, Philip walked away along the sand with Antigonus beside him. "What will you do then?" he asked.

"I will not betray my brother."

"About the Athenians," he said.

"I'm not sure, that man knew my father, but I don't trust him."

"But we aren't letting them keep supplying their ships?"

"No," he said. "Definitely not."

They waited on shore until nightfall. Then all of the men were brought around the cove. They lay hidden behind the sand dunes. The sound of the waves gently lapped up the beach.

Philip lay on the brow of the closest dune to the Athenians, staring into the darkness, listening out for any sound.

There was too much time to think lying there in the dark. He pondered Iphicrates offer. Athens would make him king. He could run things how he wanted to. He could end all this nonsense with wasting money paying for philosophers and artists. He could use it to strengthen the army. Maybe they would help him to kill Bardylis and take over Illyria. With their navy he could definitely do that; they could sail around the Peloponnese and attack Illyria from the West in the Ionian Sea, while he attacked from the land. Once that was done, he could-

"Philip… Philip," Antigonus whispered.

His line of thought was broken. Antigonus' face was just visible in the pale moonlight, and even that was partially blocked by the canopy of the trees over their heads.

"Yes?"

"Can you hear that? I think they're trying to resupply."

Philip listened carefully, all he could hear was the tide lapping in and out.

Nothing.

Then, in-between the waves, he heard hushed voices.

"They're out there," he whispered. "Tell the men to get ready, we will attack when they are out in the open."

He squinted into the darkness. He couldn't see far enough to see them; the silhouette of the boat was just visible, with the sky behind it, but the men were on the beach and could not be seen. He waited. Antigonus whispered the order to the man next to him, and it was carried down the line.

After a while, between the sound of the waves, Philip heard the muffled sound of someone cough into a fist and he signalled for them to get up. They all rose, and started to march quickly across the beach in the direction of the sailors they could not see, trying to keep their footfalls as silent as was possible.

They traversed the beach in a line and reached the Athenians in the dark. They drew their swords and charged at them in the blackness. There was no precision; they hacked like wild animals goring and thrashing. There were screams, and running; some men tripped over bodies and the sailors ran back to the ship; others panicked and ran off the beach and into the woods; it was impossible to tell how many they had killed before they fell back to the tree line.

No matter, Philip thought, killing them all was not the intention, just scare them enough to stop them sneaking out in the dark for supplies.

The Macedonians slept in shifts on the tree line. So far as they could tell, there were no more attempts at getting ashore that night.

At dawn the sun rose over the sea and revealed the bodies of the night before. They were grotesque, even in the distance. Some had been carried out by the waves, then washed back in. They were bloated and swollen. The crabs had been at all of them and were still feasting.

Swarms of gulls ripped at them; their white breast feathers now red with blood.

More of the triremes had moved close to the shore and had beached. The marines from these ships filed down onto the beach. These marines all wore the white armour and open-faced bronze helmets the marines on the deck of Iphicrates' ship had worn. None carried shields, but each of them carried a spear, an abnormally long spear, not unlike the ones the Thracian's had used to unhorse him; he stroked the bridge of his nose. They formed a phalanx, with archers behind them, facing the tree line where Philip and the Macedonians waited. What in the name of Hades is this? he thought.

The sailors from the ships came down onto the beach and hastily started to remove the bodies. They all wore cloths tied over their faces, covering their mouths and noses. A few of them stopped, bent over, lifted their masks, and threw up. Others stayed back, frozen, reluctant to go near their fallen comrades.

Philip shouted the order for them to attack. The men emerged from the tree line and formed up in their own opposing Phalanx, linking shields and raising their spears.

"Antigonus!" he shouted, and looked to his friend, who set up on the right-hand flank of the formation, the position of honour.

"Yes, Philip," he shouted, understanding the order. They began a steady march toward the Athenians. A hail of arrows flew from behind the Athenian line, but they were few in number, and mostly stuck the shields.

Philip mounted his horse and took his cavalry out. The pound of the hoofs beat in his chest like a drum. Clumps of wet sand kicked up and he spat it out, the taste of salt on his lips. They rode out as hard as they could and wheeled around to the rear of the Athenians as the two lines of infantry clashed.

He estimated from his elevated position on his horse that they outnumbered the Athenians. Excellent, he thought; and because they had come from the ships, they had no cavalry to match his.

They chased off the bowmen who were behind the Athenian line. The fools should have stayed on their trireme. The skirmishers panicked and ran in all directions; some tried to scramble back to the ship, but Philip and his cavalry rode them down. He swung his sword into the back of an archer's head, and then another on his other side. He took a moment to look around and assess their position. Almost all the skirmishers had been killed and the remaining few had either dropped their equipment and fled, or had managed to escape back to safety of the ships.

Antigonus's line was holding, but did not seem to have moved.

"Back with me!" he shouted. His trumpeter sounded and the cavalry regrouped to form a line with him.

"Charge!" he yelled. The trumpeter sounded. They charged as fast as they could into the rear of the enemy line. Philip hacked and slashed into the backs of the Athenians.

To his surprise they could not turn. These long spears prevented it. Some dropped them and tried to climb over the men in front to escape; these men had turned their heads at the screams and the surge of men rushing forward to get away. Philip could see the whites of eyes, and the spears started to get dropped. As they did, Antigonus and his men managed to push forward. Some Athenians reached for short swords, but it was too late. The Macedonians had them surrounded.

Chapter 34

"And how did the Athenians react to you attacking them?" Perdiccas said. He rubbed the back of his neck.

The men had spent the last few days sorting the recovered weapons and armour that had been looted from the bodies of the dead Athenians. Anything that was damaged that could be repaired, was, and Philip had started his men making as many of the new spears as he could while he travelled with Antigonus to Pella to report this to Perdiccas.

"What do you think? They're really angry. My men are continuing to stop them from resupplying along the coast. Soon they'll have to leave."

"Very good," he said, again rubbing his neck; he appeared restless, unable to settle. "Avoid killing them from now on, just chase them off. Disrupt them. We need to avoid actually starting a war until the Theban's fleet is complete, so no unnecessary killing," Perdiccas said, pointing a finger. Even though he had taken orders from his brother for years as a king's general should, he was, however, still his brother, so he didn't much like it.

"Very good," Philip said, biting his tongue.

"And what of these new armaments you discovered them using?"

"The white armour is made of hardened layers of linen," Philip told Perdiccas who nodded in fascination. "Where they got it from, we don't know, but it is far lighter than bronze and protects almost as well."

"And the spears?" Perdiccas asked.

"It is far longer than a doru spear that our hoplites would normally carry, allowing them to keep out of their opponents reach. Our phalanx had a lot of trouble getting to engage with them; fortunately for us, those

Athenian bastards didn't have any cavalry, and ours was able to ride around and hit them in the rear."

"How does a man wield such a long spear?" Perdiccas asked, lifting it up. His face lit up with surprise when he felt the weight; the wood creaked as he twisted the spear in his grip, and ran his fingers up it, feeling the finish.

"You feel that? The butt spike is weighted to perfectly balance the extra length, but it stops them carrying a shield."

Perdiccas lowered the spear down under control. He then made some thrusting motions forward toward an imaginary enemy.

"It's very clever," he said. "Just like when you used your reach to beat your opponents at boxing. Did you suffer many losses?"

"No," Philip said. "We beat them easily, despite not being able to engage them head on. But these Athenians were marines; they weren't prepared to fight us on such open ground. They had the extra reach, but they had nothing to protect their flanks."

"Good, so we don't need to worry about these new weapons any more then?" Perdiccas said. There was a long pause. Philip and Antigonus looked at each other.

"What is it? You recovered them all? They don't seem to be that much of a threat."

"I was in the front line, Perdiccas, we could not engage them," Antigonus said. "We could do nothing but tuck behind our shields. We could not hit them back. These weapons could be a disaster if we fought a larger force, one that was not so easily flanked. We need to start using them, so we are at least even."

"No, I don't see the need to arm all our men with these," Perdiccas said, but showed some concern.

"I have my men making as many of these as we can. I want to arm our phalanx with them. If we incorporate this new weapon with our tactics and cavalry, it is going to make our army far more formidable, our men will take far less injuries, and there will be less fatalities," Philip said.

Perdiccas didn't seem impressed, Philip thought.

"And how much is it going to cost to equip all of our men with these and retrain them all? And then what's to stop them coming back with even longer spears? And what about archers? With no shields-"

"You didn't see how it worked on the battlefield, they were only six men deep, less than a traditional phalanx," Philip said, starting to become annoyed. As he talked, he realised that his voice was becoming more heated. "Our men couldn't get near them. If we hadn't outnumbered them and if they could have protected their flanks, we could not have beaten them! If we use them in eight, or ten, or twelve ranks deep, no army will be able to hurt us! Don't you see? This is the future."

Perdiccas sighed.

"Very well. How many do you need?" he asked.

"Five thousand."

"Five thousand!"

"We recovered about five hundred already from the Athenians,"

"And how much will four thousand five hundred cost?"

"We estimate about- "

"Actually no, don't answer that. The answer is no."

"Perdiccas-" Philip said, but his brother raised a finger to him, cutting him off.

"No, will you just obey me, just once. I say it's too risky," Perdiccas said.

"I'll take care of it from Amphaxitis," Philip said, trying to keep as calm as possible. "I don't need funding from the royal treasury. In the long term, this is going to save us a fortune; the less casualties we take, the better: when soldiers are killed or injured, we have to train more."

There was a long wait while Perdiccas scratched his chin.

"Very well, you govern your own province as you wish," he said.

"I am going to start drilling the men with these, and combined with our cavalry, we will have a much greater chance in our next engagement. We will take far less casualties because the front line will simply hold theirs in place for the cavalry to crash into their opponents' rear; like a hammer hitting a sword on an anvil. I promise you. You won't regret this."

Perdiccas still seemed sceptical, Philip thought, but this was fine; he was never a soldier, more interested in talking and politics than fighting; and he was good at that. He could be the general.

"Very good," he said, rubbing the back of his neck again and shooing Philip and Antigonus. "Keep me informed of your progress. If it's successful we will make more, and you can train my soldiers in your new tactics."

…

Over the next year Macedonia's ties with Athens had become more and more strained. Perdiccas' spies in Athens reported that the Athenian blockade incident greatly angered many of the Athenian citizens, who ranted against Macedonia on the Pnyx, where their democratic assembly was held. Some even called for a takeover with military force; others argued with them that they should never have sent the blockade in the first place as it was not in their territory. This was then argued that they had to protect their own interests and that Macedonia had betrayed their alliance with Athens. Euphraeus had returned to Athens to argue in favour of Perdiccas and calm the anger towards him.

Philip had felt more settled over the past year. Philinna had warmed to him; their love of horses had been a great common ground and gave them reason to spend time together. However, she was stressed, and unhappy every time Philip had to go into the mountains and fight another battle. The raids in upper Macedonia were constant.

It was a spring morning, and they were at the stables, and together they groomed a great Sassanian charger who had been a gift from her to him; they prepared this horse and another of Philinna's to go for a ride.

"Where do you want to ride to today?" he asked.

"Head out to the coast? It's so beautiful down there."

"Of course, it will be beautiful." He watched her slender arms, as she brushed the horse's neck. His gaze crept to her shoulders and down her back. She looked up and caught him staring, opened her mouth wide in a playful gasp, and smacked him on the cheek. It stung, but it didn't bother him.

"How dare you!" she exclaimed.

"I'm sorry my lady, I couldn't help myself," he said, his grin growing. He stepped forward and put his arms around her and lifted her up as if he was going to wrestle her to the ground. She let out a playful squeal, and with her arms pinned to her sides, she wiggled her legs and slapped his sides.

"Ahem-" a loud deliberate cough came from behind them and killed the moment.

Philip put her down, and they both turned to see a young courier standing awkwardly. In his hand he held a scroll, sealed with wax.

"My apologies Philip, the King sends you this as a matter of urgency."

"Don't worry lad," Philip said taking the scroll from him. "Do you know what this is about?"

"No, but there are rumours."

Philip ran his finger across the wax seal; the sixteen-point Argead Star. He snapped it off and unrolled the letter.

Dear Brother,

This letter finds us in a worse predicament than before. Athens have now severed diplomatic ties with us altogether, and have recalled all of their ambassadors. They have not declared war formally, but it is as good as war. I have tried to keep us out of this Athenian and Theban rivalry for a long as I can, but this is no longer possible.

My friend Euphraeus has informed me that the debate over what to do was long, and that he will not be able to return here, as this would make it unsafe for his family and friends. This saddens me, but I know you will rejoice. He assured me that he remains our friend; he tells me he will always argue for Macedonia's case in Athens.

Please be most cautious when dealing with any of the southern Greeks in the future. The Thebans have found this most amusing and are happy to assist us in any way they can.

My lookouts on the coast have informed me that an Athenian fleet is on its way north. Worst of all, my spies have intercepted and tortured an agent who was on his way to Illyria. This was a secret mission to speak with

Bardylis, our great enemy. It appears that they have been talking for some time about the annexation of upper Macedonia to Illyria, and in return, the Illyrians will assist them in taking their old territory of Amphipolis back. I have sent a number of soldiers to Amphipolis to offer their assistance should Athens siege the city.

You know as well as I do that this alliance cannot be allowed to be made; if Amphipolis is taken and held, it will give them an extremely strong foothold in the North from which to strike at us, and we will find ourselves in a coordinated war on two fronts. It will also give them access to the vast gold and silver deposits there.

I request that you send scouts into the hills, to keep lookout for any more agents. I also want you to take as many men as you can spare. March them north on the road to Amphipolis to shadow this fleet and prevent them from landing any soldiers onto Macedonian soil.

I will be marching my army northwest toward Illyria. Bardylis has already begun to march, and I must make a show of strength to deter him.

Perdiccas

Philip crumpled up the letter in his fist, and took a long moment to think.

"What is it, Philip?" Philinna asked.

"I have to go," he said, and watched the joy drain from her face.

"Again?"

"I'm afraid so,"

"Another Thracian raid?"

"Not this time," he said scratching his beard.

"Then who?" she asked, looking concerned.

"It's Athens."

"Athens?" Philinna asked, her eyes were wide.

"And Illyria."

"What has happened?"

"There's no time to talk about it. They seem to be making war on us. I have to go. Here, take the scroll, you can read it." He looked to the courier. "Find Antigonus, tell him to muster his troops, and meet me at the barracks. Once lady Philinna has read this letter, take it to Polyperchon, tell him he's in charge of the city until I return. Then you must return to Pella and tell the King that we are marching."

The young man nodded. Philip kissed Philinna, climbed onto his horse and rode hard toward the barracks, leaving her standing; he looked back over his shoulder, her hand was on her mouth as she read the letter.

Chapter 35

The army marched north at a furious pace; the men walked double-time; they were not running, Philip needed them to arrive at their destination in a fit state to fight. The scouts who monitored the Athenian fleet had said they were hugging the coast, and looked as if they were searching for a good place to land an army.

The baggage train had been left far behind, and Philip had ordered a small number of men to stay with it until it caught up with them. His goal was to reach the coast and shadow the fleet; for this he had to get there as quickly as possible. The men carried only their essential equipment and a small amount of food and water in sacks slung over their backs. They marched in full armour, and although they seem tired, when Philip looked down the line, not a single man groaned or complained. This filled him with immense pride, although beneath this a growing feeling of dread gnawed at him.

If they had to keep this up for too long, it would be very difficult to keep his army fed, they numbered around three thousand, and there had not been time to take a full register of their numbers. If their supplies ran out, sustaining the army in such a turbulent province could fail, forcing them to withdraw. On top of that, only the gods knew how many men the Athenians might land, and where.

He had sent Antigonus ahead with the scout cavalry. There was no man he now trusted more. Although he was the faster rider, he decided it would be better that he stayed with the main army, and marched on foot alongside them to inspire and push them if need be.

He did not know for certain, but it seemed to be working. He stopped at the side of the road; many who seemed to be flagging nodded to him as they marched past, some whose heads had been sagging before raising them. He patted them on the shoulders and thanked them for their courage.

Philip wore new armour that had been tailored for him, metal plate, black with a gold trim. He also wore his helmet while marching, so that he could carry his own supplies, the same as he had ordered his men to do.

He was not sure how long it was going to take to get to Amphipolis, and he was nervous at what awaited them there. His stomach fluttered at the thought, it felt like he needed to empty his bowels, but he held it; they needed to press on, he forced the thought out of mind and continued to march alongside the column; he clapped his hands hard together. "Come men! Not far now!"

The Athenians were sailing. They could be anywhere by now. Were their winds favourable? Would they rendezvous with Illyrians or Thracians, or both? Or would they just attack at the same time as them, trapping his army. Where was Perdiccas? There were too many questions, and not enough answers.

His best hope was to catch them before they left their ships and shadow them on the coast as they had done before, not allowing them to properly deploy an army.

His men were hardened from fighting Thracians, who, as ferocious as they were, did not fight in the same way as a disciplined hoplite phalanx would.

He remembered vividly the battle that his father had lost against Bardylis, when he had not long earned his sword belt. He squeezed it in his grip.The leather creaked. He remembered well how the rows of linked

407

shields looked, like the scales of a snake overlapping each other, giving each other strength, and he remembered all too well how his father's soldiers could not break this line. Then the reinforcements had surged out of the woods and surrounded them.

He was not sure if his own men would hold, although he was confident in the new spears that most of them now carried.

He glanced up the road, through the dust cloud that floated over the army like a spectre. In the distance where it was thick, almost out of view, the tips of the pikes protruded out of the top of the cloud, looking like an army of shades marching from Hades. Perhaps tomorrow they would be.

He knew the Illyrians were not going to be prepared for this weapon used in this way, but thoughts of doubt plagued his mind. What if they knew what he knew? The Thracians used these long spears, and the Athenian marines, what if they knew how to defend or counter this kind of attack? No, neither had used them as a replacement for hoplites. They would be crushed, he told himself.

The men encamped for the night, and Philip strolled through the camp, in-between the tents, with Antigonus, who had returned. In the soft light of campfires, he saw the men's faces; some sang songs together; they drank; a soldier placed a log on the fire and stoked the flames. He whispered to his friend as they passed. A few men looked up, some stood up. Their banter quietened down at the visit of the prince.

"What are you drinking?" Philip asked one of the soldiers.

"Wine, Philip, from my home in Upper Macedonia," the soldier said. He was a young man, couldn't have been older than fifteen or sixteen. His hair was dark as coal, this was visible even in the soft light of the campfire.

"Sounds good," he said. The soldier waited awkwardly. "Can I have a swig?"

"Of course," the soldier said, and handed Philip the skin. He took a long swig of the wine, the men watching as he gulped and gulped. The wine began to burn his throat, and he continued to gulp. When he felt he was about to choke, he stopped swallowing and removed the skin from his lips and gasped for breath.

"It's good," he said, even though it tasted horrendous. "I feel a bit sick."

The men laughed and gave a cheer, any standing on ceremony disappearing as quickly as the wine. They returned to their drinking and songs.

"What's your name?" Philip asked.

"Cleitus."

"Cleitus. Good lad. You fought yet?"

"Yeah, I was with you the first time we fought the Greeks on the beach, spent the whole time stuck behind my shield mind."

"Ha, no matter, you will get to strike them back this time."

"Yeah, definitely, I'll stick some of those Greek bastards!"

He gave the young soldier a pat on the shoulder, and they continued their walk.

Spirits seemed high, which he did not expect; he expected them to be terrified, and the idea of going up against Athens worried him.

"The men seem relaxed?" he whispered to Antigonus. "Do they not realise that we face the most dangerous threat we have ever fought against?"

"They have faith in you, Philip. They trust you will not send them to Hades just yet," Antigonus said.

Philip put his hand on his friend's shoulder. "That's-
"

"They're used to fighting Thracian monsters. They think Greeks will be weak."

"They couldn't be more wrong. The Thracians may be more aggressive, but they do not have the same discipline as a Greek citizen army," Philip said, and shook his head; his stomach fluttered again.

"Yes and no. The Athenians do have discipline, but do you remember the battle on the beach?" Antigonus said raising an eyebrow. "We absolutely destroyed them."

"Yes, but those men had been on the ships for days being starved, and without fresh water. And we outnumbered them. Had they not been so far from home it might have ended differently. We must make the men aware of what they face."

"No. They are just as far from home Philip. Confidence is important. By the gods, we may even meet Athens on the same battlefield as before. Wouldn't that be a good omen? The men who fought that battle will have told their friends how easy the Athenians were to beat. We know that all they need to do is hold the line in the centre to buy time for the cavalry. If this gives them the confidence to do that, then so be it."

Philip nodded in agreement. "You have become wise my friend."

"We both have," Antigonus said.

The two men walked back to their tents and settled down for the night.

Philip was almost asleep when one of his scouts returned, and placed a hand on his shoulder. He grabbed the man by the throat and pulled a knife which he still kept next to his bed, almost thrusting it into the man's guts. He quickly gained his composure when he saw the petrified look on the man's face, his hands up in the air, fingers wide, like his eyes. He immediately loosened his grip and lowered the blade. He recognised the young man.

"I'm sorry boy, what news do you bring?"

"I'm sorry, I startled you. We've sighted the Athenians. They've beached their triremes a day's march north of here; they're unloading supplies, then we think they will head West in the direction of the old capital."

Philip yawned and rubbed his head. He sat up sharply when he realised what he had been told. "Aegae? What makes you think that?"

"Their scouts, we watched them heading that way. The pass is less than a day's march north of here."

"Do they know we are coming?"

"I don't know for certain, but I think so. In the darkness we could hear hoof beats and whispers. The sound carries in the night air. It may have been Athenian scouts doing the same as us."

Philip nodded again. "We had to expect that. Thank you for coming to me immediately. Get yourself fed, get some rest, and then head back out when you're fresh."

"Philip, I feel fine, I would rather head now. I can rest in the wild at a better time. We want to serve you best as we can."

"The king. You serve the king."

"Of course, of course, we serve the king," the man said, his cheeks flushed. "Gods forgive me."

"Don't worry, you are a good man; go then, we will meet you tomorrow."

The scout left and Philip sank back onto his bedroll and scratched his chin. They know we are coming he thought. It was too late to attack them while they tried to

411

land the ships. He did not settle back to sleep so easily
this time.

....

The men rose after only a few hours of rest, and
before the sun came up. They were quick marched to
take control of the mountain pass that the scout had
spoken of. The scouts had all stayed to shadow the
Athenian army and warn of any troop movements.

When the morning came, Philip deployed his army
on the slope of the valley, making sure he had the higher
ground, but the troops from Athens had not showed yet.
Philip sat and took deep breaths, slowly. He waited for
the return of the scouts, who could now be seen in the
distance returning down the other side; the hoof beats
quietened by the distance.

"Maybe they are not coming?" he said to Antigonus,
who sat by his side on their horseback. "The scouts
could have been wrong."

"They are coming, no doubt about it." Antigonus
said, adjusting the strap of his helmet by hooking his
index finger into it. Both of them were uncomfortable at
having to wear helmets so long. Boredom was surely
starting to affect the men; Philip's mind began to
wander.

The scouts came back in and rode around the lines
of the new phalanx. Most of the men were armed with
the new spears which pointed towards the sky, the butt
spikes stabbed into the ground to take the weight while
they waited.

"They're coming, General," the scout said.

"How far are they?" Philip asked.

"Just on the other side of the valley. Their leaders
requested to meet with you."

412

"Ha, no doubt to offer terms for our surrender," Antigonus said, a broad grin growing on his face. "Does he realise how many men we've got armed with the new fucking spears?"

"No sir," the scout said. "He asks why you are here, that they are here to settle a dispute in Amphipolis as is their right as the mother city."

"Interesting that they're heading in the opposite direction," Philip said, "but I do think we should be more cautious. How many men are there?"

"About three thousand Athenians and a number of Thracian mercenaries - too hard to count, maybe two thousand; they were moving through the woods; it was very difficult to keep track of them."

"What was this leader's name?"

"A General Mantias from Athens, the other, Arg… Agr-"

"Argeus? That was his name?" Philip said, feeling his nostrils flare. The anger in his voice was clear to the scout who took an uncomfortable step away from him.

"Yes Philip, he sounded- "

"Macedonian?"

"Yes. Macedonian. He was definitely not Athenian."

"He's not Athenian. You can tell them that we are merely patrolling our borders. If they still want to talk, so be it. You tell them that Philip of Macedonia leads this army, in the name of his brother King Perdiccas, and that if any of them remember what happened the last time I fought against the Athenians, they would do well to get back on the ships and go back to Athens."

"Who is this Argeus?" Antigonus asked. "Iphicrates mentioned him on the ships, and you clearly despise him."

"He's the pretender who drove my family out when we were children. If he's there, I don't plan on letting

413

him live," Philip said, and turned to the scout. "Tell them we are simply patrolling our borders."

The scout was dismissed. He saluted Philip with a nod of his head and a strike to his breastplate with a clenched fist. They watched him ride off into the distance across what was likely about to become a battlefield. The skirmishers of the enemy were now visible, loosely spaced out on the valley floor, and others could be seen traversing the steep slopes up the sides of the valley. Loose rock and dirt fell down from under some of their feet, but they did not slow, as sure footed as mountain goats. These were Thracians, Philip thought. They will have no problem crossing that kind of terrain.

The front of the column of hoplites followed behind the skirmishers and began to spread out into the valley floor.

"They outnumber us," Antigonus said.

"No matter. The valley is narrow, the flanks are well protected, almost the whole army have sarissas. They will be unable to reach us. They'll stack up behind their own lines, to try to push forward with more weight. Those at the back pushing forward will be unaware that they are driving the men at the front onto our spear points. Go to *our* Thracian mercenaries now, and tell them that I want them to get whatever equipment they need, and their best mountaineers are to climb the slopes of the valley on either side and protect our flanks. If they manage to flank the Athenians, they will get bonuses. Return to me as soon as you have done that."

"Understood," Antigonus said, and rode off as fast as he could.

The Athenians were now starting to disperse across the width of the valley, their formation beginning to take shape, their brightly polished shields and armour gleaming in the low morning sun. Philip felt admiration for these men, who were brave enough to come and fight of their own free will for the benefit of their city. He had some understanding of their democracy from his friends in Thebes; he decided then that if he routed their army, he would let any Athenians go, on condition that they turn over Argeus.

Philip ordered all the cavalry to dismount, and he joined them on foot. He passed the reins of his horse to one of his pages. "Take him to the rear, as close to the baggage as possible," he said. The boy obeyed; all the other horses were taken away as well. He gathered the officers.

"The valley is narrow, and their flanks are well protected by the sides of the valley. We will take our place in the phalanx," he said, "and because it is so narrow my plan is to use an echelon phalanx. Double the depth of one flank with sword armed men in reserve. When a gap opens, they can manoeuvre between the pikes. The rest of the front line should slope back away from the Athenian line. This will cause the whole battle line to shift and create the gap they need at the loaded end."

He slid his sword out of its scabbard on his hip, and drew the two lines facing each other in the dirt. All the officers and men were Philip's from Amphaxitis. They had been well drilled on this type of formation while they were there. He had learned this from Thebes, and explained to them that this is how the Spartans were destroyed so effectively at Leuctra, with one critical difference; the Thebans at Leuctra were armed with spears of equal length to the Spartans.

"When the Athenian hoplites get more and more anxious at being stabbed without being able to hit back it will cause discord among them. Ideally the line will try and match ours, and we will stretch their line thin, and when that happens, the men with short swords will be able to get into the gap and get behind them or into their flank. They will break."

"What will we do when they break? Shall we route them?" an officer asked.

"No. When they break, take prisoners where you can, but do not kill anyone unnecessarily or injure or mistreat them. Perdiccas will want to preserve a relationship wherever possible. Also having prisoners will help us in negotiations. The traitor Argeus is to be brought to me if he's taken alive."

They all nodded. Antigonus returned, and Philip filled him in on the plan of action. Antigonus agreed that it was the best thing to do with the terrain. They looked across the valley floor to the Athenian army now fully deployed.

They made their way to the right flank, where all the men armed with swords and large aspis shields were positioned, including all the cavalry men who had dismounted. They gathered in the straight lines behind the ten-man deep phalanx, providing it with a double depth of men.

Philip looked across the valley floor between the bronze helmets of his men, who stood in neat lines like an orchard of trees. He could see men on horseback visible behind the Athenian line because of their extra height. The sun was low and he raised his hand to shield his eyes, but it did little good; he could only make out their silhouettes. Was Argeus really out there? Or was he somewhere else?

"Should we concede the higher ground?" Antigonus asked, scratching his chin. "They'd shit themselves if we started towards them now without any warning. Give them a feel for how far we've come?"

Philip thought about the merits of this; would you be best to head straight for them, now, while you are prepared, and they are not? They have both been marching today, how far have they marched? He felt a murmur in his stomach. He then realised the murmur was because he wanted to attack. "Very well, sound the advance."

Chapter 36

Philip paced in his tent, unable to stop moving. He always found it difficult to settle after a battle; his mind and body were both in pain and invigorated at the same time.

The Athenians would finally pay for what they had done to Macedonia, he thought, invigorated by the sheer joy of the victory. He washed the blood from his hands, which shook, not from fear, but from the excitement; he now did not mind it. Before he would have thought it was fear, but now he understood his own reactions.

"Get me a scribe!" he shouted boisterously to one of his pages, who smiled, gave a short bow and then disappeared under the tent flap.

Philip dunked his head in a bowl of water and brought it back up, with a splash. The water ran down his hair, and his beard matted into one neat thick strand. The cold water was refreshing; it took away the sweat that had dried onto his skin. The water became cloudy and red. There was still blood which was caked into his hair; he ran his fingers through it, searching his scalp for wounds. If he had been hurt himself, he knew that he may not feel the pain for a while. None of the blood appeared to be his, not that on his head anyway, although he did have some small cuts on his arms and his right hand. His hair would need to be scrubbed, but he had other things to tend to first.

He gulped some wine from a skin and leant over the map that was spread out over the table in the centre of the room. He drew a line with his finger around the borders to the north. The valley they had just defended covered the north-eastern approach into Macedonia, and this now secured their dominance in the whole area. To

418

the south was Thessaly, and further south Thebes, and attack would never come from there. The only directions they needed to worry about were to the west and north; Bardylis and his sons, Philip thought, and clenched a fist.

The scribe arrived.

"Take a seat," he said, delighted to inform Perdiccas of the victory. "Take a letter to the king."

"Yes sir."

"Philip to Perdiccas. Hail Brother!" he said, and the scribe furiously scribbled. "This letter hopefully finds you in good health. The Athenians have been stopped and their generals captured, along with the leaders of their Thracian allies and, best of all, Argeus the Usurper."

After the logistics of the battle were sorted, and the casualty count taken, skirmishers were deployed into the surrounding area, ready to sound the alarm should there be a counterattack from those who had fled. It would also give them an early warning of any bandits in the area who may be planning on looting the battlefield. Philip had learned in Thrace that these vultures were never far away.

Messengers were sent to Athens informing them of what had happened and offered terms for the prisoners being returned.

Days later Philip celebrated with his officers in his tent. It was not spacious, and the air quickly became stale and hot, but it was the most spacious in the camp and they did not care; after their victory they could be in a pigsty, and they would have been happy. Antigonus was celebrated as the hero of the day.

They drank and cheered, embraced and sang songs.

They all fell silent when thunder started to rumble outside. They looked at each other. Was this a good or bad omen?

"Ha! Father Zeus is celebrating with us!" Philip shouted; he was normally wary of the gods, not pious like his father and Alexander had been, but how could this have been anything other than Zeus and the other gods on Mount Olympus celebrating their victory? They all agreed with Philip and raised their drinks, pouring the gods share onto the floor. The drunkenness became more and more boisterous, when a messenger ducked under the tent flap and headed straight to Philip.

"Philip, I have a message for you from Parmenion," he said; he would not look Philip in the eye.

Philip smiled a wide, drunken grin, eyes glazed, and embraced the messenger, who stood stiff. Philip broke off and took the scroll, tilting his head to try to make eye contact with the man who still would not. He broke the seal and started to read. He stood frozen to the spot. The sweet taste of victory turned to ash in his mouth.

Antigonus had stumbled his way over and put his arm around Philip's shoulders, using him as a prop to keep himself up. "Ha ha. Does Perdiccas send word of victory as well?" he asked.

Philip scrunched the paper up into his fist and gritted his teeth. "No… he doesn't."

The others gathered around, looks of concern across all of their faces. "What is it, Philip? Are you okay?"

"No," he said. "Perdiccas is dead."

"Dead?" Antigonus staggered back.

"He was killed in battle, along with four thousand of our soldiers."

There was silence throughout the tent.

420

Philip flew into a rage. "Get out!" he yelled. "Get out!" He shoved the courier hard, who half tripped and then fled the tent.

Philip tipped the table up. All the others looked on, stunned. He kicked the cups and plates that had fallen to the floor. The men recoiled and protected their faces from the flying debris, apart from Antigonus who didn't even blink.

Antigonus casually leant over and picked up the scroll, which had been dropped to the ground. It was dripping wet with spilt wine, and he wiped the excess off with his hand. "Four thousand," he said under his breath.

Philip turned. "Out. Everyone out! I need time to think."

They all stumbled and gathered their things, and left as quickly as they could, the sound of rainfall getting louder as the tent flap opened. Antigonus was still standing reading the parchment. He rolled it up, placed it on the ground and made his way towards the tent flap.

"Not you," Philip said.

Antigonus nodded and sat down. Philip slumped down next and continued to drink; he poured wine into Antigonus's cup. They sat in silence and listened to the thunder outside, and the crescendo of rain battering off the roof of the tent as the storm passed.

"What the fuck are we going to do?" Philip asked, taking a sip of his wine. "Our great victory here counts for absolutely nothing. We are dead. Macedonia is dead."

He looked to his old friend for some words of comfort to the contrary. Antigonus had none.

"I'm sorry, Philip," was all he had.

"Very well then, leave me my friend, get some rest, we're going to have to march back to Pella at the nearest opportunity."

Antigonus left through the flap of the tent, looking at Philip; his eyes welled, but no tears came.

Philip stared into space, not thinking about anything. The faces of his father, then Alexander, then Perdiccas flashed through his mind. Thoughts of Perdiccas cleaved and bloodied on the battlefield crept in. He managed to shake them for a moment, but they then became much worse. He thought of him being dragged by a horse, or stoned, or even crucified, in front of a crowd of cheering Illyrian soldiers.

He stepped over to the corner of the tent where his armour was neatly placed with his weapons, helmet and shield. He drew the sword from its leather scabbard and ran his fingertips along the blade and felt the point. He placed it down on the ground and then took off his tunic. He lifted the blade again, and turned it, placing the point in the centre of his chest just below the left side of his ribcage, clasping the handle in both hands. The cold steel tip licked his skin, and a hair of blood ran down from where it pricked him. His heart beat thudded. He held his breath, ready to throw his weight forward onto the sword. He waited, preparing himself.

The thoughts of his mother and sister came into his head; his mind flashed through all the faces that he'd ever seen in life, the members of his own family, the nobility, his friends, the boys from the gym and his lessons, Arsinoe, Pelopidas, Antigonus, Philinna.

He waited.

If he ended his life here, many more people may die. No, he thought, I will soldier on, as I always have.

He lowered the blade and gasped in a deep breath. He flipped the sword over, and held the grip in his hand as he would on the battlefield. No. It is not me who is going to die. Argeus. Yes, Argeus will pay for what has happened. Not me. Argeus, and then Bardylis.

He pulled his tunic back on, slotted his sword into his scabbard with a click, and fixed the sword belt around his waist. He marched out of the tent. The rain lashed at him, stinging the exposed skin of his face, arms and legs, and in moments his tunic was drenched through. Lightning flashed behind the mountains, illuminating the camp in brilliant white light. He shivered while he marched to the tent where Mantias and Argeus were being held, his feet splashing in deep puddles he couldn't see. Two guards were huddled against the side of the outside of the tent, trying to avoid the worst of the storm. They were two of the veteran men from Amphaxitis. They wore full face Corinthian style helmets; the rain bounced off the bronze. Philip could not see their faces, only their eyes, but he knew who they were. As he approached, the men saluted him.

"Philip?" the most senior guard said, his voice muffled through the metal of the helmet. It was even harder to hear over the battering rain. "What are you doing out in-"

Philip leant in and shouted into the man's ear. "I need to speak to the general Mantias, is he awake?"

"I don't know, but if he isn't, I'll wake the bastard with a slap. I'll accompany you," he said.

Philip ducked under the flap and entered the tent, and the guard followed. He shook the rainwater off his hair and tunic, and shuddered with the cold. The tent was dimly lit by candles, but it had a lot of space, probably the most of all the tents in the camp. It was dry inside apart from the path that had been commonly trodden, where the grass had been worn away and was thick with muddy footprints. The guard captain sat at a small wooden desk in the corner scribbling his paperwork. He had a few candles that were half burnt down, and leant over to squint at the paper, almost close enough for them to burn him.

Philip looked around the tent, there were about ten prisoners, spread out, all chained to their own post, which had been staked into the ground. Two more guards stood on the inside of the tent.

"What's he going to do?" he heard one of them whisper.

Philip looked from prisoner to prisoner, and found who he was looking for. Argeus sat in one corner, his back against his post, legs out straight. This was a mere shade of the arrogant man who had stood across from him on the battlefield only a few days ago and who had talked to Bardylis as if he was the dominant of the two. His whole demeanour was that of defeat, head hung low. The chains were short and the shackles on his wrists held his arms back in what looked an uncomfortable position. He knew he was a dead man.

His armour had been taken from him. He been left with his fine tunic, but it was bloodied and dirty, one of the sleeves ragged, most likely from a cut received on the battlefield, which was now bandaged. At the sight of him Philip's grip on his sword handle tightened, to the point where it became painful.

As he took a step towards him, he lethargically lifted his head, looked Philip in the eye, and then lowered it. Philip loosened his grip. Argeus now looked pathetic. He did not feel the need to kill him, he would die soon enough now that he was caught.

"General?" the captain of the guard asked from behind, breaking Philip's daze. He had got up from his desk, and was now standing with one hand outstretched, almost on Philip's shoulder, He was clearly trying to

424

dissuade him from whatever he thought he was going to do.

"Yes soldier?"

"Philip. You can't kill him. He is to be brought back to Pella. The king will decide what is to happen to him."

"Soldier. Do you realise the king-" Philip cut himself off. It was too early to tell the soldiers that the king was dead. Even he did not know what would happen next. Macedonia was certain to tear itself apart.

"Philip?"

"Very well. I won't kill him," he said. He stood and thought for a moment, looking around this makeshift prison. A few of them were clearly Thracian mercenary leaders, but it was difficult to tell the difference between the Macedonian traitors and the Athenians.

"Where is Mantias?" he asked the guard captain.

"Opposite corner," he said and pointed with his head.

Philip saw the man he was referring to. He also recognised him from the battlefield. He still retained his composure, and, unlike Argeus, he looked Philip in the eye, as if they were in any normal situation. "I see him. Have him cleaned, fed and well looked after. Unshackle him and his men."

"Sir?" the guard asked.

"Find the Athenians a dry tent to sleep in, but keep them under heavy guard. I will come and speak to them in the morning," Philip said.

The guard captain acknowledged his orders, and Philip left the tent. He returned to his own, and fell into a disturbed, restless sleep, his mind again conjuring up images of Perdiccas dead on the battlefield. And Bardylis, that smug face of his standing over the corpse.

In the morning Philip, fighting a throb in his head, got dressed and lifted a heavy leather purse from the mess on his tent floor. He hooked it to his belt and returned to the guard captain he had spoken to the night before. The rain had stopped at some point in the night; the air was cool from the downpour. The ground was sodden, his feet were drenched, and itched, he tried his hardest to keep them dry, but it was an impossible task. He asked the guard captain where the Athenian prisoners had been moved to, and was led a few tents down.

Several guards that he recognised stood outside, which pleased Philip. There was no chance of escape. He also knew that although the army was made of his own men from Amphaxitis, there may be Macedonians somewhere who would consider betraying the country and letting the prisoners escape, if they were threatened or the price offered was high enough. Every man has his price, he thought, but these men were as reliable as any he had.

He made his way into the tent, and true to his orders, it was clean and dry. Several more of the reliable guards were in the tent with these prisoners. The three Athenian prisoners lounged on beds that had been laid out for them on the ground. Next to these bedsheets were cups containing the dregs of wine, and plates with breadcrumbs and a few chicken bones on each. They wore Macedonian tunics. Philip recognised the style. Their own had been hung along the ropes that held up the tent to dry along with their shoes.

The Athenian's conversation abruptly ended as he entered. The man who he recognised as Mantias stood up as he came in. It occurred to Philip he'd only ever seen this man wearing a helmet from which the ends of the grey hairs of his beard protruded, or the night before, when it had been very dark. Nonetheless, he recognised the grey eyes, the brow and the bridge of his nose.

"Are you being treated better?" Philip said.

Mantias' jaw went from side to side, and he stared Philip in the eye. He obviously had a fine line to walk, if he did not appear grateful then he may end up back in the mud, if he appeared too grateful this would make him look weak.

"Yes. Thank you." he finally said.

"Good, I can see for myself," Philip said. "I want you to know that I want an end to hostilities between us. You will be released soon. I want you to return to Athens; tell them I want us to be friends. However, I will be keeping Argeus as a prisoner."

"We would have to speak to your king would we not? Is this not the Macedonian way?" Mantias said.

"The king is-" Philip paused, realising that these men were not aware of Perdiccas' death. He would need to keep it as quiet as possible, though they would obviously find out soon enough; but if he sent them away, they would be on the road for a while, and then back to sea. It would take a long time for the news to travel all the way to Athens. "I speak for the King. He is in agreement with me on the subject. He never wished for it to go so far. I want you to go back to Athens and make them change their policy on Macedonia."

Mantias looked back over his shoulder at the other Athenians, who still lounged, but had been listening to every word. They exchanged looks and then he turned back.

"You would send us back? I do want to go home, rather than rot in a prison, but we are not kings, I cannot guarantee that we can convince every Athenian to change their mind. We are a democ-"

427

"I know, you are a democracy. And I'm sure you're a fine orator, so you can address the assembly on the Pnyx and talk in our favour."

Mantias rolled his jaw from side to side again.

"If not an alliance, the least we can have is peace? I have the king's permission to remove our garrison from Amphipolis, or perhaps open the gates for you?" Philip said, noting the reaction. Their eyes widened and they exchanged looks; he knew that this would pique their interest. "If you were the men who returned Amphipolis back into Athenian control, like the glory days of the Delian league, surely you would be heroes of the city? They would shower you in gold, and your names would go down in history, might even soften the blow for when you have to go back and explain that your army was annihilated by a Macedonian rabble. Last count I was told, you've lost three thousand citizens. It's been a costly expedition for you. We're still counting, but *you* know how many men you brought, and how many are left. This could prevent any unpleasant repercussions. Will you be expected to kill yourselves? Or just ostracised?"

"And Argeus?" Mantias asked. "Will he face a fair trial?"

"No, but what do you care about him?" Philip said. "He will have to be taken back to Pella and explain his actions to the king. Most likely he will be executed. His Thracian mercenaries will be as well if they don't change sides, but in my experience, they will fight for whoever pays them."

Mantias again turned and looked at the other Athenians. Their expressions said they wanted to, but Philip guessed they also feared going back to Athens to face what would happen to them. They started to have a

428

small discussion among themselves, but then Mantias hushed them down.

"If you wish I can give you an hour to discuss this among yourselves, I'll let you exercise your democracy."

Mantias nodded.

Philip left the tent and headed back through the sodden ground to where Argeus and the Thracians were being held. He stood outside, holding onto one of the tent posts. His stomach lurched, hung over from the drinking the night before. He had held it together until now, but now he fought to not vomit, swallowing it back. He thought of Perdiccas death; if he did not get this right it would lead to the death of Macedonia. He felt queasy, deep in the pit of his stomach the vomit came up again and, bent over, he threw up on the grass; his throat burned. One of the guards that stood outside came to his aid, but he put up a hand, fought back the feeling, and paused for a moment. He wiped his mouth with the back of his hand, then marched straight into the tent.

He surveyed the room. Argeus still sat in the corner, head slumped. He was asleep, perfect, he did not have to deal with him right now. The Thracians were awake, all five of them. They watched him with casual indifference. From what he knew of his own Thracian mercenaries, they were not afraid of him, nor were they challenging him. He felt they were just trying to read him, curious to see what he would do next. He looked to the desk in the corner, where the captain of the guard had sat before. He was no longer there. The candles had melted all the way down to the wick and had gone out, each standing in a hardened puddle of white wax.

Philip stepped towards who he thought was the dominant Thracian, the one the others kept looking to.

He sat up and looked at Philip, sat up as tall as he could but the chains would not allow him to stand. He looked Philip straight in the eye, unflinching. He had long red hair, and a thick red beard to match, although this was streaked with grey hairs. Philip turned to the guards. "Can you undo his shackles please?"

The guards looked at each other and then the closest one approached. He produced a large ring on the end of a chain which had about twenty keys on it. "I can," he said, his voice hoarse. He coughed to clear his throat. He must not have spoken for hours. "You sure Philip?"

"Yes of course, just do it," he said, taking the keys from the guard's hand, "but be ready in case he makes a move."

Philip unlocked the man's shackles, and he stood up tall, his shoulders broad. He was taller than Philip, almost as tall as Antigonus. He did not remember this man from the battle; he was glad. The man felt his wrists and nodded his head. Philip could now see that the grey streaks were in his hair as well. Some of the hair was pulled back and tied together into a horses' tail; the rings holding it in place were made of silver, and contained symbols that weaved in and out of each other like tree branches. The craftsmanship of the metalwork was beautiful.

"Do you speak Greek?" Philip asked him.

"Enough," the man replied, his voice deep and gruff, as you would imagine Ares, God of War speaking.

"If you don't understand much Greek, I assume you will understand this?"

Philip pulled back his cloak at the hip. The heavy purse he had lifted earlier was hooked onto his belt. He unhooked it, and lifted it up. He cupped his other hand under it and felt the weight of the coin inside. He untied the leather drawstring and took a coin out; the

430

Thracian's eyes widened as he lifted one out to show him, a silver owl stared back at him, an Athenian tetra drachma. He held it in the palm of his hand.

"We seized chests full of this from your Athenian friends after the battle. If you and your men fight for me, I will make you rich."

The man stared back at him, then nodded.

Chapter 37

Philip rushed back to Pella and met with the Macedonian council. He stood around the table with Parmenion, Antigonus, Polyperchon and the others; a mixture of his and his father's generations, some men he trusted, and some he didn't.

"Thank you all for coming so quickly, we all know of my brother's fate. I thank all of you that were there with him, fighting so bravely for Macedonia. We need to act fast if we are to keep Macedonia in one piece. If we are too slow, we will be ripped apart; my spies tell me there are already pretenders ready to come out of the woodwork like worms," he said.

"We are with you, Philip," Antigonus said, and looked around at the other men, who nodded in agreement.

"I am claiming the Regency. I will have my nephew crowned Amyntas IV immediately. Parmenion make the arrangements. We also need to organise funeral games and a burial for my brother. I-"

"Philip," Parmenion said. Philip held his hand out, inviting him to speak. "with respect, that is not enough."

"What do you mean?" Philip said, not trying to hide his confusion.

Parmenion looked around to the other men, who nodded, already agreeing with whatever Parmenion was about to say. The general was still bruised along the side of his face from the battle with the Illyrians, and the eye on that side was bloodshot and a long red streak ran across the bridge of his nose. He scratched it.

"We have talked, and we all agree that we want you to be king. We can't have an infant child as king.

Perdiccas himself was not of age when he was crowned and look at what happened."

"It's not the same thing."

"Yes, it is, but this will be seen as weakness. Others will try to capture him to claim control."

Philip was taken aback and looked at them. "That is absolutely out of the question. I will not break my oath to my brother to look after his family, and I will not supplant my own nephew from his birth right."

"Philip, it will split loyalties, and there will be more fighting. I know this is something you want to avoid," Parmenion said.

Antigonus stood up and put his hand on the shoulder. "Philip, it's the best thing for Macedonia, like Parmenion says, we can't have an infant on the throne. As you said, pretenders are already starting to spring up. Look how much trouble just one of the bastards caused. This will weaken Macedonia."

Polyperchon spoke up as well. "They're right Philip, someone will kill the boy, and we will have another decade of fighting, and the fire will be stoked by Greeks, Persians, Illyrians, Thracians and whoever else."

Philip shook his head. "By Zeus and all the gods! No! I won't hear any of this. I want you to double the guards around my nephew."

"We have already agreed, all of us. We think you're the best man to lead this country, all of us know you; it's what we want," Polyperchon said, his eyes searching around the room for support.

Parmenion spoke up again. "Philip-"

He was immediately cut off by the slam of Philip's palm on the desk. He pointed his finger from man-to-man, the veins on his hand showing. "I will hear no more of this. My brother's corpse is still warm, and you will talk no more of this."

Parmenion tried again. "Philip we-"

"We need to act quickly and stall the Illyrians and their allies before they begin a full invasion. Have they advanced deeper into upper Macedonia?" Philip asked.

Parmenion looked around at the eyes of the other men, clearly none of them wanting to continue trying to argue their case. "No, they have stayed put. The bulk of their army is heading back north, but they have left enough men to guard all the passes," he said.

"We need to send envoys out to them immediately. I will meet with Bardylis, stall him, come to some sort of agreement with him. He is going to be overconfident speaking to me."

"Why do you say that?" Parmenion asked.

"We've met," Philip said, chewing his cheek. "I was his prisoner before I was in Thebes. He doesn't have a very high opinion of me. This will work to our advantage. I will act submissive and afraid, and he will relish it."

"And what are we stalling for exactly? If all you do is try and restore the peace and keep your family on the throne."

"We need time to train more men how to fight like the men in Amphaxitis, how to use sarissas, and the cavalry to work with them. We have found our new tactics most effective. When we fought the Athenians, we crushed them; they had never seen anything like it. When I look around this table, look at all of you who fought as hoplites, you're all bloodied. We were barely scratched. When we march north and invade Illyria, Bardylis will-"

"Invade Illyria?" Parmenion said, his eyes wide.

434

"Yes. When we invade Illyria, Bardylis will be the same. He will not know what he has come up against. And I will kill him." The whole room looked astonished. "If there is nothing else, I want you to make arrangements for my nephew's coronation."

He left the room followed by Antigonus and Polyperchon. The rest of them stayed, in stunned silence.

.....

Philip stood in silence, holding onto Perdiccas' cold, blue fingers.

Silence.

Silence apart from the drip from the ice brought down from the mountains to preserve the body, until the funeral games could be organised. The drips echoed round the white stone walls of the tomb. Philip looked his brother up and down; he lay on his back with his arms crossed over his chest and his eyes shut. He was in his finest armour, which had been cleaned and polished, prepared for his journey to the underworld, any sign of blood or wounds was no longer visible.

He was pale and looked at peace. In his free hand, Philip had a silver coin; he fidgeted with it in his fingers, and looked at the image of Perdiccas on one side of the mint. He placed it into his brother's palm and closed his hand around it, his fingers cold and stiff.

He kissed Perdiccas' forehead, sniffed and wiped a tear away with the back of his hand.

He was completely alone in the crypt, but it was well lit, the doors were wide open at the end of the long entrance corridor. The sunlight reflected off the various weapons, shields, armour and riches that Perdiccas would take to the afterlife; they shone like the stars.

"I don't know what to say to you, Brother. There doesn't seem to be anything I can do. I will likely be

435

joining you very soon. Bardylis wants a meeting with me, and I'm not sure what's going to happen. He'll probably have me killed while we're still trying to keep the chaos under control. Macedonia could be done as its own country. It will be part of Illyria, not even a vassal."

Philip sat down with his back to the body which was raised on an altar.

"I'm not sure what to do. Your philosopher is gone. You know we had our differences, but I wouldn't have hurt him; his advice may have been useful, then I would have allowed him to go home." There was a long pause. "The Macedonians want me to be king, and I do want to be king, I will not lie to you brother. I think that I have what it takes to finally destroy Bardylis, as long as we can gather enough men. I think I can get Macedonia under control, with the help of Thebes. Your son is the heir. Forgive me for what I have to do, I won't-"

There were footsteps behind him, lightly pattering on the marble. Philip jumped to his feet, whipped round and slid his sword out of his scabbard as fast as a viper. As he turned, he immediately looked to the hands of the person approaching to see what weapon they carried. They did not. He looked up and his eyes met with the eyes of, Perdiccas' widow. She shyly cowered back from his aggressive posture. Her eyes were wet. Philip immediately sheathed his sword and put his hands out apologetically. "I'm sorry, I expect an assassin's blade in me soon."

"And me," she said. The two of them stood in silence looking at Perdiccas' body, side-by-side. "What becomes of us now?"

Philip looked into her eyes, realising that he had just made the decision to supplant her infant son from his birthright on the throne. He wasn't quite sure how to tell her. "I have to meet with Bardylis. We need a treaty of some kind, or else Macedonia is going to be in complete chaos; the Macedonian council have named me regent."

"What will they do with my son?" she asked tearfully. "What will they do with me?"

"They want me to be king."

Her face sank into her palms, and she wept. She fell to her knees, "Philip, please, don't have us killed, please, please."

She stepped toward him, and he took a step away. He stood stiff and awkward, unsure what to do. She lowered herself down to all fours and put her hands and face on his feet. His memory flashed back to years ago when their father had died, and he had been sent with Perdiccas to find his half-brothers. Their mother had begged just like this. He could not see her face now, the tears running down her cheeks. They dripped onto his feet. History repeats itself.

"Please Philip, don't have us killed, I'll do anything you ask."

Philip squatted down, took her hands and helped her up to her feet. He looked her in the eyes, they welled up with tears and pleaded with him.

"I'm not going to have you killed. Why would I do that? I'm going to protect you. Both of you," he said.

The sign of relief on her face became immediately apparent, but she was still hesitant. She embraced him and kissed him. "Thank you, thank you," she said, her eyes locked with his. Philip suddenly became aware that she was holding on to his arms, and tenderly. She kissed him gently on the lips. He could taste the salt from her tears. He felt her hand on his knee and it slowly slid up his thigh. He tried to step back a little, but her hand kept going. She kissed him again and looked into his eyes. Hers were red from weeping, but they were beautiful.

He stared back for a moment, then pushed away, breaking it off.

"You don't need to do that," he said. The moment now became awkward. She stood looking at him. "I'll have you looked after."

"Please, Philip," she pleaded, "Take me as one of your wives."

"You're grieving, it will heal in time. I have to go now," he said.

He walked briskly away, and up the stairs, shielding his eyes from the sun, leaving her on her knees with Perdiccas' body.

Later when the funeral pyre was being lit, he looked across at her. She stared straight ahead, avoiding looking in his direction.

Chapter 38

When the funeral games concluded, the Illyrian delegation arrived in Pella. Philip did not welcome them; they were greeted by Polyperchon. Philip did not want his anger toward them to cause problems so early on in the negotiations. He also wanted to give the impression he was afraid of them.

He stood in the great hall at Pella, with Antigonus and Polyperchon either side of him, waiting for their arrival. As regent, he was surrounded by the king's personal guard. They wore full armour and carried spears and shields. The room was filled with the Macedonian nobility and ambassadors from all parts of Greece: Athens, Sparta, Thebes, and Corinth and many others; everyone who had a vested interest in Macedonia. As he looked around the room it reminded him of all the times that he had attended summits like this before, but this time it was himself who would have to negotiate. The last time he had been present, before he went to Illyria and then Thebes, Alexander had been frantically trying to keep the kingdom together. He had succeeded to a point, at Philip's expense. As Philip reflected on it, he thought that this is what made him the man he was today. He forgave Alexander for being impotent in a situation that was not of his doing. He had been thrown to the wolves when their father was killed.

The whole room was alive with chatter; the voices echoed off the walls, so Philip could not make out completely what any of them were actually saying, only fragments. Philip tried to swallow away a lump in his throat, and took a slow breath to rid himself of the fluttering in his chest. He tried to put the images of Alexander being talked over out of his mind.

He looked to his side. Antigonus looked him in the eye and gave a firm nod. "You'll do just fine," he said reassuringly. Philip put great faith in Antigonus; he trusted no one more. He chewed on the inside of his cheek and took another deep breath.

All the inane chatter around the room began to die down as the heavy main doors at one end were thrown open, and the Illyrian Royal Guards marched in in formation, their full bronze armour polished and shining. They wore helmets with tall plumes, similar to his own Royal Guard, but far more extravagant. Their sandals pounded on the marble, the fastening buckles on their armour clicked. Behind the first six rows of them, Philip could see, moving his head from side to side was Bardylis, the King of Illyria himself. The sight of him, just being in his presence made him grind his teeth. He tried to relax his jaw muscles and not to show his emotion to the room, but found it difficult.

Bardylis's Royal Guard all about faced to form an honour guard for their king to walk down. The butts of their spears banged in perfect harmony as they rested them on the ground. The old man, and he was old now, strolled down the centre. He had been elderly when Philip last saw him, but he had still been in good physical condition; he could have been mistaken for a much younger man. His condition had deteriorated, his shoulders were hunched, his skin was loose, and he walked with a limp. His eyes scanned along the line of the Macedonian nobility, first the front row, then his eyes fixed on Philip; he smirked. That smirk, that look, was what filled Philip with rage; he ground his teeth but kept his face placid and relaxed. The old king's gaze then moved across the next row, and the next, as if he was inspecting his own soldiers. They're not yours yet, Philip thought.

Bardylis mingled with the various delegates. He worked his way along the line of people, including the Athenians and Thebans. The Spartan generals who were there refused to come near him, backing Macedonia in these matters, but stretched to a nod of acknowledgement.

When he got to Philip, the two locked gazes. Everyone in the room waited with bated breath. Philip's stomach wrenched. He felt as if he was going to vomit, but managed to keep his composure. Bardylis opened his arms wide and declared in a loud voice, "My condolences Philip, I must express my deepest sympathy for your losses. Nobody wants war. I pray to the gods that we can put all this bad blood to rest, and then we will have peace."

He then stepped forward and embraced Philip, who stood with his arms by his sides unsure how to react. There was some light applause from around the room, sycophants, he thought. Philip looked around a little over Bardylis' shoulder. Certain members of his own team of delegates, including Parmenion looked on with scepticism. Bardylis then kissed him on the cheek and those who had been applauding applauded louder, and some cheered. Philip's skin prickled. He felt the urge to pull out of the embrace but resisted, he not wanting to look as though he was being troublesome.

Bardylis took a half step back, the smell of perfume and roses was on him, but when he lent in ever so slightly, just so Philip could hear what he was about to say over the cheers, his breath stank like a dog's. "Your brother died a coward, begging for mercy, begged, we didn't give it to him."

The sourness in Philip's stomach turned to pure boiling rage. He was tempted to kill Bardylis where he stood. Piece of shit, he thought, he's small and frail, I could ring his neck before anyone could react. He bent his knees slightly and gripped his belt. It was all he could do to stop himself from wrestling him to the ground and throttling him.

"Welcome to Pella, King Bardylis of Illyria. I too hope we can put all of this trouble aside and come to an agreement that will benefit everybody," he declared in a loud voice.

All the ambassadors and delegates took their places around the negotiating table. Most spoke Greek, but there were some others, Thracians, who had translators with them. Just behind Philip sat a table of scribes dipping their pens in ink and looking up, waiting for the talking to begin.

After a few hours of talking, things were not looking good. Bardylis had asked for all the money he was owed from when his father and brothers had refused tribute in the past, plus a vast amount of compensation. He warned that if this was not met, he would be forced to invade Macedonia, take direct control over its assets, and reimburse himself for damages done.

Philip sat in utter disbelief; his relationship with the Athenians was already strained, and they were willing to back any deal that resulted in them getting their timber and an acknowledgment of their right to rule Amphipolis. They seemed to want to distance themselves from having to deal with Macedonia.

Unlike anyone else in the room, the Athenians had seen Philip in battle, using the new equipment and tactics, and they did not mention it, but they showed concern. They wanted to limit the size of the Macedonian army, which resulted in a few smirks around the room. To this Philip played dumb, which seemed to work because no one else was concerned about the Macedonian army. He knew well how little the others worried about a Macedonian attack, especially with the current state of the military, having lost so many fighting men to Bardylis when Perdiccas fell.

Philip stared silently across the table at Bardylis, while the Illyrian king was busy playing the victim, and trying to convince the Thebans and the Spartans that he was the one who was in danger of attack. "-And what assurances do I have that they won't attack us again? I simply want to keep my kingdom safe from Macedonian aggression and banditry. These warmongers invaded my land. All I did was defend it."

"Did they battle not take place in Macedonia?" one of the Spartans asked.

"It was pre-emptive. Now that Macedonia has been decisively defeated. Your king is dead. I want you to increase your tribute to Illyria, and you should pay reparations to Athens for all of their men you killed," he said, and glanced over at the Athenian delegates.

"Athens concurs," said one of the Athenian delegates.

Philip stood up. "Are you serious? I should pay them? For invading my land and trying to ally themselves with you?"

"Also, I propose the betrothal of my granddaughter to infant King Amyntas; they will wed when he comes of age. This will make Philip keep the peace," Bardylis said.

A few people around the room nodded. Philip tried to hide his confusion.

"Marry your granddaughter? Why by the gods would you want that?"

Bardylis smirked, looking amused. "It is for Macedonia's benefit Philip," he said, softly, as if he was talking to a puppy, looking around to make sure he was being heard. "If I bring our families together, surely this will make you feel safer."

Philip could take it no longer. He suddenly understood what Bardylis was trying to do. He sprang up, his chair falling out from under him and clattering to the floor.

"And what happens then? Will an assassin kill my nephew in his sleep? Will you then claim your granddaughter is the rightful heir and declare yourself regent?" he shouted, pointing an accusing finger at the old man.

"These accusations are outrageous," Bardylis said calmly. "I am offended at the very idea of it."

One of the Athenian delegates stood up and Philip recognised him. He had not noticed him before in the crowd of people: Euphraeus, the man who had been Perdiccas' advisor. He cleared his throat.

"If the regent does not think this betrothal is suitable, I suggest that Philip marries into the family of Bardylis himself," he said. Philip stared in disbelief. He clenched a fist under the table, wishing he would stay out of it.

"It should be the king that gets married," Bardylis said.

"Amyntas will not be a man for many years. A marriage to Philip will still bond your families, and it will alleviate the fears of Philip," he said. Many around the room nodded and murmured approval.

"Very well." Bardylis reluctantly accepted.

The negotiations, and arguments, continued. Philip had to concede almost everything that Bardylis demanded, even his allies in Thebes and Sparta agreed, wanting to keep stability, who did they care sat on the throne, as long as they got their trade.

After the Illyrians and all the others had left, Philip stood with Antigonus in the great hall which only an hour or so ago had been a hive of activity. Now they were the only two there, save for the palace servants who were sweeping the floors. Philip stared up at the throne.

"Will you marry the girl?" Antigonus asked.

Philip sighed.

"I will have to," he said, "or face the wrath of the Illyrians."

"It didn't go as well as we'd hoped?" Antigonus asked.

"It couldn't really have gone any better, but it could have been far worse."

"What comes next? Do you still plan to kill him?"

"Yes," Philip said, without hesitation, "but we must time it carefully. I will marry Audata, but we are lucky, it will not be until the spring. This gives us much time to prepare."

Antigonus frowned. "Prepare for what?"

"Invading Illyria," Philip said.

...

When spring came, Philip wasted no time. He took the army north with Parmenion on a dry, warm morning. Polyperchon stayed in Pella to act as regent for the infant king Amyntas. Philip sat on his horse at the head of his army as they marched northwest, towards the mouth of the Erawan Valley. He was already well aware that they were out of territory that Macedonia controlled, although it was claimed by Pella

445

it was also claimed by Bardylis and his Illyrians. The local nobility was fickle.

The local peasants however, despised the Illyrians; they had been thieving, raiding and raping here for decades, maybe centuries, so Philip felt no danger from the people living around there. Out far ahead he could no longer see his scouts led by Antigonus. He remembered all too well when the scouts had given incorrect information to his father, at the first battle he had seen. Had they been bought or were they simply wrong? The question had been with him since he was a boy. He would not leave this in the hands of chance; the fate of Macedonia would not be taken so cheaply, so they were led by Antigonus. He would send only someone who he trusted with his life.

The bulk of the army, around eight thousand men, was made up of the Macedonians from Pella and the surrounding areas. They had been trained over the last year with the new longer spears that were now being called sarissas. They may not be ready, he thought, but he would find out soon enough. The rest of the army was made up of his men who had come from Amphaxitis, two thousand of them. All were well trained, drilled and fit. He would head the cavalry.

He squinted into the sun and looked up into the valley; riders were coming back down. He could make out Antigonus at the head of the group, a trail of dust in the air behind them. He turned back and looked down the road at his army, the men all carrying the sarissas over their shoulders as they marched with their small pelta shields slung over the opposite shoulder. They look confident, he thought, they know themselves how well the new tactics and weapons work. The new recruits though, they think they are going to die after what happened to Perdiccas. Almost no family in

446

Macedonia had not felt the touch of death from that battle, most had lost at least one son.

Antigonus rode straight to Philip, all the men recognised him and let him straight past. "Hail Philip!"

"Hail Antigonus!" he said. The two locked forearms. "What news do you bring me, my friend?" Antigonus took a deep breath. "He knows we are coming. He has sent an advance force forward, and is taking up a position in the valley by lake Lynkestra; it's a flat plain."

"A defensible position until the bulk of his army arrives," Philip said. "Is this where Perdiccas fell?"

Antigonus nodded. "I think so. There is evidence there was a battle there, rusty weapons and armour and some bones. Philip. Are you sure about this? Maybe we should negotiate again."

"I've never been surer of anything in my life. I know we can beat him; he is going to be overconfident. We can win this."

Half a day's march later they arrived at the valley. Philip sat on his horse next to Parmenion and Antigonus and surveyed the enemy troops already deployed. They blocked the path of his army and the road into Illyria. "Praise Zeus, it's exactly what we hoped for. They deployed themselves in a traditional hoplite formation, eight ranks deep, eight-foot spears, cavalry guarding each flank. Right out in the open where we can see. He is trying to intimidate us."

"Be careful, Philip, they may be deployed the way we would expect, but these Illyrians are hardened veterans, far more experienced than ours; these were the men we fought when your brother was killed, and they know the position well. They will hold their ground," Parmenion said.

447

"Yes, but they have not yet experienced the sarissas; they will not know what to do. Trust me Parmenion, we have them."

"I agree with Philip," Antigonus said. "You haven't seen them in action, Parmenion."

"I'm not saying we can't beat them. All I'm saying is that overconfidence was your father's undoing."

"No, Parmenion, I remember the day well. My father was not overconfident, he sought revenge, he acted rashly. Do you remember the Spartan advisor? He advised not to attack. He told them there was too much danger of being flanked, but he didn't want to miss the opportunity to kill Bardylis," Philip said. "Look how he has deployed. Overconfidence will be his undoing."

As they surveyed the army, and their own men filed into ranks to the drumbeats, Philip positioned all of his best troops on the right flank, and deployed the rest of the men carrying the sarissas, in an echelon that sloped back from the right flank. He took his position on the right flank, with the companion cavalry. "We must keep the less experienced men out of the fight for as long as possible, until our right crushes their left, just as the Thebans did at Leuctra."

Antigonus left for the far right to be with his men, commanding the phalanx.

Philip sat with Parmenion on the horses. Once his army was in position, riders from the Illyrian army emerged, riding out to the centre of the battlefield and stopping there.

"They expecting to bargain?" Parmenion asked.

"I doubt it, but let's see what they have to say," Philip said. His helmet was strapped to his hip. Instead of putting it on, he took a laurel wreath made of golden leaves, and placed it on his head. Parmenion looked at him, shocked.

"What are you doing Philip?"

"Trust me my friend; shall we go and speak to them?"

They rode out to the centre of the battlefield, accompanied by the royal standard-bearer, his banner carried the sixteen-pointed Argead star. With him were two of the companions to match the five riders that were now waiting for them.

As they approached Philip recognised Bardylis even in the distance. When they got close enough, and he saw his face, his lips began to curl up into a smile. Was Bardylis frowning? He looked confused.

"Hail Bardylis of the Illyrians, we have come to-"

"I think I'll do the talking boy. What do you think you're doing here? Take your army and march straight back to Pella, or once I've routed your army, I'll have you hung by your entrails."

"Not today. Today you will leave Macedonia, and march straight back to Illyria," Philip said. He kept his posture upright and tall, trying to appear as arrogant and regal as possible.

"Why are you wearing that crown? You are not the king, or has Perdicass' pup died?"

"I have taken the throne. We will no longer pay your tribute; you will in fact pay the same amount to us. If you don't, I will have you hung by *your* entrails."

Bardylis' mouth was wide open at Philip's words; he seemed unable to take his eyes off the laurel wreath. "I'm going to kill you now," he spat, whipped around and rode back to his army at a furious pace, his men trailing after him.

"It was a short negotiation," Philip said. Parmenion laughed. The two rode back towards their army, who were now lined up in the phalanx, sarissas pointed to the

449

sky, the tips glinting in the sun. He looked along the faces of his men.

"I hope he took the bait," he said.

"Don't worry, he did," Parmenion said. "He will be the one to act rashly today."

Chapter 39

Philip galloped his horse along the front of his army, away from the veteran troops from Amphaxitis, and down towards the left flank, followed by his companions. The forest of sarissas pointing towards the sky forced him to blink as the sun flickered between them. Some of the men banged their sarissas off the back of their shields in salute.

He positioned himself in the middle of the inexperienced men, about a third in from the left flank and glanced back over his shoulder. He looked to see if he could see Antigonus's standard on the far right to judge the distance. He tugged on his horse's reins and pointed himself across the valley to the other side of the battlefield. Bardylis and his generals sat on their horses, behind their men. He tugged again on the reins and whipped round to face his men.

"Today, we face the Illyrians once again." He paused, and the men in the front ranks, the ones who could hear him turned their heads and whispered the message back through the ranks so that those further back knew what Philip was saying. "The Illyrians who have raided and raped here further back than any of us can remember. Further back than my grandfather and great-grandfather."

He raised his arm up in the air and held his palm out towards Bardylis. He turned back to the men, who looked nervous. The points of some of the sarissas wobbled in the air, held by unsteady hands. He took a glance down to the end of his men from Amphaxitis. They stood fast.

"Today, we will defeat the Illyrians, and there will be no more raiding and no more raping. Your wives and daughters will be safe. Your crops and animals will be safe. Your homes will be safe. Today, all I ask of you is to hold fast. You hold them off as long as there is strength in your body."

Again, he paused to allow the message to be passed back. He could see some of the men starting to nod, and some of the unsteady sarissas stabilised.

"My cavalry, and my men from Amphaxitis will cripple their right flank. They will then run, or be killed, I don't care which. All I need from you is to give us the time to do that. If you hold them until that is done, I promise you that we will be victorious!"

The men cheered and raised their sarrisas.

They seemed a bit more confident as he rode back to the companion cavalry. He unsheathed his sword, raised it to the sky and galloped as fast as he could along the front line. When he arrived back at his position with the cavalry there were priests of Apollo with a bull being restrained, its head held low. The priests chanted and waved their arms.

Philip dismounted and stroked the bull's head; he whispered to it as he would to calm one of his horses. He lifted his sword up under the bull's throat and then drew it back with one hard slash that severed the beast's jugular. Blood sprayed up, and the air was thick with the salt scent. The animal bucked, kicked and screeched. Eventually this slowed, and it lay down, the blood seeping into the ground.

Philip wiped the blood from his face, climbed onto his horse's back and looked down at Antigonus, who waited to take his command on the furthest right flank of the phalanx.

"May the gods be with us," he said to his old friend.

"I think they will be, Philip," he said and nodded, "If not, wait for me at the bank of the Styx."

452

"Sound the attack," Philip said and smiled at his friend.

...

Antigonus turned to his trumpeter, who wet his lips, then blew hard, signalling the advance. The sarissas were lowered toward the enemy. The men tightened up their rank; he felt the shoulders on either side of him brush his own, and they began to march forward to the beat of the drums.

He looked through the thicket of heads, shoulders and sarissas, across to the other side of the battlefield. The skirmishers that had stood behind the phalanx slipped through the gaps and ran out into the open in front, carrying their slings and javelins. He squinted into the distance and could see the enemy doing the same. Their large round aspis shields locked into a wall; there were so many that the clunk was audible, even over the distance, and the rhythmic pounding of the Macedonian's march. He swallowed a lump in his throat, even though they had seen what happened against the Athenians when their new type of phalanx met traditional hoplites. He could not help but feel the nerves. If they failed, it would all end.

The phalanx was deeper than before, with more men behind them, ten as Philip told them, instead of the normal eight, that they had used against the Athenians. The exception was the right flank; the men from Amphaxitis were deployed twelve deep. He needed as much mass there as he could. The first five ranks of spear tips protruded well out in front of the first rank of men. The rear ranks held their sarissas at increasingly steep angles, stretching up into the sky.

Through spaces in the orchard of helmets in front, he could see the skirmishers start to dance around and launch the missiles at the Illyrians. When he looked to his right, he could see Philip's cavalry riding out to the flank, ready to protect it from any Illyrians attempting to get into their side or behind them. Philip definitely knew what he was doing. Antigonus held his head high and pumped his chest out.

As the gap between the two front lines began to get narrower, the skirmishers were getting pushed closer and closer together. Some fled back through the gaps and hid inside the phalanx. The Illyrian skirmishers stayed a little longer. If they weren't too careful, they would find themselves caught between the two lines. This would be most unfortunate, he thought, getting a free stab at some unarmoured Illyrians.

They launched a few extra volleys of missiles, before disappearing into their own army's ranks. Antigonus blinked and ducked his head slightly as the javelins, arrows and sling balls hurtled up in an arc toward his formation. Almost all of the missiles clattered off the sarissas held up from the rear ranks, and rained straight down on top of the men. These falling projectiles did not carry much speed. One man a few feet away from Antigonus was struck on the shoulder by a falling sling ball, but it merely bounced off the shoulder plate of his armour. He watched the man roll his shoulder and flex his neck from side to side and carry on. He didn't appear to shout or scream, although he could not actually hear over the rhythmic stomping of feet. His smile began to grow as he realised that the missiles were not getting through and injuring anyone. The enemy skirmishers had all disappeared behind the Illyrian phalanx.

The two front lines met. Unlike what would normally happen, there was a noticeable gap between them and their enemies. It was so wide, Antigonus thought he could lie across it and still not be able to touch the Illyrians.

The Macedonian front ranks began to lightly probe their sarissas at the Illyrian hoplites, far outreaching them. The Illyrian shields, being the large round aspis kind that the Greeks had used for centuries offered a lot of protection, and their dome-shaped structure allowed the wielder to tuck their upper body inside the protection of their shield. Their sides were protected by the overlap of their neighbours on either side.

However, because of the superior length of the sarissas, these men, as they had seen with the Athenians, did not know how to react. They could only cover up and try to defend themselves and were unable to advance.

Antigonus swallowed at the lump in his throat, remembering how this felt from their first encounter with the Athenian marines, how he had been pinned behind his shield, unable to strike back. He understood the confusion and how this then turned into panic. After a time, some of the Illyrians even lowered their spears; they could tell that they were too far out of reach. The Macedonian march slowed, and the focus became much more on the thrusting of the sarissas which, now that they were closer, began to bang off the shields of the enemy.

After a few moments, Antigonus saw the first man killed. A Macedonian thrust forward, the shaft of his sarissa stretched from somewhere behind him over his shoulder. The tip glanced off the top of the Illyrian hoplite's shield, under his helmet and penetrated deep into the man's throat. There was a spray of blood, and the man fell forward out of the formation as the thrust was pulled back. His shield dropped and he fell onto his knees, then slumped flat onto the ground, clutching his neck with both hands. The man behind him immediately stepped forward and took his place, locking his shield in with those to his left and right. Very efficient move, Antigonus thought; they are well drilled and experienced. No matter, they still don't have a hope in Hades.

The Macedonians continued to thrust, and more Illyrians began to drop, their frustration began to become clear; in desperation some began to throw their spears at the Macedonians. Some dropped their spears, drew their short swords and began to hack at the tips of the sarissas, attempting to cut the points off, but this resulted in them exposing themselves to more stabbing spear tips.

Now the lines were pressing tightly, pushing from behind, and they were getting nudged forward. Antigonus patted his trumpeter on the shoulder. The man turned, looked at him and nodded, then blew into his instrument. It could be heard over the din of pounding feet as they took short steps forward, the sounds of screams and of metal clattering metal. The message was received. The Hypaspists, the sword armed men who were standing behind the phalanx began to surge out. They lapped around the end of the enemy flank, now that their line was pinned and could not move away.

…

Philip clutched at the reins of his horse. It galloped hard, and his legs clutched at the animal's sides. The hoof beats, the breath of the horse and his own were all in rhythm.

They chased down the skirmishers who had been there to guard the army's flank. They ran now to get to safety behind their own phalanx. Most got away, but a few were cut down. He took a look back over his shoulder; the chinstrap of his helmet butted off the shoulder plate of his armour and forced him to turn at the waist to see back. The horse bounding up and down made this extremely uncomfortable. His eyes darted along the line until he found the standard-bearer of Antigonus. There he was. The phalanx was holding off the Illyrians well, the lines being held apart by the length of the sarissas; the Illyrians looked unable to manoeuvre – perfect! He could also make out his hypaspists, armed with hoplite shields and short swords, pouring round the flank to overlap the Illyrians.

The skirmishers had fled around behind the lines completely. Philip could make out the enemy cavalry coming out into open ground now to match them. They were later than he had expected; Bardylis must have pulled them from the other flank of his army. He obviously hadn't expected Philip to have all his cavalry on one flank. The Illyrian cavalry now barrelled towards them. "Pick up the pace!" Philip yelled, raising his sword and stabbing it into the air in front of him. Tugging on the reins harder, his horse sped up. He felt the heat rising from the animal. It was breathing hard, its muscular sides moving in and out like a blacksmith's bellows. The Illyrians were now coming harder and faster to meet them.

The two lines came together with a clash of metal on metal; some riders were knocked clean off their horses and trampled, and others came to a sudden halt and jostled with their enemy. Philip rode straight ahead. He dipped his head low as an Illyrian blade grazed the top of his helmet. He simultaneously swung his sword into the underside of his enemies exposed arm. He heard the man scream as he rode past. Another rider charged from his other side, and he clashed swords with him, parrying a blow and stabbing the man in the neck. The Illyrian fell back off his horse, and blood flicked up into Philip's face and eyes, the sting momentarily blinding him. He wiped the blood off with the back of his hand and blinked repeatedly until it was gone. Something hard struck him in the centre of his back, it knocked him forward, but his armour took the sharpness of the blow. He looked over his shoulder and raised his sword to swing it back at his attacker, but the Illyrian was struck by one of his companions who rode across the back of the two of them. The Illyrian fell with his arm tangled in his horse's reins; the animal grunted and rode off in fright, dragging him with it, being kicked by its legs.

What was left of the Illyrian cavalry fled. Philip took a moment to catch his breath. "We have to get back to the phalanx," he shouted. His eyes darted around in all directions. "Regroup, regroup! We're going to charge the Illyrian phalanx in the rear!"

They gathered themselves back together and rode with Philip in the lead, wheeling round behind where the two lines were locked together. They clutched their horse's sides with their thighs and charged hard toward the backs of the Illyrian hoplites.

...

"Keep pressing forward!" Antigonus yelled to his men, his voice becoming hoarse; his drummer beat in steady intervals to help keep the rhythm of their feet marching forward. It was deafening in one ear. Being taller than most of his men, he could see around quite well. The Hypaspists who had surged out were still hacking into the side of the enemy flank, but they were holding the line well, and further out the Illyrian cavalry had fled.

The pounding of his men's feet on the ground was rising like a storm, into a rumble; he could feel it all through his body and up into his chest. It drowned out

458

all the other noise of the battlefield. Behind the enemy lines dust was being kicked up and it had gathered into a huge cloud that drifted like a shade through the Illyrian line and enveloped everyone fighting on the battlefield. The dust got everywhere. Antigonus' eyes were half shut. He pushed air hard out of his nose and coughed into the back of his sword hand. All around him men were coughing and sneezing.

Then all the Illyrian hoplites surged forward, shouting, desperate. The men around him braced their sarissas hard and dug their feet into the ground against their mass. The Macedonian horses had crashed into the back of the Illyrian line. He thought he could make out Philip's silhouette by the shape of the helmet, but in the dust it was too hard to tell. "Philip's cavalry is here! Press forward harder!" he shouted then coughed. His trumpeter sounded, and the Macedonians dug their feet in and drove forward with a second wind, stabbing and thrusting.

....

Philip hacked downward at the Illyrians from his horse; for a moment he glanced up to quickly read the battle. His sword-wielding hypaspists were hacking into the side of the Illyrian flank, driving deeper into the gaps that they had created. There was a surge of men trying to escape; in such a tightly packed formation the move rippled through them like a wave. They were surrounded on three sides with the cavalry at the rear, the hypaspists to their side, and the spiked wall of sarissas in front of them. The only way out was to their right, through their own men. Some dropped their weapons and pushed and shoved, others tried to climb over the densely packed bodies, a few even cut at their own men to try and get through. It was a terrible sight to behold. It was becoming a massacre.

459

The Macedonians pushed harder and harder. It was becoming claustrophobic, with barely room to swing a sword. Philip coughed and rubbed the dust from his eyes as best as he could. He was fighting for breath and his arms were heavy, but he fought on. A man who had lost his weapon grabbed Philip and pulled him off his horse. Philip gouged his eye with his thumb to get off the man off him, then thrust his sword into his throat, his elbow held high to create enough space. More Illyrians dropped their weapons and tried to push their way to the right, through their own men. Some were stabbed in the sides with sarissas. Others lost their footing and were trampled into the ground and drowned in the puddles of blood.

A mass panic spread its way through the Illyrian line. It was becoming butchery, stabbing men in the back, and limbs were being hacked off. The Macedonians began to tire, their mouths wide open despite the dust; the heat was becoming unbearable. Sitting above the infantry on his horse, Philip could see the panic spread down the line. None of the Illyrians fought back, men scrambling in terror to escape. The whole line was falling apart and they ran towards the one direction where there were no Macedonians. Any space that opened up was filled by Macedonian hypaspists.

The rest of the cavalry had dismounted. It was becoming too dangerous being on horses with the Illyrians trying to climb over the line. Philip's feet splashed into a warm puddle up past his ankles. Now that he was on the ground, he could see there were deep puddles of blood between all the bodies; the salt scent in the hot air was almost overpowering. He wiped sweat and dust from his brow. He stood on a body and almost lost his footing. He hacked and stabbed at the backs of the Illyrians. All of a sudden, there was space in front of him. A cool breeze kissed his face. Some of the Illyrians had managed to get out. The ground they had left was piled with the dead, streams of blood running between the bodies forming tributaries that ran into the river, which was now red and cloudy.

The Macedonians gave chase to survivors, hacking them down and running them off the battlefield.

As the slaughter slowed, and the men began to rally back and gather around Philip, he realised that Bardylis was nowhere to be seen. He looked around and saw Parmenion. "Find Bardylis!" he shouted over the ringing in his ears, half deaf from the noise.

Parmenion nodded and ran back to his horse.

Chapter 40

Philip picked his way across the battlefield with Antigonus. The blood on his hands and arms had become a crust of crimson on his skin. He was able to brush some of it off, but it would not go from the lines on his hands and was matted into the hairs on his arms. Their heads were down as they stepped over bodies. All around him men were looting the slain Illyrians, taking their armour, helmets and weapons, and any jewellery or coin they could find. Some of them were only injured; they crawled away or lay still, moaning in pain. They were not put out of their misery.

No more than they deserve after years of doing it to us, he thought. These people were farmers just wanting to live their lives without the politics and the soldiers.

He remembered a day when he had not wanted to be involved at all, but this was long past. He had wanted to hurt the Illyrians and hurt them badly. They came to an Illyrian officer, who was lying flat on his face. Philip kicked him over onto his back. the officer's dead eyes looked up in Philip's direction, but straight through him. He crouched down and waved his hand in front of the man's face; he began to frisk the corpse for any coin or jewels. This was interrupted by running and panting.

Parmenion ran towards them, "Philip, they found him."

They followed Parmenion, weaving in and out of the bodies that were strewn across the battlefield, avoiding any puddles of blood that had gathered deep enough to have not been absorbed straight into the dirt.

The piled bodies drew a line along the battlefield, where the two front lines had met. Once they were outside this, they were able to walk without fear of tripping over anything apart from the streams of blood. There were prisoners being processed by the Macedonians. Some were already shackled together along a chain. Unchained prisoners were on their knees, hands tied behind their backs with leather straps, being guarded by Macedonians with spears and slings. Will I pardon them for service?

As they passed the peasants, they were nodded at. Men lowered their heads in respect of Philip; some gestured their swords towards him. Some approached and patted him on the back as he walked. "The gods were with you, Philip," one of the men said.

"They were with all of us," he said.

They got to where Parmenion and some of the Royal Guard had gathered. There was a dozen or so corpses neatly lined up on their backs, arms by their sides with all their equipment. They all wore expensive, well-kept armour. Their helmets had been removed. Philip stood over the body at the end which had been separated out from the others, an elderly man, he squatted down beside him.

Bardylis.

"That's him," Philip said, surprised at how indifferent he felt. This man had been his enemy for so long now, since before he was even born. He had been his enemy and now that he was dead Philip didn't feel anything, He looked up and surveyed the battlefield; there was no joy to be had today.

Bardylis' eyes had been closed; Philip opened one of them with his thumb and forefinger. There were specks of mud covering the bottom half of the white; it didn't blink or water. There was no life at all. He lifted an arm. The skin was still warm. It was wrinkled and loose, but the muscle underneath was still hard. He stood back up.

463

"You did it," Antigonus said. "Epaminondas and Pelopidas would be proud of you."

Philip stood quietly. "I can't believe it actually happened. I can't believe he's dead"

"He's dead all right, and well done as well."

"What do we do now?" Philip said. "What were the losses?"

"Reports are still coming in," Parmenion said, "but so far the count is 5000 or so, at least half their army. We have lost around 300 men."

"Is that all?"

"Yes, the men held well, as you asked them to."

"We'll compensate the families of the dead, and I will sacrifice to the gods for them," Philip said. "This was a great victory, and it was these men, the men of Macedonia that made it happen."

One of the officers under Parmenion came running over. "Philip, we've captured two of his sons. The bastards were running off into the hills."

Antigonus smiled at Philip who nodded his approval.

"They're not to be harmed," Philip said, causing Antigonus to raise an eyebrow.

The officer nodded and ran off back towards the prisoners. Antigonus looked at Philip. "We should make an example at least one of them. There's plenty more where they came from."

"No. We need them alive. Bardylis has gone. I don't want to tear Illyria apart; I want it whole. Macedonia will be ours again, and so will Illyria."

"I agree with Philip," Parmenion said. "Once he is married to Audata, he can stake a claim on their throne. They are much more valuable as hostages."

"Yes," Philip said. "We need to keep as much of their government intact as possible. Just like ours, you remove the king, and look at what happens: complete chaos. There will be pretenders in Illyria, just like in Macedonia. I need to send somebody to the Illyrian capital to make our claim known. They've not suffered a defeat like this in a long time. They will be in complete shock, and need someone to turn to for guidance."

"Very good," Antigonus said. "I will go to Illyria. If someone my size shows up and tells them that we have just annihilated their army, it may make them more willing to discuss things."

"Excellent. You go in the morning at dawn, once we've consolidated, and secure the whole area. Make sure there's no counter-attack."

"Will we go and see who we got then?" Parmenion asked.

"Yes, take me to them. Is it the same smug pricks that we've met before?"

"Not sure. He had quite a few sons and grandsons. I don't think they will be smug now," Parmenion said.

"Ha," Philip said and laughed. "Let's go."

The three of them walked across the clean ground, behind the main line of bodies. Philip looked to the other end of the valley. The blood draining from the bodies had formed tributaries that flowed into the river, making it a murky red. The scent of salt carried on the breeze. Not to worry, it would soon wash downriver.

"We will have to build funeral pyres soon, before the bodies start to rot," Philip said.

His skirmishers had already moved up and created a screen; they and the hypaspists had been deployed to scour the hills around for any who had fled. Men from the cavalry were rounding up the Illyrian horses whose riders had been slain; they would be taken to market in

465

Macedonia, or used to replace any of their horses, or even used to expand his own cavalry.

Philip approached a group of captured high-ranking Illyrians. They were all kneeling, their foreheads on the ground, arms raked back and tied behind their backs. There was about a dozen of them, and they were surrounded by his own elite troops from Amphaxitis. The Macedonians were laughing and joking with each other, celebrating the victory. The moment from his childhood flashed into his mind, when they had returned to Pella, the moment when the Spartans had captured the Illyrian soldiers.

The two sons of Bardylis stepped forward. One swallowed. The other looked defiant.

"You will all be left alive if you pledge your loyalty to me," Philip said.

. . . .

Philip squinted into the torchlight, treading carefully on the grimy, slippery floor. It was slick with moss and moisture. Parmenion followed, along with Antigonus. They stopped at the end of the corridor, where Arrhidaeus stood in his cell. His pale eyes caught the torchlight, and Philip's skin crawled immediately. He had not seen his half-brother in almost a decade. Arrhidaeus had been down here the entire time.

He looked up at Philip weakly. "Philip? Is that you?" he asked, his voice dry.

"Yes, it's me."

Arrhidaeus coughed and wheezed. He limped over to the bars, and entered the torchlight. Philip took a step back, and put his hand over his mouth. He stank of piss and shit, flies rested on him, lice crawled in his hair, which hung down to his waist but was thin, his head covered in bald patches.

466

"How long have I been here? You've changed, a full beard, You're a man."

Arrhidaeus squinted toward him in the flickering light. "…and a crown? Is Perdiccas dead? I always liked him."

"You've been here nearly ten years," Philip said. "Do you want out of here? I'm willing to let you go free. The only condition is you tell me where your brothers are."

"You still haven't found them?" He smiled a warm content smile, exposing his gums, most of his teeth having rotted away. "I'd spit on you, if I had spit."

"Very well," Philip said. "I didn't expect anything from you. My spies will find them."

The next day, Arrhidaeus was brought in front of a tribunal of the Macedonian council, Philip and seven of his closest companions. They discussed whether to have him executed. They all agreed he had to go.

He was half carried by two burly Royal Guards out into the sunlight with his feet dragging the ground. He shielded his eyes as they tied him to a post in the public square. Tied to the post next to him was Argeus, who had been held since they captured him. The two looked at each other but did not acknowledge each other. A large crowd had gathered. Most of the nobility was also in attendance. Antigonus stepped forward.

"Prince Arrhidaeus. You are charged with conspiring to murder King Amyntas, your own father, and for that you are sentenced to die. Argeus. You are charged with rebellion against Macedonia, and for that you are sentenced to die," Antigonus said. He then turned and addressed the crowd. "Let these men be an example that pretenders to the throne will not be tolerated."

467

Antigonus stepped to the side and the crowd began to pelt Arrhidaeus and Argeus with rocks. They squirmed from side to side in a futile attempt to avoid the missiles being thrown. Arrhidaeus was so weak that he did not last long. His tattered scrawny body went limp after a stone the size of an apple struck him on the temple. Argeus, who was still relatively healthy continued to squirm and curled up into a foetal position with rocks striking him in the back, his body jarring with every hit. After a short while he stopped reacting, and went limp, as if he had fallen asleep.

Philip sat down in the royal box; to his left sat Philinna and to his right, Audata, the granddaughter of Bardylis, who he would soon marry. He scratched his beard, feeling closure from the years of torment Arrhidaeus had given him. Antigonus looked over to him. "That bastard deserved it."

"I know," he said, chewing his cheek. Although he harboured a deep hatred for Arrhidaeus, this was not a good way to die. He would rather die on the battlefield than be tied up like an animal to be slaughtered, not given the chance to fight back.

Audata, who had never met Arrhidaeus, nor heard the stories of what they had done to Philip all those years ago looked at him, pity in her eyes. What a brute she must think I am. Never mind.

"Are you okay my dear?" he asked.

She stared wide eyed at the battered bodies of Arrhidaeus and Argeus, who lay still, sharp stones still striking them and piling up around them. They were covered in cuts and bruises. One struck Arrhidaeus in the face, and cut most of his lip back, exposing what was left of his teeth. She touched her own mouth and shuffled in her seat.

"I'm sorry you had to see this," Philip said. "I promise there will be no more blood after today."

He turned to Philinna who calmly watched, unphased by the brutality. He kissed her cheek and looked down at her belly, and ran his hand gently over it. She was starting to show, becoming rounded just below the navel.

She stroked the middle of her stomach. "No Philip. The land may be spear-won for now, but it never ends," she said.

Acknowledgements.

I want to thank all of my family and friends for their encouragement and support, and for helping with beta reading and editing. I couldn't have done it without you.

My inspirations to write historical fiction mostly came from the novels of Steven Pressfield, Bernard Cornwell, Mary Renault and Valerio Massimo Manfredi who I aspire to equal one day. Thank you all.

I also want to thank those whose books I used for research. I hope they forgive me for this humble work of fiction, which is not the match of their far more detailed and better researched histories.

If you seek to learn more of Philip, and early Macedonia in general, please read *By the Spear* and *Philip II of Macedonia* by Ian Worthington, and *Philip of Macedon* by Nicholas Hammond.

To learn more about Antigonus, read: *Antigonus the One-Eyed* by Jeff Grainger.

For insights into the infantry fighting, read *An Invisible Beast* by Christopher Mathew.

On amazon audible, the Great Courses lectures *Alexander the Great and the Macedonian Empire*, and *The Peloponnesian War* are brilliantly written and delivered by Kenneth W Harl.

Historical notes.

This novel is, first and foremost, a work of fiction, built using the frame of historical events. I have therefore tried to avoid as much "jargon" as I can and keep it focussed on the story.

It was originally undertaken as an excuse to research Philip II, and the period immediately before Alexander the Great. I loved Alexander, and wanted to know the backstory to his life, of what Macedonia was like before him. The period is extremely complexed and volatile, with alliances being constantly broken and made, like all history, however, the period is not well documented in the region, so there are many voids in our knowledge.

To make the novel completely accurate would have had to have been twenty or more volumes, so this book is the product of, sadly, many omissions, and a condensed timeline.

I have tried to apply common sense to connect the dots. Philip was known as a very pragmatic man and learned from his mistakes, so I have tried to reflect this. We know that he spent time with Iphicrates, who was known to have experimented with all sorts of weaponry, including spears longer than usual 8ft. I do think it was possible that in Philips's encounter with the Athenian marines, that he could have seen the potential for this by taking the design a step further, and combine it with tactics he may have learned from his time in Thebes in the presence of Epaminondas, Pammenes and Pelopidas.

Almost every named character in the book was real. Many were still present later when Alexander the Great was king, and I have tried my very best to capture their personalities based on how I perceive them. However, what people were actually like, we will probably never know.

Some parts are possibly more dramatic than reality, for example, the death of Alexander. We know he was assassinated, and this was frequently the case, and happened to many Macedonian Kings, but the exact circumstances are unknown.

If you are like me, since you have chosen to spend your money and time on a historical fiction novel, once you've finished (and sometimes during) reading, do your own research, and find out the truth of it. I hope this is the case, because, although I am fascinated by Alexander, his great triumphs, and eventual downfall, this novel was to explore Philip, the people around him and the kingdom that Alexander inherited.

I hope you enjoyed the novel and that it encourages you to read more about Philip, a truly remarkable man.

D William Thorburn.

Printed in Great Britain
by Amazon

68625496R00281